Persian
Myths

Persian
Myths

General Editor: Jake Jackson
Associate Editor: Taylor Bentley

**FLAME TREE
PUBLISHING**

This is a FLAME TREE Book

FLAME TREE PUBLISHING
6 Melbray Mews
Fulham, London SW6 3NS
United Kingdom
www.flametreepublishing.com

First published 2022

24 26 25
3 5 7 9 8 6 4 2

ISBN: 978-1-83964-934-9
Special ISBN: 978-1-80417-181-3

Contributors, authors, editors and sources for this series include:
James Atkinson, Loren Auerbach, William H. Barker and Cecilia Sinclair, Norman Bancroft-Hunt, George W. Bateman, James S. de Benneville, E.M. Berens, W.H.I. Bleek and L. C. Lloyd, Laura Bulbeck, J. F. Campbell, Harold Courlander, Jeremiah Curtin, F. Hadland Davis, Elphinstone Dayrell, O.B. Duane, Dr Ray Dunning, Firdusi, W.W. Gibbings, William Elliot Griffis, H. A. Guerber, Lafcadio Hearn, Stephen Hodge, James A. Honey M.D., Jake Jackson, Joseph Jacobs, Judith John, Husayn Va'iz Kashifi, Michael Kerrigan, J.W. Mackail, Alexander Mackenzie, Donald Mackenzie, Chris McNab, Minnie Martin, A.B. Mitford (Lord Redesdale), Robert Hamill Nassau, Nizami, M.I. Ogumefu, Yei Theodora Ozaki, Robert Sutherland Rattray, Elizabeth A. Reed, Professor James Riordan, Sara Robson, Jalal-uddin Rumi, Lewis Spence, Henry M. Stanley, Capt. C.H. Stigand, Rachel Storm, K.E. Sullivan, Percy Amaury Talbot, François-Marie Arouet a.k.a. Voltaire, E.A. Wallis Budge, Dr Roy Willis, Epiphanius Wilson, Alice Werner, E.T.C. Werner, Morris Meredith Williams, E.H. Whinfield.

A copy of the CIP data for this book is available from the British Library.

Printed and bound in China

Contents

Series Foreword

STRETCHING BACK to the oral traditions of thousands of years ago, tales of heroes and disaster, creation and conquest have been told by many different civilizations in many different ways. Their impact sits deep within our culture even though the detail in the tales themselves are a loose mix of historical record, transformed narrative and the distortions of hundreds of storytellers.

Today the language of mythology lives with us: our mood is jovial, our countenance is saturnine, we are narcissistic and our modern life is hermetically sealed from others. The nuances of myths and legends form part of our daily routines and help us navigate the world around us, with its half truths and biased reported facts.

The nature of a myth is that its story is already known by most of those who hear it, or read it. Every generation brings a new emphasis, but the fundamentals remain the same: a desire to understand and describe the events and relationships of the world. Many of the great stories are archetypes that help us find our own place, equipping us with tools for self-understanding, both individually and as part of a broader culture.

For Western societies it is Greek mythology that speaks to us most clearly. It greatly influenced the mythological heritage of the ancient Roman civilization and is the lens through which we still see the Celts, the Norse and many of the other great peoples and religions. The Greeks themselves learned much from their neighbours, the Egyptians, an older culture that became weak with age and incestuous leadership.

It is important to understand that what we perceive now as mythology had its own origins in perceptions of the divine and the rituals of the sacred. The earliest civilizations, in the crucible of the Middle East, in the Sumer of the third millennium BC, are the source to which many of the mythic archetypes can be traced. As humankind collected together in cities for the first time, developed writing and industrial scale agriculture, started to irrigate the rivers and attempted to control rather than be at the mercy of its environment, humanity began to write down its tentative explanations of natural events, of floods and plagues, of disease.

Early stories tell of Gods (or god-like animals in the case of tribal societies such as African, Native American or Aboriginal cultures) who are crafty and use their wits to survive, and it is reasonable to suggest that these were the first rulers of the gathering peoples of the earth, later elevated to god-like status with the distance of time. Such tales became more political as cities vied with each other for supremacy, creating new Gods, new hierarchies for their pantheons. The older Gods took on primordial roles and became the preserve of creation and destruction, leaving the new gods to deal with more current, everyday affairs. Empires rose and fell, with Babylon assuming the mantle from Sumeria in the 1800s BC, then in turn to be swept away by the Assyrians of the 1200s BC; then the Assyrians and the Egyptians were subjugated by the Greeks, the Greeks by the Romans and so on, leading to the spread and assimilation of common themes, ideas and stories throughout the world.

The survival of history is dependent on the telling of good tales, but each one must have the 'feeling' of truth, otherwise it will be ignored. Around the firesides, or embedded in a book or a computer, the myths and legends of the past are still the living materials of retold myth, not restricted to an exploration of origins. Now we have devices and global communications that give us unparalleled access to a diversity of traditions. We can find out about Native American, Indian, Chinese and tribal African mythology in a way that was denied to our ancestors, we can find connections, match the archaeology, religion and the mythologies of the world to build a comprehensive image of the human experience that is endlessly fascinating.

The stories in this book provide an introduction to the themes and concerns of the myths and legends of their respective cultures, with a short introduction to provide a linguistic, geographic and political context. This is where the myths have arrived today, but undoubtedly over the next millennia, they will transform again whilst retaining their essential truths and signs.

Jake Jackson
General Editor

Introduction to Persian Mythology and Literature

PERSIAN CIVILIZATION was to a great extent the product of Babylonian elements, and her mythology was born of a kind of sensual idolatry. But the Persians were a poetic people, and in their hands these ancient myths were refined and somewhat elevated. Every nation has a literature peculiarly her own, even though it may find its sources in foreign fields. As Persia was founded upon the ruins of more ancient monarchies, as she gathered into the halls of her kings the spoils of conquered nations, so also her literature was enriched by the philosophy and science, the poetry and mythology of her predecessors. The resistless horde, which poured down from the mountains and swept all of Western Asia into its current, formed the kindred tribes into a single monarchy, and this monarchy gathered unto herself, not only the wealth and military glory, but also the culture and learning of the nations she had conquered. The whole civilized world was taxed to maintain the splendors of her court; the imperial purple was found in the city of Tyre, and her fleets also came from Phoenicia, for the experience of this maritime people was indispensable to their Persian masters. Indian groves furnished the costly woods of aloe and of sandal that burned upon her altars, while Syria and the islands of the sea filled her flagons with wine.

Persia was a land of extremes, and the richest part of her dominions was fated to lie beneath the early snows, and feel the severity of winter, while the central portion of the country was one vast desert, whose scorching simoons were as much to be dreaded as the snows of her northern table-lands. The early settlers of Iran, therefore, were forced to win their bread and develop their resources by the most arduous labor, and the dreamy mythology of the Hindus gave way in their minds to the sterner conflict between good and evil.

The opposition between light and darkness became a prominent feature of their mythology, for the battles which raged in Hindu skies between Indra,

11

the storm king, and his constant enemy, Vritra, became to the sons of Iran a personal strife with the powers of nature, and instead of dreaming of a contest in the clouds, they sang of the daily battle in lives which were crowded with hardship. Hence it is that Ormazd and Ahriman, in their continual strife, form the background of the national mythology, although Persia took the sun for her emblem, and called her kings by his royal name; a flashing globe was the signal light above the imperial tent, and the golden eagle was perched upon the ensign that led the Persian troops to victory.

Early Literature

It is evident that the early kings of Persia possessed royal libraries, containing historical records and official decrees, for in the book of Ezra it is said that "search was made in the house of rolls," in Babylon, for the imperial decree of Cyrus concerning the rebuilding of the temple. It was afterwards found at Ecbatana "in the palace that is in the province of the Medes," the decree having been made in the first year of King Cyrus. But aside from some of the inscriptions, the earliest literature we now have belonging to this people is the Zend-Avesta, our present version of which was possibly derived from texts which already existed in the time of the Achæmenian kings. Although there are no facts to prove that the text of the Avesta as we now possess it was committed to writing previous to the Sassanian dynasty Prof. Darmesteter thinks it possible that "Herodotus may have heard the Magi sing, in the fifth century before Christ, the very same Gathas which are sung now a days by the Mobeds of Bombay."

As some of these early texts must have existed before the fifth century B.C. we place them chronologically before the inscriptions of Darius the Great.

Historians claim that ancient Persian manuscripts were destroyed, when Alexander, in a condition of drunkenness, ordered the beautiful city of Persepolis to be set on fire, in order to please the courtesan Thais.

The modern worshippers of Alexander, however, have placed around his name all the possible glory of military achievement with a vast amount of rhetoric, concerning "the young hero" and "the thunder of his tread." They claim, indeed, that he had very few faults, except cruelty, drunkenness, and some worse forms of dissipation. Their defense of this barbarous act is that "only the palace and its environs were burned" at this particular time, and that this was an act of requital for the pillage of Athens, and also to impress the Persians with a due sense of his own importance. Whatever may have been the motive, or physical condition, of the incendiary, it is highly probable that when the palace, and its environs were burned, the royal libraries went down in the flames, and certain it is, that from the time of the Macedonian conquest to the foundation of the Sassanian dynasty, the history of the Persian language and literature is almost a blank page. The legends of the Sassanian coins, the inscriptions of their emperors, and the translation of the Avesta, by Sassanian scholars, represent another phase of the language and literature of Iran.

The men who, at the rising of the new national dynasty, became the reformers, teachers, and prophets of Persia, formed their language and the whole train of their ideas upon a Semitic model. The grammar of the Sassanian dialect, however, was Persian, and "this was a period of religious and metaphysical delirium, when everything became everything, when Maya and Sophia, Mitra and Christ, Viraf and Isaiah, Belus and Kronos were mixed up in one jumbled system of inane speculation, from which at last the East was delivered by the doctrines of Mohammed, and the West by the pure Christianity of the Teutonic nations."

It was five hundred years after Alexander before Persian literature and religion were revived, and the books of the Zend-Avesta collected, either from scattered manuscripts or from oral tradition. The first collection of traditions, which finally resulted in the Shah-Namah, was made also during the Sassanian dynasty. Firdusi tells us that there was a Pahlevan, of the family of the Dihkans, who loved to study the traditions of antiquity. He therefore summoned from the provinces, all the old men who could remember portions of the ancient legends, and questioned them concerning the stories of the country. The Dihkan then wrote down the traditions of the kings and the changes in the empire as they had been recited to him. But this work, which was commenced under Nushirvan and finished under Yezdejird, the last of the Sassanians, was destroyed by the command of Omar, the Arabian chieftain.

The scanty literature of the Sassanian age was somewhat augmented by a notable collection of SanskRit fables which was brought to the court of the Persian king, Koshrou, and translated into the Persian, or Pahlavi tongue. This collection comprised the fables of the Pancatantra and the Hitopadesa, and from it the later European fables of La Fontaine probably originated. In this collection we present selections from the Persian version: Anwar-I-Suhali.

Literature of Modern Persia

After the Muslim conquest, Persia's treasures of literature were again destroyed, so far as the conquerors could complete their work of devastation, and the altar fires of the Parsis were quenched in the long night of Mohammedan rule, while the Koran supplanted the Avesta even upon its native soil.

Modern Persian literature may be said to begin with the reconstruction of the National Epic. This work marks an important era, in even the language of Persia, for it seems to close the biography of that peculiar tongue. There has been but little, of either growth or decay, in its structure since that period, although it becomes more and more encumbered with foreign words.

The Persian Epic could be reconstructed only when the national feeling began to reassert itself, and it was at this period that the patriotism of the people began to recover from the benumbing pressure of Mohammedan rule, and especially in the eastern portions of the empire, a distinctively Persian spirit was revived. It is true that Mohammedanism had taken root even in the national party, but the Arabic tongue was no longer favored by the governors of the eastern provinces. Persian again became the court language of these dignitaries, the native poets were encouraged and began to collect once more the traditions of the empire.

It is claimed that Jacob, the son of Leis, the first prince of Persian blood, who declared himself independent of the Caliphs, procured fragments of the early National Epic, and had it rearranged and continued. Then followed the dynasty of the Samanians who claimed descent from the Sassanian kings, and they pursued the same popular policy. The later dynasty of the Gaznevides also encouraged the growth of the national spirit, and the great Persian Epic was written during the reign of Mahmud the Great, who was the second king of the Gaznevide dynasty. By his command, collections of old books were made all over the empire, and men who knew the ancient poems were summoned to his court. It was from these materials that Firdusi composed his Shah-Namah. "Traditions," says the poet, "have been given me; nothing of what is worth knowing has been forgotten; all that I shall say others have said before me."

Hence the heroes in the Shah-Namah exhibit many of the traits of the Vedic deities – traits which have lived through the Zoroastrian period, the Achæmenian dynasty, the Macedonian rule, the Parthian wars, and even the Arabian conquest, to be reproduced in the poem of Firdusi.

The modern phase of their literature is emphatically an age of poetry; the Persians of these later centuries seem to have been born with a song on their lips, for their poets are numbered by thousands. Not only their books of polite literature, but their histories, ethics and science, nay, even their mathematics and grammar are written in rhyme. There are many volumes of these productions that cannot be dignified by the name of poetry, but their literature is tropical in its development and their annals bear the names of many illustrious poets. Firdusi, author of the great Epic, must always stand at the head of Persian poetry.

Nizami of the twelfth century has given us, perhaps, the best version of the beautiful Arabian tragedy of Lili and Majnun, and Hafiz says of the author:

> *"Not all the treasured lore of ancient days*
> *Can boast the sweetness of Nizami's lays."*

It was to the thirteenth century, the third period of Persian poetry, which may be called the mystic and moral age, that the mystic poet and philosopher, Jalal-Uddin Rumi, author of the series of stories with moral maxims known as the *Mesnevi* (*Masnavi*) belonged.

The clear and harmonious style of Hafiz, who belonged to the fourteenth century, has a fascination of its own, and it is claimed that the prophet Khizer carried to the waiting lips of the poet the water from the fountain of life, and therefore his words are immortal among the sons of men.

Mythical Mountains

The silent mountains standing calmly beneath the skies of blue, while the ages come and go, always command the reverence of the human heart. With forests around their feet, the gray peaks reach upward to dim and ashen heights, where the white snow lies unpolluted by the foot of man. Their frost-crowns gleam in the sunlight of noon, or change to tints of opal and crimson light beneath the farewell fires of the setting sun. No wonder, then, that in the fables of all people the gods are enthroned on wondrous heights. The old Assyrian kings wrote upon their strange tablets of "the world mountain," which, although rooted in hades, still supported the heavens with all their starry hosts. The world was bound to it with a rope, like that with which the sea was churned in the later Hindu legend, for the lost ambrosia of the gods or like the golden cord of Homer with which Zeus proposed to suspend the nether earth, after binding the cord about Olympus. This mythical mountain was the abode of the gods, and it was this of which the Babylonian king said:

> *"I will exalt my throne above the stars of God;*
> *I will sit upon the mount of the congregation in the sides of the north;*
> *I will be like the Most High."*

It was between the "Twin Mountains" that the sun passed in its rising and setting, and the rocky gates were guarded by the "scorpion men," whose heads were at the portals of heaven, and their feet in hell beneath.

In the mythology of the Hindus, Mount Meru rises in her solitary grandeur in the very centre of the earth to the height of sixty-four thousand miles; and there on her sun-kissed crown, amidst gardens of fabulous beauty, and flowers that never of winter hear – where the skies are of rose and pearl, and the dreamlike harmonies of far-off voices are borne upon the air, we find the heaven of Indra, the abode of the gods.

Among the Greeks the gates of Olympus open to receive the imperial throng, when

> *"The gods with Jove assume their thrones of gold."*

When the chambers of the east were opened, and floods of light were poured upon the peak, the Greek poet dreamt that:

> *"The sounding hinges ring on either side,*
> *The gloomy volumes pierced with light divide,*
> *The chariot mounts, where deep in ambient skies*
> *Confused Olympus' hundred heads arise—*
> *Where far apart the Thunderer fills his throne*
> *O'er all the gods, superior and alone."*

But even the storm-swept heights of Olympus, where the chariots of the gods were crushed to fragments beneath the lightnings of Jove, were not lofty enough for the spirit of the Norseman. Odin's Valhal, with its roof of shields and walls of gleaming spears, lies in heaven itself, and higher still is Gimle, the gold-roofed hall of the higher gods. Far away to the northward, on the heights of the Nida mountains, stands a hall of shining gold which is the home of the Sindre race. These are they who smelt earth's gold from her rough brown stone, and flashing through her crystals, the tints which are hidden in the hearts of the roses, they are changed to rubies and garnets. These are they who make the sapphires blue with the fresh lips of the violet, and mould earth's tears into her purest pearls.

In Persian mythology we find a trace of "the world mountain" of the old Assyrian kings, as well as a thought which is akin to the vine-clad bowers of Meru, the shining gates of Olympus, and the Nida mountains of the Norsemen, for here the Qaf mountains surround the world after the manner of the annular system described in the Maha-Bharata. This mythical range is pure emerald, and although it surrounds the world, it is placed between two of the horns of a white ox, named Kornit or Kajuta. He has four thousand horns, and the distance from one horn to another could not be traversed in five hundred years. These mountains are the abode of giants, fairies and peris, while their life-giving fountains confer immortality upon those who taste of their waters.

The highest portion of the emerald range is the Alborz, where the fabled Simurgh builds her colossal nest of sandal wood, and the woven branches of aloe and myrtle trees. Mount Alborz is represented as standing upon the earth, while her crown of light reposes in the region far beyond the stars. It is Hara-Berezaita (the lofty mountain) – the sphere of endless light, where the supreme god of Persian mythology dwells in his own temple which is the "abode of song." This is the "Mother of Mountains" and from it have grown all the heights that stand upon the earth; it is the fabled center of the world, and around it the sun, moon and stars revolve. Hence, in the Vendidad we find the following hymn:

> *"Up, rise and roll along, thou swift horsed sun,*
> *Above Hara-Berezaita and produce light for the world.*
> *Up, rise up, thou moon—*
> *Rise up, ye stars, rise up above Hara-Berezaita*
> *And produce light for the world,*
> *And mayest thou, O man, rise up along the path made by Mazda—*
> *Along the way made by the gods,*
> *The watery way they opened."*

Rivers

In the mythology of every people we find mystic rivers in connection with the worship of their divinities. They are winding everywhere through the enchanted land of fable. Often born in the highlands of the celestial mountains, they are represented as coming down to earth with the glint of the sunlight on their waves.

In Persian mythology there is a crystal stream which gushes from a golden precipice of the mythical mountain and descends to the earth from the heavens, as does the celestial Ganga of the Hindus. This is the heavenly spring from which all the waters of the earth come down.... It is the Ardvi Sura Anahita which ever flows in a life-giving current, bringing blessings unto man and receiving in return the sacrifices of the material world.

This river has a thousand cells and a thousand channels, and each of these extend as far as a swiftly mounted horseman can ride in forty days; in each channel there stands a palace gleaming with an hundred windows and a thousand columns; these palaces are surrounded with ten thousand balconies founded in the distant channels of the river, and within their courts are luxurious beds, "well scented and covered with pillows." In the golden ravines around these palace halls are the wondrous fountains of the Ardvi Sura Anahita, and the stream rushes down from the summit of the mountain with a volume greater than all the rivers of earth, and falls into the bosom of the celestial sea that lies at the foot of the Hara-Berezaita. When the waters of the river fall into the Vouru-Kasha, the waves of the sea boil over the shores, and the billows chant a song of welcome.

This celestial spring, with its mighty torrent of waters, is personified as a beautiful goddess – a maiden tall and shapely, who is born of a glorious race. She is stately and noble, strong as the current of a mighty river, and pure as the snows that lie on the mountain's crown. Her beautiful arms are white and thick, her hair is long and luxuriant, for she is large and comely, radiant with the glory of a perfect womanhood.

This glorious maid of the mountain has four white horses, which were made for her by Ahura Mazda; one is the snow, and one is the wind, while the others are the rain and the cloud; thus it happens that ever upon the earth it is snowing, or the rain is somewhere coming down to gladden the flowers with refreshing touch.

The beautiful goddess springs from a golden fissure in the highest peak, and mounting her chariot draws the reins above her white steeds and drives them down the steep incline, which is a thousand times the height of a man, and continual sacrifice is offered to her brightness and glory.

Clothed with a golden mantle and wearing a crown radiant with the light of an hundred gems, she comes dashing down the mountain side, thinking in her heart: "Who will praise me? Who will offer me a sacrifice with libations?"

The cloud-sea represents the "dewy treasures" of the Hindus – the rains which are held in the reluctant cloud, and only drawn therefrom by the lightning bolts of Indra, who is assisted in the battle by the Maruts when they "harness their deer for victory." The Persian Vendidad represents a continual interchange between the waters of the earth and sky.

> "As the Vouru-Kasha is the gathering place of the waters
> Rise up, go up the ærial way and go down upon the earth....
> The large river that is known afar
> That is as large as all the waters of earth
> Runs from the height down to the sea, Vouru-Kasha."

Persian Romance

The Arabic and even the Turkish tongue has intruded upon the classic Persian of Firdusi, but as the English has borrowed from all nations, and yet retains its own individuality, so also the Persian tongue, while absorbing and adapting the wealth of others, still retains its personal character, modified only by the changes of time.

In borrowing from the language of her neighbors, Persia has not hesitated to adopt also portions of their literature. During the reign of the Moslem kings the choicest mental productions from India, and even from Greece, found the way to their courts. Alp Arslan, around whose throne stood twelve hundred princes, was a lover of letters, and from the banks of the Euphrates to the feet of the Himalayas a wealth of literature was called, to be wrought up by Persian scholars and poets under royal patronage. There was an active rivalry in literary culture, and much of the fire of Arabian poetry brightened the pages of Persian romance. There were the mystic lights and shadows of nomadic life, and desert voices mingled with the strains of native singers.

The terrible contrasts of life and death – the unyielding resentments and jealousies – passionate loves and hates, which are so distinctively Arabian, began to fill the pages of Iranian romance with tragedy.

Even the vivid description of the Moslems could scarcely add to the gorgeousness of Persian fancy, where Oriental lovers wandered in the greenest of valleys, while around them floated the soft perfume of the orange blossoms. It could not add to the fabulous wealth of their nobles, where camels were burdened with the choicest of gems, and vines of gold were laden with grapes of amethyst. But it did add the element of fierce revenge and the tragedy of violent death, represented by the pitiless simoon and the shifting sand column, the hopeless wastes, the bitter waters, and the dry bones of perished caravans. It added the life-springs of the oasis, as well as the rushing whirlwind; it added the palm tree of the desert, with her feet in the burning sand and her head in the morning light – a symbol of the watch-fires of faith above the desert places of life. The best literature of Persia in our own age is largely the reproduction in various forms of her standard poets; her romances, however, still rival the Arabian Nights in their startling combinations and bewildering descriptions. The imagination of her writers is not bound by the rules of our northern clime, and there is nothing too wild or improbable to find a place in Oriental story. There are rayless caverns of sorcery in a wilderness of mystery; there are mountains of emerald and hills of ruby; there are enchanted valleys, rich with fabulous treasure, and rivers gushing from fairy fountains. There is always the grand uprising of the king of day and the endless cycle of the stars – for this poetic people cannot forget the teaching of the Parsi and the Sabean. In the literature found on the banks of these southern seas there is also the restfulness of night, with its coolness and dews, to be followed by the glory of the morning and the fragrance from the hearts of the roses.

Persian literature rings with voices from ruined cities, and mingles the story of the past with the dreams of her future. Her treasures are drawn from the records of Chaldean kings; her historic pictures have caught the light of early crowns and repeated the story of their magnificence. Her annals are filled with the victories of her Cyrus, with the extended dominions of her great Darius, and the gorgeousness of her later sovereigns. Her poets have immortalized her myths as well as her heroes, and the Oriental world has contributed to the pages of her romance.

Sháh Námeh
Firdusi
Translated by James Atkinson

HEN SIR JOHN LUBBOCK, in the list of a hundred books which he published, in the year 1886, as containing the best hundred worth reading, mentioned the *Sháh Námeh* or *Book of Kings*, written by the Persian poet Firdusi (Abul Kasim Mansur, *c.* 935/940–1019/1026), it is doubtful whether many of his readers had even heard of such a poem or of its author. Yet Firdusi, "The Poet of Paradise" (for such is the meaning of this pen-name), is as much the national poet of Persia as Dante is of Italy or Shakespeare of England. Abul Kasim Mansur is indeed a genuine epic poet, and for this reason his work is of genuine interest to the lovers of Homer, Vergil, and Dante.

The qualities that go to make up an epic poem are all to be found in this work of the Persian bard. In the first place, the *Sháh Námeh* is written by an enthusiastic patriot, who glorifies his country, and by that means has become recognized as the national poet of Persia. In the second place, the poem presents us with a complete view of a certain definite phase, and complete era of civilization; in other words, it is a transcript from the life; a portrait-gallery of distinct and unique individuals; a description of what was once an actual society. We find in it delineated the Persia of the heroic age, an age of chivalry, eclipsing, in romantic emotion, deeds of daring, scenes of love and violence, even the mediaeval chivalry of France and Spain.

We read this abridged version (starting with 'Zál, the Son of Sám' and ending with 'The Death of Rustem') of the Sháh Námeh with keen interest – because from its study the mind is enlarged and stimulated by new scenes, new ideas and unprecedented situations

Zál, the Son of Sám

ACCORDING TO THE traditionary histories from which Firdusi has derived his legends, the warrior Sám had a son born to him whose hair was perfectly white. On his birth the nurse went to Sám and told him that God had blessed him with a wonderful child, without a single blemish, excepting that his hair was white; but when Sám saw him he was grieved:

> *His hair was white as goose's wing,*
> *His cheek was like the rose of spring*
> *His form was straight as cypress tree—*
> *But when the sire was brought to see*
> *That child with hair so silvery white,*
> *His heart revolted at the sight.*

His mother gave him the name of Zál and the people said to Sám, "This is an ominous event, and will be to thee productive of nothing but calamity; it would be better if thou couldst remove him out of sight.

> *"No human being of this earth*
> *Could give to such a monster birth;*
> *He must be of the Demon race,*
> *Though human still in form and face.*
> *If not a Demon, he, at least,*
> *Appears a party-coloured beast."*

When Sám was made acquainted with these reproaches and sneers of the people, he determined, though with a sorrowful heart, to take him up to the mountain Alberz, and abandon him there to be destroyed by beasts of prey. Alberz was the abode of the Símúrgh or Griffin, and, whilst flying about in quest of food for his hungry young ones, that surprising animal discovered the child lying alone upon the hard rock, crying and sucking its fingers. The Símúrgh, however, felt no inclination to devour him, but compassionately took him up in the air, and conveyed him to his own habitation.

He who is blest with Heaven's grace
Will never want a dwelling-place
And he who bears the curse of Fate
Can never change his wretched state.
A voice, not earthly, thus addressed
The Símúrgh in his mountain nest—
"To thee this mortal I resign,
Protected by the power divine;
Let him thy fostering kindness share,
Nourish him with paternal care;
For from his loins, in time, will spring
The champion of the world, and bring
Honour on earth, and to thy name;
The heir of everlasting fame."

The young ones were also kind and affectionate to the infant, which was thus nourished and protected by the Símúrgh for several years.

The Dream of Sám

I T IS SAID THAT one night, after melancholy musings and reflecting on the miseries of this life, Sám was visited by a dream, and when the particulars of it were communicated to the interpreters of mysterious warnings and omens, they declared that Zál was certainly still alive, although he had been long exposed on Alberz, and left there to be torn to pieces by wild animals. Upon this interpretation being given, the natural feelings of the father returned, and he sent his people to the mountain in search of Zál, but without success. On another night Sám dreamt a second time, when he beheld a young man of a beautiful countenance at the head of an immense army, with a banner flying before him, and a Múbid on his left hand. One of them addressed Sám, and reproached him thus:

Unfeeling mortal, hast thou from thy eyes
Washed out all sense of shame? Dost thou believe
That to have silvery tresses is a crime?
If so, thy head is covered with white hair;
And were not both spontaneous gifts from Heaven?
Although the boy was hateful to thy sight,
The grace of God has been bestowed upon him;
And what is human tenderness and love
To Heaven's protection? Thou to him wert cruel,
But Heaven has blest him, shielding him from harm.

Sám screamed aloud in his sleep, and awoke greatly terrified. Without delay he went himself to Alberz, and ascended the mountain, and wept and prayed before the throne of the Almighty, saying:

"If that forsaken child be truly mine,
And not the progeny of Demon fell,
O pity me! forgive the wicked deed,
And to my eyes, my injured son restore."

His prayer was accepted. The Símúrgh, hearing the lamentations of Sám among his people, knew that he had come in quest of his son, and thus said to Zál: – "I have fed and protected thee like a kind nurse, and I have given thee the name of Dustán, like a father. Sám, the warrior, has just come upon the mountain in search of his child, and I must restore thee to him, and we must part." Zál wept when he heard of this unexpected separation, and in strong terms expressed his gratitude to his benefactor; for the Wonderful Bird had not omitted to teach him the language of the country, and to cultivate his understanding, removed as they were to such a distance from the haunts of mankind. The Símúrgh soothed him by assuring him that he was not going to abandon him to misfortune, but to increase his prosperity; and, as a striking proof of affection, gave him a feather from his own wing, with these instructions: – "Whenever thou art involved in difficulty or danger, put this feather on the fire, and I will instantly appear to thee to ensure thy safety. Never cease to remember me.

"I have watched thee with fondness by day and by night,

> *And supplied all thy wants with a father's delight;*
> *O forget not thy nurse – still be faithful to me—*
> *And my heart will be ever devoted to thee."*

Zál immediately replied in a strain of gratitude and admiration; and then the Símúrgh conveyed him to Sám, and said to him: "Receive thy son – he is of wonderful promise, and will be worthy of the throne and the diadem."

> *The soul of Sám rejoiced to hear*
> *Applause so sweet to a parent's ear;*
> *And blessed them both in thought and word,*
> *The lovely boy, and the Wondrous Bird.*

He also declared to Zál that he was ashamed of the crime of which he had been guilty, and that he would endeavor to obliterate the recollection of the past by treating him in future with the utmost respect and honor.

When Minúchihr heard from Zábul of these things, and of Sám's return, he was exceedingly pleased, and ordered his son, Nauder, with a splendid istakbál, to meet the father and son on their approach to the city. They were surrounded by warriors and great men, and Sám embraced the first moment to introduce Zál to the king.

> *Zál humbly kissed the earth before the king,*
> *And from the hands of Minúchihr received*
> *A golden mace and helm. Then those who knew*
> *The stars and planetary signs, were told*
> *To calculate the stripling's destiny;*
> *And all proclaimed him of exalted fortune,*
> *That he would be prodigious in his might,*
> *Outshining every warrior of the age.*

Delighted with this information, Minúchihr, seated upon his throne, with Kárun on one side and Sám on the other, presented Zál with Arabian horses, and armor, and gold, and splendid garments, and appointed Sám to the government of Kábul, Zábul, and Ind. Zál accompanied his father on his return; and when they arrived at Zábulistán, the most renowned instructors in every art and science were collected together to cultivate and enrich his young mind.

In the meantime Sám was commanded by the king to invade and subdue the Demon provinces of Karugsár and Mázinderán; and Zál was in consequence left by his father in charge of Zábulistán. The young nursling of the Símúrgh is said to have performed the duties of sovereignty with admirable wisdom and discretion, during the absence of his father. He did not pass his time in idle exercises, but with zealous delight in the society of accomplished and learned men, for the purpose of becoming familiar with every species of knowledge and acquirement. The city of Zábul, however, as a constant residence, did not entirely satisfy him, and he wished to see more of the world; he therefore visited several other places, and proceeded as far as Kábul, where he pitched his tents, and remained for some time.

Rúdábeh

THE CHIEF OF KÁBUL was descended from the family of Zohák. He was named Mihráb, and to secure the safety of his state, paid annual tribute to Sám. Mihráb, on the arrival of Zál, went out of the city to see him, and was hospitably entertained by the young hero, who soon discovered that he had a daughter of wonderful attractions.

Her name Rúdábeh; screened from public view,
Her countenance is brilliant as the sun;
From head to foot her lovely form is fair
As polished ivory. Like the spring, her cheek
Presents a radiant bloom, – in stature tall,
And o'er her silvery brightness, richly flow
Dark musky ringlets clustering to her feet.
She blushes like the rich pomegranate flower;
Her eyes are soft and sweet as the narcissus,
Her lashes from the raven's jetty plume
Have stolen their blackness, and her brows are bent
Like archer's bow. Ask ye to see the moon?

Look at her face. Seek ye for musky fragrance?
She is all sweetness. Her long fingers seem
Pencils of silver, and so beautiful
Her presence, that she breathes of Heaven and love.

Such was the description of Rúdábeh, which inspired the heart of Zál with the most violent affection, and imagination added to her charms.

Mihráb again waited on Zál, who received him graciously, and asked him in what manner he could promote his wishes. Mihráb said that he only desired him to become his guest at a banquet he intended to invite him to; but Zál thought proper to refuse, because he well knew, if he accepted an invitation of the kind from a relation of Zohák, that his father Sám and the King of Persia would be offended. Mihráb returned to Kábul disappointed, and having gone into his harem, his wife, Síndokht, inquired after the stranger from Zábul, the white-headed son of Sám. She wished to know what he was like, in form and feature, and what account he gave of his sojourn with the Símúrgh. Mihráb described him in the warmest terms of admiration – he was valiant, he said, accomplished and handsome, with no other defect than that of white hair. And so boundless was his praise, that Rúdábeh, who was present, drank every word with avidity, and felt her own heart warmed into admiration and love. Full of emotion, she afterwards said privately to her attendants:

"To you alone the secret of my heart
I now unfold; to you alone confess
The deep sensations of my captive soul.
I love, I love; all day and night of him
I think alone – I see him in my dreams—
You only know my secret – aid me now,
And soothe the sorrows of my bursting heart."

The attendants were startled with this confession and entreaty, and ventured to remonstrate against so preposterous an attachment.

"What! hast thou lost all sense of shame,
All value for thy honored name!
That thou, in loveliness supreme,

Of every tongue the constant theme,
Should choose, and on another's word.
The nursling of a Mountain Bird!
A being never seen before,
Which human mother never bore!
And can the hoary locks of age,
A youthful heart like thine engage?
Must thy enchanting form be prest
To such a dubious monster's breast?
And all thy beauty's rich array,
Thy peerless charms be thrown away?"

This violent remonstrance was more calculated to rouse the indignation of Rúdábeh than to induce her to change her mind. It did so. But she subdued her resentment, and again dwelt upon the ardor of her passion.

"My attachment is fixed, my election is made,
And when hearts are enchained 'tis in vain to upbraid.
Neither Kízar nor Faghfúr I wish to behold,
Nor the monarch of Persia with jewels and gold;
All, all I despise, save the choice of my heart,
And from his beloved image I never can part.
Call him aged, or young, 'tis a fruitless endeavour
To uproot a desire I must cherish for ever;
Call him old, call him young, who can passion control?
Ever present, and loved, he entrances my soul.
'Tis for him I exist – him I worship alone,
And my heart it must bleed till I call him my own."

As soon as the attendants found that Rúdábeh's attachment was deeply fixed, and not to be removed, they changed their purpose, and became obedient to her wishes, anxious to pursue any measure that might bring Zál and their mistress together. Rúdábeh was delighted with this proof of their regard.

It was spring-time, and the attendants repaired towards the halting-place of Zál, in the neighborhood of the city. Their occupation seemed to be gathering roses along the romantic banks of a pellucid streamlet, and when they purposely strayed opposite the tent of Zál, he observed them, and asked his friends – why they presumed to gather roses in his garden. He was told that they were damsels sent by the moon of Kábulistán from the palace of Mihráb to gather roses, and upon hearing this his heart was touched with emotion. He rose up and rambled about for amusement, keeping the direction of the river, followed by a servant with a bow. He was not far from the damsels, when a bird sprung up from the water, which he shot, upon the wing, with an arrow. The bird happened to fall near the rose-gatherers, and Zál ordered his servant to bring it to him. The attendants of Rúdábeh lost not the opportunity, as he approached them, to inquire who the archer was. "Know ye not," answered the servant, "that this is Ním-rúz, the son of Sám, and also called Dustán, the greatest warrior ever known." At this the damsels smiled, and said that they too belonged to a person of distinction – and not of inferior worth – to a star in the palace of Mihráb. "We have come from Kábul to the King of Zábulistán, and should Zál and Rúdábeh be of equal rank, her ruby lips may become acquainted with his, and their wished-for union be effected." When the servant returned, Zál was immediately informed of the conversation that had taken place, and in consequence presents were prepared.

> *They who to gather roses came – went back*
> *With precious gems – and honorary robes;*
> *And two bright finger-rings were secretly*
> *Sent to the princess.*

Then did the attendants of Rúdábeh exult in the success of their artifice, and say that the lion had come into their toils. Rúdábeh herself, however, had some fears on the subject. She anxiously sought to know exactly the personal appearance of Zál, and happily her warmest hopes were realized by the description she received. But one difficulty remained – how were they to meet? How was she to see with her own eyes the man whom her fancy had depicted in such glowing colors? Her attendants, sufficiently expert at intrigue, soon contrived the means of gratifying her wishes. There was a beautiful rural retreat in a sequestered situation, the apartments of which were adorned with pictures of great men, and ornamented in the most splendid manner. To this favorite place Rúdábeh retired, and most magnificently dressed, awaiting the coming of Zál, whom her attendants had previously invited to repair thither as soon as the sun had gone down. The shadows of evening were falling as he approached, and the enamoured princess thus addressed him from her balcony: –

> *"May happiness attend thee ever, thou,*
> *Whose lucid features make this gloomy night*
> *Clear as the day; whose perfume scents the breeze;*
> *Thou who, regardless of fatigue, hast come*
> *On foot too, thus to see me—"*

Hearing a sweet voice, he looked up, and beheld a bright face in the balcony, and he said to the beautiful vision:

> *"How often have I hoped that Heaven*
> *Would, in some secret place display*
> *Thy charms to me, and thou hast given*
> *My heart the wish of many a day;*
> *For now thy gentle voice I hear,*
> *And now I see thee – speak again!*
> *Speak freely in a willing ear,*
> *And every wish thou hast obtain."*

Not a word was lost upon Rúdábeh, and she soon accomplished her object. Her hair was so luxuriant, and of such a length, that casting it loose it flowed down from the balcony; and, after fastening the upper part to a ring, she requested Zál to take hold of the other end and mount up. He ardently kissed the musky tresses, and by them quickly ascended.

> *Then hand in hand within the chambers they*
> *Gracefully passed. – Attractive was the scene,*
> *The walls embellished by the painter's skill,*
> *And every object exquisitely formed,*
> *Sculpture, and architectural ornament,*
> *Fit for a king. Zál with amazement gazed*
> *Upon what art had done, but more he gazed*
> *Upon the witching radiance of his love,*
> *Upon her tulip cheeks, her musky locks,*

Breathing the sweetness of a summer garden;
Upon the sparkling brightness of her rings,
Necklace, and bracelets, glittering on her arms.
His mien too was majestic – on his head
He wore a ruby crown, and near his breast
Was seen a belted dagger. Fondly she
With side-long glances marked his noble aspect,
The fine proportions of his graceful limbs,
His strength and beauty. Her enamoured heart
Suffused her cheek with blushes, every glance
Increased the ardent transports of her soul.
So mild was his demeanour, he appeared
A gentle lion toying with his prey.
Long they remained rapt in admiration
Of each other. At length the warrior rose,
And thus addressed her: "It becomes not us
To be forgetful of the path of prudence,
Though love would dictate a more ardent course,
How oft has Sám, my father, counselled me,
Against unseeming thoughts, – unseemly deeds,—
Always to choose the right, and shun the wrong.
How will he burn with anger when he hears
This new adventure; how will Minúchihr
Indignantly reproach me for this dream!
This waking dream of rapture! but I call
High Heaven to witness what I now declare—
Whoever may oppose my sacred vows,
I still am thine, affianced thine, for ever."
And thus Rúdábeh: "Thou hast won my heart,
And kings may sue in vain; to thee devoted,
Thou art alone my warrior and my love."
Thus they exclaimed, – then Zál with fond adieus
Softly descended from the balcony,
And hastened to his tent.

As speedily as possible he assembled together his counsellors and Múbids to obtain their advice on the present extraordinary occasion, and he represented to them the sacred importance of encouraging matrimonial alliances.

For marriage is a contract sealed by Heaven—
How happy is the Warrior's lot, amidst
His smiling children; when he dies, his son
Succeeds him, and enjoys his rank and name.
And is it not a glorious thing to say—
This is the son of Zál, or this of Sám,
The heir of his renowned progenitor?

He then related to them the story of his love and affection for the daughter of Mihráb; but the Múbids, well knowing that the chief of Kábul was of the family of Zohák, the serpent-king, did not approve the union desired, which excited the indignation of Zál. They, however, recommended his writing a letter to Sám, who might, if he thought proper, refer the matter to Minúchihr. The letter was accordingly written and despatched, and when Sám received it, he immediately referred the question to his astrologers, to know whether the nuptials, if solemnized between Zál and Rúdábeh would be prosperous or not. They foretold that the nuptials would be prosperous and that the issue would be a son of wonderful strength and power, the conqueror of the world. This announcement delighted the heart of the old warrior, and he sent the messenger back with the assurance of his approbation of the proposed union but requested that the subject might be kept concealed till he returned with his army from the expedition to Karugsár, and was able to consult with Minúchihr.

Zál, exulting at his success, communicated the glad tidings to Rúdábeh by their female emissary, who had hitherto carried on successfully the correspondence between them. But as she was conveying an answer to this welcome news, and some presents to Zál, Síndokht, the mother of Rúdábeh, detected her, and examining the contents of the packet, she found sufficient evidence, she thought of something wrong.

"What treachery is this? What have we here!
Sirbund and male attire? Thou, wretch, confess!
Disclose thy secret doings."

The emissary, however, betrayed nothing; but declared that she was a dealer in jewels and dresses, and had been only showing her merchandise to Rúdábeh. Síndokht, in extreme agitation of mind, hastened to her daughter's apartment to ascertain the particulars of this affair, when Rúdábeh at once fearlessly acknowledged her unalterable affection for Zál,

> *"I love him so devotedly, all day,*
> *All night my tears have flowed unceasingly;*
> *And one hair of his head I prize more dearly*
> *Than all the world beside; for him I live;*
> *And we have met, and we have sat together,*
> *And pledged our mutual love with mutual joy*
> *And innocence of heart."*

Rúdábeh further informed her of Sám's consent to their nuptials, which in some degree satisfied the mother. But when Mihráb was made acquainted with the arrangement, his rage was unbounded, for he dreaded the resentment of Sám and Minúchihr when the circumstances became fully known to them. Trembling with indignation he drew his dagger, and would have instantly rushed to Rúdábeh's chamber to destroy her, had not Síndokht fallen at his feet and restrained him. He insisted, however, on her being brought before him; and upon his promise not to do her any harm, Síndokht complied. Rúdábeh disdained to take off her ornaments to appear as an offender and a supplicant, but, proud of her choice, went into her father's presence, gayly adorned with jewels, and in splendid apparel. Mihráb received her with surprise.

> *"Why all this glittering finery? Is the devil*
> *United to an angel? When a snake*
> *Is met with in Arabia, it is killed!"*

But Rúdábeh answered not a word, and was permitted to retire with her mother.

When Minúchihr was apprised of the proceedings between Zál and Rúdábeh, he was deeply concerned, anticipating nothing but confusion and ruin to Persia from the united influence of Zál and Mihráb. Feridún had purified the world from the abominations of Zohák, and as Mihráb was a descendant of that merciless tyrant, he feared that some attempt would be made to resume the enormities of former times;

Sám was therefore required to give his advice on the occasion.

The conqueror of Karugsár and Mázinderán was received on his return with cordial rejoicings, and he charmed the king with the story of his triumphant success. The monarch against whom he had fought was descended, on the mother's side, from Zohák, and his Demon army was more numerous than ants, or clouds of locusts, covering mountain and plain. Sám thus proceeded in his description of the conflict.

> *"And when he heard my voice, and saw what deeds*
> *I had performed, approaching me, he threw*
> *His noose; but downward bending I escaped,*
> *And with my bow I showered upon his head*
> *Steel-pointed arrows, piercing through the brain;*
> *Then did I grasp his loins, and from his horse*
> *Cast him upon the ground, deprived of life.*
> *At this, the demons terrified and pale,*
> *Shrunk back, some flying to the mountain wilds,*
> *And others, taken on the battle-field,*
> *Became obedient to the Persian king."*

Minúchihr, gratified by this result of the expedition, appointed Sám to a new enterprise, which was to destroy Kábul by fire and sword, especially the house of Mihráb; and that ruler, of the serpent-race, and all his adherents were to be put to death. Sám, before he took leave to return to his own government at Zábul, tried to dissuade him from this violent exercise of revenge, but without making any sensible impression upon him.

Meanwhile the vindictive intentions of Minúchihr, which were soon known at Kábul, produced the greatest alarm and consternation in the family of Mihráb. Zál now returned to his father, and Sám sent a letter to Minúchihr, again to deprecate his wrath, and appointed Zál the messenger. In this letter Sám enumerates his services at Karugsár and Mázinderán, and especially dwells upon the destruction of a prodigious dragon.

> *"I am thy servant, and twice sixty years*
> *Have seen my prowess. Mounted on my steed,*
> *Wielding my battle-axe, overthrowing heroes,*
> *Who equals Sám, the warrior? I destroyed*
> *The mighty monster, whose devouring jaws*

Unpeopled half the land, and spread dismay
From town to town. The world was full of horror,
No bird was seen in air, no beast of prey
In plain or forest; from the stream he drew
The crocodile; the eagle from the sky.
The country had no habitant alive,
And when I found no human being left,
I cast away all fear, and girt my loins,
And in the name of God went boldly forth,
Armed for the strife. I saw him towering rise,
Huge as a mountain, with his hideous hair
Dragging upon the ground; his long black tongue
Shut up the path; his eyes two lakes of blood;
And, seeing me, so horrible his roar,
The earth shook with affright, and from his mouth
A flood of poison issued. Like a lion
Forward I sprang, and in a moment drove
A diamond-pointed arrow through his tongue,
Fixing him to the ground. Another went
Down his deep throat, and dreadfully he writhed.
A third passed through his middle. Then I raised
My battle-axe, cow-headed, and with one
Tremendous blow, dislodged his venomous brain,
And deluged all around with blood and poison.
There lay the monster dead, and soon the world
Regained its peace and comfort. Now I'm old,
The vigour of my youth is past and gone,
And it becomes me to resign my station,
To Zál, my gallant son."

Mihráb continued in such extreme agitation, that in his own mind he saw no means of avoiding the threatened desolation of his country but by putting his wife and daughter to death. Síndokht however had a better resource, and suggested the expediency of waiting upon Sám herself, to induce him to forward her own views and the nuptials between Zál and Rúdábeh. To this Mihráb assented, and she proceeded, mounted on a richly caparisoned horse, to Zábul with most magnificent presents, consisting of three hundred thousand dínars; ten horses with golden, and thirty with silver, housings; sixty richly attired damsels, carrying golden trays of jewels and musk, and camphor, and wine, and sugar; forty pieces of figured cloth; a hundred milch camels, and a hundred others for burden; two hundred Indian swords, a golden crown and throne, and four elephants. Sám was amazed and embarrassed by the arrival of this splendid array. If he accepted the presents, he would incur the anger of Minúchihr; and if he rejected them, Zál would be disappointed and driven to despair. He at length accepted them, and concurred in the wishes of Síndokht respecting the union of the two lovers.

When Zál arrived at the court of Minúchihr, he was received with honor, and the letter of Sám being read, the king was prevailed upon to consent to the pacific proposals that were made in favor of Mihráb, and the nuptials. He too consulted his astrologers, and was informed that the offspring of Zál and Rúdábeh would be a hero of matchless strength and valor. Zál, on his return through Kábul, had an interview with Rúdábeh, who welcomed him in the most rapturous terms:

> *Be thou for ever blest, for I adore thee,*
> *And make the dust of thy fair feet my pillow.*

In short, with the approbation of all parties the marriage at length took place, and was celebrated at the beautiful summer-house where first the lovers met. Sám was present at Kábul on the happy occasion, and soon afterwards returned to Sístán, preparatory to resuming his martial labors in Karugsár and Mázinderán.

As the time drew near that Rúdábeh should become a mother, she suffered extremely from constant indisposition, and both Zál and Síndokht were in the deepest distress on account of her precarious state.

> *The cypress leaf was withering; pale she lay,*
> *Unsoothed by rest or sleep, death seemed approaching.*

At last Zál recollected the feather of the Símúrgh, and followed the instructions which he had received, by placing it on the fire. In a moment darkness surrounded them, which was however, immediately dispersed by the sudden appearance of the Símúrgh. "Why," said the Símúrgh, "do I see all this grief and sorrow? Why are the tear-drops in the warrior's eyes? A child will be born of mighty power, who will become the wonder of the world."

The Símúrgh then gave some advice which was implicitly attended to, and the result was that Rúdábeh was soon out of danger. Never was beheld so prodigious a child. The father and mother were equally amazed. They called the boy Rustem. On the first day he looked a year old, and he required the milk of ten nurses. A likeness of him was immediately worked in silk, representing him upon a horse, and armed like a warrior, which was sent to Sám, who was then fighting in Mázinderán, and it made the old champion almost delirious with joy. At Kábul and Zábul there was nothing but feasting and rejoicing, as soon as the tidings were known, and thousands of dínars were given away in charity to the poor. When Rustem was five years of age, he ate as much as a man, and some say that even in his third year he rode on horseback. In his eighth year he was as powerful as any hero of the time.

In beauty of form and in vigour of limb,
No mortal was ever seen equal to him.

Both Sám and Mihráb, though far distant from the scene of felicity, were equally anxious to proceed to Zábulistán to behold their wonderful grandson. Both set off, but Mihráb arrived first with great pomp, and a whole army for his suite, and went forth with Zál to meet Sám, and give him an honorable welcome. The boy Rustem was mounted on an elephant, wearing a splendid crown, and wanted to join them, but his father kindly prevented him undergoing the inconvenience of alighting. Zál and Mihráb dismounted as soon as Sám was seen at a distance, and performed the ceremonies of an affectionate reception. Sám was indeed amazed when he did see the boy, and showered blessings on his head.

Afterwards Sám placed Mihráb on his right hand, and Zál on his left, and Rustem before him, and began to converse with his grandson, who thus manifested to him his martial disposition.

"Thou art the champion of the world, and I
The branch of that fair tree of which thou art
The glorious root: to thee I am devoted,
But ease and leisure have no charms for me;
Nor music, nor the songs of festive joy.
Mounted and armed, a helmet on my brow,
A javelin in my grasp, I long to meet
The foe, and cast his severed head before thee."

Then Sám made a royal feast, and every apartment in his palace was richly decorated, and resounded with mirth and rejoicing. Mihráb was the merriest, and drank the most, and in his cups saw nothing but himself, so vain had he become from the countenance he had received. He kept saying:

> *"Now I feel no alarm about Sám or Zál-zer,*
> *Nor the splendour and power of the great Minúchihr;*
> *Whilst aided by Rustem, his sword, and his mace,*
> *Not a cloud of misfortune can shadow my face.*
> *All the laws of Zohák I will quickly restore,*
> *And the world shall be fragrant and blest as before."*

This exultation plainly betrayed the disposition of his race; and though Sám smiled at the extravagance of Mihráb, he looked up towards Heaven, and prayed that Rustem might not prove a tyrant, but be continually active in doing good, and humble before God.

Upon Sám departing, on his return to Karugsár and Mázinderán, Zál went with Rustem to Sístán, a province dependent on his government, and settled him there. The white elephant, belonging to Minúchihr, was kept at Sístán. One night Rustem was awakened out of his sleep by a great noise, and cries of distress when starting up and inquiring the cause, he was told that the white elephant had got loose, and was trampling and crushing the people to death. In a moment he issued from his apartment, brandishing his mace; but was soon stopped by the servants, who were anxious to expostulate with him against venturing out in the darkness of night to encounter a ferocious elephant. Impatient at being thus interrupted he knocked down one of the watchmen, who fell dead at his feet, and the others running away, he broke the lock of the gate, and escaped. He immediately opposed himself to the enormous animal, which looked like a mountain, and kept roaring like the River Nil. Regarding him with a cautious and steady eye, he gave a loud shout, and fearlessly struck him a blow, with such strength and vigor, that the iron mace was bent almost double. The elephant trembled, and soon fell exhausted and lifeless in the dust. When it was communicated to Zál that Rustem had killed the animal with one blow, he was amazed, and fervently returned thanks to heaven. He called him to him, and kissed him, and said: "My darling boy, thou art indeed unequalled in valor and magnanimity."

Then it occurred to Zál that Rustem, after such an achievement, would be a proper person to take vengeance on the enemies of his grandfather Narímán, who was sent by

Feridún with a large army against an enchanted fort situated upon the mountain Sipund, and who whilst endeavoring to effect his object, was killed by a piece of rock thrown down from above by the besieged. The fort, which was many miles high, inclosed beautiful lawns of the freshest verdure, and delightful gardens abounding with fruit and flowers; it was also full of treasure. Sám, on hearing of the fate of his father, was deeply afflicted, and in a short time proceeded against the fort himself; but he was surrounded by a trackless desert. He knew not what course to pursue; not a being was ever seen to enter or come out of the gates, and, after spending months and years in fruitless endeavors, he was compelled to retire from the appalling enterprise in despair. "Now," said Zál to Rustem, "the time is come, and the remedy is at hand; thou art yet unknown, and may easily accomplish our purpose." Rustem agreed to the proposed adventure, and according to his father's advice, assumed the dress and character of a salt-merchant, prepared a caravan of camels, and secreted arms for himself and companions among the loads of salt. Everything being ready they set off, and it was not long before they reached the fort on the mountain Sipund. Salt being a precious article, and much wanted, as soon as the garrison knew that it was for sale, the gates were opened; and then was Rustem seen, together with his warriors, surrounded by men, women, and children, anxiously making their purchases, some giving clothes in exchange, some gold, and some silver, without fear or suspicion.

> *But when the night came on, and it was dark,*
> *Rustem impatient drew his warriors forth,*
> *And moved towards the mansion of the chief—*
> *But not unheard. The unaccustomed noise,*
> *Announcing warlike menace and attack,*
> *Awoke the Kotwál, who sprung up to meet*
> *The peril threatened by the invading foe.*
> *Rustem meanwhile uplifts his ponderous mace,*
> *And cleaves his head, and scatters on the ground*
> *The reeking brains. And now the garrison*
> *Are on the alert, all hastening to the spot*
> *Where battle rages; midst the deepened gloom*
> *Flash sparkling swords, which show the crimson earth*
> *Bright as the ruby.*

Rustem continued fighting with the people of the fort all night, and just as morning dawned, he discovered the chief and slew him. Those who survived, then escaped, and not one of the inhabitants remained within the walls alive. Rustem's next object was to enter the governor's mansion. It was built of stone, and the gate, which was made of iron, he burst open with his battle-axe, and advancing onward, he discovered a temple, constructed with infinite skill and science, beyond the power of mortal man, and which contained amazing wealth, in jewels and gold. All the warriors gathered for themselves as much treasure as they could carry away, and more than imagination can conceive; and Rustem wrote to Zál to know his further commands on the subject of the capture. Zál, overjoyed at the result of the enterprise, replied:

> *Thou hast illumed the soul of Narímán,*
> *Now in the blissful bowers of Paradise,*
> *By punishing his foes with fire and sword.*

He then recommended him to load all the camels with as much of the invaluable property as could be removed, and bring it away, and then burn and destroy the whole place, leaving not a single vestige; and the command having been strictly complied with, Rustem retraced his steps to Zábulistán.

> *On his return Zál pressed him to his heart,*
> *And paid him public honors. The fond mother*
> *Kissed and embraced her darling son, and all*
> *Uniting, showered their blessings on his head.*

Nauder

UPON THE DEMISE of King Minúchihr, Nauder ascended the throne, and commenced his reign in the most promising manner; but before two months had passed, he neglected the counsels of his father, and betrayed the despotic character of his heart. To such an extreme did he carry his oppression, that to escape from his violence, the people were induced to solicit other princes to come and take possession of the empire. The courtiers labored under the greatest embarrassment, their monarch being solely occupied in extorting money from his subjects, and amassing wealth for his own coffers. Nauder was not long in perceiving the dissatisfaction that universally prevailed, and, anticipating, not only an immediate revolt, but an invading army, solicited, according to his father's advice, the assistance of Sám, then at Mázinderán. The complaints of the people, however, reached Sám before the arrival of the messenger, and when he received the letter, he was greatly distressed on account of the extreme severity exercised by the new king. The champion, in consequence, proceeded forthwith from Mázinderán to Persia, and when he entered the capital, he was joyously welcomed, and at once entreated by the people to take the sovereignty upon himself. It was said of Nauder:

> *The gloom of tyranny has hid*
> *The light his father's counsel gave;*
> *The hope of life is lost amid*
> *The desolation of the grave.*
> *The world is withering in his thrall,*
> *Exhausted by his iron sway;*
> *Do thou ascend the throne, and all*
> *Will cheerfully thy will obey.*

But Sám said, "No; I should then be ungrateful to Minúchihr, a traitor, and deservedly offensive in the eyes of God. Nauder is the king, and I am bound to do him service, although he has deplorably departed from the advice of his father." He then soothed the alarm and irritation of the chiefs, and engaging to be a mediator upon the unhappy occasion, brought them to a more pacific tone of thinking. After this he immediately repaired to Nauder, who received him with great favor and kindness. "O king," said he, "only keep Feridún in remembrance, and govern the empire in such a manner that thy name may be honored by thy subjects; for, be well assured, that he who has a just estimate of the world, will never look upon it as his place of rest. It is but an inn, where all travellers meet on their way to eternity, but must not remain. The wise consider those who fix their affections on this life, as utterly devoid of reason and reflection:

"Pleasure, and pomp, and wealth may be obtained—
And every want luxuriously supplied:
But suddenly, without a moment's warning,
Death comes, and hurls the monarch from his throne,
His crown and sceptre scattering in the dust.
He who is satisfied with earthly joys,
Can never know the blessedness of Heaven;
His soul must still be dark. Why do the good
Suffer in this world, but to be prepared
For future rest and happiness? The name
Of Feridún is honoured among men,
Whilst curses load the memory of Zohák."

This intercession of Sám produced an entire change in the government of Nauder, who promised, in future, to rule his people according to the principles of Húsheng, and Feridún, and Minúchihr. The chiefs and captains of the army were, in consequence, contented, and the kingdom reunited itself under his sway.

In the meantime, however, the news of the death of Minúchihr, together with Nauder's injustice and seventy, and the disaffection of his people, had reached Túrán, of which country Poshang, a descendant from Túr, was then the sovereign. Poshang, who had been unable to make a single successful hostile movement during the life of Minúchihr, at once conceived this to be a fit opportunity of taking revenge for the blood of Sílim and Túr, and every appearance seeming to be in his favor, he called before him his heroic son Afrásiyáb, and explained to him his purpose and views. It was not difficult to inspire the youthful mind of Afrásiyáb with the sentiments he himself cherished, and a large army was immediately collected to take the field against Nauder. Poshang was proud of the chivalrous spirit and promptitude displayed by his son, who is said to have been as strong as a lion, or an elephant, and whose shadow extended miles. His tongue was like a bright sword, and his heart as bounteous as the ocean, and his hands like the clouds when rain falls to gladden the thirsty earth. Aghríras, the brother of Afrásiyáb, however, was not so precipitate. He cautioned his father to be prudent, for though Persia could no longer boast of the presence of Minúchihr, still the great warrior Sám, and Kárun, and Garshásp, were living, and Poshang had only to look at the result of the wars in which Sílim and Túr were involved, to be convinced that the existing conjuncture required mature deliberation. "It would be better," said he, "not to begin the contest at all, than to bring ruin and desolation on our own country." Poshang, on the contrary, thought the time peculiarly fit and inviting, and contended that, as Minúchihr took vengeance for the blood of his grandfather, so ought Afrásiyáb to take vengeance for his. "The grandson," he said, "who refuses to do this act of justice, is unworthy of his family. There is nothing to apprehend from the efforts of Nauder, who is an inexperienced youth, nor from the valor of his warriors. Afrásiyáb is brave and powerful in war, and thou must accompany him and share the glory." After this no further observation was offered, and the martial preparations were completed.

Afrásiyáb Marches Against Nauder

THE BRAZEN drums on the elephants were sounded as the signal of departure, and the army proceeded rapidly to its destination, overshadowing the earth in its progress. Afrásiyáb had penetrated as far as the Jihún before Nauder was aware of his approach. Upon receiving this intelligence of the activity of the enemy, the warriors of the Persian army immediately moved in that direction, and on their arrival at Dehstán, prepared for battle.

Afrásiyáb despatched thirty thousand of his troops under the command of Shimasás and Khazervän to Zábulistán, to act against Zál, having heard on his march of the death of the illustrious Sám, and advanced himself upon Dehstán with four hundred thousand soldiers, covering the ground like swarms of ants and locusts. He soon discovered that Nauder's forces did not exceed one hundred and forty thousand men, and wrote to Poshang, his father, in high spirits, especially on account of not having to contend against Sám, the warrior, and informed him that he had detached Shimasás against Zábulistán. When the armies had approached to within two leagues of each other, Bármán, one of the Túránian chiefs, offered to challenge any one of the enemy to single combat: but Aghríras objected to it, not wishing that so valuable a hero should run the hazard of discomfiture. At this Afrásiyáb was very indignant and directed Bármán to follow the bent of his own inclinations.

"'Tis not for us to shrink from Persian foe,
Put on thy armour, and prepare thy bow."

Accordingly the challenge was given. Kárun looked round, and the only person who answered the call was the aged Kobád, his brother. Kárun and Kobád were both sons of Kavah, the blacksmith, and both leaders in the Persian army. No persuasion could restrain Kobád from the unequal conflict. He resisted all the entreaties of Kárun, who said to him—

"O, should thy hoary locks be stained with blood,
Thy legions will be overwhelmed with grief,
And, in despair, decline the coming battle."
But what was the reply of brave Kobád?
"Brother, this body, this frail tenement,
Belongs to death. No living man has ever
Gone up to Heaven – for all are doomed to die.
Some by the sword, the dagger, or the spear,
And some, devoured by roaring beasts of prey;
Some peacefully upon their beds, and others
Snatched suddenly from life, endure the lot
Ordained by the Creator. If I perish,
Does not my brother live, my noble brother,
To bury me beneath a warrior's tomb,
And bless my memory?"

Saying this, he rushed forward, and the two warriors met in desperate conflict. The struggle lasted all day; at last Bármán threw a stone at his antagonist with such force, that Kobád in receiving the blow fell lifeless from his horse. When Kárun saw that his brother was slain, he brought forward his whole army to be revenged for the death of Kobád. Afrásiyáb himself advanced to the charge, and the encounter was dreadful. The soldiers who fell among the Túránians could not be numbered, but the Persians lost fifty thousand men.

Loud neighed the steeds, and their resounding hoofs.
Shook the deep caverns of the earth; the dust

Rose up in clouds and hid the azure heavens—
Bright beamed the swords, and in that carnage wide,
Blood flowed like water. Night alone divided
The hostile armies.

When the battle ceased Kárun fell back upon Dehstán, and communicated his misfortune to Nauder, who lamented the loss of Kobád, even more than that of Sám. In the morning Kárun again took the field against Afrásiyáb, and the conflict was again terrible. Nauder boldly opposed himself to the enemy, and singling out Afrásiyáb, the two heroes fought with great bravery till night again put an end to the engagement. The Persian army had suffered most, and Nauder retired to his tent disappointed, fatigued, and sorrowful. He then called to mind the words of Minúchihr, and called for his two sons, Tús and Gustahem. With melancholy forebodings he directed them to return to Irán, with his shubistán, or domestic establishment, and take refuge on the mountain Alberz, in the hope that some one of the race of Feridún might survive the general ruin which seemed to be approaching.

The armies rested two days. On the third the reverberating noise of drums and trumpets announced the recommencement of the battle. On the Persian side Shahpúr had been appointed in the room of Kobád, and Bármán and Shíwáz led the right and left of the Túránians under Afrásiyáb.

From dawn to sunset, mountain, plain, and stream,
Were hid from view; the earth, beneath the tread
Of myriads, groaned; and when the javelins cast
Long shadows on the plain at even-tide,
The Tartar host had won the victory;
And many a Persian chief fell on that day:—
Shahpúr himself was slain.

When Nauder and Kárun saw the unfortunate result of the battle, they again fell back upon Dehstán, and secured themselves in the fort. Afrásiyáb in the meantime despatched Karúkhán to Irán, through the desert, with a body of horsemen, for the purpose of intercepting and capturing the shubistán of Nauder. As soon as Kárun heard of this expedition he was all on fire, and proposed to pursue the squadron under Karúkhán, and frustrate at once the object which the enemy had in view; and though Nauder was unfavorable to this movement, Kárun, supported by several of the chiefs and a strong volunteer force, set off at midnight, without permission, on this important enterprise. It was not long before they reached the Duz-i-Supêd, or white fort, of which Gustahem was the governor, and falling in with Bármán, who was also pushing forward to Persia, Kárun, in revenge for his brother Kobád, sought him out, and dared him to single combat. He threw his javelin with such might, that his antagonist was driven furiously from his horse; and then, dismounting, he cut off his head, and hung it at his saddle-bow. After this he attacked and defeated the Tartar troops, and continued his march towards Irán.

Nauder having found that Kárun had departed, immediately followed, and Afrásiyáb was not long in pursuing him. The Túránians at length came up with Nauder, and attacked him with great vigor. The unfortunate king, unable to parry the onset, fell into the hands of his enemies, together with upwards of one thousand of his famous warriors.

After the achievement of this victory Afrásiyáb directed that Kárun should be pursued and attacked wherever he might be found; but when he heard that he had hurried on for the protection of the shubistán, and had conquered and slain Bármán, he gnawed his hands with rage. The reign of Nauder lasted only seven years. After him Afrásiyáb was the master of Persia.

Afrásiyáb

IT HAS ALREADY BEEN said that Shimasás and Khazervár were sent by Afrásiyáb with thirty thousand men against Kábul and Zábul, and when Zál heard of this movement he forthwith united with Mihráb the chief of Kábul, and having first collected a large army in Sístán, had a conflict with the two Tartar generals.

> *Zál promptly donned himself in war attire,*
> *And, mounted like a hero, to the field*
> *Hastened, his soldiers frowning on their steeds.*
> *Now Khazervár grasps his huge battle-axe,*

And, his broad shield extending, at one blow
Shivers the mail of Zál, who calls aloud
As, like a lion, to the fight he springs,
Armed with his father's mace. Sternly he looks
And with the fury of a dragon, drives
The weapon through his adversary's head,
Staining the ground with streaks of blood, resembling
The waving stripes upon a tiger's back.

At this time Rustem was confined at home with the smallpox. Upon the death of Khazervån, Shimasås thirsted to be revenged; but when Zál meeting him raised his mace, and began to close, the chief became alarmed and turned back, and all his squadrons followed his example.

Fled Shimasás, and all his fighting train,
Like herds by tempests scattered o'er the plain.

Zál set off in pursuit, and slew a great number of the enemy; but when Afrásiyáb was made acquainted with this defeat, he immediately released Nauder from his fetters, and in his rage instantly deprived him of life.

He struck him and so deadly was the blow,
Breath left the body in a moment's space.

After this Afrásiyáb turned his views towards Tús and Gustahem in the hope of getting them into his hands; but as soon as they received intimation of his object, the two brothers retired from Irán, and went to Sístán to live under the protection of Zál. The champion received them with due respect and honor. Kárun also went, with all the warriors and people who had been supported by Nauder, and co-operated with Zál, who encouraged them with the hopes of future success. Zál, however, considered that both Tús and Gustahem were still of a tender age – that a monarch of extraordinary wisdom and energy was required to oppose Afrásiyáb – that he himself was not of the blood of the Kais, nor fit for the duties of sovereignty, and, therefore, he turned his thoughts towards Aghríras, the younger brother of Afrásiyáb, distinguished as he was for his valor, prudence, and humanity, and to whom Poshang, his father, had given the government of Raí. To him Zál sent an envoy, saying, that if he would proceed to Sístán, he should be supplied with ample resources to place him on the throne of Persia; that by the co-operation of Zál and all his warriors the conquest would be easy, and that there would be no difficulty in destroying the power of Afrásiyáb. Aghríras accepted the offer, and immediately proceeded from his kingdom of Raí towards Sístán. On his arrival at Bábel, Afrásiyáb heard of his ambitious plans, and lost no time in assembling his army and marching to arrest the progress of his brother. Aghríras, unable to sustain a battle, had recourse to negotiation and a conference, in which Afrásiyáb said to him, "What rebellious conduct is this, of which thou art guilty? Is not the country of Raí sufficient for thee, that thou art thus aspiring to be a great king?" Aghríras replied: "Why reproach and insult me thus? Art thou not ashamed to accuse another of rebellious conduct?

> *"Shame might have held thy tongue; reprove not me*
> *In bitterness; God did not give thee power*
> *To injure man, and surely not thy kin.*
> *Afrásiyáb, enraged at this reproof,*
> *Replied by a foul deed – he grasped his sword,*
> *And with remorseless fury slew his brother!"*

When intelligence of this cruel catastrophe came to Zál's ears, he exclaimed: "Now indeed has the empire of Afrásiyáb arrived at its crisis:

> *"Yes, yes, the tyrant's throne is tottering now,*
> *And past is all his glory."*

Then Zál bound his loins in hostility against Afrásiyáb, and gathering together all his warriors, resolved upon taking revenge for the death of Nauder, and expelling the tyrant from Persia. Neither Tús nor Gustahem being yet capable of sustaining the cares and duties of the throne, his anxiety was to obtain the assistance of some one of the race of Feridún.

> *These youths were for imperial rule unfit:*
> *A king of royal lineage and worth*
> *The state required, and none could he remember*
> *Save Tahmasp's son, descended from the blood*
> *Of Feridún.*

Zau

A T THE TIME when Sílim and Túr were killed, Tahmasp, the son of Sílim, fled from the country and took refuge in an island, where he died, and left a son named Zau. Zál sent Kárun, the son of Kavah, attended by a proper escort, with overtures to Zau, who readily complied, and was under favorable circumstances seated upon the throne:

> *Speedily, in arms,*
> *He led his troops to Persia, fought, and won*
> *A kingdom, by his power and bravery—*
> *And happy was the day when princely Zau*
> *Was placed upon that throne of sovereignty;*
> *All breathed their prayers upon his future reign,*
> *And o'er his head (the customary rite)*
> *Shower'd gold and jewels.*

When he had subdued the country, he turned his arms against Afrásiyáb, who in consequence of losing the co-operation of the Persians, and not being in a state to encounter a superior force, thought it prudent to retreat, and return to his father. The reign of Zau lasted five years, after which he died, and was succeeded by his son Garshásp.

Garshásp

G ARSHÁSP, whilst in his minority, being unacquainted with the affairs of government, abided in all things by the judgment and counsels of Zál. When Afrásiyáb arrived at Túrán, his father was in great distress and anger on account of the inhuman murder of Aghríras; and so exceedingly did he grieve, that he would not endure his presence.

> *And when Afrásiyáb returned, his sire,*
> *Poshang, in grief, refused to see his face.*
> *To him the day of happiness and joy*
> *Had been obscured by the dark clouds of night;*
> *And thus he said: "Why didst thou, why didst thou*
> *In power supreme, without pretence of guilt,*
> *With thy own hand his precious life destroy?*
> *Why hast thou shed thy innocent brother's blood?*
> *In this life thou art nothing now to me;*
> *Away, I must not see thy face again."*

Afrásiyáb continued offensive and despicable in the mind of his father till he heard that Garshásp was unequal to rule over Persia, and then thinking he could turn the warlike spirit of Afrásiyáb to advantage, he forgave the crime of his son. He forthwith collected an immense army, and sent him again to effect the conquest of Irán, under the pretext of avenging the death of Sílim and Túr.

> *Afrásiyáb a mighty army raised,*
> *And passing plain and river, mountain high,*
> *And desert wild, filled all the Persian realm*
> *With consternation, universal dread.*

The chief authorities of the country applied to Zál as their only remedy against the invasion of Afrásiyáb.

> *They said to Zál, "How easy is the task*
> *For thee to grasp the world – then, since thou canst*
> *Afford us succour, yield the blessing now;*
> *For, lo! the King Afrásiyáb has come,*
> *In all his power and overwhelming might."*

Zál replied that he had on this occasion appointed Rustem to command the army, and to oppose the invasion of Afrásiyáb.

> *And thus the warrior Zál to Rustem spoke—*

"Strong as an elephant thou art, my son,
Surpassing thy companions, and I now
Forewarn thee that a difficult emprize,
Hostile to ease or sleep, demands thy care.
'Tis true, of battles thou canst nothing know,
But what am I to do? This is no time
For banquetting, and yet thy lips still breathe
The scent of milk, a proof of infancy;
Thy heart pants after gladness and the sweet
Endearments of domestic life; can I
Then send thee to the war to cope with heroes
Burning with wrath and vengeance?" Rustem said—
"Mistake me not, I have no wish, not I,
For soft endearments, nor domestic life,
Nor home-felt joys. This chest, these nervous limbs,
Denote far other objects of pursuit,
Than a luxurious life of ease and pleasure."

Zál having taken great pains in the instruction of Rustem in warlike exercises, and the rules of battle, found infinite aptitude in the boy, and his activity and skill seemed to be superior to his own. He thanked God for the comfort it gave him, and was glad. Then Rustem asked his father for a suitable mace; and seeing the huge weapon which was borne by the great Sám, he took it up, and it answered his purpose exactly.

When the young hero saw the mace of Sám
He smiled with pleasure, and his heart rejoiced;
And paying homage to his father Zál,
The champion of the age, asked for a steed
Of corresponding power, that he might use
That famous club with added force and vigor.

Zál showed him all the horses in his possession, and Rustem tried many, but found not one of sufficient strength to suit him. At last his eyes fell upon a mare followed by a foal of great promise, beauty, and strength.

Seeing that foal, whose bright and glossy skin
Was dappled o'er, like blossoms of the rose
Upon a saffron lawn, Rustem prepared
His noose, and held it ready in his hand.

The groom recommended him to secure the foal, as it was the offspring of Abresh, born of a Díw, or Demon, and called Rakush. The dam had killed several persons who attempted to seize her young one.

Now Rustem flings the noose, and suddenly
Rakush secures. Meanwhile the furious mare
Attacks him, eager with her pointed teeth
To crush his brain – but, stunned by his loud cry,
She stops in wonder. Then with clenched hand
He smites her on the head and neck, and down
She tumbles, struggling in the pangs of death.

Rakush, however, though with the noose round his neck, was not so easily subdued; but kept dragging and pulling Rustem, as if by a tether, and it was a considerable time before the animal could be reduced to subjection. At last, Rustem thanked Heaven that he had obtained the very horse he wanted.

"Now am I with my horse prepared to join
The field of warriors!" Thus the hero said,
And placed the saddle on his charger. Zál
Beheld him with delight, – his withered heart
Glowing with summer freshness. Open then
He threw his treasury – thoughtless of the past
Or future – present joy absorbing all
His faculties, and thrilling every nerve.

In a short time Zál sent Rustem with a prodigious army against Afrásiyáb, and two days afterwards set off himself and joined his son. Afrásiyáb said, "The son is but a boy, and the father is old; I shall have no difficulty in recovering the empire of Persia." These observations having reached Zál, he pondered deeply, considering that Garshásp would not be able to contend against Afrásiyáb, and that no other prince of the race of Feridún was known to be in existence. However, he despatched people in every quarter to gather information on the subject, and at length Kai-kobád was understood to be residing in obscurity on the mountain Alberz, distinguished for his wisdom and valor, and his qualifications for the exercise of sovereign power. Zál therefore recommended Rustem to proceed to Alberz, and bring him from his concealment.

> *Thus Zál to Rustem spoke, "Go forth, my son,*
> *And speedily perform this pressing duty,*
> *To linger would be dangerous. Say to him,*
> *'The army is prepared – the throne is ready,*
> *And thou alone, of the Kaiánian race,*
> *Deemed fit for sovereign rule.'"*

Rustem accordingly mounted Rakush, and accompanied by a powerful force, pursued his way towards the mountain Alberz; and though the road was infested by the troops of Afrásiyáb, he valiantly overcame every difficulty that was opposed to his progress. On reaching the vicinity of Alberz, he observed a beautiful spot of ground studded with luxuriant trees, and watered by glittering rills. There too, sitting upon a throne, placed in the shade on the flowery margin of a stream, he saw a young man, surrounded by a company of friends and attendants, and engaged at a gorgeous entertainment. Rustem, when he came near, was hospitably invited to partake of the feast: but this he declined, saying, that he was on an important mission to Alberz, which forbade the enjoyment of any pleasure till his task was accomplished; in short, that he was in search of Kai-kobád: but upon being told that he would there receive intelligence of him, he alighted and approached the bank of the stream where the company was assembled. The young man who was seated upon the golden throne took hold of the hand of Rustem, and filling up a goblet with wine, gave another to his guest, and asked him at whose command or suggestion he was in search of Kai-kobád. Rustem replied, that he was sent by his father Zál, and frankly communicated to him the special object they had in view. The young man, delighted with the information, immediately discovered himself, acknowledged that he was Kai-kobád, and then Rustem respectfully hailed him as the sovereign of Persia.

The banquet was resumed again—
And, hark, the softly warbled strain,
As harp and flute, in union sweet,
The voices of the singers meet.
The black-eyed damsels now display
Their art in many an amorous lay;
And now the song is loud and clear,
And speaks of Rustem's welcome here.
"This is a day, a glorious day,
That drives ungenial thoughts away;
This is a day to make us glad,
Since Rustem comes for Kai-kobád;
O, let us pass our time in glee,
And talk of Jemshíd's majesty,
The pomp and glory of his reign,
And still the sparkling goblet drain.
Come, Sakí, fill the wine-cup high,
And let not even its brim be dry;
For wine alone has power to part
The rust of sorrow from the heart.
Drink to the king, in merry mood,
Since fortune smiles, and wine is good;
Quaffing red wine is better far
Than shedding blood in strife, or war;
Man is but dust, and why should he
Become a fire of enmity?
Drink deep, all other cares resign.
For what can vie with ruby wine?"

In this manner ran the song of the revellers. After which, and being rather merry with wine, Kai-kobád told Rustem of the dream that had induced him to descend from his place of refuge on Alberz, and to prepare a banquet on the occasion. He dreamt the night before that two white falcons from Persia placed a splendid crown upon his head, and this vision was interpreted by Rustem as symbolical of his father and himself, who at that moment were engaged in investing him with kingly power.

The hero then solicited the young sovereign to hasten his departure for Persia, and preparations were made without delay. They travelled night and day, and fell in with several detachments of the enemy, which were easily repulsed by the valor of Rustem. The fiercest attack proceeded from Kelún, one of Afrásiyáb's warriors, near the confines of Persia, who in the encounter used his spear with great dexterity and address.

> *But Rustem with his javelin soon transfixed*
> *The Tartar knight – who in the eyes of all*
> *Looked like a spitted chicken – down he sunk,*
> *And all his soldiers fled in wild dismay.*
> *Then Rustem turned aside, and found a spot*
> *Where verdant meadows smiled, and streamlets flowed,*
> *Inviting weary travellers to rest.*
> *There they awhile remained – and when the sun*
> *Went down, and night had darkened all the sky,*
> *The champion joyfully pursued his way,*
> *And brought the monarch to his father's house.*
> *– Seven days they sat in council – on the eighth*
> *Young Kai-kobád was crowned – and placed upon*
> *The ivory throne in presence of his warriors,*
> *Who all besought him to commence the war*
> *Against the Tartar prince, Afrásiyáb.*

Kai-kobád

KAI-KOBÁD having been raised to the throne at a council of the warriors, and advised to oppose the progress of Afrásiyáb, immediately assembled his army. Mihráb, the ruler of Kábul, was appointed to one wing, and Gustahem to the other – the centre was given to Kárun and Kishwád, and Rustem was placed in front, Zál with Kai-kobád remaining in the rear. The glorious standard of Kavah streamed upon the breeze.

On the other side, Afrásiyáb prepared for battle, assisted by his heroes Akbás, Wísah, Shimasás, and Gersíwaz; and so great was the clamor and confusion which proceeded from both armies, that earth and sky seemed blended together. The clattering of hoofs, the shrill roar of trumpets, the rattle of brazen drums, and the vivid glittering of spear and shield, produced indescribable tumult and splendor.

Kárun was the first in action, and he brought many a hero to the ground. He singled out Shimasás; and after a desperate struggle, laid him breathless on the field. Rustem, stimulated by these exploits, requested his father, Zál, to point out Afrásiyáb, that he might encounter him; but Zál endeavored to dissuade him from so hopeless an effort, saying,

> *"My son, be wise, and peril not thyself;*
> *Black is his banner, and his cuirass black—*
> *His limbs are cased in iron – on his head*
> *He wears an iron helm – and high before him*
> *Floats the black ensign; equal in his might*
> *To ten strong men, he never in one place*
> *Remains, but everywhere displays his power.*
> *The crocodile has in the rolling stream*
> *No safety; and a mountain, formed of steel,*
> *Even at the mention of Afrásiyáb,*
> *Melts into water. Then, beware of him."*
> *Rustem replied: – "Be not alarmed for me—*
> *My heart, my arm, my dagger, are my castle,*
> *And Heaven befriends me – let him but appear,*
> *Dragon or Demon, and the field is mine."*

Then Rustem valiantly urged Rakush towards the Túránian army, and called out aloud. As soon as Afrásiyáb beheld him, he inquired who he could be, and he was told, "This is Rustem, the son of Zál. Seest thou not in his hand the battle-axe of Sám? The youth has come in search of renown." When the combatants closed, they struggled for some time together, and at length Rustem seized the girdle-belt of his antagonist, and threw him from his saddle. He wished to drag the captive as a trophy to Kai-kobád, that his first great victory might be remembered, but unfortunately the belt gave way, and Afrásiyáb fell on the ground. Immediately the fallen chief was surrounded and rescued by his own warriors, but not before Rustem had snatched off his crown, and carried it away with the broken girdle which was left in his hand. And now a general engagement took place. Rustem being reinforced by the advance of the king, with Zál and Mihráb at his side—

Both armies seemed so closely waging war,
Thou wouldst have said, that they were mixed together.
The earth shook with the tramping of the steeds,
Rattled the drums; loud clamours from the troops
Echoed around, and from the iron grasp
Of warriors, many a life was spent in air.
With his huge mace, cow-headed, Rustem dyed
The ground with crimson – and wherever seen,
Urging impatiently his fiery horse,
Heads severed fell like withered leaves in autumn.
If, brandishing his sword, he struck the head,
Horseman and steed were downward cleft in twain—
And if his side-long blow was on the loins,
The sword passed through, as easily as the blade
Slices a cucumber. The blood of heroes
Deluged the plain. On that tremendous day,
With sword and dagger, battle-axe and noose,
He cut, and tore, and broke, and bound the brave,
Slaying and making captive. At one swoop
More than a thousand fell by his own hand.

Zál beheld his son with amazement and delight. The Túránians left the fire-worshippers in possession of the field, and retreated towards the Jihún with precipitation, not a sound of drum or trumpet denoting their track. After halting three days in a state of deep dejection and misery, they continued their retreat along the banks of the Jihún. The Persian army, upon the flight of the enemy, fell back with their prisoners of war, and Rustem was received by the king with distinguished honor. When Afrásiyáb returned to his father, he communicated to him, with a heavy heart, the misfortunes of the battle, and the power that had been arrayed against him, dwelling with wonder and admiration on the stupendous valor of Rustem.

Seeing my sable banner,
He to the fight came like a crocodile,
Thou wouldst have said his breath scorched up the plain;
He seized my girdle with such mighty force
As if he would have torn my joints asunder;
And raised me from my saddle – that I seemed
An insect in his grasp – but presently
The golden girdle broke, and down I fell
Ingloriously upon the dusty ground;
But I was rescued by my warrior train!
Thou knowest my valour, how my nerves are strung,
And may conceive the wondrous strength, which thus
Sunk me to nothing. Iron is his frame,
And marvellous his power; peace, peace, alone
Can save us and our country from destruction.

Poshang, considering the luckless state of affairs, and the loss of so many valiant warriors, thought it prudent to acquiesce in the wishes of Afrásiyáb, and sue for peace. To this end Wísah was intrusted with magnificent presents, and the overtures which in substance ran thus: "Minúchihr was revenged upon Túr and Sílim for the death of Irij. Afrásiyáb again has revenged their death upon Nauder, the son of Minúchihr, and now Rustem has conquered Afrásiyáb. But why should we any longer keep the world in confusion – Why should we not be satisfied with what Feridún, in his wisdom, decreed? Continue in the empire which he appropriated to Irij, and let the Jihún be the boundary between us, for are we not connected by blood, and of one family? Let our kingdoms be gladdened with the blessings of peace."

When these proposals of peace reached Kai-kobád, the following answer was returned:

"Well dost thou know that I was not the first
To wage this war. From Túr, thy ancestor,
The strife began. Bethink thee how he slew
The gentle Irij – his own brother; – how,
In these our days, thy son, Afrásiyáb,
Crossing the Jihún, with a numerous force

> *Invaded Persia – think how Nauder died!*
> *Not in the field of battle, like a hero,*
> *But murdered by thy son – who, ever cruel,*
> *Afterwards stabbed his brother, young Aghríras,*
> *So deeply mourned by thee. Yet do I thirst not*
> *For vengeance, or for strife. I yield the realm*
> *Beyond the Jihún – let that river be*
> *The boundary between us; but thy son,*
> *Afrásiyáb, must take his solemn oath*
> *Never to cross that limit, or disturb*
> *The Persian throne again; thus pledged, I grant*
> *The peace solicited."*

The messenger without delay conveyed this welcome intelligence to Poshang, and the Túránian army was in consequence immediately withdrawn within the prescribed line of division, Rustem, however, expostulated with the king against making peace at a time the most advantageous for war, and especially when he had just commenced his victorious career; but Kai-kobád thought differently, and considered nothing equal to justice and tranquillity. Peace was accordingly concluded, and upon Rustem and Zál he conferred the highest honors, and his other warriors engaged in the late conflict also experienced the effects of his bounty and gratitude in an eminent degree.

Kai-kobád then moved towards Persia, and establishing his throne at Istakhar, he administered the affairs of his government with admirable benevolence and clemency, and with unceasing solicitude for the welfare of his subjects. In his eyes every one had an equal claim to consideration and justice. The strong had no power to oppress the weak. After he had continued ten years at Istakhar, building towns and cities, and diffusing improvement and happiness over the land, he removed his throne into Irán. His reign lasted one hundred years, which were passed in the continued exercise of the most princely virtues, and the most munificent liberality. He had four sons: Kai-káús, Arish, Poshín and Aramín; and when the period of his dissolution drew nigh, he solemnly enjoined the eldest, whom he appointed his successor, to pursue steadily the path of integrity and justice, and to be kind and merciful in the administration of the empire left to his charge.

Kai-káús

WHEN KAI-KÁÚS ascended the throne of his father, the whole world was obedient to his will; but he soon began to deviate from the wise customs and rules which had been recommended as essential to his prosperity and happiness. He feasted and drank wine continually with his warriors and chiefs, so that in the midst of his luxurious enjoyments he looked upon himself as superior to every being upon the face of the earth, and thus astonished the people, high and low, by his extravagance and pride.

One day a Demon, disguised as a musician, waited upon the monarch, and playing sweetly on his harp, sung a song in praise of Mázinderán.

> *And thus he warbled to the king—*
> *"Mázinderán is the bower of spring,*
> *My native home; the balmy air*
> *Diffuses health and fragrance there;*
> *So tempered is the genial glow,*
> *Nor heat nor cold we ever know;*
> *Tulips and hyacinths abound*
> *On every lawn; and all around*
> *Blooms like a garden in its prime,*
> *Fostered by that delicious clime.*
> *The bulbul sits on every spray,*
> *And pours his soft melodious lay;*
> *Each rural spot its sweets discloses,*
> *Each streamlet is the dew of roses;*
> *And damsels, idols of the heart,*
> *Sustain a more bewitching part.*
> *And mark me, that untravelled man*
> *Who never saw Mázinderán,*
> *And all the charms its bowers possess,*
> *Has never tasted happiness!"*

No sooner had Kai-káús heard this description of the country of Mázinderán than he determined to lead an army thither, declaring to his warriors that the splendor and glory of his reign should exceed that of either Jemshíd, Zohák, or Kai-kobád. The warriors, however, were alarmed at this precipitate resolution, thinking it certain destruction to make war against the Demons; but they had not courage or confidence enough to disclose their real sentiments. They only ventured to suggest, that if his majesty reflected a little on the subject, he might not ultimately consider the enterprise so advisable as he had at first imagined. But this produced no impression, and they then deemed it expedient to despatch a messenger to Zál, to inform him of the wild notions which the Evil One had put into the head of Kai-káús to effect his ruin, imploring Zál to allow of no delay, otherwise the eminent services so lately performed by him and Rustem for the state would be rendered utterly useless and vain. Upon this summons, Zál immediately set off from Sístán to Irán; and having arrived at the royal court, and been received with customary respect and consideration, he endeavored to dissuade the king from the contemplated expedition into Mázinderán.

Kai-káús, however, was not to be diverted from his purpose; and with respect to what his predecessors had not done, he considered himself superior in might and influence to either Feridún, Jemshíd, Minúchihr, or Kai-kobád, who had never aspired to the conquest of Mázinderán. He further observed, that he had a bolder heart, a larger army, and a fuller treasury than any of them, and the whole world was under his sway—

> *And what are all these Demon-charms,*
> *That they excite such dread alarms?*
> *What is a Demon-host to me,*
> *Their magic spells and sorcery?*
> *One effort, and the field is won;*
> *Then why should I the battle shun?*
> *Be thou and Rustem (whilst afar*
> *I wage the soul-appalling war),*
> *The guardians of the kingdom; Heaven*
> *To me hath its protection given;*
> *And, when I reach the Demon's fort,*
> *Their severed heads shall be my sport!*

When Zál became convinced of the unalterable resolution of Kai-káús, he ceased to oppose his views, and expressed his readiness to comply with whatever commands he might receive for the safety of the state.

> *May all thy actions prosper – may'st thou never*
> *Have cause to recollect my warning voice,*
> *With sorrow or repentance. Heaven protect thee!*

Zál then took leave of the king and his warrior friends, and returned to Sístán, not without melancholy forebodings respecting the issue of the war against Mázinderán.

As soon as morning dawned, the army was put in motion. The charge of the empire, and the keys of the treasury and jewel-chamber were left in the hands of Mílad, with injunctions, however, not to draw a sword against any enemy that might spring up, without the consent and assistance of Zál and Rustem. When the army had arrived within the limits of Mázinderán, Kai-káús ordered Gíw to select two thousand of the bravest men, the boldest wielders of the battle-axe, and proceed rapidly towards the city. In his progress, according to the king's instructions, he burnt and destroyed everything of value, mercilessly slaying man, woman, and child. For the king said:

> *Kill all before thee, whether young or old,*
> *And turn their day to night; thus free the world*
> *From the magician's art.*

Proceeding in his career of desolation and ruin, Gíw came near to the city, and found it arrayed in all the splendor of heaven; every street was crowded with beautiful women, richly adorned, and young damsels with faces as bright as the moon. The treasure-chamber was full of gold and jewels, and the country abounded with cattle. Information of this discovery was immediately sent to Kai-káús, who was delighted to find that Mázinderán was truly a blessed region, the very garden of beauty, where the cheeks of the women seemed to be tinted with the hue of the pomegranate flower, by the gate-keeper of Paradise.

This invasion filled the heart of the king of Mázinderán with grief and alarm, and his first care was to call the gigantic White Demon to his aid. Meanwhile Kai-káús, full of the wildest anticipations of victory, was encamped on the plain near the city in splendid state and preparing to commence the final overthrow of the enemy on the following day. In the night, however, a cloud came, and deep darkness like pitch overspread the earth, and tremendous hail-stones poured down upon the Persian host, throwing them into the greatest confusion. Thousands were destroyed, others fled, and were scattered abroad in the gloom. The morning dawned, but it brought no light to the eyes of Kai-káús; and amidst the horrors he experienced, his treasury was captured, and the soldiers of his army either killed or made prisoners of war. Then did he bitterly lament that he had not followed the wise counsel of Zál. Seven days he was involved in this dreadful affliction, and on the eighth day he heard the roar of the White Demon, saying:

> *"O king, thou art the willow-tree, all barren,*
> *With neither fruit, nor flower. What could induce*
> *The dream of conquering Mázinderán?*
> *Hadst thou no friend to warn thee of thy folly?*
> *Hadst thou not heard of the White Demon's power—*
> *Of him, who from the gorgeous vault of Heaven*
> *Can charm the stars? From this mad enterprise*
> *Others have wisely shrunk – and what hast thou*
> *Accomplished by a more ambitious course?*
> *Thy soldiers have slain many, dire destruction*
> *And spoil have been their purpose – thy wild will*
> *Has promptly been obeyed; but thou art now*
> *Without an army, not one man remains*
> *To lift a sword, or stand in thy defence;*
> *Not one to hear thy groans and thy despair."*

There were selected from the army twelve thousand of the demon-warriors, to take charge of and hold in custody the Iránian captives, all the chiefs, as well as the soldiers, being secured with bonds, and only allowed food enough to keep them alive. Arzang, one of the demon-leaders, having got possession of the wealth, the crown and jewels, belonging to Kai-káús, was appointed to escort the captive king and his troops, all of whom were deprived of sight, to the city of Mázinderán, where they were delivered into the hands of the monarch of that country. The White Demon, after thus putting an end to hostilities, returned to his own abode.

Kai-káús, strictly guarded as he was, found an opportunity of sending an account of his blind and helpless condition to Zál, in which he lamented that he had not followed his advice, and urgently requested him, if he was not himself in confinement, to come to his assistance, and release him from captivity. When Zál heard the melancholy story, he gnawed the very skin of his body with vexation, and turning to Rustem, conferred with him in private.

> *"The sword must be unsheathed, since Kai-káús*
> *Is bound a captive in the dragon's den,*
> *And Rakush must be saddled for the field,*
> *And thou must bear the weight of this emprize;*
> *For I have lived two centuries, and old age*
> *Unfits me for the heavy toils of war.*
> *Should'st thou release the king, thy name will be*
> *Exalted o'er the earth. – Then don thy mail,*
> *And gain immortal honor."*

Rustem replied that it was a long journey to Mázinderán, and that the king had been six months on the road. Upon this Zál observed that there were two roads – the most tedious one was that which Kai-káús had taken; but by the other, which was full of dangers and difficulty, and lions, and demons, and sorcery, he might reach Mázinderán in seven days, if he reached it at all.

On hearing these words Rustem assented, and chose the short road, observing:

> *"Although it is not wise, they say,*
> *With willing feet to track the way*
> *To hell; though only men who've lost,*
> *All love of life, by misery crossed,*
> *Would rush into the tiger's lair,*
> *And die, poor reckless victims, there;*
> *I gird my loins, whate'er may be,*
> *And trust in God for victory."*

On the following day, resigning himself to the protection of Heaven, he put on his war attire, and with his favorite horse, Rakush, properly caparisoned, stood prepared for the journey. His mother, Rúdábeh, took leave of him with great sorrow; and the young hero departed from Sístán, consoling himself and his friends, thus:

"O'er him who seeks the battle-field,
Nobly his prisoned king to free,
Heaven will extend its saving shield,
And crown his arms with victory."

The Seven Labors of Rustem

FIRST STAGE. He rapidly pursued his way, performing two days' journey in one, and soon came to a forest full of wild asses. Oppressed with hunger, he succeeded in securing one of them, which he roasted over a fire, lighted by sparks produced by striking the point of his spear, and kept in a blaze with dried grass and branches of trees. After regaling himself, and satisfying his hunger, he loosened the bridle of Rakush, and allowed him to graze; and choosing a safe place for repose during the night, and taking care to have his sword under his head, he went to sleep among the reeds of that wilderness. In a short space a fierce lion appeared, and attacked Rakush with great violence; but Rakush very speedily with his teeth and heels put an end to his furious assailant. Rustem, awakened by the confusion, and seeing the dead lion before him, said to his favorite companion:

"Ah! Rakush, why so thoughtless grown,
To fight a lion thus alone;
For had it been thy fate to bleed,
And not thy foe, my gallant steed!
How could thy master have conveyed
His helm, and battle-axe, and blade,
Kamund, and bow, and buberyán,
Unaided, to Mázinderán?
Why didst thou fail to give the alarm,
And save thyself from chance of harm,
By neighing loudly in my ear;
But though thy bold heart knows no fear,

> *From such unwise exploits refrain,*
> *Nor try a lion's strength again."*

Saying this, Rustem laid down to sleep, and did not awake till the morning dawned. As the sun rose, he remounted Rakush, and proceeded on his journey towards Mázinderán.

Second Stage. After travelling rapidly for some time, he entered a desert, in which no water was to be found, and the sand was so burning hot, that it seemed to be instinct with fire. Both horse and rider were oppressed with the most maddening thirst. Rustem alighted, and vainly wandered about in search of relief, till almost exhausted, he put up a prayer to Heaven for protection against the evils which surrounded him, engaged as he was in an enterprise for the release of Kai-káús and the Persian army, then in the power of the demons. With pious earnestness he besought the Almighty to bless him in the great work; and whilst in a despairing mood he was lamenting his deplorable condition, his tongue and throat being parched with thirst, his body prostrate on the sand, under the influence of a raging sun, he saw a sheep pass by, which he hailed as the harbinger of good. Rising up and grasping his sword in his hand, he followed the animal, and came to a fountain of water, where he devoutly returned thanks to God for the blessing which had preserved his existence, and prevented the wolves from feeding on his lifeless limbs. Refreshed by the cool water, he then looked out for something to allay his hunger and killing a gor, he lighted a fire and roasted it, and regaled upon its savory flesh which he eagerly tore from the bones.

When the period of rest arrived, Rustem addressed Rakush, and said to him angrily

> *"Beware, my steed, of future strife.*
> *Again thou must not risk thy life;*
> *Encounter not with lion fell,*
> *Nor demon still more terrible;*
> *But should an enemy appear,*
> *Ring loud the warning in my ear."*

After delivering these injunctions, Rustem laid down to sleep, leaving Rakush unbridled, and at liberty to crop the herbage close by.

Third Stage. At midnight a monstrous dragon-serpent issued from the forest; it was eighty yards in length, and so fierce, that neither elephant, nor demon, nor lion, ever ventured to pass by its lair. It came forth, and seeing the champion asleep, and a horse near him, the latter was the first object of attack. But Rakush retired towards his master, and neighed and beat the ground so furiously, that Rustem soon awoke; looking around on every side, however, he saw nothing – the dragon had vanished, and he went to sleep again. Again the dragon burst out of the thick darkness, and again Rakush was at the pillow of his master, who rose up at the alarm: but anxiously trying to penetrate the dreary gloom, he saw nothing – all was a blank; and annoyed at this apparently vexatious conduct of his horse, he spoke sharply:

> *"Why thus again disturb my rest,*
> *When sleep had softly soothed my breast?*
> *I told thee, if thou chanced to see*
> *Another dangerous enemy,*
> *To sound the alarm; but not to keep*
> *Depriving me of needful sleep;*
> *When nothing meets the eye nor ear,*
> *Nothing to cause a moment's fear!*
> *But if again my rest is broke,*
> *On thee shall fall the fatal stroke,*
> *And I myself will drag this load*
> *Of ponderous arms along the road;*
> *Yes, I will go, a lonely man,*
> *Without thee, to Mázinderán."*

Rustem again went to sleep, and Rakush was resolved this time not to move a step from his side, for his heart was grieved and afflicted by the harsh words that had been addressed to him. The dragon again appeared, and the faithful horse almost tore up the earth with his heels, to rouse his sleeping master. Rustem again awoke, and sprang to his feet, and was again angry; but fortunately at that moment sufficient light was providentially given for him to see the prodigious cause of alarm.

> *Then swift he drew his sword, and closed in strife*
> *With that huge monster. – Dreadful was the shock*

And perilous to Rustem; but when Rakush
Perceived the contest doubtful, furiously,
With his keen teeth, he bit and tore away
The dragon's scaly hide; whilst quick as thought
The Champion severed off the ghastly head,
And deluged all the plain with horrid blood.
Amazed to see a form so hideous
Breathless stretched out before him, he returned
Thanks to the Omnipotent for his success,
Saying – "Upheld by thy protecting arm,
What is a lion's strength, a demon's rage,
Or all the horrors of the burning desert,
With not one drop to quench devouring thirst?
Nothing, since power and might proceed from Thee."

Fourth Stage. Rustem having resumed the saddle, continued his journey through an enchanted territory, and in the evening came to a beautifully green spot, refreshed by flowing rivulets, where he found, to his surprise, a ready-roasted deer, and some bread and salt. He alighted, and sat down near the enchanted provisions, which vanished at the sound of his voice, and presently a tambourine met his eyes, and a flask of wine. Taking up the instrument he played upon it, and chanted a ditty about his own wanderings, and the exploits which he most loved. He said that he had no pleasure in banquets, but only in the field fighting with heroes and crocodiles in war. The song happened to reach the ears of a sorceress, who, arrayed in all the charms of beauty suddenly approached him, and sat down by his side. The champion put up a prayer of gratitude for having been supplied with food and wine, and music, in the desert of Mázinderán, and not knowing that the enchantress was a demon in disguise, he placed in her hands a cup of wine in the name of God; but at the mention of the Creator the enchanted form was converted into a black fiend. Seeing this, Rustem threw his kamund, and secured the demon; and, drawing his sword, at once cut the body in two.

Fifth Stage.

From thence proceeding onward, he approached
A region destitute of light, a void
Of utter darkness. Neither moon nor star

Peep'd through the gloom; no choice of path remained,
And therefore, throwing loose the rein, he gave
Rakush the power to travel on, unguided.
At length the darkness was dispersed, the earth
Became a scene, joyous and light, and gay,
Covered with waving corn – there Rustem paused
And quitting his good steed among the grass,
Laid himself gently down, and, wearied, slept;
His shield beneath his head, his sword before him.

When the keeper of the forest saw the stranger and his horse, he went to Rustem, then asleep, and struck his staff violently on the ground, and having thus awakened the hero, he asked him, devil that he was, why he had allowed his horse to feed upon the green corn-field. Angry at these words, Rustem, without uttering a syllable, seized hold of the keeper by the ears, and wrung them off. The mutilated wretch, gathering up his severed ears, hurried away, covered with blood, to his master, Aúlád, and told him of the injury he had sustained from a man like a black demon, with a tiger-skin cuirass and an iron helmet; showing at the same time the bleeding witnesses of his sufferings. Upon being informed of this outrageous proceeding, Aúlád, burning with wrath, summoned together his fighting men, and hastened by the directions of the keeper to the place where Rustem had been found asleep. The champion received the angry lord of the land, fully prepared, on horseback, and heard him demand his name, that he might not slay a worthless antagonist, and why he had torn off the ears of his forest-keeper! Rustem replied that the very sound of his name would make him shudder with horror. Aúlád then ordered his troops to attack Rustem, and they rushed upon him with great fury; but their leader was presently killed by the master-hand, and great numbers were also scattered lifeless over the plain. The survivors running away, Rustem's next object was to follow and secure, by his kamund, the person of Aúlád, and with admirable address and ingenuity, he succeeded in dismounting him and taking him alive. He then bound his hands, and said to him:

"If thou wilt speak the truth unmixed with lies,
Unmixed with false prevaricating words,
And faithfully point out to me the caves
Of the White Demon and his warrior chiefs—

And where Káús is prisoned – thy reward
Shall be the kingdom of Mázinderán;
For I, myself, will place thee on that throne.
But if thou play'st me false – thy worthless blood
Shall answer for the foul deception."

"Stay,
Be not in wrath," Aúlád at once replied—
"Thy wish shall be fulfilled – and thou shalt know
Where king Káús is prisoned – and, beside,
Where the White Demon reigns. Between two dark
And lofty mountains, in two hundred caves
Immeasurably deep, his people dwell.
Twelve hundred Demons keep the watch by night
And Baid, and Sinja. Like a reed, the hills
Tremble whenever the White Demon moves.
But dangerous is the way. A stony desert
Lies full before thee, which the nimble deer
Has never passed. Then a prodigious stream
Two farsangs wide obstructs thy path, whose banks
Are covered with a host of warrior-Demons,
Guarding the passage to Mázinderán;
And thou art but a single man – canst thou
O'ercome such fearful obstacles as these?"

At this the Champion smiled. "Show but the way,
And thou shalt see what one man can perform,
With power derived from God! Lead on, with speed,
To royal Káús." With obedient haste
Aúlád proceeded, Rustem following fast,
Mounted on Rakush. Neither dismal night
Nor joyous day they rested – on they went
Until at length they reached the fatal field,
Where Káús was o'ercome. At midnight hour,
Whilst watching with attentive eye and ear,

A piercing clamor echoed all around,
And blazing fires were seen, and numerous lamps
Burnt bright on every side. Rustem inquired
What this might be. "It is Mázinderán,"
Aúlád rejoined, "and the White Demon's chiefs
Are gathered there." Then Rustem to a tree
Bound his obedient guide – to keep him safe,
And to recruit his strength, laid down awhile
And soundly slept.

When morning dawned, he rose,
And mounting Rakush, put his helmet on,
The tiger-skin defended his broad chest,
And sallying forth, he sought the Demon chief,
Arzang, and summoned him with such a roar
That stream and mountain shook. Arzang sprang up,
Hearing a human voice, and from his tent
Indignant issued – him the champion met,
And clutched his arms and ears, and from his body
Tore off the gory head, and cast it far
Amidst the shuddering Demons, who with fear
Shrunk back and fled, precipitate, lest they
Should likewise feel that dreadful punishment.

Sixth Stage. After this achievement Rustem returned to the place where he had left Aúlád, and having released him, sat down under the tree and related what he had done. He then commanded his guide to show the way to the place where Kaikáús was confined; and when the champion entered the city of Mázinderán, the neighing of Rakush was so loud that the sound distinctly reached the ears of the captive monarch. Káús rejoiced, and said to his people: "I have heard the voice of Rakush, and my misfortunes are at an end;" but they thought he was either insane or telling them a dream. The actual appearance of Rustem, however, soon satisfied them. Gúdarz, and Tús, and Báhrám, and Gíw, and Gustahem, were delighted to meet him, and the king embraced him with great warmth and affection, and heard from him with admiration the story of his wonderful progress and exploits. But Káús and his warriors, under the influence and spells of the Demons, were still blind, and he cautioned Rustem particularly to conceal Rakush from the sight of the sorcerers, for if the White Demon should hear of the slaughter of Arzang, and the conqueror being at Mázinderán, he would immediately assemble an overpowering army of Demons, and the consequences might be terrible.

Rustem accordingly, after having warned his friends and companions in arms to keep on the alert, prepared for the enterprise, and guided by Aúlád, hurried on till he came to the Haft-koh, or Seven Mountains. There he found numerous companies of Demons; and coming to one of the caverns, saw it crowded with the same awful beings. And now consulting with Aúlád, he was informed that the most advantageous time for attack would be when the sun became hot, for then all the Demons were accustomed to go to sleep, with the exception of a very small number who were appointed to keep watch. He therefore waited till the sun rose high in the firmament; and as soon as he had bound Aúlád to a tree hand and foot, with the thongs of his kamund, drew his sword, and rushed among the prostrate Demons, dismembering and slaying all that fell in his way. Dreadful was the carnage, and those who survived fled in the wildest terror from the champion's fury.

Seventh Stage. Rustem now hastened forward to encounter the White Demon.

> *Advancing to the cavern, he looked down*
> *And saw a gloomy place, dismal as hell;*
> *But not one cursed, impious sorcerer*
> *Was visible in that infernal depth.*
> *Awhile he stood – his falchion in his grasp,*
> *And rubbed his eyes to sharpen his dim sight,*
> *And then a mountain-form, covered with hair,*
> *Filling up all the space, rose into view.*
> *The monster was asleep, but presently*
> *The daring shouts of Rustem broke his rest,*
> *And brought him suddenly upon his feet,*
> *When seizing a huge mill-stone, forth he came,*
> *And thus accosted the intruding chief:*
> *"Art thou so tired of life, that reckless thus*
> *Thou dost invade the precincts of the Demons?*
> *Tell me thy name, that I may not destroy*

A *nameless thing!" The champion stern replied,*
"My name is Rustem – sent by Zál, my father,
Descended from the champion Sám Súwár,
To be revenged on thee – the King of Persia
Being now a prisoner in Mázinderán."
When the accursed Demon heard the name
Of Sám Súwár, he, like a serpent, writhed
In agony of spirit; terrified
At that announcement – then, recovering strength,
He forward sprang, and hurled the mill-stone huge
Against his adversary, who fell back
And disappointed the prodigious blow.
Black frowned the Demon, and through Rustem's heart
A wild sensation ran of dire alarm;
But, rousing up, his courage was revived,
And wielding furiously his beaming sword,
He pierced the Demon's thigh, and lopped the limb;
Then both together grappled, and the cavern
Shook with the contest – each, at times, prevailed;
The flesh of both was torn, and streaming blood
Crimsoned the earth. "If I survive this day,"
Said Rustem in his heart, in that dread strife,
"My life must be immortal." The White Demon,
With equal terror, muttered to himself:
"I now despair of life – sweet life; no more
Shall I be welcomed at Mázinderán."
And still they struggled hard – still sweat and blood
Poured down at every strain. Rustem, at last,
Gathering fresh power, vouchsafed by favouring Heaven
And bringing all his mighty strength to bear,
Raised up the gasping Demon in his arms,
And with such fury dashed him to the ground,
That life no longer moved his monstrous frame.
Promptly he then tore out the reeking heart,
And crowds of demons simultaneous fell

As part of him, and stained the earth with gore;
Others who saw this signal overthrow,
Trembled, and hurried from the scene of blood.
Then the great victor, issuing from that cave
With pious haste – took off his helm, and mail,
And royal girdle – and with water washed
His face and body – choosing a pure place
For prayer – to praise his Maker – Him who gave
The victory, the eternal source of good;
Without whose grace and blessing, what is man!
With it his armor is impregnable.

The Champion having finished his prayer, resumed his war habiliments, and going to Aúlád, released him from the tree, and gave into his charge the heart of the White Demon. He then pursued his journey back to Káús at Mázinderán. On the way Aúlád solicited some reward for the services he had performed, and Rustem again promised that he should be appointed governor of the country.

"But first the monarch of Mázinderán,
The Demon-king, must be subdued, and cast
Into the yawning cavern – and his legions
Of foul enchanters, utterly destroyed."

Upon his arrival at Mázinderán, Rustem related to his sovereign all that he had accomplished, and especially that he had torn out and brought away the White Demon's heart, the blood of which was destined to restore Kai-káús and his warriors to sight. Rustem was not long in applying the miraculous remedy, and the moment the blood touched their eyes, the fearful blindness was perfectly cured.

The champion brought the Demon's heart,
And squeezed the blood from every part,
Which, dropped upon the injured sight,
Made all things visible and bright;
One moment broke that magic gloom,
Which seemed more dreadful than the tomb.

The monarch immediately ascended his throne surrounded by all his warriors, and seven days were spent in mutual congratulations and rejoicing. On the eighth day they all resumed the saddle, and proceeded to complete the destruction of the enemy. They set fire to the city, and burnt it to the ground, and committed such horrid carnage among the remaining magicians that streams of loathsome blood crimsoned all the place.

Káús afterwards sent Ferhád as an ambassador to the king of Mázinderán, suggesting to him the expediency of submission, and representing to him the terrible fall of Arzang, and of the White Demon with all his host, as a warning against resistance to the valor of Rustem. But when the king of Mázinderán heard from Ferhád the purpose of his embassy, he expressed great astonishment, and replied that he himself was superior in all respects to Káús; that his empire was more extensive, and his warriors more numerous and brave. "Have I not," said he, "a hundred war-elephants, and Káús not one? Wherever I move, conquest marks my way; why then should I fear the sovereign of Persia? Why should I submit to him?"

This haughty tone made a deep impression upon Ferhád, who returning quickly, told Káús of the proud bearing and fancied power of the ruler of Mázinderán. Rustem was immediately sent for; and so indignant was he on hearing the tidings, that "every hair on his body started up like a spear," and he proposed to go himself with a second dispatch. The king was too much pleased to refuse, and another letter was written more urgent than the first, threatening the enemy to hang up his severed head on the walls of his own fort, if he persisted in his contumacy and scorn of the offer made.

As soon as Rustem had come within a short distance of the court of the king of Mázinderán, accounts reached his majesty of the approach of another ambassador, when a deputation of warriors was sent to receive him. Rustem observing them, and being in sight of the hostile army, with a view to show his strength, tore up a large tree on the road by the roots, and dexterously wielded it in his hand like a spear. Tilting onwards, he flung it down before the wondering enemy, and one of the chiefs then thought it incumbent upon him to display his own prowess. He advanced, and offered to grasp hands with Rustem: they met; but the gripe of the champion was so excruciating that the sinews of his adversary cracked, and in agony he fell from his horse. Intelligence of this discomfiture was instantly conveyed to the king, who then summoned his most valiant and renowned chieftain, Kálahúr, and directed him to go and punish, signally, the warrior who had thus presumed to triumph over one of his heroes. Accordingly Kálahúr appeared, and boastingly stretched out his hand, which Rustem wrung with such grinding force, that the very nails dropped off, and blood started from his body. This was enough, and Kálahúr hastily returned to the king, and anxiously recommended him to submit to terms, as it would be in vain to oppose such invincible strength. The king was both grieved and angry at this situation of affairs, and invited the ambassador to his presence. After inquiring respecting Káús and the Persian army, he said:

> "And thou art Rustem, clothed with mighty power,
> Who slaughtered the White Demon, and now comest
> To crush the monarch of Mázinderán!"
> "No!" said the champion, "I am but his servant,
> And even unworthy of that noble station;
> My master being a warrior, the most valiant
> That ever graced the world since time began.
> Nothing am I; but what doth he resemble!
> What is a lion, elephant, or demon!
> Engaged in fight, he is himself a host!"

The ambassador then tried to convince the king of the folly of resistance, and of his certain defeat if he continued to defy the power of Káús and the bravery of Rustem; but the effort was fruitless, and both states prepared for battle.

The engagement which ensued was obstinate and sanguinary, and after seven days of hard fighting, neither army was victorious, neither defeated. Afflicted at this want of success, Káús grovelled in the dust, and prayed fervently to the Almighty to give him the triumph. He addressed all his warriors, one by one, and urged them to increased exertions; and on the eighth day, when the battle was renewed, prodigies of valor were performed. Rustem singled out, and encountered the king of Mázinderán, and fiercely they fought together with sword and javelin; but suddenly, just as he was rushing on with overwhelming force, his adversary, by his magic art, transformed himself into a stony rock. Rustem and the Persian warriors were all amazement. The fight had been suspended for some time, when Káús came forward to inquire the cause; and hearing with astonishment of the transformation, ordered his soldiers to drag the enchanted mass towards his own tent; but all the strength that could be applied was unequal to move so great a weight, till Rustem set himself to the task, and amidst the wondering army, lifted up the rock and conveyed it to the appointed place.

He then addressed the work of sorcery, and said: "If thou dost not resume thy original shape, I will instantly break thee, flinty-rock as thou now art, into atoms, and scatter thee in the dust." The magician-king was alarmed by this threat, and reappeared in his own form, and then Rustem, seizing his hand, brought him to Káús, who, as a punishment for his wickedness and atrocity, ordered him to be slain, and his body to be cut into a thousand pieces! The wealth of the country was immediately afterwards secured; and at the recommendation of Rustem, Aúlád was appointed governor of Mázinderán. After the usual thanksgivings and rejoicings on account of the victory, Káús and his warriors returned to Persia, where splendid honors and rewards were bestowed on every soldier for his heroic services. Rustem having received the highest acknowledgments of his merit, took leave, and returned to his father Zál at Zábulistán.

Suddenly an ardent desire arose in the heart of Káús to survey all the provinces and states of his empire. He wished to visit Túrán, and Chín, and Mikrán, and Berber, and Zirra. Having commenced his royal tour of inspection, he found the King of Berberistán in a state of rebellion, with his army prepared to dispute his authority. A severe battle was the consequence; but the refractory sovereign was soon compelled to retire, and the elders of the city came forward to sue for mercy and protection. After this triumph, Káús turned towards the mountain Káf, and visited various other countries, and in his progress became the guest of the son of Zál in Zábulistán where he stayed a month, enjoying the pleasures of the festive board and the sports of the field.

The disaffection of the King of Hámáverán, in league with the King of Misser and Shám, and the still hostile King of Berberistán, soon, however, drew him from Nímrúz, and quitting the principality of Rustem, his arms were promptly directed against his new enemy, who in the contest which ensued, made an obstinate resistance, but was at length overpowered, and obliged to ask for quarter. After the battle, Káús was informed that the Sháh had a daughter of great beauty, named Súdáveh, possessing a form as graceful as the tall cypress, musky ringlets, and all the charms of Heaven. From the description of this damsel he became enamoured, and through the medium of a messenger, immediately offered himself to be her husband. The father did not seem to be glad at this proposal, observing to the messenger, that he had but two things in life valuable to him, and those were his daughter and his property; one was his solace and delight, and the other his support; to be deprived of both would be death to him; still he could not gainsay the wishes of a king of such power, and his conqueror. He then sorrowfully communicated the overture to his child, who, however, readily consented; and in the course of a week, the bride was sent escorted by soldiers, and accompanied by a magnificent cavalcade, consisting of a thousand horses and mules, a thousand camels, and numerous female attendants. When Súdáveh descended from her litter, glowing with beauty, with her rich dark tresses flowing to her feet, and cheeks like the rose, Káús regarded her with admiration and rapture; and so impatient was he to possess that lovely treasure, that the marriage rites were performed according to the laws of the country without delay.

The Sháh of Hámáverán, however, was not satisfied, and he continually plotted within himself how he might contrive to regain possession of Súdáveh, as well as be revenged upon the king. With this view he invited Káús to be his guest for a while; but Súdáveh cautioned the king not to trust to the treachery which dictated the invitation, as she apprehended from it nothing but mischief and disaster. The warning, however, was of no avail, for Káús accepted the proffered hospitality of his new father-in-law. He accordingly proceeded with his bride and his most famous warriors to the city, where he was received and entertained in the most sumptuous manner, seated on a gorgeous throne, and felt infinitely exhilarated with the magnificence and the hilarity by which he was surrounded. Seven days were passed in this glorious banqueting and delight; but on the succeeding night, the sound of trumpets and the war-cry was heard. The intrusion of soldiers changed the face of the scene; and the king, who had just been waited on, and pampered with such respect and devotion, was suddenly seized, together with his principal warriors, and carried off to a remote fortress, situated on a high mountain, where they were imprisoned, and guarded by a thousand valiant men. His tents were plundered, and all his treasure taken away. At this event his wife was inconsolable and deaf to all entreaties from her father, declaring that she preferred death to separation from her husband; upon which she was conveyed to the same dungeon, to mingle groans with the captive king.

Invasion of Irán by Afrásiyáb

THE INTELLIGENCE of Káús's imprisonment was very soon spread through the world, and operated as a signal to all the inferior states to get possession of Irán. Afrásiyáb was the most powerful aspirant to the throne; and gathering an immense army, he hurried from Túrán, and made

a rapid incursion into the country, which after three months he succeeded in conquering, scattering ruin and desolation wherever he came.

Some of those who escaped from the field bent their steps towards Zábulistán, by whom Rustem was informed of the misfortunes in which Káús was involved; it therefore became necessary that he should again endeavor to effect the liberation of his sovereign; and accordingly, after assembling his troops from different quarters, the first thing he did was to despatch a messenger to Hámáverán, with a letter, demanding the release of the prisoners; and in the event of a refusal, declaring the king should suffer the same fate as the White Demon and the magician-monarch of Mázinderán. Although this threat produced considerable alarm in the breast of the king of Hámáverán, he arrogantly replied, that if Rustem wished to be placed in the same situation as Káús, he was welcome to come as soon as he liked.

Upon hearing this defiance, Rustem left Zábulistán, and after an arduous journey by land and water, arrived at the confines of Hámáverán. The king of that country, roused by the noise and uproar, and bold aspect of the invading army, drew up his own forces, and a battle ensued, but he was unequal to stand his ground before the overwhelming courage of Rustem. His troops fled in confusion, and then almost in despair he anxiously solicited assistance from the chiefs of Berber and Misser, which was immediately given. Thus three kings and their armies were opposed to the power and resources of one man. Their formidable array covered an immense space.

But when the King of Hámáverán beheld the person of Rustem in all its pride and strength, and commanding power, he paused with apprehension and fear, and intrenched himself well behind his own troops. Rustem, on the contrary, was full of confidence.

> *"What, though there be a hundred thousand men*
> *Pitched against one, what use is there in numbers*
> *When Heaven is on my side: with Heaven my friend,*
> *The foe will soon be mingled with the dust."*

Having ordered the trumpets to sound, he rushed on the enemy, mounted on Rakush, and committed dreadful havoc among them.

The chief of Hámáverán and his legions were the first to shrink from the conflict; and then the King of Misser, ashamed of their cowardice, rapidly advanced towards the champion with the intention of punishing him for his temerity, but he had no sooner received one of Rustem's hard blows on his head, than he turned to flight, and thus hoped to escape the fury of his antagonist. That fortune, however, was denied him, for being instantly pursued, he was caught with the kamund, or noose, thrown round his loins, dragged from his horse, and safely delivered into the hands of Báhrám, who bound him, and kept him by his side.

Ring within ring the lengthening kamund flew,
And from his steed the astonished monarch drew.

Having accomplished this signal capture, Rustem proceeded against the troops under the Sháh of Berberistán, which, valorously aided as he was, by Zúára, he soon vanquished and dispatched; and impelling Rakush impetuously forward upon the sháh himself, made him and forty of his principal chiefs prisoners of war. The King of Hámáverán, seeing the horrible carnage, and the defeat of all his expectations, speedily sent a messenger to Rustem, to solicit a suspension of the fight, offering to deliver up Káús and all his warriors, and all the regal property and treasure which had been plundered from him. The troops of the three kingdoms also urgently prayed for quarter and protection, and Rustem readily agreed to the proffered conditions.

"Káús to liberty restore,
With all his chiefs, I ask no more;
For him alone I conquering came;
Than him no other prize I claim."

The Return of Kai-káús

IT WAS A JOYOUS day when Káús and his illustrious heroes were released from their fetters, and removed from the mountain-fortress in which they were confined. Rustem forthwith reseated him on his throne, and did not fail to collect for the public treasury all the valuables of the three states which had submitted to his power. The troops of Misser, Berberistán, and Hámáverán, having declared their allegiance to the Persian king, the accumulated numbers increased Káús's army to upwards of three hundred thousand men, horse and foot, and with this immense force he moved towards Irán. Before marching, however, he sent a message to Afrásiyáb, commanding him to quit the country he had so unjustly invaded, and recommending him to be contented with the territory of Túrán.

> "Hast thou forgotten Rustem's power,
> When thou wert in that perilous hour
> By him overthrown? Thy girdle broke,
> Or thou hadst felt the conqueror's yoke.
> Thy crowding warriors proved thy shield,
> They saved and dragged thee from the field;
> By them unrescued then, wouldst thou
> Have lived to vaunt thy prowess now?"

This message was received with bitter feelings of resentment by Afrásiyáb, who prepared his army for battle without delay, and promised to bestow his daughter in marriage and a kingdom upon the man who should succeed in taking Rustem alive.

This proclamation was a powerful excitement: and when the engagement took place, mighty efforts were made for the reward; but those who aspired to deserve it were only the first to fall. Afrásiyáb beholding the fall of so many of his chiefs, dashed forward to cope with the champion: but his bravery was unavailing; for, suffering sharply under the overwhelming attacks of Rustem, he was glad to effect his escape, and retire from the field. In short, he rapidly retraced his steps to Túrán, leaving Káús in full possession of the kingdom.

> With anguish stricken, he regained his home,
> After a wild and ignominious flight;
> The world presenting nothing to his lips
> But poison-beverage; all was death to him.

Káús being again seated on the throne of Persia, he resumed the administration of affairs with admirable justice and liberality, and despatched some of his most distinguished warriors to secure the welfare and prosperity of the states of Mervi, and Balkh, and Níshapúr, and Hírát. At the same time he conferred on Rustem the title of Jaháni Pahlván, or, Champion of the World.

In safety now from foreign and domestic enemies, Káús turned his attention to pursuits very different from war and conquest. He directed the Demons to construct two splendid palaces on the mountain Alberz, and separate mansions for the accommodation of his household, which he decorated in the most magnificent manner. All the buildings were beautifully arranged both for convenience and pleasure; and gold and silver and precious stones were used so lavishly, and the brilliancy produced by their combined effect was so great, that night and day appeared to be the same.

Iblís, ever active, observing the vanity and ambition of the king, was not long in taking advantage of the circumstance, and he soon persuaded the Demons to enter into his schemes. Accordingly one of them, disguised as a domestic servant, was instructed to present a nosegay to Káús; and after respectfully kissing the ground, say to him:

> *"Thou art great as king can be,*
> *Boundless in thy majesty;*
> *What is all this earth to thee,*
> *All beneath the sky?*
> *Peris, mortals, demons, hear*
> *Thy commanding voice with fear;*
> *Thou art lord of all things here,*
> *But, thou canst not fly!*
> *That remains for thee; to know*
> *Things above, as things below,*
> *How the planets roll;*
> *How the sun his light displays,*
> *How the moon darts forth her rays;*
> *How the nights succeed the days;*
> *What the secret cause betrays,*
> *And who directs the whole!"*

This artful address of the Demon satisfied Káús of the imperfection of his nature, and the enviable power which he had yet to obtain. To him, therefore, it became matter of deep concern, how he might be enabled to ascend the Heavens without wings, and for that purpose he consulted his astrologers, who presently suggested a way in which his desires might be successfully accomplished.

They contrived to rob an eagle's nest of its young, which they reared with great care, supplying them well with invigorating food, till they grew large and strong. A framework of aloes-wood was then prepared; and at each of the four corners was fixed perpendicularly, a javelin, surmounted on the point with flesh of a goat. At each corner again one of the eagles was bound, and in the middle Káús was seated in great pomp with a goblet of wine before him. As soon as the eagles became hungry, they endeavored to get at the goat's flesh upon the javelins, and by flapping their wings and flying upwards, they quickly raised up the throne from the ground. Hunger still pressing them, and still being distant from their prey, they ascended higher and higher in the clouds, conveying the astonished king far beyond his own country; but after long and fruitless exertion their strength failed them, and unable to keep their way, the whole fabric came tumbling down from the sky, and fell upon a dreary solitude in the kingdom of Chín. There Káús was left, a prey to hunger, alone, and in utter despair, until he was discovered by a band of Demons, whom his anxious ministers had sent in search of him.

Rustem, and Gúdarz, and Tús, at length heard of what had befallen the king, and with feelings of sorrow not unmixed with indignation, set off to his assistance. "Since I was born," said Gúdarz, "never did I see such a man as Káús. He seems to be entirely destitute of reason and understanding; always in distress and affliction. This is the third calamity in which he has wantonly involved himself. First at Mázinderán, then at Hámáverán, and now he is being punished for attempting to discover the secrets of the Heavens!" When they reached the wilderness into which Káús had fallen, Gúdarz repeated to him the same observations, candidly telling him that he was fitter for a mad-house than a throne, and exhorting him to be satisfied with his lot and be obedient to God, the creator of all things. The miserable king was softened to tears, acknowledged his folly; and as soon as he was escorted back to his palace, he shut himself up, remaining forty days, unseen, prostrating himself in shame and repentance. After that he recovered his spirits, and resumed the administration of affairs with his former liberality, clemency, and justice, almost rivalling the glory of Feridún and Jemshíd.

One day Rustem made a splendid feast; and whilst he and his brother warriors, Gíw and Gúdarz, and Tús, were quaffing their wine, it was determined upon to form a pretended hunting party, and repair to the sporting grounds of Afrásiyáb. The feast lasted seven days; and on the eighth, preparations were made for the march, an advance party being pushed on to reconnoitre the motions of the enemy. Afrásiyáb was soon informed of what was going on, and flattered himself with the hopes of getting Rustem and his seven champions into his thrall, for which purpose he called together his wise men and warriors, and said to them: "You have only to secure these invaders, and Káús will soon cease to be the sovereign of Persia." To accomplish this object, a Túránian army of thirty thousand veterans was assembled, and ordered to occupy all the positions and avenues in the vicinity of the sporting grounds. An immense clamor, and thick clouds of dust, which darkened the skies, announced their approach; and when intelligence of their numbers was brought to Rustem, the undaunted champion smiled, and said to Garáz: "Fortune favors me; what cause is there to fear the king of Túrán? his army does not exceed a hundred thousand men. Were I alone, with Rakush, with my armor, and battle-axe, I would not shrink from his legions. Have I not seven companions in arms, and is not one of them equal to five hundred Túránian heroes? Let Afrásiyáb dare to cross the boundary-river, and the contest will presently convince him that he has only sought his own defeat." Promptly at a signal the cup-bearer produced goblets of the red wine of Zábul; and in one of them Rustem pledged his royal master with loyalty, and Tús and Zúára joined in the convivial and social demonstration of attachment to the king.

The champion arrayed in his buburiyán, mounted Rakush, and advanced towards the Túránian army. Afrásiyáb, when he beheld him in all his terrible strength and vigor, was amazed and disheartened, accompanied, as he was, by Tús, and Gúdarz, and Gurgín, and Gíw, and Báhrám, and Berzín, and Ferhád. The drums and trumpets of Rustem were now heard, and immediately the hostile forces engaged with dagger, sword, and javelin. Dreadful was the onset, and the fury with which the conflict was continued. In truth, so sanguinary and destructive was the battle that Afrásiyáb exclaimed in grief and terror: "If this carnage lasts till the close of day, not a man of my army will remain alive. Have I not one warrior endued with sufficient bravery to oppose and subdue this mighty Rustem? What! not one fit to be rewarded with a diadem, with my own throne and kingdom, which I will freely give to the victor!" Pílsum heard the promise, and was ambitious of earning the reward; but fate decreed it otherwise. His prodigious efforts were of no avail. Alkús was equally unsuccessful, though the bravest of the brave among the Túránian warriors. Encountering Rustem, his brain was pierced by a javelin wielded by the Persian hero, and he fell dead from his saddle. This signal achievement astonished and terrified the Túránians, who, however, made a further despairing effort against the champion and his seven conquering companions, but with no better result than before, and nothing remained to them excepting destruction or flight. Choosing the latter they wheeled round, and endeavored to escape from the sanguinary fate that awaited them.

Seeing this precipitate movement of the enemy, Rustem impelled Rakush forward in pursuit, addressing his favorite horse with fondness and enthusiasm:

> "My valued friend – put forth thy speed,
> This is a time of pressing need;
> Bear me away amidst the strife,
> That I may take that despot's life;
> And with my mace and javelin, flood
> This dusty plain with foe-man's blood."

> Excited by his master's cry,
> The war-horse bounded o'er the plain,
> So swiftly that he seemed to fly,
> Snorting with pride, and tossing high
> His streaming mane.

> And soon he reached that despot's side,
> "Now is the time!" the Champion cried,
> "This is the hour to victory given,"
> And flung his noose – which bound the king
> Fast for a moment in its ring;
> But soon, alas! the bond was riven.

> Haply the Tartar-monarch slipt away,
> Not doomed to suffer on that bloody day;
> And freed from thrall, he hurrying led
> His legions cross the boundary-stream,
> Leaving his countless heaps of dead
> To rot beneath the solar beam.

Onward he rushed with heart opprest,
And broken fortunes; he had quaffed
Bright pleasure's cup – but now, unblest,
Poison was mingled with the draught!

The booty in horses, treasure, armor, pavilions, and tents, was immense; and when the whole was secured, Rustem and his companions fell back to the sporting-grounds already mentioned, from whence he informed Kai-káús by letter of the victory that had been gained. After remaining two weeks there, resting from the toils of war and enjoying the pleasures of hunting, the party returned home to pay their respects to the Persian king:

And this is life! Thus conquest and defeat,
Vary the lights and shades of human scenes,
And human thought. Whilst some, immersed in pleasure,
Enjoy the sweets, others again endure
The miseries of the world. Hope is deceived
In this frail dwelling; certainty and safety
Are only dreams which mock the credulous mind;
Time sweeps o'er all things; why then should the wise
Mourn o'er events which roll resistless on,
And set at nought all mortal opposition?

Kai-khosráu

THE TIDINGS of Khosráu's accession to the throne were received at Sístán by Zál and Rustem with heartfelt pleasure, and they forthwith hastened to court with rich presents, to pay him their homage, and congratulate him on the occasion of his elevation. The heroes were met on the road with suitable honors, and Khosráu embracing Rustem affectionately, lost no time in asking for his assistance in taking vengeance for the death of Saiáwush. The request was no sooner made than granted, and the champion having delivered his presents, then proceeded with his father Zál to wait upon Káús, who prepared a royal banquet, and entertained Khosráu and them in the most sumptuous manner. It was there agreed to march a large army against Afrásiyáb; and all the warriors zealously came forward with their best services, except Zál, who on account of his age requested to remain tranquilly in his own province. Khosráu said to Káús:

> *"The throne can yield no happiness for me,*
> *Nor can I sleep the sleep of health and joy*
> *Till I have been revenged on that destroyer.*
> *The tyrant of Túrán; to please the spirit*
> *Of my poor butchered father."*

Káús, on delivering over to him the imperial army, made him acquainted with the character and merits of every individual of importance. He appointed Fríburz, and a hundred warriors, who were the prince's friends and relatives, to situations of trust and command, and Tús was among them. Gúdarz and his seventy-eight sons and grandsons were placed on the right, and Gustahem, the brother of Tús, with an immense levy on the left. There were also close to Khosráu's person, in the centre of the hosts, thirty-three warriors of the race of Poshang, and a separate guard under Byzun.

In their progress Khosráu said to Fríburz and Tús, "Ferúd, who is my brother, has built a strong fort in Bokhára, called Kulláb, which stands on the way to the enemy, and there he resides with his mother, Gúlshaher. Let him not be molested, for he is also the son of Saiáwush, but pass on one side of his possessions." Fríburz did pass on one side as requested; but Tús, not liking to proceed by the way of the desert, and preferring a cultivated and pleasant country, went directly on through the places which led to the very fort in question. When Ferúd was informed of the approach of Tús with an armed force, he naturally concluded that he was coming to fight him, and consequently determined to oppose his progress. Tús, however, sent Ríú, his son-in-law, to explain to Ferúd that he had no quarrel or business with him, and only wished to pass peaceably through his province; but Ferúd thought this was merely an idle pretext, and proceeding to hostilities, Ríú was killed by him in the conflict that ensued. Tús, upon being informed of this result, drew up his army, and besieged the fort into which Ferúd had precipitately retired. When Ferúd, however, found that Tús himself was in the field, he sallied forth from his fastness, and assailed him with his bow and arrows. One of the darts struck and killed the horse of Tús, and tumbled his rider to the ground. Upon this occurrence Gíw rushed forward in the hopes of capturing the prince; but it so happened that he was unhorsed in the same way. Byzun, the son of Gíw, seeing with great indignation this signal overthrow, wished to be revenged on the victor; and though his father endeavored to restrain him, nothing could control his wrath. He sprung speedily forward to fulfil his menace, but by the bravery and expertness of Ferúd, his horse was killed, and he too was thrown headlong from his saddle. Unsubdued, however, he rose upon his feet, and invited his antagonist to single combat. In consequence of this challenge, they fought a short time with spears till Ferúd deemed it advisable to retire into his fort, from the lofty walls of which he cast down so many stones, that Byzun was desperately wounded, and compelled to leave the place. When he informed Tús of the misfortune which had befallen him, that warrior vowed that on the following day not a man should remain alive in the fort. The mother of Ferúd, who was the daughter of Wísah, had at this period a dream which informed her that the fortress had taken fire, and that the whole of the inhabitants had been consumed to death. This dream she communicated to Ferúd, who said in reply:

> *"Mother! I have no dread of death;*
> *What is there in this vital breath?*
> *My sire was wounded, and he died;*
> *And fate may lay me by his side!*
> *Was ever man immortal? – never!*
> *We cannot, mother, live for ever.*
> *Mine be the task in life to claim*
> *In war a bright and spotless name.*
> *What boots it to be pale with fear,*
> *And dread each grief that waits us here?*
> *Protected by the power divine,*
> *Our lot is written – why repine?"*

Tús, according to his threat, attacked the fort, and burst open the gates. Ferúd defended himself with great valor against Byzun; and whilst they were engaged in deadly battle, Báhrám, the hero, sprang up from his ambuscade, and striking furiously upon the head of Ferúd, killed that unfortunate youth on the spot. The mother, the beautiful Gúlshaher, seeing what had befallen her son, rushed out of the fort in a state of frenzy, and flying to him, clasped him in her arms in an agony of grief. Unable to survive his loss, she plunged a dagger in her own breast, and died at his feet. The Persians then burst open the gates, and plundered the city. Báhrám, when he saw what had been done, reproached Tús with being the cause of this melancholy tragedy, and asked him what account he would give of his conduct to Kai-khosráu. Tús was extremely concerned, and remaining three days at that place, erected a lofty monument to the memory of the unfortunate youth, and scented it with musk and camphor. He then pushed forward his army to attack another fort. That fort gave way, the commandant being killed in the attack; and he then hastened on toward Afrásiyáb, who had ordered Nizád with thirty thousand horsemen to meet him. Byzun distinguished himself in the contest which followed, but would have fallen into the hands of the enemy if he had not been rescued by his men, and conveyed from the field of battle. Afrásiyáb pushed forward another force of forty thousand horsemen under Pírán-wísah, who suffered considerable loss in an engagement with Gíw; and in consequence fell back for the purpose of retrieving himself by a shubkhún, or night attack. The resolution proved to be a good one; for when night came on, the Persians were found off their guard, many of them being intoxicated, and the havoc and destruction committed among them by the Tartars was dreadful. The survivors were in a miserable state of despondency, but it was not till morning dawned that Tús beheld the full extent of his defeat and the ruin that surrounded him. When Kai-khosráu heard of this heavy reverse, he wrote to Fríburz, saying, "I warned Tús not to proceed by the way of Kulláb, because my brother and his mother dwelt in that place, and their residence ought to have been kept sacred. He has not only despised my orders, but he has cruelly occasioned the untimely death of both. Let him be bound, and sent to me a prisoner, and do thou assume the command of the army." Fríburz accordingly placed Tús in confinement, and sent him to Khosráu, who received and treated him with reproaches and wrath, and consigned him to a dungeon. He then wrote to Pírán, reproaching him for resorting to a night attack so unworthy of a brave man, and challenging him to resume the battle with him. Pírán said that he would meet him after the lapse of a month, and at the expiration of that period both armies were opposed to each other. The contest commenced with arrows, then swords, and then with javelins; and Gíw and Byzun were the foremost in bearing down the warriors of the enemy, who suffered so severely that they turned aside to attack Fríburz, against whom they hoped to be more successful. The assault which they made was overwhelming, and vast numbers were slain, so that Fríburz, finding himself driven to extremity, was obliged to shelter himself and his remaining troops on the skirts of a mountain. In the meantime Gúdarz and Gíw determined to keep their ground or perish, and sent Byzun to Fríburz to desire him to join them, or if that was impracticable, to save the imperial banner by despatching it to their care. To this message, Fríburz replied: "The traitors are triumphant over me on every side, and I cannot go, nor will I give up the imperial banner, but tell Gúdarz to come to my aid." Upon receiving this answer, Byzun struck the standard-bearer dead, and snatching up the Derafsh Gávahní, conveyed it to Gúdarz, who, raising it on high, directed his troops against the enemy; and so impetuous was the charge, that the carnage on both sides was prodigious. Only eight of the sons of Gúdarz remained alive, seventy of his kindred having been slain on that day, and many of the family of Káús were also killed. Nor did the relations of Afrásiyáb and Pírán suffer in a less degree, nine hundred of them, warriors and cavaliers, were sent out of the world; yet victory remained with the Túránians.

When Afrásiyáb was informed of the result of this battle, he sent presents and honorary dresses to his officers, saying, "We must not be contented with this triumph; you have yet to obscure the martial glory of Rustem and Khosráu." Pírán replied, "No doubt that object will be accomplished with equal facility."

After the defeat of the Persian army, Fríburz retired under the cover of night, and at length arrived at the court of Khosráu, who was afflicted with the deepest sorrow, both on account of his loss in battle and the death of his brother Ferúd. Rustem was now as usual applied to for the purpose of consoling the king, and extricating the empire from its present misfortunes. Khosráu was induced to liberate Tús from his confinement, and requested Rustem to head the army against Pírán, but Tús offered his services, and the champion observed, "He is fully competent to oppose the arms of Pírán; but if Afrásiyáb takes the field, I will myself instantly follow to the war." Khosráu accordingly deputed Tús and Gúdarz with a large army, and the two hostile powers were soon placed in opposition to each other. It is said that they were engaged seven days and nights, and that on the eighth Húmán came forward, and challenged several warriors to fight singly, all of whom he successively slew. He then called upon Tús, but Gúdarz not permitting him to accept the challenge, sent Gíw in his stead. The combatants met; and after being wounded and exhausted by their struggles for mastery, each returned to his own post. The armies again engaged with arrows, and again the carnage was great, but the battle remained undecided.

Pírán had now recourse to supernatural agency, and sent Barú, a renowned magician, perfect in his art, upon the neighboring mountains, to involve them in darkness, and produce by his conjuration tempestuous showers of snow and hail. He ordered him to direct all their intense severity against the enemy, and to avoid giving any annoyance to the Túránian army. Accordingly when Húmán and Pírán-wísah made their attack, they had the co-operation of the elements, and the consequence was a desperate overthrow of the Persian army.

> *So dreadful was the carnage, that the plain*
> *Was crimsoned with the blood of warriors slain.*

In this extremity, Tús and Gúdarz piously put up a prayer to God, earnestly soliciting protection from the horrors with which they were surrounded.

> *O Thou! the clement, the compassionate,*
> *We are thy servants, succor our distress,*
> *And save us from the sorcery that now*
> *Yields triumph to the foe. In thee alone*
> *We place our trust; graciously hear our prayer!*

Scarcely had this petition been uttered, when a mysterious person appeared to Rehám from the invisible world, and pointed to the mountain from whence the tempest descended. Rehám immediately attended to the sign, and galloped forward to the mountain, where he discovered the magician upon its summit, deeply engaged in incantations and witchcraft. Forthwith he drew his sword and cut off this wizard's arms. Suddenly a whirlwind arose, which dissipated the utter darkness that prevailed; and then nothing remained of the preternatural gloom, not a particle of the hail or snow was to be seen: Rehám, however, brought him down from the mountain and after presenting him before Tús, put an end to his wicked existence. The armies were now on a more equal footing: they beheld more clearly the ravages that had been committed by each, and each had great need of rest. They accordingly retired till the following day, and then again opposed each other with renewed vigor and animosity. But fortune would not smile on the exertions of the Persian hosts, they being obliged to fall back upon the mountain Hamáwun, and in the fortress situated there Tús deposited all his sick and wounded, continuing himself in advance to ensure their protection. Pírán seeing this, ordered his troops to besiege the place where Tús had posted himself. This was objected to by Húmán, but Pírán was resolved upon the measure, and had several conflicts with the enemy without obtaining any advantage over them. In the mountain-fortress there happened to be wells of water and abundance of grain and provisions, so that the Persians were in no danger of being reduced by starvation. Khosráu, however, being informed of their situation, sent Rustem, accompanied by Fríburz, to their assistance, and they were both welcomed, and received with rejoicing, and cordial satisfaction. The fortress gates were thrown open, and Rustem was presently seen seated upon a throne in the public hall, deliberating on the state of affairs, surrounded by the most distinguished leaders of the army.

In the meanwhile Pírán-wísah had written to Afrásiyáb, informing him that he had reduced the Persian army to great distress, had forced them to take refuge in a mountain fort, and requested a further reinforcement to complete the victory, and make them all prisoners. Afrásiyáb in consequence despatched three illustrious confederates from different regions. There was Shinkul of Sugsar, the Khakán of Chín, whose crown was the starry heavens, and Kámús of Kushán, a hero of high renown and wondrous in every deed.

> *For when he frowned, the air grew freezing cold;*
> *And when he smiled, the genial spring showered down*
> *Roses and hyacinths, and all was brightness!*

Pírán went first to pay a visit to Kámús, to whom he, almost trembling, described the amazing strength and courage of Rustem: but Kámús was too powerful to express alarm; on the contrary, he said:

> *"Is praise like this to Rustem due?*
> *And what, if all thou say'st be true?*
> *Are his large limbs of iron made?*
> *Will they resist my trenchant blade?*
> *His head may now his shoulders grace,*
> *But will it long retain its place?*
> *Let me but meet him in the fight,*
> *And thou shalt see Kamus's might!"*

Pírán's spirits rose at this bold speech, and encouraged by its effects, he repaired to the Khakán of Chín, with whom he settled the necessary arrangements for commencing battle on the following day. Early in the morning the different armies under Kámús, the Khakán, and Pírán-wísah, were drawn out, and Rustem was also prepared with the troops under his command for the impending conflict. He saw that the force arrayed against him was prodigious, and most tremendous in aspect; and offering a prayer to the Creator, he plunged into the battle.

> 'Twas at mid-day the strife began,
> With steed to steed and man to man;
> The clouds of dust which rolled on high,
> Threw darkness o'er the earth and sky.
> Each soldier on the other rushed,
> And every blade with crimson blushed;
> And valiant hearts were trod upon,
> Like sand beneath the horse's feet,
> And when the warrior's life was gone,
> His mail became his winding sheet.

The first leader who advanced conspicuously from among the Tartar army was Ushkabús, against whom Rehám boldly opposed himself; but after a short conflict, in which he had some difficulty in defending his life from the assaults of his antagonist, he thought it prudent to retire. When Ushkabús saw this he turned round with the intention of rejoining his own troops; but Rustem having witnessed the triumph over his friend, sallied forth on foot, taking up his bow, and placing a few arrows in his girdle, and asked him whither he was going.

> Astonished, Ushkabús cried, "Who art thou?
> What kindred hast thou to lament thy fall?"
> Rustem replied: – "Why madly seek to know
> That which can never yield thee benefit?
> My name is death to thee, thy hour is come!"
> "Indeed! and thou on foot, mid mounted warriors,
> To talk so bravely!" – "Yes," the champion said;
> "And hast thou never heard of men on foot,
> Who conquered horsemen? I am sent by Tús,
> To take for him the horse of Ushkabús."

"What! and unarmed?" inquired the Tartar chief;
"No!" cried the champion, "Mark, my bow and arrow!
Mark, too, with what effect they may be used!"
So saying, Rustem drew the string, and straight
The arrow flew, and faithful to its aim,
Struck dead the foeman's horse. This done, he laughed,
But Ushkabús was wroth, and showered upon
His bold antagonist his quivered store—
Then Rustem raised his bow, with eager eye
Choosing a dart, and placed it on the string,
A thong of elk-skin; to his ear he drew
The feathered notch, and when the point had touched
The other hand, the bended horn recoiled,
And twang the arrow sped, piercing the breast
Of Ushkabús, who fell a lifeless corse,
As if he never had been born! Erect,
And firm, the champion stood upon the plain,
Towering like mount Alberz, immovable,
The gaze and wonder of the adverse host!

When Rustem, still unknown to the Túránian forces, returned to his own army, the Tartars carried away the body of Ushkabús, and took it to the Khakán of Chin, who ordered the arrow to be drawn out before him; and when he and Kámús saw how deeply it had penetrated, and that the feathered end was wet with blood, they were amazed at the immense power which had driven it from the bow; they had never witnessed or heard of anything so astonishing. The fight was, in consequence, suspended till the following day. The Khakán of Chin then inquired who was disposed or ready to be revenged on the enemy for the death of Ushkabús, when Kámús advanced, and, soliciting permission, urged forward his horse to the middle of the plain. He then called aloud for Rustem, but a Kábul hero, named Alwund, a pupil of Rustem's, asked his master's permission to oppose the challenger, which being granted, he rushed headlong to the combat. Luckless however were his efforts, for he was soon overthrown and slain, and then Rustem appeared in arms before the conqueror, who hearing his voice, cried: "Why this arrogance and clamor! I am not like Ushkabús, a trembler in thy presence." Rustem replied:

> *"When the lion sees his prey,*
> *Sees the elk-deer cross his way,*
> *Roars he not? The very ground*
> *Trembles at the dreadful sound.*
> *And art thou from terror free,*
> *When opposed in fight to me?"*

Kámús now examined him with a stern eye, and was satisfied that he had to contend against a powerful warrior: he therefore with the utmost alacrity threw his kamund, which Rustem avoided, but it fell over the head of his horse Rakush. Anxious to extricate himself from this dilemma, Rustem dexterously caught hold of one end of the kamund, whilst Kámús dragged and strained at the other; and so much strength was applied that the line broke in the middle, and Kámús in consequence tumbled backwards to the ground. The boaster had almost succeeded in remounting his horse, when he was secured round the neck by Rustem's own kamund, and conveyed a prisoner to the Persian army, where he was put to death!

The fate of Kámús produced a deep sensation among the Túránians, and Pírán-wísah, partaking of the general alarm, and thinking it impossible to resist the power of Rustem, proposed to retire from the contest, but the Khakán of Chín was of a different opinion, and offered himself to remedy the evil which threatened them all. Moreover the warrior, Chingush, volunteered to fight with Rustem; and having obtained the Khakán's permission, he took the field, and boldly challenged the champion. Rustem received the foe with a smiling countenance, and the struggle began with arrows. After a smart attack on both sides, Chingush thought it prudent to fly from the overwhelming force of Rustem, who, however, steadily pursued him, and adroitly seizing the horse by the tail, hurled him from his saddle.

> *He grasped the charger's flowing tail,*
> *And all were struck with terror pale,*
> *To see a sight so strange; the foe,*
> *Dismounted by one desperate blow;*
> *The captive asked for life in vain,*
> *His recreant blood bedewed the plain.*
> *His head was from his shoulders wrung,*
> *His body to the vultures flung.*

Rustem, after this exploit, invited some other hero to single combat; but at the moment not one replied to his challenge. At last Húmán came forward, not however to fight, but to remonstrate, and make an effort to put an end to the war which threatened total destruction to his country. "Why such bitter enmity? why such a whirlwind of resentment?" said he; "to this I ascribe the calamities under which we suffer; but is there no way by which this sanguinary career of vengeance can be checked or moderated?" Rustem, in answer, enumerated the aggressions and the crimes of Afrásiyáb, and especially dwelt on the atrocious murder of Saiáwush, which he declared could never be pardoned. Húmán wished to know his name; but Rustem refused to tell him, and requested Pírán-wísah might be sent to him, to whom he would communicate his thoughts, and the secrets of his heart freely. Húmán accordingly returned, and informed Pírán of the champion's wishes.

> "This must be Rustem, stronger than the pard,
> The lion, or the Egyptian crocodile,
> Or fell Iblís; dreams never painted hero
> Half so tremendous on the battle plain."

The old man said to him:

> "If this be Rustem, then the time has come,
> Dreaded so long – for what but fire and sword,
> Can now await us? Every town laid waste,
> Soldier and peasant, husband, wife, and child,
> Sharing the miseries of a ravaged land!"

With tears in his eyes and a heavy heart, Pírán repaired to the Khakán, who, after some discussion, permitted him in these terms to go and confer with Rustem.

> "Depart then speedful on thy embassy,
> And if he seeks for peace, adjust the terms,
> And presents to be sent us. If he talks
> Of war and vengeance, and is clothed in mail,
> No sign of peace, why we must trust in Heaven
> For strength to crush his hopes of victory.

He is not formed of iron, nor of brass,
But flesh and blood, with human nerves and hair,
He does not in the battle tread the clouds,
Nor can he vanish, like the demon race—
Then why this sorrow, why these marks of grief?
He is not stronger than an elephant;
Not he, but I will show him what it is
To fight or gambol with an elephant!
Besides, for every man his army boasts,
We have three hundred – wherefore then be sad?"

Notwithstanding these expressions of confidence, Pírán's heart was full of alarm and terror; but he hastened to the Persian camp, and made himself known to the champion of the host, who frankly said, after he had heard Pírán's name, "I am Rustem of Zábul, armed as thou seest for battle!" Upon which Pírán respectfully dismounted, and paid the usual homage to his illustrious rank and distinction. Rustem said to him, "I bring thee the blessings of Kai-khosráu and Ferangís, his mother, who nightly see thy face in their dreams."

"Blessings from me, upon that royal youth!"
Exclaimed the good old man. "Blessings on her,
The daughter of Afrásiyáb, his mother,
Who saved my life – and blessings upon thee,
Thou matchless hero! Thou hast come for vengeance,
In the dear name of gallant Saiáwush,
Of Saiáwush, the husband of my child,
(The beautiful Gúlshaher), of him who loved me
As I had been his father. His brave son,
Ferúd, was slaughtered, and his mother too,
And Khosráu was his brother, now the king,
By whom he fell, or if not by his sword,
Whose was the guilty hand? Has punishment
Been meted to the offender? I protected,
In mine own house, the princess Ferangís;
And when her son was born, Kai-khosráu, still
I, at the risk of my existence, kept them

97

Safe from the fury of Afrásiyáb,
Who would have sacrificed the child, or both!
And night and day I watched them, till the hour
When they escaped and crossed the boundary-stream.
Enough of this! Now let us speak of peace,
Since the confederates in this mighty war
Are guiltless of the blood of Saiáwush!"

Rustem, in answer to Pírán, observed, that in negotiating the terms of pacification, several important points were to be considered, and several indispensable matters to be attended to. No peace could be made unless the principal actors in the bloody tragedy of Saiáwush's death were first given up, particularly Gersíwaz; vast sums of money were also required to be presented to the king of kings; and, moreover, Rustem said he would disdain making peace at all, but that it enabled Pírán to do service to Kai-khosráu. Pírán saw the difficulty of acceding to these demands, but he speedily laid them before the Khakán, who consulted his confederates on the subject, and after due consideration, their pride and shame resisted the overtures, which they thought ignominious. Shinkul, a king of Ind, was a violent opposer of the terms, and declared against peace on any such conditions. Several other warriors expressed their readiness to contend against Rustem, and they flattered themselves that by a rapid succession of attacks, one after the other, they would easily overpower him. The Khakán was pleased with this conceit and permitted Shinkul to begin the struggle. Accordingly he entered the plain, and summoned Rustem to renew the fight. The champion came and struck him with a spear, which, penetrating his breast, threw him off his horse to the ground. The dagger was already raised to finish his career, but he sprang on his feet, and quickly ran away to tell his misfortune to the Khakán of Chín.

And thus he cried, in look forlorn,
"This foe is not of mortal born;
A furious elephant in fight,
A very mountain to the sight;
No warrior of the human race,
That ever wielded spear or mace,
Alone this dragon could withstand,
Or live beneath his conquering brand!"

The Khakán reminded him how different were his feelings and sentiments in the morning, and having asked him what he now proposed to do, he said that without a considerable force it would be useless to return to the field; five thousand men were therefore assigned to him, and with them he proceeded to engage the champion. Rustem had also been joined by his valiant companions, and a general battle ensued. The heavens were obscured by the dust which ascended from the tramp of the horses, and the plain was crimsoned with the blood of the slain. In the midst of the contest, Sáwa, a relation of Kámús, burst forward and sought to be revenged on Rustem for the fate of his friend. The champion raised his battle-axe, and giving Rakush the rein, with one blow of his mace removed him to the other world. No sooner had he killed this assailant than he was attacked by another of the kindred of Kámús, named Kahár, whom he also slew, and thus humbled the pride of the Kushanians. Elated with his success, and having further displayed his valor among the enemy's troops, he vowed that he would now encounter the Khakán himself, and despoil him of all his pomp and treasure. For this purpose he selected a thousand horsemen, and thus supported, approached the kulub-gah, or headquarters of the monarch of Chín. The clamor of the cavalry, and the clash of spears and swords, resounded afar. The air became as dark as the visage of an Ethiopian, and the field was covered with several heads, broken armor, and the bodies of the slain. Amidst the conflict Rustem called aloud to the Khakán:

> *"Surrender to my arms those elephants,*
> *That ivory throne, that crown, and chain of gold;*
> *Fit trophies for Kai-khosráu, Persia's king;*
> *For what hast thou to do with diadem*
> *And sovereign power! My noose shall soon secure thee,*
> *And I will send thee living to his presence;*
> *Since, looking on my valour and my strength,*
> *Life is enough to grant thee. If thou wilt not*
> *Resign thy crown and throne – thy doom is sealed."*

The Khakán, filled with indignation at these haughty words, cautioned Rustem to parry off his own danger, and then commanded his troops to assail the enemy with a shower of arrows. The attack was so tremendous and terrifying, even beyond the picturings of a dream, that Gúdarz was alarmed for the safety of Rustem, and sent

Rehám and Gíw to his aid. Rustem said to Rehám: – "I fear that my horse Rakush is becoming weary of exertion, in which case what shall I do in this conflict with the enemy? I must attack on foot the Khakán of Chín, though he has an army here as countless as legions of ants or locusts; but if Heaven continues my friend, I shall stretch many of them in the dust, and take many prisoners. The captives I will send to Khosráu, and all the spoils of Chín." Saying this he pushed forward, roaring like a tiger, towards the Khakán, and exclaiming with a stern voice: "The Turks are allied to the devil, and the wicked are always unprosperous. Thou hast not yet fallen in with Rustem, or thy brain would have been bewildered. He is a never-dying dragon, always seeking the strongest in battle. But thou hast not yet had enough of even me!" He then drew his kamund from the saddle-strap, and praying to God to grant him victory over his foes, urged on Rakush, and wherever he threw the noose, his aim was successful. Great was the slaughter, and the Khakán, seeing from the back of his white elephant the extent of his loss, and beginning to be apprehensive about his own safety, ordered one of his warriors, well acquainted with the language of Irán, to solicit from the enemy a cessation of hostilities.

> *"Say whence this wrath on us, this keen revenge?*
> *We never injured Saiáwush; the kings*
> *Of Ind and Chín are guiltless of his blood;*
> *Then why this wrath on strangers? Spells and charms,*
> *Used by Afrásiyáb – the cause of all—*
> *Have brought us hither to contend against*
> *The champion Rustem; and since peace is better*
> *Than war and bloodshed, let us part in peace."*

The messenger having delivered his message, Rustem replied:

> *"My words are few. Let him give up his crown,*
> *His golden collar, throne, and elephants;*
> *These are the terms I grant. He came for plunder,*
> *And now he asks for peace. Tell him again,*
> *Till all his treasure and his crown are mine,*
> *His throne and elephants, he seeks in vain*
> *For peace with Rustem, or the Persian king!"*

When the Khakán was informed of these reiterated conditions, he burst out into bitter reproaches and abuse; and with so loud a voice, that the wind conveyed them distinctly to Rustem's ear. The champion immediately prepared for the attack; and approaching the enemy, flung his kamund, by which he at once dragged the Khakán from his white elephant. The hands of the captured monarch were straightway bound behind his back. Degraded and helpless he stood, and a single stroke deprived him of his crown, and throne, and life.

> Such are, since time began, the ways of Heaven;
> Such the decrees of fate! Sometimes raised up,
> And sometimes hunted down by enemies,
> Men, struggling, pass through this precarious life,
> Exalted now to sovereign power; and now
> Steeped in the gulf of poverty and sorrow.
> To one is given the affluence of Kárun;
> Another dies in want. How little know we
> What form our future fortune may assume!
> The world is all deceit, deception all!

Pírán-wísah beheld the disasters of the day, he saw the Khakán of Chín delivered over to Tús, his death, and the banners of the confederates overthrown; and sorrowing said: "This day is the day of flight, not of victory to us! This is no time for son to protect father, nor father son – we must fly!" In the meanwhile Rustem, animated by feelings of a very different kind, gave a banquet to his warrior friends, in celebration of the triumph.

When the intelligence of the overthrow and death of Kámús and the Khakán of Chín, and the dispersion of their armies, reached Afrásiyáb, he was overwhelmed with distress and consternation, and expressed his determination to be revenged on the conquerors. Not an Iránian, he said, should remain alive; and the doors of his treasury were thrown open to equip and reward the new army, which was to consist of a hundred thousand men.

Rustem having communicated to Kai-khosráu, through Fríburz, the account of his success, received the most satisfactory marks of his sovereign's applause; but still anxious to promote the glory of his country, he engaged in new exploits. He went against Kafúr, the king of the city of Bidád, a cannibal, who feasted on human flesh, especially on the young women of his country, and those of the greatest beauty, being the richest morsels, were first destroyed. He soon overpowered and slew the monster, and having given his body to be devoured by dogs, plundered and razed his castle to the ground. After this he invaded and ravaged the province of Khoten, one of the dependencies of Túrán, and recently the possession of Saiáwush, which was a new affliction to Afrásiyáb, who, alarmed about his own empire, dispatched a trusty person secretly to Rustem's camp, to obtain private intelligence of his hostile movements. The answer of the spy added considerably to his distress, and in the dilemma he consulted with Pírán-wísah, that he might have the benefit of the old man's experience and wisdom. Pírán told him that he had failed to make an impression upon the Persians, even assisted by Kámús the Kashánian, and the Khakán of Chin; both had been slain in battle, and therefore it would be in vain to attempt further offensive measures without the most powerful aid. There was, he added, a neighboring king, named Púladwund, who alone seemed equal to contend with Rustem. He was of immense stature, and of prodigious strength, and might by the favor of heaven, be able to subdue him. Afrásiyáb was pleased with this information, and immediately invited Púladwund, by letter, to assist him in exterminating the champion of Persia. Púladwund was proud of the honor conferred upon him, and readily complied; hastening the preparation of his own army to cooperate with that of Afrásiyáb. He presently joined him, and the whole of the combined forces rapidly marched against the enemy. The first warrior he encountered was Gíw, whom he caught with his kamund. Rehám and Byzun seeing this, instantly rushed forward to extricate their brother and champion in arms; but they too were also secured in the same manner! In the struggle, however, the kamunds gave way, and then Púladwund drew his sword, and by several strokes wounded them all. The father, Gúdarz, apprised of this disaster, which had unfortunately happened to three of his sons, applied to Rustem for succor. The champion, the refuge, the protector of all, was, as usual, ready to repel the enemy. He forthwith advanced, liberated his friends, and dreadful was the conflict which followed. The club was used with great dexterity on both sides; but at length Púladwund struck his antagonist such a blow that the sound of it was heard by the troops at a distance, and Rustem, stunned by its severity, thought himself opposed with so much vigor, that he prayed to the Almighty for a prosperous issue to the engagement.

> *"Should I be in this struggle slain,*
> *What stay for Persia will be left?*
> *None to defend Kai-khosráu's reign,*

> *Of me, his warrior-chief, bereft.*
> *Then village, town, and city gay,*
> *Will feel the cruel Tartar's sway!"*

Púladwund wishing to follow up the blow by a final stroke of his sword, found to his amazement that it recoiled from the armor of Rustem, and thence he proposed another mode of fighting, which he hoped would be more successful. He wished to try his power in wrestling. The challenge was accepted. By agreement both armies retired, and left the space of a farsang between them, and no one was allowed to afford assistance to either combatant. Afrásiyáb was present, and sent word to Púladwund, the moment he got Rustem under him, to plunge a sword in his heart. The contest began, but Púladwund had no opportunity of fulfilling the wishes of Afrásiyáb. Rustem grasped him with such vigor, lifted him up in his arms, and dashed him so furiously on the plain, that the boaster seemed to be killed on the spot. Rustem indeed thought he had put a period to his life; and with that impression left him, and remounted Rakush: but the crafty Púladwund only pretended to be dead: and as soon as he found himself released, sprang up and escaped, flying like an arrow to his own side. He then told Afrásiyáb how he had saved his life by counterfeiting death, and assured him that it was useless to contend against Rustem. The champion having witnessed this subterfuge, turned round in pursuit, and the Tartars received him with a shower of arrows; but the attack was well answered, Púladwund being so alarmed that, without saying a word to Afrásiyáb, he fled from the field. Pírán now counselled Afrásiyáb to escape also to the remotest part of Tartary. As the flight of Púladwund had disheartened the Túránian troops, and there was no chance of profiting by further resistance, Afrásiyáb took his advice, and so precipitate was his retreat, that he entirely abandoned his standards, tents, horses, arms, and treasure to an immense amount. The most valuable booty was sent by Rustem to the king of Irán, and a considerable portion of it was divided among the chiefs and the soldiers of the army. He then mounted Rakush, and proceeded to the court of Kai-khosráu, where he was received with the highest honors and with unbounded rejoicings. The king opened his jewel chamber, and gave him the richest rubies, and vessels of gold filled with musk and aloes, and also splendid garments; a hundred beautiful damsels wearing crowns and ear-rings, a hundred horses, and a hundred camels. Having thus terminated triumphantly the campaign, Rustem carried with him to Zábul the blessings and admiration of his country.

Akwán Díw

And now we come to Akwán Díw,
Whom Rustem next in combat slew.

ONE DAY AS Kai-khosráu was sitting in his beautiful garden, abounding in roses and the balmy luxuriance of spring, surrounded by his warriors, and enjoying the pleasures of the banquet with music and singing, a peasant approached, and informed him of a most mysterious apparition. A wild ass, he said, had come in from the neighboring forest; it had at least the external appearance of a wild ass, but possessed such supernatural strength, that it had rushed among the horses in the royal stables with the ferocity of a lion or a demon, doing extensive injury, and in fact appeared to be an evil spirit! Kai-khosráu felt assured that it was something more than it seemed to be, and looked round among his warriors to know what should be done. It was soon found that Rustem was the only person capable of giving effectual assistance in this emergency, and accordingly a message was forwarded to request his services. The champion instantly complied, and it was not long before he occupied himself upon the important enterprise.

Guided by the peasant, he proceeded in the first place towards the spot where the mysterious animal had been seen; but it was not till the fourth day of his search that he fell in with him, and then, being anxious to secure him alive, and send him as a trophy to Kai-khosráu, he threw his kamund; but it was in vain: the wild ass in a moment vanished out of sight! From this circumstance Rustem observed, "This can be no other than Akwán Díw, and my weapon must now be either dagger or sword." The next time the wild ass appeared he pursued him with his drawn sword: but on lifting it up to strike, nothing was to be seen. He tried again, when he came near him, both spear and arrow: still the animal vanished, disappointing his blow; and thus three days and nights he continued fighting, as it were against a shadow. Wearied at length with his exertions, he dismounted, and leading Rakush to a green spot near a limpid fountain or rivulet of spring water, allowed him to graze, and then went to sleep. Akwán Díw seeing from a distance that Rustem had fallen asleep, rushed towards him like a whirlwind, and rapidly digging up the ground on every side of him, took up the plot of ground and the champion together, placed them upon his head, and walked away with them. Rustem being awakened with the motion, he was thus addressed by the giant-demon:

> *"Warrior! now no longer free!*
> *Tell me what thy wish may be;*
> *Shall I plunge thee in the sea,*
> *Or leave thee on the mountain drear,*
> *None to give thee succour, near?*
> *Tell thy wish to me!"*

Rustem, thus deplorably in the power of the demon, began to consider what was best to be done, and recollecting that it was customary with that supernatural race to act by the rule of contraries, in opposition to an expressed desire, said in reply, for he knew that if he was thrown into the sea there would be a good chance of escape:

> *"O, plunge me not in the roaring sea,*
> *The maw of a fish is no home for me;*
> *But cast me forth on the mountain; there*
> *Is the lion's haunt and the tiger's lair;*
> *And for them I shall be a morsel of food,*
> *They will eat my flesh and drink my blood;*
> *But my bones will be left, to show the place*
> *Where this form was devoured by the feline race;*
> *Yes, something will then remain of me,*
> *Whilst nothing escapes from the roaring sea!"*

Akwán Díw having heard this particular desire of Rustem, determined at once to thwart him, and for this purpose he raised him up with his hands, and flung him from his lofty position headlong into the deep and roaring ocean. Down he fell, and a crocodile speedily darted upon him with the eager intention of devouring him alive; but Rustem drew his sword with alacrity, and severed the monster's head from his body. Another came, and was put to death in the same manner, and the water was crimsoned with blood. At last he succeeded in swimming safely on shore, and instantly returned thanks to Heaven for the signal protection he had experienced.

> *Breasting the wave, with fearless skill*
> *He used his glittering brand;*
> *And glorious and triumphant still,*
> *He quickly reached the strand.*

He then moved towards the fountain where he had left Rakush; but, to his great alarm and vexation his matchless horse was not there. He wandered about for some time, and in the end found him among a herd of horses belonging to Afrásiyáb. Having first caught him, and resumed his seat in the saddle, he resolved upon capturing and driving away the whole herd, and conveying them to Kai-khosráu. He was carrying into effect this resolution when the noise awoke the keepers specially employed by Afrásiyáb, and they, indignant at this outrageous proceeding, called together a strong party to pursue the aggressor. When they had nearly reached him, he turned boldly round, and said aloud: "I am Rustem, the descendant of Sám. I have conquered Afrásiyáb in battle, and after that dost thou presume to oppose me?" Hearing this, the keepers of the Tartar stud instantly turned their backs, and ran away.

It so happened that at this period Afrásiyáb paid his annual visit to his nursery of horses, and on his coming to the meadows in which they were kept, neither horses nor keepers were to be seen. In a short time, however, he was informed by those who had returned from the pursuit, that Rustem was the person who had carried off the herd, and upon hearing of this outrage, he proceeded with his troops at once to attack him. Impatient at the indignity, he approached Rustem with great fury, but was presently compelled to fly to save his life, and thus allow his herd of favorite steeds, together with four elephants, to be placed in the possession of Kai-khosráu. Rustem then returned to the meadows and the fountain near the habitation of Akwán Díw; and there he again met the demon, who thus accosted him:

> *"What! art thou then aroused from death's dark sleep?*
> *Hast thou escaped the monsters of the deep?*
> *And dost thou seek upon the dusty plain*
> *To struggle with a demon's power again?*

> *Of flint, or brass, or iron is thy form?*
> *Or canst thou, like the demons, raise the dreadful battle storm?"*

Rustem, hearing this taunt from the tongue of Akwán Díw, prepared for fight, and threw his kamund with such precision and force, that the demon was entangled in it, and then he struck him such a mighty blow with his sword, that it severed the head from the body. The severed head of the unclean monster he transmitted as a trophy to Kai-khosráu, by whom it was regarded with amazement, on account of its hideous expression and its vast size. After this extraordinary feat, Rustem paid his respects to the king, and was received as usual with distinguished honor and affection; and having enjoyed the magnificent hospitality of the court for some time, he returned to Zábulistán, accompanied part of the way by Kai-khosráu himself and a crowd of valiant warriors, ever anxious to acknowledge his superior worth and prodigious strength.

The Story of Byzun and Maníjeh

ONE DAY THE PEOPLE of Armán petitioned Kai-khosráu to remove from them a grievous calamity. The country they inhabited was overrun with herds of wild boars, which not only destroyed the produce of their fields, but the fruit and flowers in their orchards and gardens, and so extreme was the ferocity of the animals that it was dangerous to go abroad; they therefore solicited protection from this disastrous visitation, and hoped for relief. The king was at the time enjoying himself amidst his warriors at a banquet, drinking wine, and listening to music and the songs of bewitching damsels.

> *The glance of beauty, and the charm*
> *Of heavenly sounds, so soft and thrilling,*
> *And ruby wine, must ever warm*
> *The heart, with love and rapture filling.*
> *Can aught more sweet, more genial prove,*
> *Than melting music, wine, and love?*

The moment he was made acquainted with the grievances endured by the Armánians, he referred the matter to the consideration of his counsellors and nobles, in order that a remedy might be immediately applied. Byzun, when he heard what was required, and had learned the disposition of the king, rose up at once with all the enthusiasm of youth, and offered to undertake the extermination of the wild boars himself. But Gíw objected to so great a hazard, for he was too young, he said; a hero of greater experience being necessary for such an arduous enterprise. Byzun, however, was not to be rejected on this account, and observed, that though young, he was mature in judgment and discretion, and he relied on the liberal decision of the king, who at length permitted him to go, but he was to be accompanied by the veteran warrior Girgín. Accordingly Byzun and Girgín set off on the perilous expedition; and after a journey of several days arrived at the place situated between Irán and Túrán, where the wild boars were the most destructive. In a short time a great number were hunted down and killed, and Byzun, utterly to destroy the sustenance of the depredators, set fire to the forest, and reduced the whole of the cultivation to ashes. His exertions were, in short, entirely successful, and the country was thus freed from the visitation which had occasioned so much distress and ruin. To give incontestable proof of this exploit, he cut off the heads of all the wild boars, and took out the tusks, to send to Kai-khosráu. When Girgín had witnessed the intrepidity and boldness of Byzun, and found him determined to send the evidence of his bravery to Kai-khosráu, he became envious of the youth's success, and anticipated by comparison the ruin of his own name and the gratification of his foes. He therefore attempted to dissuade him from sending the trophies to the king, and having failed, he resolved upon getting him out of the way. To effect this purpose he worked upon the feelings and the passions of Byzun with consummate art, and whilst his victim was warm with wine, praised him beyond all the warriors of the age. He then told him he had heard that at no great distance from them there was a beautiful place, a garden of perpetual spring, which was visited every vernal season by Maníjeh, the lovely daughter of Afrásiyáb.

> *"It is a spot beyond imagination*
> *Delightful to the heart, where roses bloom,*
> *And sparkling fountains murmur – where the earth*
> *Is rich with many-colored flowers; and musk*
> *Floats on the gentle breezes, hyacinths*
> *And lilies add their perfume – golden fruits*

> *Weigh down the branches of the lofty trees,*
> *The glittering pheasant moves in stately pomp,*
> *The bulbul warbles from the cypress bough,*
> *And love-inspiring damsels may be seen*
> *O'er hill and dale, their lips all winning smiles,*
> *Their cheeks like roses – in their sleepy eyes*
> *Delicious languor dwelling. Over them*
> *Presides the daughter of Afrásiyáb,*
> *The beautiful Maníjeh; should we go,*
> *('Tis but a little distance), and encamp*
> *Among the lovely groups – in that retreat*
> *Which blooms like Paradise – we may secure*
> *A bevy of fair virgins for the king!"*

Byzun was excited by this description; and impatient to realize what it promised, repaired without delay, accompanied by Girgín, to the romantic retirement of the princess. They approached so close to the summer-tent in which she dwelt that she had a full view of Byzun, and immediately becoming deeply enamoured of his person despatched a confidential domestic, her nurse, to inquire who he was, and from whence he came.

> *"Go, and beneath that cypress tree,*
> *Where now he sits so gracefully,*
> *Ask him his name, that radiant moon,*
> *And he may grant another boon!*
> *Perchance he may to me impart*
> *The secret wishes of his heart!*
> *Tell him he must, and further say,*
> *That I have lived here many a day;*
> *That every year, whilst spring discloses*
> *The fragrant breath of budding roses,*
> *I pass my time in rural pleasure;*
> *But never – never such a treasure,*
> *A mortal of such perfect mould,*
> *Did these admiring eyes behold!*

Never, since it has been my lot
To dwell in this sequestered spot,
A youth by nature so designed
To soothe a love-lorn damsel's mind!
His wondrous looks my bosom thrill
Can Saiáwush be living still?"

The nurse communicated faithfully the message of Maníjeh, and Byzun's countenance glowed with delight when he heard it. "Tell thy fair mistress," he said in reply, "that I am not Saiáwush, but the son of Gív. I came from Irán, with the express permission of the king, to exterminate a terrible and destructive herd of wild boars in this neighborhood; and I have cut off their heads, and torn out their tusks to be sent to Kai-khosráu, that the king and his warriors may fully appreciate the exploit I have performed. But having heard afterwards of thy mistress's beauty and attractions, home and my father were forgotten, and I have preferred following my own desires by coming hither. If thou wilt therefore forward my views; if thou wilt become my friend by introducing me to thy mistress, who is possessed of such matchless charms, these precious gems are thine and this coronet of gold. Perhaps the daughter of Afrásiyáb may be induced to listen to my suit." The nurse was not long in making known the sentiments of the stranger, and Maníjeh was equally prompt in expressing her consent. The message was full of ardor and affection.

"O gallant youth, no farther roam,
This summer-tent shall be thy home;
Then will the clouds of grief depart
From this enamoured, anxious heart.
For thee I live – thou art the light
Which makes my future fortune bright.
Should arrows pour like showers of rain
Upon my head – 'twould be in vain;
Nothing can ever injure me,
Blessed with thy love – possessed of thee!"

Byzun therefore proceeded unobserved to the tent of the princess, who on meeting and receiving him, pressed him to her bosom; and taking off his Kaiáni girdle, that he might be more at his ease, asked him to sit down and relate the particulars of his enterprise among the wild boars of the forest. Having done so, he added that he had left Girgín behind him.

> *"Enraptured, and impatient to survey*
> *Thy charms, I brook'd no pause upon the way."*

He was immediately perfumed with musk and rose-water, and refreshments of every kind were set before him; musicians played their sweetest airs, and dark-eyed damsels waited upon him. The walls of the tent were gorgeously adorned with amber, and gold, and rubies; and the sparkling old wine was drunk out of crystal goblets. The feast of joy lasted three nights and three days, Byzun and Maníjeh enjoying the precious moments with unspeakable rapture. Overcome with wine and the felicity of the scene, he at length sunk into repose, and on the fourth day came the time of departure; but the princess, unable to relinquish the society of her lover, ordered a narcotic draught to be administered to him, and whilst he continued in a state of slumber and insensibility, he was conveyed secretly and in disguise into Túrán. He was taken even to the palace of Afrásiyáb, unknown to all but to the emissaries and domestics of the princess, and there he awoke from the trance into which he had been thrown, and found himself clasped in the arms of his idol. Considering, on coming to his senses, that he had been betrayed by some witchery, he made an attempt to get out of the seclusion: above all, he was apprehensive of a fatal termination to the adventure; but Maníjeh's blandishments induced him to remain, and for some time he was contented to be immersed in continual enjoyment – such pleasure as arises from the social banquet and the attractions of a fascinating woman.

> *"Grieve not my love – be not so sad,*
> *'Tis now the season to be glad;*
> *There is a time for war and strife,*
> *A time to soothe the ills of life.*
> *Drink of the cup which yields delight,*
> *The ruby glitters in thy sight;*
> *Steep not thy heart in fruitless care,*
> *But in the wine-flask sparkling there."*

At length, however, the love of the princess for a Persian youth was discovered, and the keepers and guards of the palace were in the greatest terror, expecting the most signal punishment for their neglect or treachery. Dreadful indeed was the rage of the king when he was first told the tidings; he trembled like a reed in the wind, and the color fled from his cheeks. Groaning, he exclaimed:

> *"A daughter, even from a royal stock,*
> *Is ever a misfortune – hast thou one?*
> *The grave will be thy fittest son-in-law!*
> *Rejoice not in the wisdom of a daughter;*
> *Who ever finds a daughter good and virtuous?*
> *Who ever looks on woman-kind for aught*
> *Save wickedness and folly? Hence how few*
> *Ever enjoy the bliss of Paradise:*
> *Such the sad destiny of erring woman!"*

Afrásiyáb consulted the nobles of his household upon the measures to be pursued on this occasion, and Gersíwaz was in consequence deputed to secure Byzun, and put him to death. The guilty retreat was first surrounded by troops, and then Gersíwaz entered the private apartments, and with surprise and indignation saw Byzun in all his glory, Maníjeh at his side, his lips stained with wine, his face full of mirth and gladness, and encircled by the damsels of the shubistán. He accosted him in severe terms, and was promptly answered by Byzun, who, drawing his sword, gave his name and family, and declared that if any violence or insult was offered, he would slay every man that came before him with hostile intentions. Gersíwaz, on hearing this, thought it prudent to change his plan, and conduct him to Afrásiyáb, and he was permitted to do so on the promise of pardon for the alleged offence. When brought before Afrásiyáb, he was assailed with further opprobrium, and called a dog and a wicked remorseless demon.

> *"Thou caitiff wretch, of monstrous birth,*
> *Allied to hell, and not of earth!"*

But he thus answered the king:

"Listen awhile, if justice be thy aim,
And thou wilt find me guiltless. I was sent
From Persia to destroy herds of wild boars,
Which laid the country waste. That labour done,
I lost my way, and weary with the toil,
Weary with wandering in a wildering maze,
Haply reposed beneath a shady cypress;
Thither a Peri came, and whilst I slept,
Lifted me from the ground, and quick as thought
Conveyed me to a summer-tent, where dwelt
A princess of incomparable beauty.
From thence, by hands unknown, I was removed,
Still slumbering in a litter – still unconscious;
And when I woke, I found myself reclining
In a retired pavilion of thy palace,
Attended by that soul-entrancing beauty!
My heart was filled with sorrow, and I shed
Showers of vain tears, and desolate I sate,
Thinking of Persia, with no power to fly
From my imprisonment, though soft and kind,
Being the victim of a sorcerer's art.
Yes, I am guiltless, and Maníjeh too,
Both by some magic influence pursued,
And led away against our will or choice!"

Afrásiyáb listened to this speech with distrust, and hesitated not to charge him with falsehood and cowardice. Byzun's indignation was roused by this insulting accusation; and he said to him aloud, "Cowardice, what! cowardice! I have encountered the tusks of the formidable wild boar and the claws of the raging lion. I have met the bravest in battle with sword and arrow; and if it be thy desire to witness the strength of my arm, give me but a horse and a battle-axe, and marshal twice five hundred Túránians against me, and not a man of them shall survive the contest. If this be not thy pleasure, do thy worst, but remember my blood will be avenged. Thou knowest the power of Rustem!" The mention of Rustem's name renewed all the deep feelings of resentment and animosity in the mind of Afrásiyáb, who, resolved upon the immediate execution of his purpose, commanded Gersíwaz to bind the youth, and put an end to his life on the gallows tree. The good old man Pírán-wísah happened to be passing by the place to which Byzun had just been conveyed to suffer death; and seeing a great concourse of people, and a lofty dar erected, from which hung a noose, he inquired for whom it was intended. Gersíwaz heard the question, and replied that it was for a Persian, an enemy of Túrán, a son of Gíw, and related to Rustem. Pírán straightway rode up to the youth, who was standing in deep affliction, almost naked, and with his hands bound behind his back, and he said to him:

> "Why didst thou quit thy country, why come hither,
> Why choose the road to an untimely grave?"

Upon this Byzun told him his whole story, and the treachery of Girgín. Pírán wept at the recital, and remembering the circumstances under which he had encountered Gíw, and how he had been himself delivered from death by the interposition of Ferangís, he requested the execution to be stayed until he had seen the king, which was accordingly done. The king received him with honor, praised his wisdom and prudence, and conjecturing from his manner that something was heavy at his heart, expressed his readiness to grant any favor which he might have come to solicit. Pírán said: "Then, my only desire is this: do not put Byzun to death; do not repeat the tragedy of Saiáwush, and again consign Túrán and Irán to all the horrors of war and desolation. Remember how I warned thee against taking the life of that young prince; but malignant and evil advisers exerted their influence, were triumphant, and brought upon thee and thy kingdom the vengeance of Káús, of Rustem, and all the warriors of the Persian empire. The swords now sleeping in their scabbards are ready to flash forth again, for assuredly if the blood of Byzun be spilt the land will be depopulated by fire and sword. The honor of a king is sacred; when that is lost, all is lost." But Afrásiyáb replied: "I fear not the thousands that can be brought against me. Byzun has committed an offence which can never be pardoned; it covers me with shame, and I shall be universally despised if I suffer him to live. Death were better for me than life in disgrace. He must die." – "That is not necessary," rejoined Pírán, "let him be imprisoned in a deep cavern; he will never be heard of more, and then thou canst not be accused of having shed his blood." After some deliberation, Afrásiyáb altered his determination, and commanded Gersíwaz to bind the youth with chains from head to foot, and hang him within a deep pit with his head downwards, that he might never see sun or moon again; and he sentenced

Maníjeh to share the same fate: and to make their death more sure, he ordered the enormous fragment of rock which Akwán Díw had dragged out of the ocean and flung upon the plain of Tartary, to be placed over the mouth of the pit. In respect to Byzun, Gersíwaz did as he was commanded; but the lamentations in the shubistán were so loud and distressing upon Maníjeh being sentenced to the same punishment, that the tyrant was induced to change her doom, allowing her to dwell near the pit, but forbidding, by proclamation, anyone going to her or supplying her with food. Gersíwaz conducted her to the place; and stripping her of her rich garments and jewels, left her bareheaded and barefooted, weeping torrents of tears.

> *He left her – the unhappy maid;*
> *Her head upon the earth was laid,*
> *In bitterness of grief, and lone,*
> *Beside that dreadful demon-stone.*

There happened, however, to be a fissure in the huge rock that covered the mouth of the pit, which allowed of Byzun's voice being heard, and bread and water was let down to him, so that they had the melancholy satisfaction of hearing each other's woes.

The story now relates to Girgín, who finding after several days that Byzun had not returned, began to repent of his treachery; but what is the advantage of such repentance? it is like the smoke that rises from a conflagration.

> *When flames have done their worst, thick clouds arise*
> *Of lurid smoke, which useless mount the skies.*

He sought everywhere for him; went to the romantic retreat where the daughter of Afrásiyáb resided; but the place was deserted, nothing was to be seen, and nothing to be heard. At length he saw Byzun's horse astray, and securing him with his kamund, thought it useless to remain in Túrán, and therefore proceeded in sorrow back to Irán. Gív, finding that his son had not returned with him from Armán, was frantic with grief; he tore his garments and his hair, and threw ashes over his head; and seeing the horse his son had ridden, caressed it in the fondest manner, demanding from Girgín a full account of what he knew of his fate. "O Heaven forbid," said he, "that my son should have fallen into the power of the merciless demons!" Girgín could not safely confess the truth, and therefore told a falsehood, in the hope of escaping from the consequences of his own guilt. "When we arrived at Armán," said he, "we entered a large forest, and cutting down the trees, set them on fire. We then attacked the wild boars, which were found in vast numbers; and as soon as they were all destroyed, left the place on our return. Sporting all the way, we fell in with an elk, of a most beautiful and wonderful form. It was like the Símúrgh; it had hoofs of steel, and the head and ears and tail of a horse. It was strong as a lion and fleet as the wind, and came fiercely before us, yet seemed to be a thing of air. Byzun threw his kamund over him; and when entangled in the noose, the animal became furious and sprung away, dragging Byzun after him. Presently the prospect was enveloped in smoke, the earth looked like the ocean, and Byzun and the phantom-elk disappeared. I wandered about in search of my companion, but found him not: his horse only remained. My heart was rent with anguish, for it seemed to me that the furious elk must have been the White Demon." But Gíw was not to be deceived by this fabricated tale; on the contrary, he felt convinced that treachery had been at work, and in his rage seized Girgín by the beard, dragged him to and fro, and inflicted on him two hundred strokes with a scourge. The unhappy wretch, from the wounds he had received, fell senseless on the ground. Gíw then hastened to Kai-khosráu to inform him of his misfortune; and though the first resolve was to put the traitor to death, the king was contented to load him with chains and cast him into prison. The astrologers being now consulted, pronounced that Byzun was still living, and Gíw was consoled and cheered by the promptitude with which the king despatched troops in every quarter in search of his son.

Kai-khosráu, thinking the services of Rustem requisite on this occasion, dispatched Gíw with an invitation to him, explaining the circumstance of Byzun's capture. Rustem had made up his mind to continue in peace and tranquillity at his Zábul principality, and not to be withdrawn again from its comforts by any emergency; but the reported situation of his near relative altered his purpose, and he hesitated not to give his best aid to restore him to freedom. Gíw rejoiced at this, and both repaired without delay to the royal residence, where Khosráu gratified the champion with the most cordial welcome, placing him on a throne before him. The king asked him what force he would require, and he replied that he did not require any army; he preferred going in disguise as a merchant. Accordingly the necessary materials were prepared; a thousand camels were laden with jewels and brocades, and other merchandise, and a thousand warriors were habited like camel-drivers. Girgín had prayed to be released from his bonds, and by the intercession of Rustem was allowed to be of the party; but his children were kept in prison as hostages and security for his honorable conduct.

When the champion, with his kafila, arrived within the territory of the enemy, and approached the spot where Byzun was imprisoned, a loud clamor arose that a caravan of merchandise had come from Irán, such as was never seen before. The tidings having reached the ear of Maníjeh, she went immediately to Rustem, and inquired whether the imprisonment of Byzun was yet known at the Persian court? Rustem replied in anger: "I am a merchant employed in traffic, what can I know of such things? Go away, I have no acquaintance with either the king or his warriors." This answer overwhelmed Maníjeh with disappointment and grief, and she wept bitterly. Her tears began to soften the heart of Rustem, and he said to her in a soothing voice: – "I am not an inhabitant of the city in which the court is held, and on that account I know nothing of these matters; but tell me the cause of thy grief." Maníjeh sighed deeply, and endeavored to avoid giving him any reply, which increased the curiosity of the champion; but she at length complied. She told him who she was, the daughter of Afrásiyáb, the story of her love, and the misfortunes of Byzun, and pointed out to him the pit in which he was imprisoned and bound down with heavy chains.

> "For the sake of him has been my fall
> From royal state, and bower, and hall,
> And hence this pale and haggard face,
> This saffron hue thy eye may trace,
> Where bud of rose was wont to bloom,
> But withered now and gone;
> And I must sit in sorrow's gloom
> Unsuccoured and alone."

Rustem asked with deep interest if any food could be conveyed to him, and she said that she had been accustomed to supply him with bread and water through a fissure in the huge stone which covered the mouth of the pit. Upon receiving this welcome information, Rustem brought a roasted fowl, and inclosing in it his own seal-ring, gave it to Maníjeh to take to Byzun. The poor captive, on receiving it, inquired by whom such a blessing could have been sent, and when she informed him that it had been given to her by the chief of a caravan from Irán, who had manifested great anxiety about him, his smiles spoke the joyous feelings of his heart, for the name of Rustem was engraved on the ring. Maníjeh was surprised to see him smile, considering his melancholy situation, and could not imagine the cause. "If thou wilt keep my secret," said he, "I will tell thee the cause." "What!" she replied, "have I not devoted my heart and soul to thee? – have I not sacrificed everything for thy love, and is my fidelity now to be suspected?

> *"Can I be faithless, then, to thee,*
> *The choice of this fond heart of mine;*
> *Why sought I bonds, when I was free,*
> *But to be thine – forever thine?"*

"True, true! then hear me: – the chief of the caravan is Rustem, who has undoubtedly come to release me from this dreadful pit. Go to him, and concert with him the manner in which my deliverance may be soonest effected." Maníjeh accordingly went and communicated with the champion; and it was agreed between them that she should light a large fire to guide him on his way. He was prompt as well as valiant, and repaired in the middle of the following night, accompanied by seven of his warriors, directed by the blaze, to the place where Byzun was confined. The neighborhood was infested by demons with long nails, and long hair on their bodies like the hair of a goat, and horny feet, and with heads like dogs, and the chief of them was the son of Akwán Díw. The father having been slain by Rustem, the son nourished the hope of revenge, and perpetually longed for an opportunity of meeting him in battle. Well knowing that the champion was engaged in the enterprise to liberate Byzun, he commanded his demons to give him intelligence of his approach. His height was tremendous, his face was black, his mouth yawned like a cavern, his eyes were fountains of blood, his teeth like those of a wild boar, and the hair on his body like needles. The monster advanced, and reproaching Rustem disdainfully for having slain Akwán Díw, and many other warriors in the Túránian interest, pulled up a tree by the roots and challenged him to combat. The struggle began, but the Demon frequently escaped the fury of the champion by vanishing into air. At length Rustem struck a fortunate blow, which cut the body of his towering adversary in two. His path being now free from interruption, he sped onward, and presently beheld the prodigious demon-stone which covered the mouth of the pit, in which Byzun was imprisoned.

> *And praying to the Almighty to infuse*
> *Strength through his limbs, he raised it up, and flung*
> *The ponderous mass of rock upon the plain,*
> *Which shuddered to receive that magic load!*

The mouth of the cavern being thus exposed, Rustem applied himself to the extrication of Byzun from his miserable condition, and letting down his kamund, he had soon the pleasure of drawing up the unfortunate captive, whom he embraced with great affection; and instantly stripped off the chains with which he was bound. After mutual congratulations had been exchanged, Rustem proposed that Byzun and Maníjeh should go immediately to Irán, whilst he and his companions in arms attacked the palace of Afrásiyáb; but though wasted as he was by long suffering, Byzun could not on any consideration consent to avoid the perils of the intended assault, and determined, at all hazards, to accompany his deliverer.

> *"Full well I know thy superhuman power*
> *Needs no assistance from an arm like mine;*
> *But grateful as I am for this great service,*
> *I cannot leave thee now, and shrink from peril,*
> *That would be baseness which I could not bear."*

It was on the same night that Rustem and Byzun, and seven of his warriors, proceeded against that part of the palace in which the tyrant slept. He first put to death the watchman, and also killed a great number of the guard, and a loud voice presently resounded in the chamber of the king: – "Awake from thy slumbers, Afrásiyáb, Byzun has been freed from his chains." Rustem now entered the royal palace, and openly declaring his name, exclaimed: – "I am come, Afrásiyáb, to destroy thee, and Byzun is also here to do thee service for thy cruelty to him." The death-note awoke the trembling Afrásiyáb, and he rose up, and fled in dismay. Rustem and his companions rushed into the inner apartments, and captured all the blooming damsels of the shubistán, and all the jewels and golden ornaments which fell in their way. The moon-faced beauties were sent to Zábul; but the jewels and other valuable property were reserved for the king.

In the morning Afrásiyáb hastily collected together his troops and marched against Rustem, who, with Byzun and his thousand warriors, met him on the plain prepared for battle. The champion challenged any one who would come forward to single combat; but though frequently repeated, no attention was paid to the call. At length Rustem said to Afrásiyáb: "Art thou not ashamed to avoid a contest with so inferior a force, a hundred thousand against one thousand? We two, and our armies, have often met, and dost thou now shrink from the fight?" The reproach had its effect,

> *For the tyrant at once, and his heroes, began*
> *Their attack like the demons of Mázinderán.*

But the valor and the bravery of Rustem were so eminently shown, that he overthrew thousands of the enemy.

> *In the tempest of battle, disdaining all fear,*
> *With his kamund, and khanjer, his garz, and shamshír,*
> *How he bound, stabbed, and crushed, and dissevered the foe,*
> *So mighty his arm, and so fatal his blow.*

And so dreadful was the carnage, that Afrásiyáb, unable to resist his victorious career, was compelled to seek safety in flight.

> *The field was red with blood, the Tartar banners*
> *Cast on the ground, and when, with grief, he saw*
> *The face of Fortune turned, his cohorts slain,*
> *He hurried back, and sought Túrán again.*

Rustem having obtained another triumph, returned to Irán with the spoils of his conquest, and was again honored with the smiles and rewards of his sovereign. Maníjeh was not forgotten; she, too, received a present worthy of the virtue and fidelity she had displayed, and of the magnanimity of her spirit; and the happy conclusion of the enterprise was celebrated with festivity and rejoicing.

Barzú, and his Conflict with Rustem

AFRÁSIYÁB AFTER HIS DEFEAT pursued his way in despair towards Chín and Má-chín, and on the road happened to fall in with a man of huge and terrific stature. Amazed at the sight of so extraordinary a being, he asked him who and what he was. "I am a villager," replied the stranger. "And thy father?" – "I do not know my father. My mother has never mentioned his name, and my birth is wrapped in mystery." Afrásiyáb then addressed him as follows: – "It is my misfortune to have a bitter and invincible enemy, who has plunged me into the greatest distress. If he could be subdued, there would be no impediment to my conquest of Irán; and I feel assured that thou, apparently endued with such prodigious strength, hast the power to master him. His name is Rustem." "What!" rejoined Barzú, "is all this concern and affliction about one man – about one man only?" "Yes," answered Afrásiyáb; "but that one man is equal to a hundred strong men. Upon him neither sword, nor mace, nor javelin has any effect. In battle he is like a mountain of steel."

At this Barzú exclaimed in gamesome mood: – "A mountain of steel! – I can reduce to dust a hundred mountains of steel! – What is a mountain of steel to me!" Afrásiyáb rejoiced to find such confidence in the stranger, and instantly promised him his own daughter in marriage, and the monarchy of Chín and Má-chín, if he succeeded in destroying Rustem. Barzú replied:

> *"Thou art but a coward slave,*
> *Thus a stranger's aid to crave.*
> *And thy soldiers, what are they?*
> *Heartless on the battle-day.*
> *Thou, the prince of such a host!*
> *What, alas! hast thou to boast?*
> *Art thou not ashamed to wear*
> *The regal crown that glitters there?*
> *And dost thou not disgrace the throne*
> *Thus to be awed, and crushed by one;*
> *By one, whate'er his name or might,*
> *Thus to be put to shameful flight!"*

Afrásiyáb felt keenly the reproaches which he heard; but, nevertheless, solicited the assistance of Barzú, who declared that he would soon overpower Rustem, and place the empire of Irán under the dominion of the Tartar king. He would, he said, overflow the land of Persia with blood, and take possession of the throne! The despot was intoxicated with delight, and expecting his most sanguine wishes would be realized, made him the costliest presents, consisting of gold and jewels, and horses, and elephants, so that the besotted stranger thought himself the greatest personage in all the world. But his mother, when she heard these things, implored him to be cautious:

> *"My son, these presents, though so rich and rare,*
> *Will be thy winding-sheet; beware, beware!*
> *They'll drive to madness thy poor giddy brain,*
> *And thou wilt never be restored again.*
> *Never; for wert thou bravest of the brave,*
> *They only lead to an untimely grave.*
> *Then give them back, nor such a doom provoke,*
> *Beware of Rustem's host-destroying stroke.*
> *Has he not conquered demons! – and, alone,*
> *Afrásiyáb's best warriors overthrown!*
> *And canst thou equal them? – Alas! the day*
> *That thy sweet life should thus be thrown away."*

Barzú, however, was too much dazzled by the presents he had received, and too vain of his own personal strength to attend to his mother's advice. "Certainly," said he, "the disposal of our lives is in the hands of the Almighty, and as certain it is that my strength is superior to that of Rustem. Would it not then be cowardly to decline the contest with him?" The mother still continued to dissuade him from the enterprise, and assured him that Rustem was above all mankind distinguished for the art, and skill, and dexterity, with which he attacked his enemy, and defended himself; and that there was no chance of his being overcome by a man entirely ignorant of the science of fighting; but Barzú remained unmoved: yet he told the king what his mother had said; and Afrásiyáb, in consequence, deemed it proper to appoint two celebrated masters to instruct him in the use of the bow, the sword, and the javelin, and also in wrestling and throwing the noose. Every day, clothed in armor, he tried his skill and strength with the warriors, and after ten days he was sufficiently accomplished to overthrow eighteen of them at one time. Proud of the progress he had made, he told the king that he would seize and bind eighteen of his stoutest and most experienced teachers, and bring them before him, if he wished, when all the assembly exclaimed: – "No doubt he is fully equal to the task;

> *"He does not seem of human birth, but wears*
> *The aspect of the Evil One; and looks*

> *Like Alberz mountain, clad in folds of mail;*
> *Unwearied in the fight he conquers all."*

Afrásiyáb's satisfaction was increased by this testimony to the merit of Barzú, and he heaped upon him further tokens of his good-will and munificence. The vain, newly-made warrior was all exultation and delight, and said impatiently:

> *"Delays are ever dangerous – let us meet*
> *The foe betimes, this Rustem and the king,*
> *Kai-khosráu. If we linger in a cause*
> *Demanding instant action, prompt appliance,*
> *And rapid execution, we are lost.*
> *Advance, and I will soon lop off the heads*
> *Of this belauded champion and his king,*
> *And cast them, with the Persian crown and throne*
> *Trophies of glory, at thy royal feet;*
> *So that Túrán alone shall rule the world."*

Speedily ten thousand experienced horsemen were selected and placed under the command of Barzú; and Húmán and Bármán were appointed to accompany him; Afrásiyáb himself intending to follow with the reserve.

When the intelligence of this new expedition reached the court of Kai-khosráu, he was astonished, and could not conceive how, after so signal a defeat and overthrow, Afrásiyáb had the means of collecting another army, and boldly invading his kingdom. To oppose this invasion, however, he ordered Tús and Fríburz, with twelve thousand horsemen, and marched after them himself with a large army. As soon as Tús fell in with the enemy the battle commenced, and lasted, with great carnage, a whole day and night, and in the end Barzú was victorious. The warriors of the Persian force fled, and left Tús and Fríburz alone on the field, where they were encountered by the conqueror, taken prisoners, and bound, and placed in the charge of Húmán. The tidings of the result of this conflict were received with as much rejoicing by Afrásiyáb, as with sorrow and consternation by Kai-khosráu. And now the emergency, on the Persian side, demanded the assistance of Rustem, whose indignation was roused, and who determined on revenge for the insult that had been given. He took with him Gustahem, the brother of Tús, and at midnight thought he had come to the tent of Barzú, but it proved to be the pavilion of Afrásiyáb, who was seen seated on his throne, with Barzú on his right hand, and Pírán-wísah on his left, and Tús and Fríburz standing in chains before them. The king said to the captive warriors: "To-morrow you shall both be put to death in the manner I slew Saiáwush." He then retired. Meanwhile Rustem returned thanks to Heaven that his friends were still alive, and requesting Gustahem to follow cautiously, he waited awhile for a fit opportunity, till the watchman was off his guard, and then killing him, he and Gustahem took up and conveyed the two prisoners to a short distance, where they knocked off their chains, and then conducted them back to Kai-khosráu.

When Afrásiyáb arose from sleep, he found his warriors in close and earnest conversation, and was told that a champion from Persia had come and killed the watchman, and carried off the prisoners. Pírán exclaimed: "Then assuredly that champion is Rustem, and no other." Afrásiyáb writhed with anger and mortification at this intelligence, and sending for Barzú, despatched his army to attack the enemy, and challenge Rustem to single combat. Rustem was with the Persian troops, and, answering the summons, said: "Young man, if thou art calling for Rustem, behold I come in his place to lay thee prostrate on the earth." "Ah!" rejoined Barzú, "and why this threat? It is true I am but of tender years, whilst thou art aged and experienced. But if thou art fire, I am water, and able to quench thy flames." Saying this he wielded his bow, and fixed the arrow in its notch, and commenced the strife. Rustem also engaged with bow and arrows; and then they each had recourse to their maces, which from repeated strokes were soon bent as crooked as their bows, and they were themselves nearly exhausted. Their next encounter was by wrestling, and dreadful were the wrenches and grasps they received from each other. Barzú finding no advantage from this struggle, raised his mace, and struck Rustem such a prodigious blow on the head, that the champion thought a whole mountain had fallen upon him. One arm was disabled, but though the wound was desperate, Rustem had the address to conceal its effects, and Barzú wondered that he had made apparently so little impression on his antagonist. "Thou art," said he, "a surprising warrior, and seemingly invulnerable. Had I struck such a blow on a mountain, it would have been broken into a thousand fragments, and yet it makes no impression upon thee. Heaven forbid!" he continued to himself, "that I should ever receive so bewildering a stroke upon my own head!" Rustem having successfully concealed the anguish of his wound, artfully observed that it would be better to finish the combat on the following day, to which Barzú readily agreed, and then they both parted.

Barzú declared to Afrásiyáb that his extraordinary vigor and strength had been of no account, for both his antagonist and his horse appeared to be composed of materials as hard as flint. Every blow was without effect; and "Heaven only knows," added he, "what may be the result of to-morrow's conflict." On the other hand Rustem showed his lacerated arm to Khosráu, and said: "I have escaped from him; but who else is there now to meet him, and finish the struggle? Ferámurz, my son, cannot fulfil my promise with Barzú, as he, alas! is fighting in Hindústán. Let me, however, call him hither, and in the meanwhile, on some pretext or other, delay the engagement." The king, in great sorrow and affliction, sanctioned his departure, and then said to his warriors: "I will fight this Barzú myself to-morrow;" but Gúdarz would not consent to it, saying: "As long as we live, the king must not be exposed to such hazard. Gíw and Byzun, and the other chiefs, must first successively encounter the enemy."

When Rustem reached his tent, he told his brother Zúára to get ready a litter, that he might proceed to Sístán for the purpose of obtaining a remedy for his wound from the Símúrgh. Pain and grief kept him awake all night, and he prayed incessantly to the Supreme Being. In the morning early, Zúára brought him intelligence of the welcome arrival of Ferámurz, which gladdened his heart; and as the youth had undergone great fatigue on his long journey, Rustem requested him to repose awhile, and he himself, freed from anxiety, also sought relief in a sound sleep.

A few hours afterwards both armies were again drawn up, and Barzú, like a mad elephant, full of confidence and pride, rode forward to resume the combat; whilst Rustem gave instructions to Ferámurz how he was to act. He attired him in his own armor, supplied him with his own weapons, and mounted him on Rakush, and told him to represent himself to Barzú as the warrior who had engaged him the day before. Accordingly Ferámurz entered the middle space, clothed in his father's mail, raised his bow, ready bent, and shot an arrow at Barzú, crying: "Behold thy adversary! I am the man come to try thy strength again. Advance!" To this Barzú replied: "Why this hilarity, and great flow of spirits? Art thou reckless of thy life?" "In the eyes of warriors," said Ferámurz, "the field of fight is the mansion of pleasure. After I yesterday parted from thee I drank wine with my companions, and the impression of delight still remains on my heart.

> "Wine exhilarates the soul,
> Makes the eye with pleasure roll;
> Lightens up the darkest mien,
> Fills with joy the dullest scene;

Hence it is I meet thee now
With a smile upon my brow,"

Barzú, however, thought that the voice and action of his adversary were not the same as he had heard and seen the preceding day, although there was no difference in the armor or the horse, and therefore he said: "Perhaps the cavalier whom I encountered yesterday is wounded or dead, that thou hast mounted his charger, and attired thyself in his mail." "Indeed," rejoined Ferámurz, "perhaps thou hast lost thy wits; I am certainly the person who engaged thee yesterday, and almost extinguished thee; and with God's favor thou shalt be a dead man to-day." "What is thy name?" "My name is Rustem, descended from a race of warriors, and my pleasure consists in contending with the lions of battle, and shedding the blood of heroes." Thus saying, Ferámurz rushed on his adversary, struck him several blows with his battle-axe, and drawing his noose from the saddle-strap with the quickness of lightning, secured his prize. He might have put an end to his existence in a moment, but preferred taking him alive, and showing him as a captive. Afrásiyáb seeing the perilous condition of Barzú, came up with his whole army to his rescue; but Kai-khosráu was equally on the alert, accompanied by Rustem, who, advancing to the support of Ferámurz, threw another noose round the neck of the already-captured Barzú, to prevent the possibility of his escape. Both armies now engaged, and the Túránians made many desperate efforts to recover their gigantic leader, but all their manoeuvres were fruitless. The struggle continued fiercely, and with great slaughter, till it was dark, and then ceased; the two kings returned back to the respective positions they had taken up before the conflict took place. The Túránians were in the deepest grief for the loss of Barzú; and Pírán-wísah having recommended an immediate retreat across the Jihún, Afrásiyáb followed his counsel, and precipitately quitted Persia with all his troops.

Kai-khosráu ordered a grand banquet on the occasion of the victory; and when Barzú was brought before him, he commanded his immediate execution; but Rustem, seeing that he was very young, and thinking that he had not yet been corrupted and debased by the savage example of the Túránians, requested that he might be spared, and given to him to send into Sístán; and his request was promptly complied with.

When the mother of Barzú, whose name was Sháh-rú, heard that her son was a prisoner, she wept bitterly, and hastened to Irán, and from thence to Sístán. There happened to be in Rustem's employ a singing-girl, an old acquaintance of hers, to whom she was much attached, and to whom she made large presents, calling her by the most endearing epithets, in order that she might be brought to serve her in the important matter she had in contemplation. Her object was soon explained, and the preliminaries at once adjusted, and by the hands of this singing-girl she secretly sent some food to Barzú, in which she concealed a ring, to apprise him of her being near him. On finding the ring, he asked who had supplied him with the food, and her answer was: "A woman recently arrived from Má-chín." This was to him delightful intelligence, and he could not help exclaiming, "That woman is my mother, I am grateful for thy services, but another time bring me, if thou canst, a large file, that I may be able to free myself from these chains." The singing-girl promised her assistance; and having told Sháh-rú what her son required, conveyed to him a file, and resolved to accompany him in his flight. Barzú then requested that three fleet horses might be provided and kept ready under the walls, at a short distance; and this being also done, in the night, he and his mother, and the singing-girl, effected their escape, and pursued their course towards Túrán.

It so happened that Rustem was at this time in progress between Irán and Sístán, hunting for his own pleasure the elk or wild ass, and he accidentally fell in with the refugees, who made an attempt to avoid him, but, unable to effect their purpose, thought proper to oppose him with all their might, and a sharp contest ensued. Both parties becoming fatigued, they rested awhile, when Rustem asked Barzú how he had obtained his liberty. "The Almighty freed me from the bondage I endured." "And who are these two women?" "One of them," replied Barzú, "is my mother, and that is a singing-girl of thy own house." Rustem went aside, and called for breakfast, and thinking in his own mind that it would be expedient to poison Barzú, mixed up a deleterious substance in some food, and sent it to him to eat. He was just going to take it, when his mother cried, "My son, beware!" and he drew his hand from the dish. But the singing-girl did eat part of it, and died on the spot. Upon witnessing this appalling scene, Barzú sprang forward with indignation, and reproached Rustem for his treachery in the severest terms.

> "Old man! hast thou mid warrior-chiefs a place,
> And dost thou practice that which brings disgrace?
> Hast thou no fear of a degraded name,
> No fear of lasting obloquy and shame?
> O, thou canst have no hope in God, when thou
> Stand'st thus defiled – dishonoured, false, as now;
> Unfair, perfidious, art thou too, in strife,
> By any pretext thou wouldst take my life!"

He then in a menacing attitude exclaimed: "If thou art a man, rise and fight!" Rustem felt ashamed on being thus detected, and rose up frowning in scorn. They met, brandishing their battle-axes, and looking as black as the clouds of night. They then dismounted to wrestle, and fastening the bridles, each to his own girdle, furiously grasped each other's loins and limbs, straining and struggling for the mastery. Whilst they were thus engaged, their horses betrayed equal animosity, and attacked each other with great violence. Rakush bit and kicked Barzú's steed so severely that he strove to gallop away, dragging his master, who was at the same time under the excruciating grip of Rustem. "O, release me for a moment till I am disentangled from my horse," exclaimed Barzú; but Rustem heeding him not, now pressed him down beneath him, and was preparing to give him the finishing blow by cutting off his head, when the mother seeing the fatal moment approach, shrieked, and cried out, "Forbear, Rustem! this youth is the son of Sohráb, and thy own grandchild! Forbear, and bring not on thyself the devouring anguish which followed the death of his unhappy father.

> *"Think of Sohráb! take not the precious life*
> *Of sire and son – unnatural is the strife;*
> *Restrain, for mercy's sake, that furious mood,*
> *And pause before thou shedd'st a kinsman's blood."*

"Ah!" rejoined Rustem, "can that be true?" upon which Sháh-rú showed him Sohráb's brilliant finger-ring and he was satisfied. He then pressed Barzú warmly and affectionately to his breast, and kissed his head and eyes, and took him along with him to Sístán, where he placed him in a station of honor, and introduced him to his great-grandfather Zál, who received and caressed him with becoming tenderness and regard.

Súsen and Afrásiyáb

SOON AFTER AFRÁSIYÁB had returned defeated into Túrán, grievously lamenting the misfortune which had deprived him of the assistance of Barzú, a woman named Súsen, deeply versed in magic and sorcery, came to him, and promised by her potent art to put him in the way of destroying Rustem and his whole family.

> *"Fighting disappointment brings,*
> *Sword and mace are useless things;*
> *If thou wouldst a conqueror be,*
> *Monarch! put thy trust in me;*
> *Soon the mighty chief shall bleed—*
> *Spells and charms will do the deed!"*

Afrásiyáb at first refused to avail himself of her power, but was presently induced, by a manifestation of her skill, to consent to what she proposed. She required that a distinguished warrior should be sent along with her, furnished with abundance of treasure, honorary tokens and presents, so that none might be aware that she was employed on the occasion. Afrásiyáb appointed Pílsam, duly supplied with the requisites, and the warrior and the sorceress set off on their journey, people being stationed conveniently on the road to hasten the first tidings of their success to the king. Their course was towards Sístán, and arriving at a fort, they took possession of a commodious residence, in which they placed the wealth and property they had brought, and, establishing a house of entertainment, all travellers who passed that way were hospitably and sumptuously regaled by them.

It is recorded that Rustem had invited to a magnificent feast at his palace in Sístán a large company of the most celebrated heroes of the kingdom, and amongst them happened to be Tús, whom the king had deputed to the champion on some important state affairs. Gúdarz was also present; and between him and Tús ever hostile to each other, a dispute as usual took place. The latter, always boasting of his ancestry, reviled the old warrior and said, "I am the son of Nauder, and the grandson of Feridún, whilst thou art but the son of Kavah, the blacksmith; – why then dost thou put thyself on a footing with me?" Gúdarz, in reply, poured upon him reproaches equally irritating, accused him of ignorance and folly, and roused the anger of the prince to such a degree that he drew his dagger to punish the offender, when Rehám started up and prevented the intended bloodshed. This interposition increased his rage, and in serious dudgeon he retired from the banquet, and set off on his return to Irán.

Rustem was not present at the time, but when he heard of the altercation and the result of it, he was very angry, saying that Gúdarz was a relation of the family, and

Tús his guest, and therefore wrong had been done, since a guest ought always to be protected. "A guest," he said, "ought to be held as sacred as the king, and it is the custom of heroes to treat a guest with the most scrupulous respect and consideration—

"For a guest is the king of the feast."

He then requested Gúdarz to go after Tús, and by fair words and proper excuses bring him back to his festive board. Accordingly Gúdarz departed. No sooner had he gone than Gíw rose up, and said, "Tús is little better than a madman, and my father of a hasty temper; I should therefore wish to follow, to prevent the possibility of further disagreement." To this Rustem consented. Byzun was now also anxious to go, and he too got permission. When all the three had departed, Rustem began to be apprehensive that something unpleasant would occur, and thought it prudent to send Ferámurz to preserve the peace. Zál then came forward, and thinking that Tús, the descendant of the Kais and his revered guest, might not be easily prevailed upon to return either by Gúdarz, Gíw, Byzun, or Ferámurz, resolved to go himself and soothe the temper which had been so injudiciously and rudely ruffled at the banquet.

When Tús, on his journey from Rustem's palace, approached the residence of Súsen the sorceress, he beheld numerous cooks and confectioners on every side, preparing all kinds of rich and rare dishes of food, and every species of sweetmeat; and enquiring to whom they belonged, he was told that the place was occupied by the wife of a merchant from Túrán, who was extremely wealthy, and who entertained in the most sumptuous manner every traveller who passed that way. Hungry, and curious to see what was going on, Tús dismounted, and leaving his horse with the attendants, entered the principal apartment, where he saw a fascinating female, and was transported with joy. – She was

> *Tall as the graceful cypress, and as bright,*
> *As ever struck a lover's ravished sight;*
> *Why of her musky locks or ringlets tell?*
> *Each silky hair itself contained a spell.*
> *Why of her face so beautifully fair?*
> *Wondering he saw the moon's refulgence there.*

As soon as his transports had subsided he sat down before her, and asked her who she was, and upon what adventure she was engaged; and she answered that she was a singing-girl, that a wealthy merchant some time ago had fallen in love with and married her, and soon afterwards died; that Afrásiyáb, the king, had since wished to take her into his harem, which alarmed her, and she had in consequence fled from his country; she was willing, however, she said, to become the handmaid of Kai-khosráu, he being a true king, and of a sweet and gentle temper.

> "A persecuted damsel I,
> Thus the detested tyrant fly,
> And hastening from impending woes,
> In happy Persia seek repose;
> For long as cherished life remains,
> Pleasure must smile where Khosráu reigns.
> Thence did I from my home depart,
> To please and bless a Persian heart."

The deception worked effectually on the mind of Tús, and he at once entered into the notion of escorting her to Kai-khosráu. But he was immediately supplied with charmed viands and goblets of rich wine, which he had not the power to resist, till his senses forsook him, and then Pílsam appeared, and, binding him with cords, conveyed him safely and secretly into the interior of the fort. In a short time Gúdarz arrived, and he too was received and treated in the same manner. Then Gíw and Byzun were seized and secured; and after them came Zál: but notwithstanding the enticements that were used, and the attractions that presented themselves, he would neither enter the enchanted apartment, nor taste the enchanted food or wine.

> The bewitching cup was filled to the brim,
> But the magic draught had no charms for him.

A person whispered in his ear that the woman had already wickedly got into her power several warriors, and he felt assured that they were his own friends. To be revenged for this treachery he rushed forward, and would have seized hold of the sorceress, but she fled into the fort and fastened the gate. He instantly sent a messenger to Rustem, explaining the perplexity in which he was involved, and exerting all his strength, broke down the gate that had just been closed against him as soon as the passage was opened, out rushed Pílsam, who with his mace commenced a furious battle with Zál, in which he nearly overpowered him, when Ferámurz reached the spot, and telling the venerable old warrior to stand aside, took his place, and fought with Pílsam without intermission all day, and till they were parted by the darkness of night.

Early in the morning Rustem, accompanied by Barzú, arrived from Sístán, and entering the fort, called aloud for Pílsam. He also sent Ferámurz to Kai-khosráu to inform him of what had occurred. Pílsam at length issued forth, and attacked the champion. They first fought with bows and arrows, with javelins next, and then successively with maces, and swords, and daggers. The contest lasted the whole day, and when at night they parted, neither had gained the victory. The next morning immense clouds of dust were seen, and they were found to be occasioned by Afrásiyáb and his army marching to the spot. Rustem appointed Barzú to proceed with his Zábul troops against him, whilst he himself encountered Pílsam. The strife between the two was dreadful. Rustem struck him several times furiously upon the head, and at length stretched him lifeless on the sand. He then impelled Rakush towards the Túránian army, and aided by Zál and Barzú, committed tremendous havoc among them.

> So thick the arrows fell, helmet, and mail,
> And shield, pierced through, looked like a field of reeds.
> In the meantime Súsen, the sorceress, escaped from the fort, and fled to
> Afrásiyáb.

Another cloud of dust spreading from earth to heaven, was observed in the direction of Persia, and the waving banners becoming more distinct, presently showed the approach of the king, Kai-khosráu.

> The steely javelins sparkled in the sun,
> Helmet and shield, and joyous seemed the sight.
> Banners, all gorgeous, floating on the breeze,
> And horns shrill echoing, and the tramp of steeds,
> Proclaimed to dazzled eye and half-stunned ear,
> The mighty preparation.

The hostile armies soon met, and there was a sanguinary conflict, but the Túránians were obliged to give way. Upon this common result, Pírán-wísah declared to Afrásiyáb that perseverance was as ridiculous as unprofitable. "Our army has no heart, nor confidence, when opposed to Rustem; how often have we been defeated by him – how often have we been scattered like sheep before that lion in battle! We have just lost the aid of Barzú, and now is it not deplorable to put any trust in the dreams of a singing-girl, to accelerate on her account the ruin of the country, and to hazard thy own personal safety.

"What! risk an empire on a wo man's word!"

Afrásiyáb replied, "So it is;" and instantly urged his horse into the middle of the plain, where he loudly challenged Kai-khosráu to single combat, saying, "Why should we uselessly shed the blood of our warriors and people. Let us ourselves decide the day. God will give the triumph to him who merits it." Kai-khosráu was ashamed to refuse this challenge, and descending from his elephant, mounted his horse and prepared for the onset. But his warriors seized the bridle, and would not allow him to fight. He declared, however, that he would himself take revenge for the blood of Saiáwush, and struggled to overcome the friends who were opposing his progress. "Forbear awhile," said Rustem, "Afrásiyáb is expert in all the arts of the warrior, fighting with the sword, the dagger, in archery, and wrestling. When I wrestled with him, and held him down, he could not have escaped, excepting by the exercise of the most consummate dexterity. Allow thy warriors to fight for thee." But the king was angry, and said, "The monarch who does not fight for himself, is unworthy of the crown." Upon hearing this, Rustem wept tears of blood. Barzú now took hold of the king's stirrup, and knocked his forehead against it, and drawing his dagger, threatened to put an end to himself, saying, "My blood will be upon thy neck, if thou goest;" and he continued in a strain so eloquent and persuasive that Khosráu relaxed in his determination, and observed to Rustem: "There can be no doubt that Barzú is descended from thee." Barzú now respectfully kissed the ground before the king, and vaulting on his saddle with admirable agility, rushed onwards to the middle space where Afrásiyáb was waiting, and roared aloud. Afrásiyáb burned with indignation at the sight, and said in his heart: "It seems that I have nurtured and instructed this ingrate, to shed my own blood. Thou wretch of demon-birth, thou knowest not thy father's name! and yet thou comest to wage war against me! Art thou not ashamed to look upon the king of Túrán after what he has done for thee?" Barzú replied: "Although thou didst protect me, thou spilt the blood of Saiáwush and Aghríras unjustly. When I ate thy salt, I served thee faithfully, and fought for thee. I now eat the salt of Kai-khosráu, and my allegiance is due to him."

He spoke, and raised his battle-axe, and rushed,
Swift as a demon of Mázinderán,

Against Afrásiyáb, who, frowning, cried:—
"Approach not like a furious elephant,
Heedless what may befall thee – nor provoke
The wrath of him whose certain aim is death."
Then placed he on the string a pointed dart,
And shot it from the bow; whizzing it flew,
And pierced the armor of the wondering youth,
Inflicting on his side a painful wound,
Which made his heart with trepidation throb;
High exultation marked the despot's brow,
Seeing the gush of blood his loins distain.

Barzú was now anxious to assail Afrásiyáb with his mace, instead of arrows; but whenever he tried to get near enough, he was disappointed by the adroitness of his adversary, whom he could not reach. He was at last compelled to lay aside the battle-axe, and have recourse to his bow, but every arrow was dexterously received by Afrásiyáb on his shield; and Barzú, on his part, became equally active and successful. Afrásiyáb soon emptied his quiver, and then he grasped his mace with the intention of extinguishing his antagonist at once, but at the moment Húmán came up, and said: "O, king! do not bring thyself into jeopardy by contending against a person of no account; thy proper adversary is Kai-khosráu, and not him, for if thou gainest the victory, it can only be a victory over a fatherless soldier, and if thou art killed, the whole of Túrán will be at the feet of Persia." Both Pírán and Húmán dissuaded the king from continuing the engagement singly, and directed the Túránians to commence a general attack. Afrásiyáb told them that if Barzú was not slain, it would be a great misfortune to their country; in consequence, they surrounded him, and inflicted on him many severe wounds. But Rustem and Ferámurz, beholding the dilemma into which Barzú was thrown, hastened to his support, and many of the enemy were killed by them, and great carnage followed the advance of the Persian army.

The noise of clashing swords, and ponderous maces
Ringing upon the iron mail, seemed like
The busy work-shop of an armorer;
Tumultuous as the sea the field appeared,
All crimsoned with the blood of heroes slain.

Kai-khosráu himself hurried to the assistance of Barzú, and the powerful force which he brought along with him soon put the Túránians to flight. Afrásiyáb too made his escape in the confusion that prevailed. The king wished to pursue the enemy, but Rustem observed that their defeat and dispersion was enough. The battle having ceased, and the army being in the neighborhood of Sístán, the champion solicited permission to return to his home; "for I am now," said he, "four hundred years old, and require a little rest. In the meantime Ferámurz and Barzú may take my place." The king consented, and distributing his favors to each of his distinguished warriors for their prodigious exertions, left Zál and Rustem to proceed to Sístán, and returned to the capital of his kingdom.

The Expedition of Gúdarz

THE OVERTHROW of the sovereign of Túrán had only a temporary effect, as it was not long before he was enabled to collect further supplies, and another army for the defence of his kingdom; and Kai-khosráu's ambition to reduce the power of his rival being animated by new hopes of success, another expedition was entrusted to the command of Gúdarz. Rustem, he said, had done his duty in repeated campaigns against Afrásiyáb, and the extraordinary gallantry and wisdom with which they were conducted, entitled him to the highest applause. "It is now, Gúdarz, thy turn to vanquish the enemy." Accordingly Gúdarz, accompanied by Gíw, and Tús, and Byzun, and an immense army, proceeded towards Túrán. Ferámurz was directed previously to invade and conquer Hindústán, and from thence to march to the borders of Chín and Má-chín, for the purpose of uniting and co-operating with the army under Gúdarz, and, finally, to capture Afrásiyáb.

As soon as it was known in Túrán that Gúdarz was in motion to resume hostilities against the king, Húmán was appointed with a large force to resist his progress, and a second army of reserve was gathered together under the command of Pírán. The first conflict which occurred was between the troops of Gúdarz and Húmán. Gúdarz directed Byzun to attack Húmán. The two chiefs joined in battle, when Húmán fell under the sword of his adversary, and his army, being defeated, retired, and united in the rear with the legions of Pírán. The enemy thus became of formidable strength, and in consequence it was thought proper to communicate the inequality to Kai-khosráu, that reinforcements might be sent without loss of time. The king immediately complied, and also wrote to Sístán to request the aid of Rustem. The war lasted two years, the army on each side being continually recruited as necessity required, so that the numbers were regularly kept up, till a great battle took place, in which the venerable Pírán was killed, and nearly the whole of his army destroyed. This victory was obtained without the assistance of Rustem, who, notwithstanding the message of the king, had still remained in Sístán. The loss of Pírán, the counsellor and warrior, proved to be a great affliction to Afrásiyáb: he felt as if his whole support was taken away, and deemed it the signal of approaching ruin to his cause.

"Thou wert my refuge, thou my friend and brother;
Wise in thy counsel, gallant in the field,
My monitor and guide – and thou art gone!
The glory of my kingdom is eclipsed,
Since thou hast vanished from this world, and left me
All wretched to myself. But food, nor sleep
Nor rest will I indulge in, till just vengeance
Has been inflicted on the cruel foe."

When the news of Pírán's death reached Kai-khosráu, he rapidly marched forward, crossed the Jihún without delay, and passed through Samerkánd and Bokhára, to encounter the Túránians. Afrásiyáb, in the meantime, had not been neglectful. He had all his hidden treasure dug up, with which he assembled a prodigious army, and appointed his son Shydah-Poshang to the command of a hundred thousand horsemen. To oppose this force, Khosráu appointed his young relative, Lohurásp, with eight thousand horsemen, and passing through Sístán, desired Rustem, on account of Lohurásp's tender age and inexperience, to afford him such good counsel as he required. When Afrásiyáb heard this, he added to the force of Shydah another hundred thousand men, but first sent his son to Kai-khosráu in the character of an ambassador to offer terms of peace. "Tell him," said he, "that to secure this object, I will deliver to him one of my sons as a hostage, and a number of troops for his service, with the sacred promise never to depart from my engagements again. – But, a word in thy ear, Shydah; if Khosráu is not disposed to accept these terms, say, to prevent unnecessary bloodshed, he and I must personally decide the day by single combat. If he refuses to fight with me, say that thou wilt meet him; and shouldst thou be slain in the strife, I will surrender to him the kingdom of Túrán, and retire myself from the world." He further commanded him to propound these terms with a gallant and fearless bearing, and not to betray the least apprehension. Shydah entered fully into the spirit of his father's instructions, and declared that he would devote his life to the cause, that he would boldly before the whole assembly dare Kai-khosráu to battle; so that Afrásiyáb was delighted with the valorous disposition he displayed.

Kai-khosráu smiled when he heard of what Afrásiyáb intended, and viewed the proposal as a proof of his weakness. "But never," said he, "will I consent to a peace till I have inflicted on him the death which Saiáwush was made to suffer." When Shydah arrived, and with proper ceremony and respect had delivered his message, Kai-khosráu invited him to retire to his chamber and go to rest, and he would send an answer by one of his people. Shydah accordingly retired, and the king proceeded to consult his warrior-friends on the offers that had been made. "Afrásiyáb tells me," said he, "that if I do not wish for peace, I must fight either him or his son. I have seen Shydah – his eyes are red and blood-shot, and he has a fierce expression of feature; if I do not accept his terms, I shall probably soon have a dagger lodged in my breast." Saying this, he ordered his mail to be got ready; but Rustem and all the great men about him exclaimed, unanimously: "This must not be allowed; Afrásiyáb is full of fraud, artifice, and sorcery, and notoriously faithless to his engagements. The sending of Shydah is all a trick, and his letter of proposal all deceit: his object is simply to induce thee to fight him alone.

> "If thou shouldst kill this Shydah – what of that!
> There would be one Túránian warrior less,
> To vex the world withal; would that be triumph?
> And to a Persian king? But if it chanced,
> That thou shouldst meet with an untimely death,
> By dart or javelin, at the stripling's hands,
> What scathe and ruin would this realm befall!"

By the advice of Rustem, Kai-khosráu gave Shydah permission to depart, and said that he would send his answer to Afrásiyáb by Kárun. "But," observed the youth, "I have come to fight thee!" which touched the honor of the king, and he replied: "Be it so, let us then meet to-morrow."

In the meantime Khosráu prepared his letter to Afrásiyáb, in which he said:

> *"Our quarrel now is dark to view,*
> *It bears the fiercest, gloomiest hue;*
> *And vain have speech and promise been*
> *To change for peace the battle scene;*
> *For thou art still to treachery prone,*
> *Though gentle now in word and tone;*
> *But that imperial crown thou wearest,*
> *That mace which thou in battle bearest,*
> *Thy kingdom, all, thou must resign;*
> *Thy army too – for all are mine!*
> *Thou talk'st of strength, and might, and power,*
> *When revelling in a prosperous hour;*
> *But know, that strength of nerve and limb*
> *We owe to God – it comes from Him!*
> *And victory's palm, and regal sway,*
> *Alike the will of Heaven obey.*
> *Hence thy lost throne, no longer thine,*
> *Will soon, perfidious king! be mine!"*

In giving this letter to Kárun, Kai-khosráu directed him, in the first place, to deliver a message from him to Shydah, to the following effect:

> *"Driven art thou out from home and life,*
> *Doomed to engage in mortal strife,*
> *For deeply lours misfortune's cloud;*
> *That gay attire will be thy shroud;*
> *Blood from thy father's eyes will gush,*
> *As Káús wept for Saiáwush."*

In the morning Khosráu went to the appointed place, and when he approached Shydah, the latter said, "Thou hast come on foot, let our trial be in wrestling;" and the proposal being agreed to, both applied themselves fiercely to the encounter, at a distance from the troops.

> *The youth appeared with joyous mien,*
> *And bounding heart, for life was new;*
> *By either host the strife was seen,*
> *And strong and fierce the combat grew.*

Shydah exerted his utmost might, but was unable to move his antagonist from the ground; whilst Khosráu lifted him up without difficulty, and, dashing him on the plain,

> *He sprang upon him as the lion fierce*
> *Springs on the nimble gor, then quickly drew*
> *His deadly dagger, and with cruel aim,*
> *Thrust the keen weapon through the stripling's heart.*

Khosráu, immediately after slaying him, ordered the body to be washed with musk and rose-water, and, after burial, a tomb to be raised to his memory.

When Kárun reached the court of Afrásiyáb with the answer to the offer of peace, intelligence had previously arrived that Shydah had fallen in the combat, which produced in the mind of the father the greatest anguish. He gave no reply to Kárun, but ordered the drums and trumpets to be sounded, and instantly marched with a large army against the enemy. The two hosts were soon engaged, the anger of the Túránians being so much roused and sharpened by the death of the prince, that they were utterly regardless of their lives. The battle, therefore, was fought with unusual fury.

> *Two sovereigns in the field, in desperate strife,*
> *Each by a grievous cause of wrath, urged on*
> *To glut revenge; this, for a father's life*
> *Wantonly sacrificed; that for a son*
> *Slain in his prime. – The carnage has begun,*
> *And blood is seen to flow on every side;*
> *Thousands are slaughtered ere the day is done,*
> *And weltering swell the sanguinary tide;*
> *And why? To soothe man's hate, his cruelty, and pride.*

The battle terminated in the discomfiture and defeat of the Túránians, who fled from the conquerors in the utmost confusion. The people seized hold of the bridle of Afrásiyáb's horse, and obliged him to follow his scattered army.

Kai-khosráu having despatched an account of his victory to Káús, went in pursuit of Afrásiyáb, traversing various countries and provinces, till he arrived on the borders of Chín. The Khakán, or sovereign of that state, became in consequence greatly alarmed, and presented to him large presents to gain his favor, but the only object of Khosráu was to secure Afrásiyáb, and he told the ambassador that if his master dared to afford him protection, he would lay waste the whole kingdom. The Khakán therefore withdrew his hospitable services, and the abandoned king was compelled to seek another place of refuge.

The Death of Afrásiyáb

MELANCHOLY AND AFFLICTED, Afrásiyáb penetrated through wood and desert, and entered the province of Mikrán, whither he was followed by Kai-khosráu and his army. He then quitted Mikrán, but his followers had fallen off to a small number and to whatever country or region he repaired for rest and protection, none was given, lest the vengeance of Kai-khosráu should be hurled upon the offender. Still pursued and hunted like a wild beast, and still flying from his enemies, the small retinue which remained with him at last left him, and he was left alone, dejected, destitute, and truly forlorn. In this state of desertion he retired into a cave, where he hoped to continue undiscovered and unseen.

It chanced, however, that a man named Húm, of the race of Feridún, dwelt hard by. He was remarkable for his strength and bravery, but had peacefully taken up his abode upon the neighboring mountain, and was passing a religious life without any communication with the busy world. His dwelling was a little way above the cave of Afrásiyáb. One night he heard a voice of lamentation below, and anxious to ascertain from whom and whence it proceeded, he stole down to the spot and listened. The mourner spoke in the Turkish language, and said: – "O king of Túrán and Chín, where is now thy pomp and power! How has Fortune cast away thy throne and thy treasure to the winds?" Hearing these words Húm conjectured that this must be Afrásiyáb; and as he had suffered severely from the tyranny of that monarch, his feelings of vengeance were awakened, and he approached nearer to be certain that it was he. The same lamentations were repeated, and he felt assured that it was Afrásiyáb himself. He waited patiently, however, till morning dawned, and then he called out at the mouth of the cave: – "O, king of the world! come out of thy cave, and obtain thy desires! I have left the invisible sphere to accomplish thy wishes. Appear!" Afrásiyáb thinking this a spiritual call, went out of the cave and was instantly recognized by Húm, who at the same moment struck him a severe blow on the forehead, which felled him to the earth, and then secured his hands behind his back. When the monarch found himself in fetters and powerless, he complained of the cruelty inflicted upon him, and asked Húm why he had treated a stranger in that manner. Húm replied: "How many a prince of the race of Feridún hast thou sacrificed to thy ambition? How many a heart hast thou broken? I, too, am one who was compelled to fly from thy persecutions, and take refuge here on this desert mountain, and constantly have I prayed for thy ruin that I might be released from this miserable mode of existence, and be permitted to return to my paternal home. My prayer has been heard at last, and God has delivered thee into my hands. But how earnest thou hither, and by what strange vicissitudes art thou thus placed before me?" Afrásiyáb communicated to him the story of his misfortunes, and begged of him rather to put him to death on the spot than convey him to Kai-khosráu. But Húm was too much delighted with having the tyrant under his feet to consider either his safety or his feelings, and was not long in bringing him to the Persian king. Kai-khosráu received the prisoner with exultation, and made Húm a magnificent present. He well recollected the basin and the dagger used in the murder of Saiáwush, and commanded the presence of the treacherous Gersíwaz, that he and Afrásiyáb might suffer, in every respect, the same fate together. The basin was brought, and the two victims were put to death, like two goats, their heads being chopped off from their bodies.

After this sanguinary catastrophe, Kai-khosráu returned to Irán, leaving Rustem to proceed to his own principality. Kai-káús quitted his palace, according to his established custom, to welcome back the conqueror. He kissed his head and face, and showered upon him praises and blessings for the valor he had displayed, and the deeds he had done, and especially for having so signally revenged the cruel murder of his father Saiáwush.

The Death of Kai-khosráu

KAI-KHOSRÁU AT LAST BECAME inspired by an insurmountable attachment to a religious life, and thought only of devotion to God. Thus influenced by a disposition peculiar to ascetics, he abandoned the duties of sovereignty, and committed all state affairs to the care of his ministers. The chiefs and warriors remonstrated respectfully against this mode of government, and trusted that he would devote only a few hours in the day to the transactions of the kingdom, and the remainder to prayer and religious exercises; but this he refused, saying: – "One heart is not equal to both duties; my affections indeed are not for this transitory world, and I trust to be an inhabitant of the world to come." The nobles were in great sorrow at this declaration, and anxiously applied to Zál and Rustem, in the hopes of working some change in the king's disposition. On their arrival the people cried to them:

> *"Some evil eye has smote the king; – Iblís*
> *By wicked wiles has led his soul astray,*
> *And withered all life's pleasures. O release*
> *Our country from the sorrow, the dismay*
> *Which darkens every heart: – his ruin stay.*
> *Is it not mournful thus to see him cold*
> *And gloomy, casting pomp and joy away?*
> *Restore him to himself; let us behold*
> *Again the victor-king, the generous, just and bold."*

Zál and Rustem went to the palace of the king in a melancholy mood, and Khosráu having heard of their approach, enquired of them why they had left Sístán. They replied that the news of his having relinquished all concern in the affairs of the kingdom had induced them to wait upon him. "I am weary of the troubles of this life," said he composedly, "and anxious to prepare for a future state." "But death," observed Zál, "is a great evil. It is dreadful to die!" Upon this the king said: "I cannot endure any longer the deceptions and the perfidy of mankind. My love of heaven is so great that I cannot exist one moment without devotion and prayer. Last night a mysterious voice whispered in my ear: The time of thy departure is nigh, prepare the load for thy journey, and neglect not thy warning angel, or the opportunity will be lost." When Zál and Rustem saw that Khosráu was resolved, and solemnly occupied in his devotions, they were for some time silent. But Zál was at length moved, and said: "I will go into retirement and solitude with the king, and by continual prayer, and through his blessing, I too may be forgiven." "This, indeed," said the king, "is not the place for me. I must seek out a solitary cell, and there resign my soul to heaven." Zál and Rustem wept, and quitted the palace, and all the warriors were in the deepest affliction.

The next day Kai-khosráu left his apartment, and called together his great men and warriors, and said to them:

> *"That which I sought for, I have now obtained.*
> *Nothing remains of worldly wish, or hope,*
> *To disappoint or vex me. I resign*
> *The pageantry of kings, and turn away*
> *From all the pomp of the Kaiánian throne,*
> *Sated with human grandeur. – Now, farewell!*
> *Such is my destiny. To those brave friends,*
> *Who, ever faithful, have my power upheld,*
> *I will discharge the duty of a king,*
> *Paying the pleasing debt of gratitude."*

He then ordered his tents to be pitched in the desert, and opened his treasury, and for seven days made a sumptuous feast, and distributed food and money among the indigent, the widows, and orphans, and every destitute person was abundantly supplied with the necessaries of life, so that there was no one left in a state of want throughout the empire. He also attended to the claims of his warriors. To Rustem he gave Zábul, and Kábul, and Ním-rúz. He appointed Lohurásp, the son-in-law of Kai-káús, successor to his throne, and directed all his people to pay the same allegiance to him as they had done to himself; and they unanimously consented, declaring their firm attachment to his person and government. He appointed Gúdarz the chief minister, and Gíw to the chief command of the armies. To Tús he gave Khorassán; and he said to Fríburz, the son of Káús: – "Be thou obedient, I beseech thee, to the commands of Lohurásp, whom I have instructed, and brought up with paternal care;

for I know of no one so well qualified in the art of governing a kingdom." The warriors of Irán were surprised, and murmured together, that the son of Kai-káús should be thus placed under the authority of Lohurásp. But Zál observed to them: – "If it be the king's will, it is enough!" The murmurs of the warriors having reached Kai-khosráu, he sent for them, and addressed them thus: – "Fríburz is well known to be unequal to the functions of sovereignty; but Lohurásp is enlightened, and fully comprehends all the duties of regal sway. He is a descendant of Húsheng, wise and merciful, and God is my witness, I think him perfectly calculated to make a nation happy." Hearing this eulogium on the character of the new king from Kai-khosráu, all the warriors expressed their satisfaction, and anticipated a glorious reign. Khosráu further said: – "I must now address you on another subject. In my dreams a fountain has been pointed out to me; and when I visit that fountain, my life will be resigned to its Creator." He then bid farewell to all the people around him, and commenced his journey; and when he had accomplished one stage he pitched his tent. Next day he resumed his task, and took leave of Zál and Rustem; who wept bitterly as they parted from him.

> *"Alas!" they said, "that one on whom*
> *Heaven has bestowed a mind so great,*
> *A heart so brave, should seek the tomb,*
> *And not his hour in patience wait.*
> *The wise in wonder gaze, and say,*
> *No mortal being ever trod*
> *Before, the dim supernal way,*
> *And living, saw the face of God!"*

After Zál and Rustem, then Khosráu took leave of Gúdarz and Gíw and Tús, and Gustahem, but unwilling to go back, they continued with him. He soon arrived at the promised fountain, in which he bathed. He then said to his followers: – "Now is the time for our separation; – you must go;" but they still remained. Again he said: – "You must go quickly; for presently heavy showers of snow will fall, and a tempestuous wind will arise, and you will perish in the storm." Saying this, he went into the fountain, and vanished!

The king having disappeared in this extraordinary manner, a loud lamentation ascended from his followers; and when the paroxysm of amazement and sorrow had ceased, Fríburz said: – "Let us now refresh ourselves with food, and rest awhile." Accordingly those that remained ate a little, and were soon afterwards overcome with sleep. Suddenly a great wind arose, and the snow fell and clothed the earth in white, and all the warriors and soldiers who accompanied Kai-khosráu to the mysterious fountain, and amongst them Tús and Fríburz, and Gíw, were while asleep overwhelmed in the drifts of snow. Not a man survived. Gúdarz had returned when about half-way on the road; and not hearing for a long time any tidings of his companions, sent a person to ascertain the cause of their delay. Upon proceeding to the fatal place, the messenger, to his amazement and horror, found them all stiff and lifeless under the snow!

Lohurásp

THE REPUTATION OF LOHURÁSP was of the highest order, and it is said that his administration of the affairs of his kingdom was more just and paternal than even that of Kai-khosráu. "The counsel which Khosráu gave me," said he, "was wise and admirable; but I find that I must go beyond him in moderation and clemency to the poor." Lohurásp had four sons, two by the daughter of Kai-káús, one named Ardshír, and the other Shydasp; and two by another woman, and they were named Gushtásp and Zarír. But Gushtásp was intrepid, acute, and apparently marked out for sovereignty, and on account of his independent conduct, no favorite with his father; in defiance of whom, with a rebellious spirit, he collected together a hundred thousand horsemen, and proceeded with them towards Hindústán of his own accord. Lohurásp sent after him his brother Zarír, with a thousand horsemen, in the hopes of influencing him to return; but when Zarír overtook him and endeavored to persuade him not to proceed any further, he said to him, with an animated look:

> *"Proceed no farther! – Well thou know'st*
> *We've no Kaiánian blood to boast,*
> *And, therefore, but a minor part*
> *In Lohurásp's paternal heart.*

Nor thou, nor I, can ever own
From him the diadem or throne.
The brothers of Káús's race
By birth command the brightest place,
Then what remains for us? We must
To other means our fortunes trust.
We cannot linger here, and bear
A life of discontent – despair."

Zarír, however, reasoned with him so winningly and effectually, that at last he consented to return; but only upon the condition that he should be nominated heir to the throne, and treated with becoming respect and ceremony. Zarír agreed to interpose his efforts to this end, and brought him back to his father; but it was soon apparent that Lohurásp had no inclination to promote the elevation of Gushtásp in preference to the claims of his other sons; and indeed shortly afterwards manifested to what quarter his determination on this subject was directed. It was indeed enough that his determination was unfavorable to the views of Gushtásp, who now, in disgust, fled from his father's house, but without any attendants, and shaped his course towards Rúm. Lohurásp again sent Zarír in quest of him; but the youth, after a tedious search, returned without success. Upon his arrival in Rúm, Gushtásp chose a solitary retirement, where he remained some time, and was at length compelled by poverty and want, to ask for employment in the establishment of the sovereign of that country, stating that he was an accomplished scribe, and wrote a beautiful hand. He was told to wait a few days, as at that time there was no vacancy. But hunger was pressing, and he could not suffer delay; he therefore went to the master of the camel-drivers and asked for service, but he too had no vacancy. However, commiserating the distressed condition of the applicant, he generously supplied him with a hearty meal. After that, Gushtásp went into a blacksmith's shop, and asked for work, and his services were accepted. The blacksmith put the hammer into his hands, and the first blow he struck was given with such force, that he broke the anvil to pieces. The blacksmith was amazed and angry, and indignantly turned him out of his shop, uttering upon him a thousand violent reproaches.

Disconsolate and wretched, he proceeded on his journey, and observing a husbandman standing in a field of corn, he approached the spot and sat down. The husbandman seeing a strong muscular youth, apparently a Túránian, sitting in sorrow and tears, went up to him and asked him the cause of his grief, and he soon became acquainted with all the circumstances of the stranger's life. Pitying his distress, he took him home and gave him some food.

After having partaken sufficiently of the refreshments placed before him, Gushtásp inquired of his host to what tribe he belonged, and from whom he was descended. "I am descended from Feridún," rejoined he, "and I belong to the Kaiánian tribe. My occupation in this retired spot is, as thou seest, the cultivation of the ground, and the customs and duties of husbandry." Gushtásp said, "I am myself descended from Húsheng, who was the ancestor of Feridún; we are, therefore, of the same origin." In consequence of this connection, Gushtásp and the husbandman lived together on the most friendly footing for a considerable time. At length the star of his fortune began to illumine his path, and the favor of Heaven became manifest.

It was the custom of the king of Rúm, when his daughters came of age, to give a splendid banquet, and to invite to it all the youths of illustrious birth in the kingdom, in order that each might select one of them most suited to her taste, for her future husband. His daughter Kitabún was now of age, and in conformity with the established practice, the feast was prepared, and the youths of royal descent invited; but it so happened that not one of them was sufficiently attractive for her choice, and the day passed over unprofitably. She had been told in a dream that a youth of a certain figure and aspect had arrived in the kingdom from Irán, and that to him she was destined to be married. But there was not one at her father's banquet who answered to the description of the man she had seen in her dream, and in consequence she was disappointed. On the following day the feast was resumed. She had again dreamt of the youth to whom she was to be united. She had presented to him a bunch of roses, and he had given her a rose-branch, and each regarded the other with smiles of mutual satisfaction. In the morning Kitabún issued a proclamation, inviting all the young men of royal extraction, whether natives of the kingdom or strangers, to her father's feast. On that day Gushtásp and the husbandman had come into the city from the country, and hearing the proclamation the latter said: "Let us go, for in this lottery the prize may be drawn in thy name." They accordingly went. Kitabún's handmaid was in waiting at the door, and kept every young man standing awhile, that her mistress might mark him well before she allowed him to pass into the banquet. The keen eyes of Kitabún soon saw Gushtásp, and her heart instantly acknowledged him as her promised lord, for he was the same person she had seen in her dream.

She presently descended from her balcony, and gave him a bunch of roses, the token by which her choice was made known, and then retired. The king, when he heard of what she had done, was exceedingly irritated, thinking that her affections were placed on a beggar, or some nameless stranger of no birth or fortune, and his first impulse was to have her put to death. But his people assembled around him, and said: – "What can be the use of killing her? – It is in vain to resist the flood of destiny, for what will be, will be.

> *"The world itself is governed still by Fate,*
> *Fate rules the warrior's and the monarch's state;*
> *And woman's heart, the passions of her soul,*
> *Own the same power, obey the same control;*
> *For what can love's impetuous force restrain?*
> *Blood may be shed, but what will be thy gain?"*

After this remonstrance he desired enquiries to be made into the character and parentage of his proposed son-in-law, and was told his name, the name of his father, and of his ancestors, and the causes which led to his present condition. But he would not believe a word of the narration. He was then informed of his daughter's dream, and other particulars: and he so far relented as to sanction the marriage; but indignantly drove her from his house, with her husband, without a dowry, or any money to supply themselves with food.

Gushtásp and his wife took refuge in a miserable cell, which they inhabited, and when necessity pressed, he used to cross the river, and bring in an elk or wild ass from the forest, give half of it to the ferryman for his trouble, and keep the remainder for his own board, so that he and the ferryman became great friends by these mutual obligations. It is related that a person of distinction, named Mabrín, solicited the king's second daughter in marriage; and Ahrun, another man of rank, was anxious to be espoused to the third, or youngest; but the king was unwilling to part with either of them, and openly declared his sentiments to that effect. Mabrín, however, was most assiduous and persevering in his attentions, and at last made some impression on the father, who consented to permit the marriage of the second daughter, but only on the following conditions: "There is," said he, "a monstrous wolf in the neighboring forest, extremely ferocious, and destructive to my property. I have frequently endeavored to hunt him down, but without success. If Mabrín can destroy the animal, I will give him my daughter." When these conditions were communicated to Mabrín, he considered it impossible that they could be fulfilled, and looked upon the proposal as an evasion of the question. One day, however, the ferryman having heard of Mabrín's disappointment, told him that there was no reason to despair, for he knew a young man, married to one of the king's daughters, who crossed the river every day, and though only a pedestrian, brought home regularly an elk-deer on his back. "He is truly," added he, "a wonderful youth, and if you can by any means secure his assistance, I have no doubt but that his activity and strength will soon put an end to the wolfs depredations, by depriving him of life."

This intelligence was received with great pleasure by Mabrín, who hastened to Gushtásp, and described to him his situation, and the conditions required. Gushtásp in reply said, that he would be glad to accomplish for him the object of his desires, and at an appointed time proceeded towards the forest, accompanied by Mabrín and the ferryman. When the party arrived at the borders of the wilderness which the wolf frequented, Gushtásp left his companions behind, and advanced alone into the interior, where he soon found the dreadful monster, in size larger than an elephant, and howling terribly, ready to spring upon him. But the hand and eye of Gushtásp were too active to allow of his being surprised, and in an instant he shot two arrows at once into the foaming beast, which, irritated by the deep wound, now rushed furiously upon him, without, however, doing him any serious injury; then with the rapidity of lightning, Gushtásp drew his sharp sword, and with one tremendous stroke cut the wolf in two, deluging the ground with bubbling blood. Having performed this prodigious exploit, he called Mabrín and the ferryman to see what he had done, and they were amazed at his extraordinary intrepidity and muscular power, but requested, in order that the special object of the lover might be obtained, that he would conceal his name, for a time at least. Mabrín, satisfied on this point, then repaired to the emperor, and claimed his promised bride, as the reward for his labor. The king of Rúm little expected this result, and to assure himself of the truth of what he had heard, bent his way to the forest, where he was convinced, seeing with astonishment and delight that the wolf was really killed. He had now no further pretext, and therefore fulfilled his engagement, by giving his daughter to Mabrín.

It was now Ahrun's turn to repeat his solicitations for the youngest daughter. The king of Rúm had another evil to root out, so that he was prepared to propose another condition. This was to destroy a hideous dragon that had taken possession of a neighboring mountain. Ahrun, on hearing the condition was in as deep distress as Mabrín had been, until he accidentally became acquainted with the ferryman, who described to him the generosity and fearless bravery of Gushtásp. He immediately applied to him, and the youth readily undertook the enterprise, saying: – "No doubt the monster's teeth are long and sharp, bring me therefore a dagger, and fasten round it a number of knives." Ahrun did so accordingly, and Gushtásp proceeded to the mountain. As soon as the dragon smelt the approach of a human being, flames issued from his nostrils, and he darted forward to devour the intruder, but was driven back by a number of arrows, rapidly discharged into his head and mouth. Again he advanced, but Gushtásp dodged round him, and continued driving arrows into him to the extent of forty, which subdued his strength, and made him writhe in agony. He then fixed the dagger, which was armed at right angles with knives, upon his spear, and going nearer, thrust it down his gasping throat.

> *Dreadful the weapon each two-edged blade*
> *Cut deep into the jaws on either side,*
> *And the fierce monster, thinking to dislodge it,*
> *Crushed it between his teeth with all his strength,*
> *Which pressed it deeper in the flesh, when blood*
> *And poison issued from the gaping wounds;*
> *Then, as he floundered on the earth exhausted,*
> *Seizing the fragment of a flinty rock,*
> *Gushtásp beat out the brains, and soon the beast*
> *In terrible struggles died. Two deadly fangs*
> *Then wrenched he from the jaws, to testify*
> *The wonderful exploit he had performed.*

When he descended from the mountain, these two teeth were delivered to Ahrun, and they were afterwards conveyed to the king, who could not believe his own eyes, but ascended the mountain himself to ascertain the fact, and there he beheld with amazement the dragon lifeless, and covered with blood. "And didst thou thyself kill this terrific dragon?" said he. "Yes," replied Ahrun. "And wilt thou swear to God that this is thy own achievement? It must be either the exploit of a demon, or of a certain Kaiánian, who resides in this neighborhood." But there was no one to disprove his assertion, and therefore the king could no longer refuse to surrender to him his youngest daughter.

And now between Gushtásp, and Mabrín, and Ahrun, the warmest friendship subsisted. Indeed they were seldom parted; and the three sisters remained together with equal affection. One day Kitabún, the wife of Gushtásp, in conversation with some of her female acquaintance, let out the secret that her husband was the person who killed the wolf and the dragon.

No sooner was this story told, than it spread, and in the end reached the ears of the queen, who immediately communicated it to the king, saying: – "This is the work of Gushtásp, thy son-in-law, of him thou hast banished from thy presence – of him who nobly would not disclose his name, before Mabrín and Ahrun had attained the object of their wishes." The king said in reply that it was just as he had suspected; and sending for Gushtásp, conferred upon him great honor, and appointed him to the chief command of his army.

Having thus possessed himself of a leader of such skill and intrepidity, he thought it necessary to turn his attention to external conquest, and accordingly addressed a letter to Alíás, the ruler of Khuz, in which he said: – "Thou hast hitherto enjoyed thy kingdom in peace and tranquillity; but thou must now resign it to me, or prepare for war." Alíás on receiving this imperious and haughty menace collected his forces together, and advanced to the contest, and the king of Rúm assembled his own troops with equal expedition, under the direction of Gushtásp. The battle was fought with great valor on both sides, and blood flowed in torrents. Gushtásp challenged Alíás to single combat, and the warriors met; but in a short time the enemy was thrown from his horse, and dragged by the young conqueror, in fetters, before the king. The troops witnessing the prowess of Gushtásp, quickly fled; and the king commencing a hot pursuit, soon entered their city victoriously, subdued the whole kingdom, and plundered it of all its property and wealth. He also gained over the army, and with this powerful addition to his own forces, and with the booty he had secured, returned triumphantly to Rúm.

In consequence of this brilliant success, the king conferred additional honors on Gushtásp, who now began to display the ambition which he had long cherished. Aspiring to the sovereignty of Irán, he spoke to the Rúmí warriors on the subject of an invasion of that country, but they refused to enter into his schemes, conceiving that there was no chance of success. At this Gushtásp took fire, and declared that he knew the power and resources of his father perfectly, and that the conquest would be attended with no difficulty. He then went to the king, and said: "Thy chiefs are afraid to fight against Lohurásp; I will myself undertake the task with even an inconsiderable army." The king was overjoyed, and kissed his head and face, and loaded him with presents, and ordered his secretary to write to Lohurásp in the following terms: "I am anxious to meet thee in battle, but if thou art not disposed to fight, I will permit thee to remain at peace, on condition of surrendering to me half thy kingdom. Should this be refused, I will myself deprive thee of thy whole sovereignty." When this letter was conveyed by the hands of Kabús to Irán, Lohurásp, upon reading it, was moved to laughter, and exclaimed, "What is all this? The king of Rúm has happened to obtain possession of the little kingdom of Khuz, and he has become insane with pride!" He then asked Kabús by what means he accomplished the capture of Khuz, and how he managed to kill Alíás. The messenger replied, that his success was owing to a youth of noble aspect and invincible courage, who had first destroyed a ferocious wolf, then a dragon, and had afterwards dragged Alíás from his horse, with as much ease as if he had been a chicken, and laid him prostrate at the feet of the king of Rúm. Lohurásp enquired his name, and he answered, Gushtásp. "Does he resemble in feature any person in this assembly?" Kabús looked round about him, and pointed to Zarír, from which Lohurásp concluded that it must be his own son, and sat silent. But he soon determined on what answer to send, and it was contained in the following words: "Do not take me for an Alíás, nor think that one hero of thine is competent to oppose me. I have a hundred equal to him. Continue, therefore, to pay me tribute, or I will lay waste thy whole country." With this letter he dismissed Kabús; and as soon as the messenger had departed, addressed himself to Zarír, saying: "Thou must go in the character of an ambassador from me to the king of Rúm, and represent to him the justice and propriety of preserving peace. After thy conference with him repair to the house of Gushtásp, and in my name ask his forgiveness for what I have done. I was not before aware of his merit, and day and night I think of him with repentance and sorrow. Tell him to pardon his old father's infirmities, and come back to Irán, to his own country and home, that I may resign to him my crown and throne, and like Kai-khosráu, take leave of the world. It is my desire to deliver myself up to prayer and devotion, and to appoint Gushtásp my successor, for he appears to be eminently worthy of that honor." Zarír acted scrupulously, in conformity with his instructions; and having first had an interview with the king, hastened to the house of his brother, by whom he was received with affection and gladness. After the usual interchange of congratulations and enquiry, he stated to him the views and the resolutions of his father, who on the faith of his royal word promised to appoint him his successor, and thought of him with the most cordial attachment. Gushtásp was as much astonished as delighted with this information, and his anxiety being great to return to his own country, he that very night, accompanied by his wife Kitabún, and Zarír, set out for Irán. Approaching the city, he was met by an istakbál, or honorary deputation of warriors, sent by the king; and when he arrived at court, Lohurásp descended from his throne and embraced him with paternal affection, shedding tears of contrition for having previously treated him not only with neglect but severity. However he now made him ample atonement, and ordering a golden chair of royalty to be constructed and placed close to his own, they both sat together, and the people by command tendered to him unanimously their respect and allegiance. Lohurásp repeatedly said to him:

> *"What has been done was Fate's decree,*
> *Man cannot strive with destiny.*
> *To be unfeeling once was mine,*
> *At length to be a sovereign thine."*
> *Thus spoke the king, and kissed the crown,*
> *And gave it to his valiant son.*

Soon afterwards he relinquished all authority in the empire, assumed the coarse habit of a recluse, retired to a celebrated place of pilgrimage, near Balkh. There, in a solitary cell, he devoted the remainder of his life to prayer and the worship of God. The period of Lohurásp's government lasted one hundred and twenty years.

Gushtásp, and the Faith of Zerdusht

GUSHTÁSP HAD BY his wife Kitabún, the daughter of the king of Rúm, two sons named Isfendiyár and Bashútan, who were remarkable for their piety and devotion to the Almighty. Being the great king, all the minor sovereigns paid him tribute, excepting Arjásp, the ruler of Chín and Má-chín, whose army consisted of Díws, and Peris, and men; for considering him of superior importance, he sent him yearly the usual tributary present.

In those days lived Zerdusht, the Guber, who was highly accomplished in the knowledge of divine things; and having waited upon Gushtásp, the king became greatly pleased with his learning and piety, and took him into his confidence. The philosopher explained to him the doctrines of the fire-worshippers, and by his art he reared a tree before the house of Gushtásp, beautiful in its foliage and branches, and whoever ate of the leaves of that tree became learned and accomplished in the mysteries of the future world, and those who ate of the fruit thereof became perfect in wisdom and holiness. In consequence of the illness of Lohurásp, who was nearly at the point of death, Zerdusht went to Balkh for the purpose of administering relief to him, and he happily succeeded in restoring him to health. On his return he was received with additional favor by Gushtásp, who immediately afterwards became his disciple. Zerdusht then told him that he was the prophet of God, and promised to show him miracles. He said he had been to heaven and to hell. He could send anyone, by prayer, to heaven; and whomsoever he was angry with he could send to hell. He had seen the seven mansions of the celestial regions, and the thrones of sapphires, and all the secrets of heaven were made known to him by his attendant angel. He said that the sacred book, called Zendavesta, descended from above expressly for him, and that if Gushtásp followed the precepts in that blessed volume, he would attain celestial felicity. Gushtásp readily became a convert to his principles, forsaking the pure adoration of God for the religion of the fire-worshippers.

The philosopher further said that he had prepared a ladder, by which he had ascended into heaven and had seen the Almighty. This made the disciple still more obedient to Zerdusht. One day he asked Gushtásp why he condescended to pay tribute to Arjásp; "God is on thy side," said he, "and if thou desirest an extension of territory, the whole country of Chin may be easily conquered." Gushtásp felt ashamed at this reproof, and to restore his character, sent a dispatch to Arjásp, in which he said, "Former kings who paid thee tribute did so from terror only, but now the empire is mine; and it is my will, and I have the power, to resist the payment of it in future." This letter gave great offence to Arjásp; who at once suspected that the fire-worshipper, Zerdusht, had poisoned his mind, and seduced him from his pure and ancient religion, and was attempting to circumvent and lead him to his ruin. He answered him thus: "It is well known that thou hast now forsaken the right path, and involved thyself in darkness. Thou hast chosen a guide possessed of the attributes of Iblís, who with the art of a magician has seduced thee from the worship of the true God, from that God who gave thee thy kingdom and thy grandeur. Thy father feared God, and became a holy Dírvesh, whilst thou hast lost thy way in wickedness and impiety. It will therefore be a meritorious action in me to vindicate the true worship and oppose thy blasphemous career with al my demons. In a month or two I will enter thy kingdom with fire and sword, and destroy thy authority and thee. I would give thee good advice; do not be influenced by a wicked counsellor, but return to thy former religious practices. Weigh well, therefore, what I say." Arjásp sent this letter by two of his demons, familiar with sorcery; and when it was delivered into the hands of Gushtásp, a council was held to consider its contents, to which Zerdusht was immediately summoned. Jamásp, the minister, said that the subject required deep thought, and great prudence was necessary in framing a reply; but Zerdusht observed, that the only reply was obvious – nothing but war could be thought of. At this moment Isfendiyár gallantly offered to lead the army, but Zarír, his uncle, objected to him on account of his extreme youth, and proposed to take the command himself, which Gushtásp agreed to, and the two demon-envoys were dismissed. The answer was briefly as follows:

> *"Thy boast is that thou wilt in two short months*
> *Ravage my country, scathe with fire and sword*
> *The empire of Irán; but on thyself*
> *Heap not destruction; pause before thy pride*
> *Hurries thee to thy ruin. I will open*
> *The countless treasures of the realm; my warriors,*
> *A thousand thousand, armed with shining steel,*
> *Shall overrun thy kingdom; I myself*
> *Will crush that head of thine beneath my feet."*

The result of these menaces was the immediate prosecution of the war, and no time was lost by Arjásp in hastening into Irán.

> *Plunder and devastation marked his course,*
> *The villages were all involved in flames,*
> *Palace of pride, low cot, and lofty tower;*
> *The trees dug up, and root and branch destroyed.*
> *Gushtásp then hastened to repel his foes;*
> *But to his legions they seemed wild and strange,*
> *And terrible in aspect, and no light*
> *Could struggle through the gloom they had diffused,*
> *To hide their progress.*

Zerdusht said to Gushtásp, "Ask thy vizir, Jamásp, what is written in thy horoscope, that he may relate to thee the dispensations of heaven." Jamásp, in reply to the inquiry, took the king aside and whispered softly to him: "A great number of thy brethren, thy relations, and warriors will be slain in the conflict, but in the end thou wilt be victorious." Gushtásp deeply lamented the coming event, which involved the destruction of his kinsmen, but did not shrink from the battle, for he exulted in the anticipation of obtaining the victory. The contest was begun with indescribable eagerness and impetuosity.

Ardshír, the son of Lohurásp, and descended from Kai-káús, was one of the first to engage; he killed many, and was at last killed himself. After him, his brother Shydasp was killed. Then Bishú, the son of Jamásp, urged on his steed, and with consummate bravery destroyed a great number of warriors. Zarír, equally bold and intrepid, also rushed amidst the host, and whether demons or men opposed him, they were all laid lifeless on the field. He then rode up towards Arjásp, scattered the ranks, and penetrated the headquarters, which put the king into great alarm: for he exclaimed: – "What, have ye no courage, no shame! whoever kills Zarír shall have a magnificent reward." Bai-derafsh, one of the demons, animated by this offer, came forward, and with remorseless fury attacked Zarír. The onset was irresistible, and the young prince was soon overthrown and bathed in his own blood. The news of the unfortunate catastrophe deeply affected Gushtásp, who cried, in great grief: "Is there no one to take vengeance for this?" when Isfendiyár presented himself, kissed the ground before his father, and anxiously asked permission to engage the demon. Gushtásp assented, and told him that if he killed the demon and defeated the enemy, he would surrender to him his crown and throne.

> "When we from this destructive field return,
> Isfendiyár, my son, shall wear the crown,
> And be the glorious leader of my armies."

Saying this, he dismounted from his famous black horse, called Behzád, the gift of Kai-khosráu, and presented it to Isfendiyár. The greatest clamor and lamentation had arisen among the Persian army, for they thought that Bai-derafsh had committed such dreadful slaughter, the moment of utter defeat was at hand, when Isfendiyár galloped forward, mounted on Behzád, and turned the fortunes of the day. He saw the demon with the mail of Zarír on his breast, foaming at the mouth with rage, and called aloud to him, "Stand, thou murderer!" The stern voice, the valor, and majesty of Isfendiyár made the demon tremble, but he immediately discharged a blow with his dagger at his new opponent, who however seized the weapon with his left hand, and with his right plunged a spear into the monster's breast, and drove it through his body. Isfendiyár then cut off his head, remounted his horse, and that instant was by the side of Bishú, the son of the vizir, into whose charge he gave the severed head of Bai-derafsh, and the armor of Zarír. Bishú now attired himself in his father's mail, and fastening the head on his horse, declared that he would take his post close by Isfendiyár, whatever might betide. Firshaid, another Iránian warrior, came to the spot at the same moment, and expressed the same resolution, so that all three, thus accidentally met, determined to encounter Arjásp and capture him. Isfendiyár led the way, and the other two followed. Arjásp, seeing that he was singled out by three warriors, and that the enemy's force was also advancing to the attack in great numbers, gave up the struggle, and was the first to retreat. His troops soon threw away their arms and begged for quarter, and many of them were taken prisoners by the Iránians. Gushtásp now approached the dead body of Zarír, and lamenting deeply over his unhappy fate, placed him in a coffin, and built over him a lofty monument, around which lights were ever afterwards kept burning, night and day; and he also taught the people the worship of fire, and was anxious to establish everywhere the religion of Zerdusht.

Jamásp appointed officers to ascertain the number of killed in the battle. Of Iránians there were thirty thousand, among whom were eight hundred chiefs; and the enemy's loss amounted to nine hundred thousand, and also eleven hundred and sixty-three chiefs. Gushtásp rejoiced at the glorious result, and ordered the drums to be sounded to celebrate the victory, and he increased his favor upon Zerdusht, who originated the war, and told him to call his triumphant son, Isfendiyár, near him.

> *The gallant youth the summons hears,*
> *And midst the royal court appears,*
> *Close by his father's side,*
> *The mace, cow-headed, in his hand;*
> *His air and glance express command,*
> *And military pride.*
> *Gushtásp beholds with heart elate.*
> *The conqueror so young, so great,*
> *And places round his brows the crown,*
> *The promised crown, the high reward,*

Proud token of a mighty king's regard,
Conferred upon his own.

After Gushtásp had crowned his son as his successor, he told him that he must not now waste his time in peace and private gratification, but proceed to the conquest of other countries. Zerdusht was also deeply interested in his further operations, and recommended him to subdue kingdoms for the purpose of diffusing everywhere the new religion, that the whole world might be enlightened and edified. Isfendiyár instantly complied, and the first kingdom he invaded was Rúm. The sovereign of that country having no power nor means to resist the incursions of the enemy, readily adopted the faith of Zerdusht, and accepted the sacred book named Zendavesta, as his spiritual instructor. Isfendiyár afterwards invaded Hindústán and Arabia, and several other countries, and successfully established the religion of the fire-worshippers in them all.

Where'er he went he was received
With welcome, all the world believed,
And all with grateful feelings took
The Holy Zendavesta-book,
Proud their new worship to declare,
The worship of Isfendiyár.

The young conqueror communicated by letters to his father the success with which he had disseminated the religion of Zerdusht, and requested to know what other enterprises required his aid. Gushtásp rejoiced exceedingly, and commanded a grand banquet to be prepared. It happened that Gurzam a warrior, was particularly befriended by the king, but retaining secretly in his heart a bitter enmity to Isfendiyár, now took an opportunity to gratify his malice, and privately told Gushtásp that he had heard something highly atrocious in the disposition of the prince. Gushtásp was anxious to know what it was; and he said, "Isfendiyár has subdued almost every country in the world: he is a dangerous person at the head of an immense army, and at this very moment meditates taking Balkh, and making even thee his prisoner!

"Thou know'st not that thy son Isfendiyár
Is hated by the army. It is said
Ambition fires his brain, and to secure

The empire to himself, his wicked aim
Is to rebel against his generous father.
This is the sum of my intelligence;
But thou'rt the king, I speak but what I hear."

These malicious accusations by Gurzam insidiously made, produced great vexation in the mind of Gushtásp. The banquet went on, and for three days he drank wine incessantly, without sleep or rest because his sorrow was extreme. On the fourth day he said to his minister: "Go with this letter to Isfendiyár, and accompany him hither to me." Jamásp, the minister, went accordingly on the mission, and when he arrived, the prince said to him, "I have dreamt that my father is angry with me." – "Then thy dream is true," replied Jamásp, "thy father is indeed angry with thee." – "What crime, what fault have I committed?

"Is it because I have with ceaseless toil
Spread wide the Zendavesta, and converted
Whole kingdoms to that faith? Is it because
For him I conquered those far-distant kingdoms,
With this good sword of mine? Why clouds his brow
Upon his son – some demon must have changed
His temper, once affectionate and kind,
Calling me to him thus in anger! Thou
Hast ever been my friend, my valued friend
Say, must I go? Thy counsel I require."

"The son does wrong who disobeys his father,
Despising his command," Jamásp replied.

"Yet," said Isfendiyár, "why should I go?
He is in wrath, it cannot be for good."

"Know'st thou not that a father's wrath is kindness?
The anger of a father to his child
Is far more precious than the love and fondness
Felt by that child for him. 'Tis good to go,

> *Whatever the result, he is the king,*
> *And more – he is thy father!"*

Isfendiyár immediately consented, and appointed Bahman, his eldest son, to fill his place in the army during his absence. He had four sons: the name of the second was Mihrbús; of the third, Avir; and of the fourth, Núsháhder; and these three he took along with him on his journey.

Before he had arrived at Balkh, Gushtásp had concerted measures to secure him as a prisoner, with an appearance of justice and impartiality. On his arrival, he waited on the king respectfully, and was thus received: "Thou hast become the great king! Thou hast conquered many countries, but why am I unworthy in thy sight? Thy ambition is indeed excessive." Isfendiyár replied: "However great I may be, I am still thy servant, and wholly at thy command." Upon hearing this, Gushtásp turned towards his courtiers, and said, "What ought to be done with that son, who in the lifetime of his father usurps his authority, and even attempts to eclipse him in grandeur? What! I ask, should be done with such a son!"

> *"Such a son should either be*
> *Broken on the felon tree,*
> *Or in prison bound with chains,*
> *Whilst his wicked life remains,*
> *Else thyself, this kingdom, all*
> *Will be ruined by his thrall!"*

To this heavy denunciation Isfendiyár replied: "I have received all my honors from the king, by whom I am appointed to succeed to the throne; but at his pleasure I willingly resign them." However, concession and remonstrance were equally fruitless and he was straightway ordered to be confined in the tower-prison of the fort situated on the adjacent mountain, and secured with chains.

Having thus made Isfendiyár secure in the mountain-prison, and being entirely at ease about the internal safety of the empire, Gushtásp was anxious to pay a visit to Zál and Rustem at Sístán, and to convert them to the religion of Zerdusht. On his approach to Sístán he was met and respectfully welcomed by Rustem. who afterwards in open assembly received the Zendavesta and adopted the new faith, which he propagated throughout his own territory; but, according to common report it was fear of Gushtásp alone which induced him to pursue this course. Gushtásp remained two years his guest, enjoying all kinds of recreation, and particularly the sports of the field and the forests.

When Bahman, the son of Isfendiyár, heard of the imprisonment of his father, he, in grief and alarm, abandoned his trust, dismissed the army, and proceeded to Balkh, where he joined his two brothers, and wept over the fate of their unhappy father.

In the meantime the news of the confinement of Isfendiyár, and the absence of Gushtásp at Sístán, and the unprotected state of Balkh, stimulated Arjásp to a further effort, and he despatched his son Kahram with a large army towards the capital of the enemy, to carry into effect his purpose of revenge. Lohurásp was still in religious retirement at Balkh. The people were under great apprehension, and being without a leader, anxiously solicited the old king to command them, but he said that he had abandoned all earthly concerns, and had devoted himself to God, and therefore could not comply with their entreaties. But they would hear no denial, and, as it were, tore him from his place of refuge and prayer. There were assembled only about one thousand horsemen, and with these he advanced to battle; but what were they compared to the hundred thousand whom they met, and by whom they were soon surrounded. Their bravery was useless. They were at once overpowered and defeated, and Lohurásp himself was unfortunately among the slain.

Upon the achievement of his victory, Kahram entered Balkh in triumph, made the people prisoners, and destroyed all the places of worship belonging to the Gubers. He also killed the keeper of the altar, and burnt the Zendavesta, which contained the formulary of their doctrines and belief.

One of the women of Gushtásp's household happened to elude the grasp of the invader, and hastened to Sístán to inform the king of the disaster that had occurred. 'Thy father is killed, the city is taken, and thy women and daughters in the power of the conqueror." Gushtásp received the news with consternation, and prepared with the utmost expedition for his departure. He invited Rustem to accompany him, but the champion excused himself at the time, and afterwards declined altogether on the plea of sickness. Before he had yet arrived at Balkh, Kahram hearing of his approach, went out to meet him with his whole army, and was joined on the same day by Arjásp and his demon-legions.

> *Great was the uproar, loud the brazen drums*
> *And trumpets rung, the earth shook, and seemed rent*

> *By that tremendous conflict, javelins flew*
> *Like hail on every side, and the warm blood*
> *Streamed from the wounded and the dying men.*
> *The claim of kindred did not check the arm*
> *Lifted in battle – mercy there was none,*
> *For all resigned themselves to chance or fate,*
> *Or what the ruling Heavens might decree.*

At last the battle terminated in the defeat of Gushtásp, who was pursued till he was obliged to take refuge in a mountain-fort. He again consulted Jamásp to know what the stars foretold, and Jamásp replied that he would recover from the defeat through the exertions of Isfendiyár alone. Pleased with this interpretation, he on that very day sent Jamásp to the prison with a letter to Isfendiyár, in which he hoped to be pardoned for the cruelty he had been guilty of towards him, in consequence, he said, of being deceived by the arts and treachery of those who were only anxious to effect his ruin. He declared too that he would put those enemies to death in his presence, and replace the royal crown upon his head. At the same time he confined in chains Gurzam, the wretch who first practised upon his feelings. Jamásp rode immediately to the prison, and delivering the letter, urged the prince to comply with his father's entreaties, but Isfendiyár was incredulous and not so easily to be moved.

> *"Has he not at heart disdained me?*
> *Has he not in prison chained me?*
> *Am I not his son, that he*
> *Treats me ignominiously?*
> *Why should Gurzam's scorn and hate*
> *Rouse a loving father's wrath?*
> *Why should he, the foul ingrate,*
> *Cast destruction in my path?"*

Jamásp, however, persevered in his anxious solicitations, describing to him how many of his brethren and kindred had fallen, and also the perilous situation of his own father if he refused his assistance. By a thousand various efforts he at length effected his purpose, and the blacksmith was called to take off his chains; but in removing them the anguish of the wounds they had inflicted was so great that Isfendiyár fainted away

Upon his recovery he was escorted to the presence of his father, who received him with open arms, and the strongest expressions of delight. He begged to be forgiven for his unnatural conduct to him, again resigned to him the throne of the empire, and appointed him to the command of the imperial armies. He then directed Gurzam, upon whose malicious counsel he had acted, to be brought before him, and the wicked minister was punished with death on the spot, and in the presence of the injured prince.

> *Wretch! more relentless even than wolf or pard,*
> *Thou hast at length received thy just reward!*

When Arjásp heard that Isfendiyár had been reconciled to his father, and was approaching at the head of an immense army, he was affected with the deepest concern, and forthwith sent his son Kahram to endeavor to resist the progress of the enemy. At the same time Kurugsar, a gladiator of the demon race, requested that he might be allowed to oppose Isfendiyár; and permission being granted, he was the very first on the field, where instantly wielding his bow, he shot an arrow at Isfendiyár, which pierced through the mail, but fortunately for him did no serious harm. The prince drew his sword with the intention of attacking him, but seeing him furious with rage, and being doubtful of the issue, thought it more prudent and safe to try his success with the noose. Accordingly he took the kamund from his saddle-strap, and dexterously flung it round the neck of his arrogant foe, who was pulled headlong from his horse: and, as soon as his arms were bound behind his back, dragged a prisoner in front of the Persian ranks. Isfendiyár then returned to the battle, attacked a body of the enemy's auxiliaries, killed a hundred and sixty of their warriors, and made the division of which Kahram was the leader fly in all directions. His next feat was to attack another force, which had confederated against him.

> *With slackened rein he galloped o'er the field;*
> *Blood gushed from every stroke of his sharp sword,*
> *And reddened all the plain; a hundred warriors*
> *Eighty and five, in treasure rich and mail,*
> *Sunk underneath him, such his mighty power.*

His remaining object was to assail the centre, where Arjásp himself was stationed; and thither he rapidly hastened. Arjásp, angry and alarmed at this success, cried out,

"What! is one man allowed to scathe all my ranks, cannot my whole army put an end to his dreadful career?" The soldiers replied, "No! he has a body of brass, and the vigor of an elephant: our swords make no impression upon him, whilst with his sword he can cut the body of a warrior, cased in mail, in two, with the greatest ease. Against such a foe, what can we do?" Isfendiyár rushed on; and after an overwhelming attack, Arjásp was compelled to quit his ground and effect his escape. The Iránian troops were then ordered to pursue the fugitives, and in revenge for the death of Lohurásp, not to leave a man alive. The carnage was in consequence terrible, and the remaining Túránians were in such despair that they flung themselves from their exhausted horses, and placing straw in their mouths to show the extremity of their misfortune, called aloud for quarter. Isfendiyár was moved at last to compassion, and put an end to the fight; and when he came before Gushtásp, the mail on his body, from the number of arrows sticking in it, looked like a field of reeds; about a thousand arrows were taken out of its folds. Gushtásp kissed his head and face, and blessed him, and prepared a grand banquet, and the city of Balkh resounded with rejoicings on account of the great victory

Many days had not elapsed before a further enterprise was to be undertaken. The sisters of Isfendiyár were still in confinement, and required to be released. The prince readily complied with the wishes of Gushtásp, who now repeated to him his desire to relinquish the cares of sovereignty, and place the reins of government in his hands that he might devote himself entirely to the service of God.

> *"To thee I yield the crown and throne,*
> *Fit to be held by thee alone;*
> *From worldly care and trouble free,*
> *A hermit's cell is enough for me,"*

But Isfendiyár replied, that he had no desire to be possessed of the power; he rather wished for the prosperity of the king, and no change.

> *"O, may thy life be long and blessed,*
> *And ever by the good caressed;*
> *For 'tis my duty still to be*
> *Devoted faithfully to thee!*
> *I want no throne, nor diadem;*
> *My soul has no delight in them.*

I only seek to give thee joy,
And gloriously my sword employ.
I thirst for vengeance on Arjásp:
To crush him in my iron grasp,
That from his thrall I may restore
My sisters to their home again,
Who now their heavy fate deplore,
And toiling drag a slavish chain."
"Then go!" the smiling monarch said,
Invoking blessings on his head,
"And may kind Heaven thy refuge be,
And lead thee on to victory."

Isfendiyár now told his father that his prisoner Kurugsar was continually requesting him to represent his condition in the royal ear, saying, "Of what use will it be to put me to death? No benefit can arise from such a punishment. Spare my life, and you will see how largely I am able to contribute to your assistance." Gushtásp expressed his willingness to be merciful, but demanded a guarantee on oath from the petitioner that he would heart and soul be true and faithful to his benefactor. The oath was sworn, after which his bonds were taken from his hands and feet, and he was set at liberty. The king then called him, and pressed him with goblets of wine, which made him merry. "I have pardoned thee," said Gushtásp, "at the special entreaty of Isfendiyár – be grateful to him, and be attentive to his commands." After that, Isfendiyár took and conveyed him to his own house, that he might have an opportunity of experiencing and proving the promised fidelity of his new ally.

The Heft-khan of Isfendiyár

THE PRINCE, who had determined to undertake the new expedition, and appeared confident of success, now addressed himself to Kurugsar, and said, "If I conquer the kingdom of Arjásp, and restore my sisters to liberty, thou shalt have for thyself any principality

thou may'st choose within the boundaries of Irán and Túrán, and thy name shall be exalted; but beware of treachery or fraud, for falsehood shall certainly be punished with death." To this Kurugsar replied, "I have already sworn a solemn oath to the king, and at thy intercession he has spared my life – why then should I depart from the truth, and betray my benefactor?"

"Then tell me the road to the brazen fortress, and how far it is distant from this place?" said Isfendiyár.

"There are three different routes," replied Kurugsar. "One will occupy three months; it leads through a beautiful country, adorned with cities, and gardens, and pastures, and is pleasant to the traveller. The second is less attractive, the prospects less agreeable, and will only employ two months; the third, however, may be accomplished in seven days, and is thence called the Heft-khan, or seven stages; but at every stage some monster, or terrible difficulty, must be overcome. No monarch, even supported by a large army, has ever yet ventured to proceed by this route; and if it is ever attempted, the whole party will be assuredly lost.

> *"Nor strength, nor juggling, nor the sorcerer's art*
> *Can help him safely through that awful path,*
> *Beset with wolves and dragons, wild and fierce,*
> *From whom the fleetest have no power to fly.*
> *There an enchantress, doubly armed with spells,*
> *The most accomplished of that magic brood,*
> *Spreads wide her snares to charm and to destroy,*
> *And ills of every shape, and horrid aspect,*
> *Cross the tired traveller at every step."*

At this description of the terrors of the Heft-khan, Isfendiyár became thoughtful for awhile, and then, resigning himself to the providence of God, resolved to take the shortest route. "No man can die before his time," said he; "heaven is my protector, and I will fearlessly encounter every difficulty on the road." "It is full of perils," replied Kurugsar, and endeavored to dissuade him from the enterprise. "But with the blessing of God," rejoined Isfendiyár, "it will be easy." The prince then ordered a sumptuous banquet to be served, at which he gave Kurugsar abundant draughts of wine, and even in a state of intoxication the demon-guide still warned him against his proposed journey. "Go by the route which takes two months," said he, "for that will be convenient and safe;" but Isfendiyár replied: "I neither fear the difficulties of the route, nor the perils thou hast described."

> And though destruction spoke in every word,
> Enough to terrify the stoutest heart,
> Still he adhered to what he first resolved.
> "Thou wilt attend me," said the dauntless prince;
> And thus Kurugsar, without a pause, replied:
> "Undoubtedly, if by the two months' way,
> And do thee ample service; but if this
> Heft-khan be thy election; if thy choice
> Be fixed on that which leads to certain death,
> My presence must be useless. Can I go
> Where bird has never dared to wing its flight?"

Isfendiyár, upon hearing these words, began to suspect the fidelity of Kurugsar, and thought it safe to bind him in chains. The next day as he was going to take leave of his father, Kurugsar called out to him, and said: "After my promises of allegiance, and my solemn oath, why am I thus kept in chains?" "Not out of anger assuredly; but out of compassion and kindness, in order that I may take thee along with me on the enterprise of the Heft-khan; for wert thou not bound, thy faint heart might induce thee to run away.

> "Safe thou art when bound in chains,
> Fettered foot can never fly.
> Whilst thy body here remains,
> We may on thy faith rely.
> Terror will in vain assail thee;
> For these bonds shall never fail thee.
> Guarded by a potent charm,
> They will keep thee free from harm."

Isfendiyár having received the parting benediction of Gushtásp, was supplied with a force consisting of twelve thousand chosen horsemen, and abundance of treasure, to enable him to proceed on his enterprise, and conquer the kingdom of Arjásp.

First Stage. – Isfendiyár placed Kurugsar in bonds among his retinue, and took with him his brother Bashútan. But the demon-guide complained that he was unable to walk, and in consequence he was mounted on a horse, still bound, and the bridle given into the hands of one of the warriors. In this manner they proceeded, directed from time to time by Kurugsar, till they arrived at the uttermost limits of the kingdom, and entered a desert wilderness. Isfendiyár now asked what they would meet with, and the guide answered, "Two monstrous wolves are in this quarter, as large as elephants, and whose teeth are of immense length." The prince told his people, that as soon as they saw the wolves, they must at once attack them with arrows. The day passed away, and in the evening they came to a forest and a murmuring stream, when suddenly the two enormous wolves appeared, and rushed towards the legions of Isfendiyár. The people seeing them advance, poured upon them a shower of arrows. Several, however, were wounded, but the wolves were much exhausted by the arrows which had penetrated their bodies. At this moment Bashútan attacked one of them, and Isfendiyár the other; and so vigorous was their charge, that both the monsters were soon laid lifeless in the dust. After this signal overthrow, Isfendiyár turned to Kurugsar, and exclaimed: "Thus, through the favor of Heaven, the first obstacle has been easily extinguished!" The guide regarded him with amazement, and said: – "I am indeed astonished at the intrepidity and valor that has been displayed."

The warriors and the party now dismounted, and regaled themselves with feasting and wine. They then reposed till the following morning.

Second Stage. – Proceeding on the second journey, Isfendiyár inquired what might now be expected to oppose their progress, and Kurugsar replied: "This stage is infested by lions." "Then," rejoined Isfendiyár, "thou shalt see with what facility I can destroy them." At about the close of the day they met with a lion and a lioness. Bashútan said: "Take one and I will engage the other." But Isfendiyár observed, that the animals seemed very wild and ferocious, and he preferred attacking them both himself, that his brother might not be exposed to any harm. He first sallied forth against the lion, and with one mighty stroke put an end to his life. He then approached the lioness, which pounced upon him with great fury, but was soon compelled to desist, and the prince, rapidly wielding his sword, in a moment cut off her head. Having thus successfully accomplished the second day's task, he alighted from his horse, and refreshments being spread out, the warriors and the troops enjoyed themselves with great satisfaction, exhilarated by plenteous draughts of ruby wine. Again Isfendiyár addressed Kurugsar, and said: "Thou seest with what facility all opposition is removed, when I am assisted by the favor of Heaven!" "But there are other and more terrible difficulties to surmount, and amazing as thy achievements certainly have been, thou wilt have still greater exertions to make before thy enterprise is complete." "What is the next evil I have to subdue?" "An enormous dragon,

> *"With power to fascinate, and from the deep*
> *To lure the finny tribe, his daily food.*
> *Fire sparkles round him; his stupendous bulk*
> *Looks like a mountain. When incensed, his roar*
> *Makes the surrounding country shake with fear.*
> *White poison-foam drops from his hideous jaws,*
> *Which yawning wide, display a dismal gulf,*
> *The grave of many a hapless being, lost*
> *Wandering amidst that trackless wilderness."*

Kurugsar described or magnified the ferocity of the animal in such a way, that Isfendiyár thought it necessary to be cautious, and with that view he ordered a curious apparatus to be constructed on wheels, something like a carriage, to which he fastened a large quantity of pointed instruments, and harnessed horses to it to drag it on the road. He then tried its motion, and found it admirably calculated for his purpose. The people were astonished at the ingenuity of the invention, and lauded him to the skies.

Third Stage – Away went the prince, and having travelled a considerable distance, Kurugsar suddenly exclaimed: "I now begin to smell the stench of the dragon." Hearing this, Isfendiyár dismounted, ascended the machine, and shutting the door fast, took his seat and drove off. Bashútan and all the warriors upon witnessing this extraordinary act, began to weep and lament, thinking that he was hurrying himself to certain destruction, and begged that for his own sake, as well as theirs, he would come out of the machine. But he replied: "Peace, peace! what know ye of the matter;" and as the warlike apparatus was so excellently contrived, that he could direct the movements of the horses himself, he drove on with increased velocity, till he arrived in the vicinity of the monster.

> *The dragon from a distance heard*
> *The rumbling of the wain,*
> *And snuffing every breeze that stirred*
> *Across the neighbouring plain,*

Smelt something human in his power,
A welcome scent to him;
For he was eager to devour
Hot reeking blood, or limb.

And darkness now is spread around,
No pathway can be traced;
The fiery horses plunge and bound
Amid the dismal waste.

And now the dragon stretches far
His cavern throat, and soon
Licks in the horses and the car,
And tries to gulp them down.

But sword and javelin, sharp and keen,
Wound deep each sinewy jaw;
Midway, remains the huge machine,
And chokes the monster's maw.
In agony he breathes, a dire
Convulsion fires his blood,
And struggling, ready to expire,
Ejects a poison-flood!

And then disgorges wain and steeds,
And swords and javelins bright;
Then, as the dreadful dragon bleeds,
Up starts the warrior-knight,
And from his place of ambush leaps,
And, brandishing his blade,
The weapon in the brain he steeps,
And splits the monster's head.

But the foul venom issuing thence,
Is so o'erpowering found,

Isfendiyár, deprived of sense,
Falls staggering to the ground!

Upon seeing this result, and his brother in so deplorable a situation, Bashútan and the troops also were in great alarm, apprehending the most fatal consequences. They sprinkled rose-water over his face, and administered other remedies, so that after some time he recovered; then he bathed, purifying himself from the filth of the monster, and poured out prayers of thankfulness to the merciful Creator for the protection and victory he had given him. But it was matter of great grief to Kurugsar that Isfendiyár had succeeded in his exploit, because under present circumstances, he would have to follow him in the remaining arduous enterprises; whereas, if the prince had been slain, his obligations would have ceased forever.

"What may be expected to-morrow?" inquired Isfendiyár. "To-morrow," replied the demon-guide, "thou wilt meet with an enchantress, who can convert the stormy sea into dry land, and the dry land again into the ocean. She is attended by a gigantic ghoul, or apparition." "Then thou shalt see how easily this enchantress and her mysterious attendant can be vanquished."

Fourth Stage. – On the fourth day Isfendiyár and his companions proceeded on the destined journey, and coming to a pleasant meadow, watered by a transparent rivulet, the party alighted, and they all refreshed themselves heartily with various kinds of food and wine. In a short space of time the enchantress appeared, most beautiful in feature and elegant in attire, and approaching our hero with a sad but fascinating expression of countenance, said to him (the ghoul, her pretended paramour, being at a little distance):

"I am a poor unhappy thing,
The daughter of a distant king.
This monster with deceit and fraud,
By a fond parent's power unawed,
Seduced me from my royal home,
Through wood and desert wild to roam;
And surely Heaven has brought thee now
To cheer my heart, and smooth my brow,
And free me from his loathed embrace,
And bear me to a fitter place,

Where, in thy circling arms more softly prest,
I may at last be truly loved, and blest."

Isfendiyár immediately called her to him, and requested her to sit down. The enchantress readily complied, anticipating a successful issue to her artful stratagems; but the intended victim of her sorcery was too cunning to be imposed upon. He soon perceived what she was, and forthwith cast his kamund over her, and in spite of all her entreaties, bound her too fast to escape. In this extremity, she successively assumed the shape of a cat, a wolf, and a decrepit old man: and so perfect were her transformations, that any other person would have been deceived, but Isfendiyár detected her in every variety of appearance; and, vexed by her continual attempts to cheat him, at last took out his sword and cut her in pieces. As soon as this was done, a thick dark cloud of dust and vapor arose, and when it subsided, a black apparition of a demon burst upon his sight, with flames issuing from its mouth. Determined to destroy this fresh antagonist, he rushed forward, sword in hand, and though the flames, in the attack, burnt his cloth-armor and dress, he succeeded in cutting off the threatening monster's head. "Now," said he to Kurugsar, "thou hast seen that with the favor of Heaven, both enchantress and ghoul are exterminated, as well as the wolves, the lions, and the dragon." "Very well," replied Kurugsar, "thou hast achieved this prodigious labor, but to-morrow will be a heavy day, and thou canst hardly escape with life. To-morrow thou wilt be opposed by the Símúrgh, whose nest is situated upon a lofty mountain. She has two young ones, each the size of an elephant, which she conveys in her beak and claws from place to place." "Be under no alarm," said Isfendiyár, "God will make the labor easy."

Fifth Stage. – On the fifth day, Isfendiyár resumed his journey, travelling with his little army over desert, plain, mountain, and wilderness, until he reached the neighborhood of the Símúrgh. He then adopted the same stratagem which he had employed before, and the machine supplied with swords and spears, and drawn by horses, was soon in readiness for the new adventure. The Símúrgh, seeing with surprise an immense vehicle, drawn by two horses, approach at a furious rate, and followed by a large company of horsemen, descended from the mountain, and endeavored to take up the whole apparatus in her claws to carry it away to her own nest; but her claws were lacerated by the sharp weapons, and she was then obliged to try her beak. Both beak and claws were injured in the effort, and the animal became extremely weakened by the loss of blood. Isfendiyár seizing the happy moment, sprang out of the carriage, and with his trenchant sword divided the Símúrgh in two parts; and the young ones, after witnessing the death of their parent, precipitately fled from the fatal scene. When Bashútan, with the army, came to the spot, they were amazed at the prodigious size of the Símúrgh, and the valor by which it had been subdued. Kurugsar turned pale with astonishment and sorrow. "What will be our next adventure?" said Isfendiyár to him. "To-morrow more pressing ills will surround thee. Heavy snow will fall, and there will be a violent tempest of wind, and it will be wonderful if even one man of thy legions remains alive. That will not be like fighting against lions, a dragon, or the Símúrgh, but against the elements, against the Almighty, which never can be successful. Thou hadst better therefore, return unhurt." The people on hearing this warning were alarmed, and proposed to go back; "for if the advice of Kurugsar is not taken, we shall all perish like the companions of Kai-khosráu, and lie buried under drifts of snow.

> *"Let us return then, whilst we may;*
> *Why should we throw our lives away?"*

But Isfendiyár replied that he had already overcome five of the perils of the road, and had no fear about the remaining two. The people, however, were still discontented, and still murmured aloud; upon which the prince said, "Return then, and I will go alone.

> *"I never can require the aid*
> *Of men so easily dismayed."*

Finding their leader immovable, the people now changed their tone, and expressed their devotion to his cause; declaring that whilst life remained, they would never forsake him, no never.

Sixth Stage. – On the following morning, the sixth, Isfendiyár continued his labors, and hurried on with great speed. Towards evening he arrived on the skirts of a mountain, where there was a running stream, and upon that spot, he pitched his tents.

Presently from the mountain there rushed down
A furious storm of wind, then heavy showers
Of snow fell, covering all the earth with whiteness,
And making desolate the prospect round.
Keen blew the blast, and pinching was the cold;
And to escape the elemental wrath,
Leader and soldier, in the caverned rock
Scooped out by mouldering time, took shelter, there
Continuing three long days. Three lingering days
Still fell the snow, and still the tempest raged,
And man and beast grew faint for want of food.

Isfendiyár and his warriors, with heads exposed, now prostrated themselves in solemn prayer to the Almighty, and implored his favor and protection from the calamity which had befallen them. Happily their prayers were heard, Heaven was compassionate, and in a short space the snow and the mighty wind entirely ceased. By this fortunate interference of Providence, the army was enabled to quit the caves of the mountain; and then Isfendiyár again addressed Kurugsar triumphantly: "Thus the sixth labor is accomplished. What have we now to fear?" The demon-guide answered him and said: "From hence to the Brazen Fortress it is forty farsangs. That fortress is the residence of Arjásp; but the road is full of peril. For three farsangs the sand on the ground is as hot as fire, and there is no water to be found during the whole journey." This information made a serious impression upon the mind of Isfendiyár; who said to him sternly: "If I find thee guilty of falsehood, I will assuredly put thee to death." Kurugsar replied: "What! after six trials? Thou hast no reason to question my veracity. I shall never depart from the truth, and my advice is, that thou hadst better return; for the seventh stage is not to be ventured upon by human strength.

"Along those plains of burning sand
No bird can move, nor ant, nor fly;
No water slakes the fiery land,
Intensely glows the flaming sky.
No tiger fierce, nor lion ever
Could breathe that pestilential air;

> *Even the unsparing vulture never*
> *Ventures on blood-stained pinions there.*

"At the distance of three farsangs beyond this inaccessible belt of scorching country lies the Brazen Fortress, to which there is no visible path; and if an army of a hundred thousand strong were to attempt its reduction, there would not be the least chance of success."

Seventh Stage. – When Isfendiyár heard these things, enough to alarm the bravest heart, he turned towards his people to ascertain their determination; when they unanimously repeated their readiness to sacrifice their lives in his service, and to follow wherever he might be disposed to lead the way. He then put Kurugsar in chains again, and prosecuted his journey, until he reached the place said to be covered with burning sand. Arrived on the spot, he observed to the demon-guide: "Thou hast described the sand as hot, but it is not so." "True; and it is on account of the heavy showers of snow that have fallen and cooled the ground, a proof that thou art under the protection of the Almighty." Isfendiyár smiled, and said: "Thou art all insincerity and deception, thus to play upon my feelings with false or imaginary terrors." Saying this he urged his soldiers to pass rapidly on, so as to leave the sand behind them, and they presently came to a great river. Isfendiyár was now angry with Kurugsar, and said: "Thou hast declared that for the space of forty farsangs there was no water, every drop being everywhere dried up by the burning heat of the sun, and here we find water! Why didst thou also idly fill the minds of my soldiers with groundless fears?" Kurugsar replied: "I will confess the truth. Did I not swear a solemn oath to be faithful, and yet I was still doubted, and still confined in irons, though the experience of six days of trial had proved the correctness of my information and advice. For this reason I was disappointed and displeased; and I must confess that I did, therefore, exaggerate the dangers of the last day, in the hope too of inducing thee to return and release me from my bonds."

Isfendiyár now struck off the irons from the hands and feet of his demon-guide and treated him with favor and kindness, repeating to him his promise to reward him at the close of his victorious career with the government of a kingdom. Kurugsar was grateful for this change of conduct to him, and again acknowledging the deception he had been guilty of, hoped for pardon, engaging at the same time to take the party in safety across the great river which had impeded their progress. This was accordingly done, and the Brazen Fortress was now at no great distance. At the close of the day they were only one farsang from the towers, but Isfendiyár preferred resting till the next morning. "What is thy counsel now?" said he to his guide. "What sort of a fortress is this which fame describes in such dreadful colors?" "It is stronger than imagination can conceive, and impregnable." – "Then how shall I get to Arjásp?

> *"How shall I cleave the oppressor's form asunder,*
> *The murderer of my grandsire, Lohurásp?*
> *The bravest heroes of Túrán shall fall*
> *Under my conquering sword; their wives and children*
> *Led captive to Irán; and desolation*
> *Scathe the whole realm beneath the tyrant's sway."*

But these words only exasperated the feelings of Kurugsar, who bitterly replied:

> *"Then may calamity be thy reward,*
> *Thy stars malignant, and thy life all sorrow;*
> *And may'st thou perish, weltering in thy blood,*
> *And the bare desert be thy lonely grave*
> *For that inhuman thought, that cruel menace."*

Isfendiyár, upon hearing this unexpected language, became furious with indignation, and instantly punished the offender on the spot; with one stroke of his sword he cleft Kurugsar in twain.

When the clouds of night had darkened the sky, Isfendiyár, with a number of his warriors, proceeded towards the Brazen Fortress, and secretly explored it on every side. He found it constructed entirely of iron and brass; and, notwithstanding a strict examination at every point, discovered no accessible part for attack. It was three farsangs high, and forty wide; and such a place as was never before beheld by man.

Capture of the Brazen Fortress

ISFENDIYÁR RETURNED from reconnoitring the fortress with acute feelings of sorrow and despair. He was at last convinced that Kurugsar had spoken the truth; for there seemed to be no chance whatever of

taking the place by any stratagem he could invent. Revolving the enterprise seriously in his mind, he now began to repent of his folly, and the overweening confidence which had led him to undertake the journey.

Returning thus to his tent in a melancholy mood, he saw a Fakír sitting down on the road, and him he anxiously accosted. "What may be the number of the garrison in this fort?" "There are a hundred thousand veteran warriors in the service of Arjásp in the fort, with abundance of supplies of every kind, and streams of pure water, so that nothing is wanted to foil an enemy." This was very unwelcome intelligence to Isfendiyár, who now assembled his officers to consider what was best to be done. They all agreed that the reduction of the fortress was utterly impracticable, and that the safest course for him would be to return. But he could not bring himself to acquiesce in this measure, saying: "God is almighty, and beneficent, and with him is the victory." He then reflected deeply and long, and finally determined upon entering the fort disguised as a merchant. Having first settled the mode of proceeding, he put Bashútan in temporary charge of the army, saying:

> *"This Brazen Fortress scorns all feats of arms,*
> *Nor sword nor spear, nor battle-axe, can here*
> *Be wielded to advantage; stratagem*
> *Must be employed, or we shall never gain*
> *Possession of its wide-extended walls,*
> *Placing my confidence in God alone*
> *I go with rich and curious wares for sale,*
> *To take the credulous people by surprise,*
> *Under the semblance of a peaceful merchant."*

Isfendiyár then directed a hundred dromedaries to be collected, and when they were brought to him he disposed of them in the following manner. He loaded ten with embroidered cloths, five with rubies and sapphires, and five more with pearls and other precious jewels. Upon each of the remaining eighty he placed two chests, and in each chest a warrior was secreted, making in all one hundred and sixty; and one hundred more were disposed as camel-drivers and servants. Thus the whole force, consisting of a hundred dromedaries and two hundred and sixty warriors, set off towards the Brazen Fortress, Isfendiyár having first intimated to his brother Bashútan to march with his army direct to the gates of the fort, as soon as he saw a column of flame and smoke ascend from the interior. On the way they gave out that they were merchants come with valuable goods from Persia, and hoped for custom. The tidings of travellers having arrived with rubies and gold-embroidered garments for sale, soon reached the ears of Arjásp, the king, who immediately gave them permission to enter the fort. When Isfendiyár, the reputed master of the caravan, had got within the walls, he said that he had brought rich presents for the king, and requested to be introduced to him in person. He was accordingly allowed to take the presents himself, was received with distinguished attention, and having stated his name to be Kherád, was invited to go to the royal palace, whenever, and as often as, he might please. At one of the interviews the king asked him, as he had come from Persia, if he knew whether the report was true or not that Kurugsar had been put to death, and what Gushtásp and Isfendiyár were engaged upon. The hero in disguise replied that it was five months since he left Persia; but he had heard on the road from many persons that Isfendiyár intended proceeding by the way of the Heft-khan with a vast army, towards the Brazen Fortress. At these words Arjásp smiled in derision, and said: "Ah! ah! by that way even the winged tribe are afraid to venture; and if Isfendiyár had a thousand lives, he would lose them all in any attempt to accomplish that journey." After this interview Isfendiyár daily continued to attend to the sale of his merchandise, and soon found that his sisters were employed in the degrading office of drawing and carrying water for the kitchen of Arjásp. When they heard that a caravan had arrived from Irán, they went to Isfendiyár (who recognized them at a distance, but hid his face that they might not know him), to inquire what tidings he had brought about their father and brother. Alarmed at the hazard of discovery, he replied that he knew nothing, and desired them to depart; but they remained, and said: "On thy return to Irán, at least, let it be known that here we are, two daughters of Gushtásp, reduced to the basest servitude, and neither father nor brother takes compassion upon our distresses.

> *"Whilst with bare head, and naked feet, we toil,*
> *They pass their time in peace and happiness,*
> *Regardless of the misery we endure."*

Isfendiyár again, in assumed anger, told them to depart, saying: "Talk not to me of Gushtásp and Isfendiyár – what have I to do with them?" At that moment the sound of his voice was recognized by the elder sister, who, in a transport of joy, instantly communicated her discovery to the younger; but they kept the secret till night, and then they returned to commune with their brother. Isfendiyár finding that he was known, acknowledged himself, and informed them that he had undertaken to restore them to liberty, and that he was now engaged in the enterprise, opposing every obstacle in his way; but it was necessary that they should continue their usual labor at the wells, till a fitting opportunity occurred.

For the purpose of accelerating the moment of release, Isfendiyár represented to the king that at a period of great adversity, he had made a vow that he would give a splendid banquet if ever Heaven again smiled upon him, and as he then was in the way to prosperity, and wished to fulfil his vow, he hoped that his majesty would honor him with his presence on the occasion. The king accepted the invitation with satisfaction, and said: "To-morrow I will be thy guest, at thy own house, and with all my warriors and soldiers." But this did not suit the scheme of the pretended merchant, who apologized on account of his house being too small, and proposed that the feast should be held upon the loftiest part of the fortress, where spacious tents and pavilions might be erected for the purpose, and a large fire lighted to give splendor to the scene. The king assented, and every requisite preparation being made, all the royal and warrior guests assembled in the morning, and eagerly partook of the rich viands set before them. They all drank wine with such relish and delight, that they soon became intoxicated, and Kherád seizing the opportunity, ordered the logs of wood which had been collected, to be set on fire, and rapidly the smoke and flame sprung up, and ascended to the sky. Bashútan saw the looked-for sign, and hastened with two thousand horsemen to the gates of the fortress, where he slew every one that he met, calling himself Isfendiyár. Arjásp had enjoyed the banquet exceedingly; the music gave him infinite pleasure, and the wine had intoxicated him; but in the midst of his hilarity and merriment, he was told that Isfendiyár had reached the gates, and entered the fort, killing immense numbers of his people. This terrible intelligence roused him and quitting the festive board of Kherád, he ordered his son Kahram, with fifty thousand horsemen, to repel the invader. He also ordered forty thousand horsemen to protect different parts of the walls, and ten thousand to remain as his own personal guard. Kahram accordingly issued forth without delay, and soon engaged in battle with the force under Bashútan.

When night came, Isfendiyár opened the lids of the chests, and let out the hundred and sixty warriors, whom he supplied with swords and spears, and armor, and also the hundred who were disguised as camel-drivers and servants.

With this bold band he sped,
Whither Arjásp had fled;
And all who fought around,
To keep untouched that sacred ground;
(Resistance weak and vain,)
By him were quickly slain.

The sisters of Isfendiyár now arrived, and pointed out to him the chamber of Arjásp, to which place he immediately repaired, and roused up the king, who was almost insensible with the fumes of wine. Arjásp, however, sprang upon his feet,

And grappled stoutly with Isfendiyár,
And desperate was the conflict: head and loins
Alternately received deep gaping wounds
From sword and dagger. Wearied out at length,
Arjásp shrunk back, when with one mighty blow,
Isfendiyár, exulting in his power,
Cleft him asunder.

Two of the wives, two daughters, and one sister of Arjásp fell immediately into the hands of the conqueror, who delivered them into the custody of his son, to be conveyed home. He then quitted the palace, and turning his steps towards the gates of the fortress, slew a great number of the enemy.

Kahram, in the meantime, had been fiercely engaged with Bashútan, and was extremely reduced. At the very moment too of his discomfiture, he heard the watchmen call out aloud that Arjásp had been slain by Kherád. Confounded and alarmed by these tidings, he approached the fort, where he heard the confirmation of his misfortune from every mouth, and also that the garrison had been put to the sword. Leading on the remainder of his troops he now came in contact with Isfendiyár and his two hundred and sixty warriors, and a sharp engagement ensued; but the coming up of Bashútan's force on his rear, placed him in such a predicament on every side, that defeat and destruction were almost inevitable. In short, Kahram was left with only a few of his soldiers near him, when Isfendiyár, observing his situation, challenged him to personal combat, and the challenge was accepted.

> *So closely did the eager warriors close,*
> *They seemed together joined, and but one man.*
> *At last Isfendiyár seized Kahram's girth,*
> *And flung him to the ground, and bound his hands;*
> *And as a leaf is severed from its stalk,*
> *So he the head cleft from its quivering trunk;*
> *Thus one blow wins, and takes away a throne,*
> *In battle heads are trodden under hoofs,*
> *Crowns under heads.*

After the death of Kahram, Isfendiyár issued a proclamation, offering full pardon to all who would unite under his banners. They had no king.

Having first written to his father an account of the great victory which he had gained, he occupied himself in reducing all the surrounding provinces and their inhabitants to subjection. Those people who continued hostile to him he deemed it necessary to put to death. He took all the women of Arjásp into his own service, and their daughters he presented to his own sons.

> *Not a warrior of Chín remained;*
> *The king of Túrán was swept away;*
> *And the realm where in pomp he had reigned,*
> *Where he basked in prosperity's ray,*
> *Was spoiled by the conqueror's brand,*
> *Desolation marked every scene,*
> *And a stranger now governed the mountainous land,*
> *Where the splendour of Poshang had been.*
> *Not a dirhem of treasure was left;*
> *For nothing eluded the conqueror's grasp;*
> *Of all was the royal pavilion bereft;*
> *All followed the fate of Arjásp!*

When Gushtásp received information of this mighty conquest, he sent orders to Isfendiyár to continue in the government of the new empire; but the prince replied that he had settled the country, and was anxious to see his father. This request being permitted, he was desired to bring away all the immense booty, and return by the road of the Heft-khan. Arriving at the place where he was overtaken by the dreadful winter-storm, he again found all the property he had lost under the drifts of snow; and when he had accomplished his journey, he was received with the warmest welcome and congratulations, on account of his extraordinary successes. A royal feast was prepared, and the king filled his son's goblet with wine so repeatedly, and drank himself so frequently, and with such zest, that both of them at length became intoxicated. Gushtásp then asked Isfendiyár to describe to him the particulars of his expedition by the road of the Heft-khan; for though he had heard the story from others, he wished to have it from his own mouth. But Isfendiyár replied: "We have both drank too much wine, and nothing good can proceed from a drunken man; I will recite my adventures to-morrow, when my head is clear." The next day Gushtásp, seated upon his throne, and Isfendiyár placed before him on a golden chair, again asked for the prince's description of his triumphant progress by the Heft-khan, and according to his wish every incident that merited notice was faithfully detailed to him. The king expressed great pleasure at the conclusion; but envy and suspicion lurked in his breast, and writhing internally like a serpent, he still delayed fulfilling his promise to invest Isfendiyár, upon the overthrow of Arjásp, with the sovereignty of Irán.

The prince could not fail to observe the changed disposition of his father, and privately went to Kitabún, his mother, to whom he related the solemn promise and engagement of Gushtásp, and requested her to go to him, and say: "Thou hast given thy royal word to Isfendiyár, that when he had conquered and slain Arjásp, and restored his own sisters to liberty, thou wouldst place upon his head the crown of Irán; faith and honor are indispensable in princes, they are inculcated by religion, and yet thou hast failed to make good thy word." But the mother had more prudence, and said: "Let me give thee timely counsel, and breathe not a syllable to any one on the subject. God forbid that thou shouldst again be thrown into prison, and confined in chains. Recollect thine is the succession; the army is in thy favor; thy father is old and infirm. Have a little patience and in the end thou wilt undoubtedly be the King of Persia.

Isfendiyár, however, was not contented with his mother's counsel, and suspecting that she would communicate to the king what he had said, he one day, as if under the influence of wine, thus addressed his father: "In what way have I failed to accomplish thy wishes? Have I not performed such actions as never were heard of, and never will be performed again, in furtherance of thy glory? I have overthrown thy greatest enemy, and supported thy honor with ceaseless toil and exertion. Is it not then incumbent on thee to fulfil thy promise?" Gushtásp replied: "Do not be impatient – the throne is thine;" but he was deeply irritated at heart on being thus reproached by his own son. When he retired he consulted with Jamásp, and was anxious to know what the stars foretold. The answer was: "He is of exalted fortune, of high destiny; he will overcome all his enemies, and finally obtain the sovereignty of the heft-aklím, or seven climes." This favorable prophecy aggravated the spleen of the father against the son, and he inquired with bitter and unnatural curiosity: "What will be his death? Look to that."

> *"A deadly dart from Rustem's bow,*
> *Will lay the glorious warrior low."*

These tidings gladdened the heart of Gushtásp, and he said: "If this miscreant had been slain in his expedition to the Brazen Fortress I should not now have been insulted with his claim to my throne." The king then having resolved upon a scheme of deep dissimulation, ordered a gorgeous banquet, and invited to it all his relations and warriors; and when the guests were assembled he said to Isfendiyár: "The crown and the throne are thine; indeed, who is there so well qualified for imperial sway?" and turning to his warriors, he spoke of him with praise and admiration, and added: "When I was entering upon the war against Arjásp, before I quitted Sístán, I said to Rustem: 'Lohurásp, my father, is dead, my wife and children made prisoners, wilt thou assist me in punishing the murderer and oppressor?' but he excused himself, and remained at home, and although I have since been involved in numberless perils, he has not once by inquiry shown himself interested in my behalf; in short, he boasts that Kai-khosráu gave him the principalities of Zábul and Kábul, and Ním-rúz, and that he owes no allegiance to me! It behooves me, therefore, to depute Isfendiyár to go and put him to death, or bring him before me in bonds alive. After that I shall have no enemy to be revenged upon, and I shall retire from the world, and leave to Isfendiyár the crown and the throne of Persia, with confidence and satisfaction." All the nobles and heroes present approved of the measure, and the king, gratified by their approbation, then turned to Isfendiyár, and said: "I have sworn on the Zendavesta, to relinquish my power, and place it in thy hands, as soon as Rustem is subdued. Take whatever force the important occasion may require, for the whole resources of the empire shall be at thy command." But Isfendiyár thus replied: "Remember the first time I defeated Arjásp – what was my reward? Through the machinations of Gurzam I was thrown into prison and chained. And what is my reward now that I have slain both Arjásp and his son in battle? Thy solemn promise to me is forgotten, or disregarded. The prince who forgets one promise will forget another, if it be convenient for his purpose.

"Whenever the Heft-khan is brought to mind,
I feel a sense of horror. But why should I
Repeat the story of those great exploits!
God is my witness, how I slew the wolf,
The lion, and the dragon; how I punished
That fell enchantress with her thousand wiles;
And how I suffered, midst the storm of snow,
Which almost froze the blood within my veins;
And how that vast unfathomable deep
We crossed securely. These are deeds which awaken
Wonder and praise in others, not in thee!
The treasure which I captured now is thine;
And what is my reward? – the interest, sorrow.
Thus am I cheated of my recompense.
It is the custom for great kings to keep
Religiously their pledged, affianced word;
But thou hast broken thine, despite of honour.

"I do remember in my early youth,
It was in Rúm, thou didst perform a feat
Of gallant daring; for thou didst destroy
A dragon and a wolf, but thou didst bear
Thyself most proudly, thinking human arm
Never before had done a deed so mighty;
Yes, thou wert proud and vain, and seemed exalted
Up to the Heavens; and for that noble act
What did thy father do? The king for that
Gave thee with joyous heart his crown and throne.
Now mark the difference; think what I have done,
What perils I sustained, and for thy sake!
Thy foes I vanquished, clearing from thy mind
The gnawing rust of trouble and affliction.
Monsters I slew, reduced the Brazen Fortress,
And laid Arjásp's whole empire at thy feet,
And what was my reward? Neglect and scorn.

Did I deserve this at a father's hands?"

Gushtásp remained unmoved by this sharp rebuke, though he readily acknowledged its justice. "The crown shall be thine," said he, "but consider my position. Think, too, what services Zál and Rustem performed for Kai-khosráu, and shall I expect less from my own son, gifted as he is with a form of brass, and the most prodigious valor? Forbid it, Heaven! that any rumor of our difference should get abroad in the world, which would redound to the dishonor of both! Nearly half of Irán is in the possession of Rustem." "Give me the crown," said Isfendiyár, "and I will immediately proceed against the Zabúl champion." "I have given thee both the crown and the throne, take with thee my whole army, and all my treasure. – What wouldst thou have more? He who has conquered the terrific obstacles of the Heft-khan, and has slain Arjásp and subdued his entire kingdom, can have no cause to fear the prowess of Rustem, or any other chief." Isfendiyár replied that he had no fear of Rustem's prowess; he was now old, and therefore not equal to himself in strength; still he had no wish to oppose him:

> *"For he has been the monitor and friend*
> *Of our Kaiánian ancestors; his care*
> *Enriched their minds, and taught them to be brave;*
> *And he was ever faithful to their cause.*
> *Besides," said he, "thou wert the honoured guest*
> *Of Rustem two long years; and at Sístán*
> *Enjoyed his hospitality and friendship,*
> *His festive, social board; and canst thou now,*
> *Forgetting that delightful intercourse,*
> *Become his bitterest foe?"*

Gushtásp replied:

> *"'Tis true he may have served my ancestors;*
> *But what is that to me? His spirit is proud,*
> *And he refused to yield me needful aid*
> *When danger pressed; that is enough, and thou*
> *Canst not divert me from my settled purpose.*
> *Therefore, if thy aim be still*

To rule, thy father's wish fulfil;
Quickly trace the distant road;
Quick invade the chiefs abode;
Bind his feet, and bind his hands
In a captive's galling bands;
Bring him here, that all may know
Thou hast quelled the mighty foe."

But Isfendiyár was still reluctant, and implored him to relinquish his design.

"For if resolved, a gloomy cloud
Will quickly all thy glories shroud,
And dim thy brilliant throne;
I would not thus aspire to reign,
But rather, free from crime, remain
Sequestered and alone."

Again Gushtásp spoke, and said: "There is no necessity for any further delay. Thou art appointed my successor, and the crown and the throne are thine; thou hast therefore only to march to the scene of action, and accomplish the object of the war." Hearing this, Isfendiyár sullenly retired to his own house, and Gushtásp, perceiving that he was in an angry mood, requested Jamásp (his minister) to ascertain the state of his mind, and whether he intended to proceed to Sístán or not. Jamásp immediately went, and Isfendiyár asked him, as his friend, what he would advise. "The commands of a father," he replied, "must be obeyed." There was now no remedy, and the king being informed that the prince consented to undertake the expedition, no further discussion took place.

But Kitabún was deeply affected when she heard of these proceedings, and repaired instantly to her son, to represent to him the hopelessness of the enterprise he had engaged to conduct.

"A mother's counsel is a golden treasure,
Consider well, and listen not to folly.
Rustem, the champion of the world, will never
Suffer himself to be confined in bonds.

Did he not conquer the White Demon, fill
The world with blood, in terrible revenge,
When Saiáwush was by Afrásiyáb
Cruelly slain? O, curses on the throne,
And ruin seize the country, which returns
Evil for good, and spurns its benefactor.
Restrain thy steps, engage not in this war;
It cannot do thee honour. Hear my voice!
For Rustem still can conquer all the world."
Hear the safe counsel of thy anxious mother!
Thus spoke Kitabún, shedding ceaseless tears;
And thus Isfendiyár: "I fear not Rustem;
I fear not his prodigious power and skill;
But never can I on so great a hero
Place ignominious bonds; it must not be.
Yet, mother dear, my faithful word is pledged;
My word Jamásp has taken to the king,
And I must follow where my fortune leads."

The next morning Isfendiyár took leave of the king, and with a vast army, and immense treasure, commenced his march towards Sístán. It happened that one of the camels in advance laid down, and though beaten severely, could not be made to get up on its legs. Isfendiyár, seeing the obstinacy of the animal, ordered it to be killed, and passed on. The people, however, interpreted the accident as a bad omen, and wished him not to proceed; but he could not attend to their suggestions, as he thought the king would look upon it as a mere pretence, and therefore continued his journey.

When he approached Sístán, he sent Bahman, his eldest son, to Rustem, with a flattering message, to induce the champion to honor him with an istakbál, or deputation to receive him. Upon Bahman's arrival, however, he hesitated and delayed, being reluctant to give a direct answer; but Zál interposed, saying: "Why not immediately wait upon the prince? – have we not always been devoted to the Kaiánian dynasty? – Go and bring him hither, that we may tender him our allegiance, and entertain him at our mansion as becomes his illustrious birth," Accordingly Rustem went out to welcome Isfendiyár, and alighting from Rakush, proceeded respectfully on foot to embrace him. He then invited him to his house, but Isfendiyár said: "So strict are my father's commands, that after having seen thee, I am not permitted to delay my departure." Rustem, however, pressed him to remain with him, but all in vain. On the contrary the prince artfully conducted him to his own quarters, where he addressed him thus: "If thou wilt allow me to bind thee, hand and foot, in chains, I will convey thee to the king my father, whose humor it is to see thee once in fetters, and then to release thee!" Rustem was silent. Again Isfendiyár said: "If thou art not disposed to comply with this demand, go thy ways," Rustem replied: "First be my guest, as thy father once was, and after that I will conform to thy will." Again the prince said: "My father visited thee under other circumstances; I have come for a different purpose. If I eat thy bread and salt, and after that thou shouldst refuse thy acquiescence, I must have recourse to force. But if I become thy guest, how can I in honor fight with thee? and if I do not take thee bound into my father's presence, according to his command, what answer shall I give to him?" "For the same reason," said Rustem; "how can I eat thy bread and salt?" Isfendiyár then replied: "Thou needest not eat my bread and salt, but only drink wine. – Bring thy own pure ruby." To this Rustem agreed, and they drank, each his own wine, together.

In a short space Rustem observed that he wished to consult his father Zál; and being allowed to depart, he, on his return home, described in strong terms of admiration the personal appearance and mental qualities of Isfendiyár.

> "In wisdom ripe, and with a form
> Of brass to meet the battle-storm,
> Thou wouldst confess his every boon,
> Had been derived from Feridún."

Bashútan in the meanwhile observed to his brother, with some degree of dissatisfaction, that his enemy had come into his power, on his own feet too, but had been strangely permitted to go away again. To this gentle reproof Isfendiyár confidently replied, "If he does fail to return, I will go and secure him in bonds, even in his own house," – "Ah!" said Bashútan, "that might be done by gentleness, but not by force, for the descendant of Sám, the champion of the world, is not to be subdued so easily." These words had a powerful effect upon the mind of Isfendiyár, and he became apprehensive that Rustem would not return; but whilst he was still murmuring at his own want of vigilance, the champion appeared, and at this second interview repeated his desire that the prince would become his guest. "I am sent here by my father, who relies upon thy accepting his proffered hospitality." – "That may be," said Isfendiyár, "but I am at my utmost limit, I cannot go farther. From this place, therefore, thou hadst better prepare to accompany me to Irán." Here Rustem paused, and at length artfully began to enumerate his various achievements, and to blazon his own name.

"I fettered fast the emperor of Chin,
And broke the enchantment of the Seven Khans;
I stood the guardian of the Persian kings,
Their shield in danger. I have cleared the world
Of all their foes, enduring pain and toil
Incalculable. Such exploits for thee
Will I achieve, such sufferings will I bear,
And hence we offer thee a social welcome.
But let not dark suspicion cloud thy mind,
Nor think thyself exalted as the heavens,
Because I thus invite thee to our home."

Isfendiyár felt so indignant and irritated by this apparent boasting and self-sufficiency of Rustem, that his first impulse was to cast a dagger at him; but he kept down his wrath, and satisfied himself with giving him a scornful glance, and telling him to take a seat on his left hand. But Rustem resented this affront, saying that he never yet had sat down on the left of any king, and placed himself, without permission, on the right hand of Isfendiyár. The unfavorable impression on the prince's mind was increased by this independent conduct, and he was provoked to say to him, "Rustem! I have heard that Zál, thy father, was of demon extraction, and that Sám cast him into the desert because of his disgusting and abominable appearance; that even the hungry Símúrgh, on the same account, forebore to feed upon him, but conveyed him to her nest among her own young ones, who, pitying his wretched condition, supplied him with part of the carrion they were accustomed to devour. Naked and filthy, he is thus said to have subsisted on garbage, till Sám was induced to commiserate his wretchedness, and take him to Sástán, where, by the indulgence of his family and royal bounty, he was instructed in human manners and human science." This was a reproach and an insult too biting for Rustem to bear with any degree of patience, and frowning with strong indignation, he said, "Thy father knows, and thy grandfather well knew that Zál was the son of Sám, and Sám of Narímán, and that Narímán was descended from

Húsheng. Thou and I, therefore, have the same origin. Besides, on my mother's side, I am descended from Zohák, so that by both parents I am of a race of princes. Knowest thou not that the Iránian empire was for some time in my hands, and that I refused to retain it, though urged by the nobles and the army to exercise the functions of royalty? It was my sense of justice, and attachment to the Kais and to thy family, which have enabled thee to possess thy present dignity and command. It is through my fidelity and zeal that thou art now in a situation to reproach me. Thou hast slain one king, Arjásp, how many kings have I slain? Did I not conquer Afrásiyáb, the greatest and bravest king that ever ruled over Túrán? And did I not also subdue the king of Hámáverán, and the Khakán of Chín? Káús, thy own ancestor, I released from the demons of Mázinderán. I slew the White Demon, and the tremendous giant, Akwán Díw. Can thy insignificant exploits be compared with mine? Never!" Rustem's vehemence, and the disdainful tone of his voice, exasperated still more the feelings of Isfendiyár, who however recollected that he was under his roof, otherwise he would have avenged himself instantly on the spot. Restraining his anger, he then said softly to him, "Wherefore dost thou raise thy voice so high? For though thy head be exalted to the skies, thou wert, and still art, but a dependent on the Kais. And was thy Heft-khan equal in terrible danger to mine? Was the capture of Mázinderán equal in valorous exertion to the capture of the Brazen Fortress? And did I not, by the power of my sword, diffuse throughout the world the blessings of my own religion, the faith of the fire-worshipper, which was derived from Heaven itself? Thou hast performed the duties of a warrior and a servant, whilst I have performed the holy functions of a sovereign and a prophet!" Rustem, in reply, said:

> *"In thy Heft-khan thou hadst twelve thousand men*
> *Completely armed, with ample stores and treasure,*
> *Whilst Rakush and my sword, my conquering sword,*
> *Were all the aid I had, and all I sought,*
> *In that prodigious enterprise of mine.*
> *Two sisters thou released – no arduous task,*
> *Whilst I recovered from the demon's grasp*
> *The mighty Káús, and the monsters slew,*
> *Roaring like thunder in their dismal caves.*

> *"This great exploit my single arm achieved;*
> *And when Kai-khosráu gave the regal crown*

To Lohurásp, the warriors were incensed,
And deemed Fríburz, Káús's valiant son,
Fittest by birth to rule. My sire and I
Espoused the cause of Lohurásp; else he
Had never sat upon the throne, nor thou
Been here to treat with scorn thy benefactor.
And now Gushtásp, with foul ingratitude,
Would bind me hand and foot! But who on earth
Can do that office? I am not accustomed
To hear harsh terms, and cannot brook their sting,
Therefore desist. Once in Káús's court,
When I was moved to anger, I poured out
Upon him words of bitterest scorn and rage,
And though surrounded by a thousand chiefs,
Not one attempted to repress my fury,
Not one, but all stood silent and amazed."

"Smooth that indignant brow," the prince replied
"And measure not my courage nor my strength
With that of Káús; had he nerve like mine?
Thou might'st have kept the timorous king in awe,
But I am come myself to fetter thee!"
So saying, he the hand of Rustem grasped,
And wrung it so intensely, that the champion
Felt inwardly surprised, but careless said,
"The time is not yet come for us to try
Our power in battle." Then Isfendiyár
Dropped Rustem's hand, and spoke, "To-day let wine
Inspire our hearts, and on the field to-morrow
Be ours the strife, with battle-axe and sword,
And my first aim shall be to bind thee fast,
And show thee to my troops, Rustem in fetters!"

At this the champion smiled, and thus exclaimed,
"Where hast thou seen the deeds of warriors brave?

Where hast thou heard the clash of mace and sword
Wielded by men of valour? I to-morrow
Will take thee in my arms, and straight convey thee
To Zál, and place thee on the ivory throne,
And on thy head a crown of gold shall glitter.
The treasury I will open, and our troops
Shall fight for thee, and I will gird my loins
As they were girt for thy bold ancestors;
And when thou art the chosen king, and I
Thy warrior-chief, the world will be thy own;
No other sovereign need attempt to reign."

"So much time has been spent in vain boasting, and extravagant self-praise," rejoined Isfendiyár, "that the day is nearly done, and I am hungry; let us therefore take some refreshment together." Rustem's appetite being equally keen, the board was spread, and every dish that was brought to him he emptied at once, as if at one swallow; then he threw aside the goblets, and called for the large flagon that he might drink his fill without stint. When he had finished several dishes and as many flagons of wine, he paused, and Isfendiyár and the assembled chiefs were astonished at the quantity he had devoured. He now prepared to depart, and the prince said to him, "Go and consult with thy father: if thou art contented to be bound, well; if not, thou wilt have cause to repent, for I will assuredly attend to the commands of Gushtásp." – "Do thou also consult with thy brethren and friends," replied Rustem, "whether thou wilt be our guest to-morrow, or not; if not, come to this place before sunrise, that we may decide our differences in battle." Isfendiyár said, "My most anxious desire, my wish to heaven, is to meet thee, for I shall have no difficulty in binding thee hand and foot. I would indeed willingly convey thee without fetters to my father, but if I did so, he would say that I was unable to put thee in bonds, and that would disgrace my name." Rustem observed that the immense number of men and demons he had contended against was as nothing in the balance of his mind compared with the painful subject of his present thoughts and fears. He was ready to engage, but afraid of meriting a bad name.

"If in the battle thou art slain by me,
Will not my cheek turn pale among the princes
Of the Kaiánian race, having cut off

A lovely branch of that illustrious tree?
Will not reproaches hang upon my name
When I am dead, and shall I not be cursed
For perpetrating such a horrid deed?
Thy father, too, is old, and near his end,
And thou upon the eve of being crowned;
And in thy heart thou knowest that I proffered,
And proffer my allegiance and devotion,
And would avoid the conflict. Sure, thy father
Is practising some trick, some foul deception,
To urge thee on to an untimely death,
To rid himself of some unnatural fear,
He stoops to an unnatural, treacherous act,
For I have ever been the firm support
Of crown and throne, and perfectly he knows
No mortal ever conquered me in battle,
None ever from my sword escaped his life."

Then spoke Isfendiyár: "Thou wouldst be generous
And bear a spotless name, and tarnish mine;
But I am not to be deceived by thee:
In fetters thou must go!" Rustem replied:
"Banish that idle fancy from thy brain;
Dream not of things impossible, for death
Is busy with thee; pause, or thou wilt die."
"No more!" exclaimed the prince, "no more of this.
Nor seek to frighten me with threatening words;
Go, and to-morrow bring with thee thy friends,
Thy father and thy brother, to behold
With their own eyes thy downfall, and lament
In sorrow over thy impending fate."
"So let it be," said Rustem, and at once
Mounted his noble horse, and hastened home.

The champion immediately requested his father's permission to go and fight

Isfendiyár the following day, but the old man recommended reconciliation and peace. "That cannot be," said Rustem, "for he has reviled thee so severely, and heaped upon me so many indignities, that my patience is exhausted, and the contest unavoidable." In the morning Zál, weeping bitterly, tied on Rustem's armor himself, and in an agony of grief, said: "If thou shouldst kill Isfendiyár, thy name will be rendered infamous throughout the world; and if thou shouldst be killed, Sístán will be prostrate in the dust, and extinguished forever! My heart shudders at the thoughts of this battle, but there is no remedy." Rustem said to him: "Put thy trust in God, and be not sorrowful, for when I grasp my sword the head of the enemy is lost; but my desire is to take Isfendiyár alive, and not to kill him. I would serve him, and not sever his head from his body." Zál was pleased with this determination, and rejoiced that there was a promise of a happy issue to the engagement.

In the morning Rustem arrayed himself in his war-attire, helmet and breast-plate, and mounted Rakush, also armed in his barguṣtuwan. His troops, too, were all assembled, and Zál appointed Zúára to take charge of them, and be careful of his brother on all occasions where assistance might be necessary. The old man then prostrated himself in prayer, and said, "O God, turn from us all affliction, and vouchsafe to us a prosperous day." Rustem being prepared for the struggle, directed Zúára to wait with the troops at a distance, whilst he went alone to meet Isfendiyár. When Bashútan first saw him, he thought he was coming to offer terms of peace, and said to Isfendiyár, "He is coming alone, and it is better that he should go to thy father of his own accord, than in bonds." – "But," replied Isfendiyár, "he is coming completely equipped in mail – quick, bring me my arms." – "Alas!" rejoined Bashútan, "thy brain is wild, and thou art resolved upon fighting. This impetuous spirit will break my heart." But Isfendiyár took no notice of the gentle rebuke. Presently he saw Rustem ascend a high place, and heard his summons to single combat. He then told his brother to keep at a distance with the army, and not to interfere till aid was positively required. Insisting rigidly on these instructions, he mounted his night-black charger, and hastened towards Rustem, who now proposed to him that they should wait awhile, and that in the meantime the two armies might be put in motion against each other. "Though," said he, "my men of Zábul are few, and thou hast a numerous host."

> *"This is a strange request," replied the prince,*
> *"But thou art all deceit and artifice;*
> *Mark thy position, lofty and commanding,*

And mine, beneath thee – in a spreading vale.
Now, Heaven forbid that I, in reckless mood,
Should give my valiant legions to destruction,
And look unpitying on! No, I advance,
Whoever may oppose me; and if thou
Requirest aid, select thy friend, and come,
For I need none, save God, in battle – none."
And Rustem said the same, for he required
No human refuge, no support but Heaven.

The battle rose, and numerous javelins whizzed
Along the air, and helm and mail were bruised;
Spear fractured spear, and then with shining swords
The strife went on, till, trenched with many a wound,
They, too, snapped short. The battle-axe was next
Wielded, in furious wrath; each bending forward
Struck brain-bewildering blows; each tried in vain
To hurl the other from his fiery horse.
Wearied, at length, they stood apart to breathe
Their charges panting from excessive toil,
Covered with foam and blood, and the strong armor,
Of steed and rider rent. The combatants
Thus paused, in mutual consternation lost.

In the meantime Zúára, impatient at this delay, advanced towards the Iránians, and reproached them for their cowardice so severely, that Núsháwer, the younger son of Isfendiyár, felt ashamed, and immediately challenged the bravest of the enemy to fight. Alwaí, one of Rustem's followers, came boldly forward, but his efforts only terminated in his discomfiture and death. After him came Zúára himself:

Who galloped to the charge incensed, and, high
Lifting his iron mace, upon the head
Of bold Núsháwer struck a furious blow,
Which drove him from his steed a lifeless corse.
Seeing their gallant leader thus overthrown,

The troops in terror fled, and in their flight
Thousands were slain, among them brave Mehrnús,
Another kinsman of Isfendiyár.

Bahman, observing the defeat and confusion of the Iránians, went immediately to his father, and told him that two of his own family were killed by the warriors of Zábul, who had also attacked him and put his troops to the rout with great slaughter. Isfendiyár was extremely irritated at this intelligence, and called aloud to Rustem: "Is treachery like this becoming in a warrior?" The champion being deeply concerned, shook like a branch, and swore by the head and life of the king, by the sun, and his own conquering sword, that he was ignorant of the event, and innocent of what had been done. To prove what he said, he offered to bind in fetters his brother Zúára, who must have authorized the movement; and also to secure Ferámurz, who slew Mehrnús, and deliver them over to Gushtásp, the fire-worshipper. "Nay," said he, "I will deliver over to thee my whole family, as well as my brother and son, and thou mayest sacrifice them all as a punishment for having commenced the fight without permission." Isfendiyár replied: "Of what use would it be to sacrifice thy brother and thy son? Would that restore my own to me? No. Instead of them, I will put thee to death, therefore come on!" Accordingly both simultaneously bent their bows, and shot their arrows with the utmost rapidity; but whilst Rustem's made no impression, those of Isfendiyár's produced great effect on the champion and his horse. So severely was Rakush wounded, that Rustem, when he perceived how much his favorite horse was exhausted, dismounted, and continued to impel his arrows against the enemy from behind his shield. But Rakush brooked not the dreadful storm, and galloped off unconscious that his master himself was in as bad a plight. When Zúára saw the noble animal, riderless, crossing the plain, he gasped for breath, and in an agony of grief hurried to the fatal spot, where he found Rustem desperately hurt, and the blood flowing copiously from every wound. The champion observed, that though he was himself bleeding so much, not one drop of blood appeared to have issued from the veins of his antagonist. He was very weak, but succeeded in dragging himself up to his former position, when Isfendiyár, smiling to see them thus, exclaimed:

"Is this the valiant Rustem, the renowned,
Quitting the field of battle? Where is now
The raging tiger, the victorious chief?

Was it from thee the Demons shrunk in terror,
And did thy burning sword sear out their hearts?
What has become of all thy valour now?
Where is thy matchless mace, and why art thou,
The roaring lion, turned into a fox,
An animal of slyness, not of courage,
Losing thy noble character and name?"

Zúára, when he came to Rustem, alighted and resigned his horse to his brother; and placing an arrow on his bow-string, wished himself to engage Isfendiyár, who was ready to fight him, but Rustem cried, "No, I have not yet done with thee." Isfendiyár replied: "I know thee well, and all thy dissimulation, but nothing yet is accomplished. Come and consent to be fettered, or I must compel thee." Rustem, however, was not to be overcome, and he said: "If I were really subdued by thee, I might agree to be bound like a vanquished slave; but the day is now closing, to-morrow we will resume the fight!" Isfendiyár acquiesced, and they separated, Rustem going to his own tent, and the prince remaining on the field. There he affectionately embraced the severed heads of his kinsmen, placed them himself on a bier, and sent them to his father, the king, with a letter in which he said, "Thy commands must be obeyed, and such is the result of to-day; Heaven only knows what may befall to-morrow." Then he spoke privately to Bashútan: "This Rustem is not human, he is formed of rock and iron, neither sword nor javelin has done him mortal harm; but the arrows went deep into his body, and it will indeed be wonderful if he lives throughout the night. I know not what to think of to-morrow, or how I shall be able to overcome him."

When Rustem arrived at his quarters, Zál soon discovered that he had received many wounds, which occasioned great affliction in his family, and he said: "Alas! that in my old age such a misfortune should have befallen us, and that with my own eyes I should see these gaping wounds!" He then rubbed Rustem's feet, and applied healing balm to the wounds, and bound them up with the skill and care of a physician. Rustem said to his father: "I never met with a foe, warrior or demon, of such amazing strength and bravery as this! He seems to have a brazen body, for my arrows, which I can drive through an anvil, cannot penetrate his chest. If I had applied the power which I have exerted to a mountain, the mountain would have moved from its base, but he sat firmly upon his saddle and scorned my efforts. I thank God that it is night, and that I have escaped from his grasp. To-morrow I cannot fight, and my secret wish is to retire unseen from the struggle, that no trace of me may be discovered." – "In that case," replied Zál, "the victor will come and take me and all my family into bondage. But let us not despair. Did not the Símúrgh promise that whenever I might be overcome by adversity, if I burned one of her feathers, she would instantly appear? Shall we not then solicit assistance in this awful extremity?" So saying, Zál went up to a high place, and burnt the feather in a censer, and in a short time the Símúrgh stood before him. After due praise and acknowledgment, he explained his wants. "But," said he, "may the misfortune we endure be far from him who has brought it upon us. My son Rustem is wounded almost unto death, and I am so helpless that I can do him no good." He then brought forward Rakush, pierced by numerous arrows; upon which the wonderful Bird said to him, "Be under no alarm on that account, for I will soon cure him;" and she immediately plucked out the rankling weapons with her beak, and the wounds, on passing a feather over them, were quickly healed.

Being thus reinvigorated by the magic influence of the Símúrgh, he solicits further aid in the coming strife with Isfendiyár; but the mysterious animal laments that she cannot assist him. "There never appeared in the world," said she, "so brave and so perfect a hero as Isfendiyár. The favor of Heaven is with him, for in his Heft-khan he, by some artifice, succeeded in killing a Símúrgh, and the further thou art removed from his invincible arm, the greater will be thy safety." Here Zál interposed and said: "If Rustem retires from the contest, his family will all be enslaved, and I shall equally share their bondage and affliction." The Símúrgh, hearing these words, fell into deep thought, and remained some time silent. At length she told Rustem to mount Rakush and follow her. Away she went to a far distance; and crossing a great river, arrived at a place covered with reeds, where the Kazú-tree abounded. The Símúrgh then rubbed one of her feathers upon the eyes of Rustem, and directed him to take a branch of the Kazú-tree, and make it straight upon the fire, and form that wand into a forked arrow; after which he was to advance against Isfendiyár, and, placing the arrow on his bowstring, shoot it into the eyes of his enemy. "The arrow will only make him blind," said the Símúrgh, "but he who spills the blood of Isfendiyár will never be free from calamity during his whole life. The Kazú-tree has also this peculiar quality: an arrow made of it is sure to accomplish its intended errand – it never misses the aim of the archer." Rustem expressed his boundless gratitude for this information and assistance; and the Símúrgh having transported him back to his tent, and affectionately kissed his face, returned to her own habitation. The champion now prepared the arrow according to the instructions he had received; and when morning dawned, mounted his horse, and hastened to the field. He found Isfendiyár still sleeping, and exclaimed aloud: "Warrior, art thou still slumbering? Rise, and see Rustem before thee!" When the prince heard his stern voice, he started up, and in great anxiety hurried on his armor. He said to Bashútan, "I had uncharitably thought he would have died of his wounds in the night, but this clear and bold voice seems to indicate perfect health – go and see whether his wounds are bound up or not, and whether he is mounted on Rakush or on some other horse." Rustem perceived Bashútan approach with an inquisitive look, and conjectured that his object was to ascertain the condition of himself and Rakush. He therefore vociferated to him: "I am now wholly free from wounds, and so is my horse, for I possess an elixir which heals the most cruel lacerations of the flesh the moment it is applied; but no such wounds were inflicted upon me, the arrows of Isfendiyár being only like needles sticking in my body." Bashútan now reported to his brother that Rustem appeared to be more fresh and vigorous than the day before, and, thinking from the spirit and gallantry of his demeanor that he would be victorious in another contest, he strongly recommended a reconciliation.

The Death of Isfendiyár

I SFENDIYÁR, blind to the march of fate, treated the suggestion of his brother with scorn, and mounting his horse, was soon in the presence of Rustem, whom he thus hastily addressed: "Yesterday thou wert wounded almost to death by my arrows, and to-day there is no trace of them. How is this?

> *"But thy father Zál is a sorcerer,*
> *And he by charm and spell*
> *Has cured all the wounds of the warrior,*
> *And now he is safe and well.*
> *For the wounds I gave could never be*
> *Closed up, excepting by sorcery.*
> *Yes, the wounds I gave thee in every part,*
> *Could never be cured but by magic art."*

Rustem replied, "If a thousand arrows were shot at me, they would all drop harmless to the ground, and in the end thou wilt fall by my hands. Therefore, if thou seekest thy own welfare, come at once and be my guest, and I swear by the Almighty, by Zerdusht, and the Zendavesta, by the sun and moon, that I will go with thee, but unfetterd, to thy father, who may do with me what he lists." – "That is not enough," replied Isfendiyár, "thou must be fettered." – "Then do not bind my arms, and take whatever thou wilt from me." – "And what hast thou to give?"

> *"A thousand jewels of brilliant hue,*
> *And of unknown price, shall be thine;*
> *A thousand imperial diadems too,*
> *And a thousand damsels divine,*
> *Who with angel-voices will sing and play,*
> *And delight thy senses both night and day;*
> *And my family wealth shall be brought thee, all*
> *That was gathered by Narímán, Sám, and Zál."*

"This is all in vain," said Isfendiyár. "I may have wandered from the way of Heaven, but I will not disobey the commands of the king. And of what use would thy treasure and property be to me? I must please my father, that he may surrender to me his crown and throne, and I have solemnly sworn to him that I will place thee before him in fetters." Rustem replied, "And in the hopes of a crown and throne thou wouldst sacrifice thyself!" – "Thou shalt see!" said Isfendiyár, and seized his bow to commence the combat. Rustem did the same, and when he had placed the forked arrow in the bow-string, he imploringly turned up his face towards Heaven, and fervently exclaimed, "O God, thou knowest how anxiously I have wished for a reconciliation, how I have suffered, and that I would now give all my treasures and wealth and go with him to Irán, to avoid this conflict; but my offers are disdained, for he is bent upon consigning me to bondage and disgrace. Thou art the redresser of grievances – direct the flight of this arrow into his eyes, but do not let me be punished for the involuntary deed." At this moment Isfendiyár shot an arrow with great force at Rustem, who dexterously eluded its point, and then, in return, instantly lodged the charmed weapon in the eyes of his antagonist.

> *And darkness overspread his sight,*
> *The world to him was hid in night;*

> *The bow dropped from his slackened hand,*
> *And down he sunk upon the sand.*

"Yesterday," said Rustem, "thou discharged at me a hundred and sixty arrows in vain, and now thou art overthrown by one arrow of mine." Bahman, the son of Isfendiyár, seeing his father bleeding on the ground, uttered loud lamentations, and Bashútan, followed by the Iránian troops, also drew nigh with the deepest sorrow marked on their countenances. The fatal arrow was immediately drawn from the wounded eyes of the prince, and some medicine being first applied to them, they conveyed him mournfully to his own tent.

The conflict having thus terminated, Rustem at the same time returned with his army to where Zál remained in anxious suspense about the result. The old man rejoiced at the issue, but said, "O, my son, thou hast killed thy enemy, but I have learnt from the wise men and astrologers that the slayer of Isfendiyár must soon come to a fatal end. May God protect thee!" Rustem replied, "I am guiltless, his blood is upon his own head." The next day they both proceeded to visit Isfendiyár, and offer to him their sympathy and condolence, when the wounded prince thus spoke to Rustem: "I do not ascribe my misfortune to thee, but to an all-ruling power. Fate would have it so, and thus it is! I now consign to thy care and guardianship my son Bahman: instruct him in the science of government, the customs of kings, and the rules and stratagems of the warrior, for thou art exceedingly wise and experienced, and perfect in all things," Rustem readily complied, and said:

> *"That duty shall be mine alone,*
> *To seat him firmly on the throne."*

Then Isfendiyár murmured to Bashútan, that the anguish of his wound was wearing him away, and that he had but a short time to live. He now groaned heavily, and his last words were:

> *"I die, pursued by unrelenting fate,*
> *The hapless victim of a father's hate."*

Life having departed, his body was placed upon a bier, and conveyed to Irán, amidst the tears and lamentations of the people.

Rustem now took charge of Bahman, according to the dying request of Isfendiyár, and brought him to Sístán. This was, however, repugnant to the wishes of Zúára, who observed to his brother: "Thou hast slain the father of this youth; do not therefore nurture and instruct the son of thy enemy, for, mark me, in the end he will be avenged." "But did not Isfendiyár, with his last breath, consign him to my guardianship? how can I refuse it now? It must be so written and determined in the dispensations of Heaven."

The arrival of the bier in Persia, at the palace of Gushtásp, produced a melancholy scene of public and domestic affliction. The king took off the covering and wept bitterly, and the mother and sisters exclaimed, "Alas! thy death is not the work of human hands; it is not the work of Rustem, nor of Zál, but of the Símúrgh. Thou hast not lived long enough to be ashamed of a gray beard, nor to witness the maturity and attainments of thy children. Alas! thou art snatched away at a moment of the highest promise, even at the commencement of thy glory." In the meanwhile the curses and imprecations of the people were poured upon the devoted head of Gushtásp on account of his cruel and unnatural conduct, so that he was obliged to confine himself to his palace till after the interment of Isfendiyár.

Rustem scrupulously fulfilled his engagement, and instructed Bahman in all manly exercises; in the use of bow and javelin, in the management of sword and buckler, and in all the arts and accomplishments of the warrior. He then wrote to Gushtásp, repeating that he was unblamable in the conflict which terminated in the death of his son Isfendiyár, that he had offered him presents and wealth to a vast extent, and moreover was ready to return with him to Irán, to his father; but every overture was rejected. Relentless fate must have hurried him on to a premature death. "I have now," continued Rustem, "completed the education of Bahman, according to the directions of his father, and await thy further commands." Gushtásp, after reading this letter, referred to Bashútan, who confirmed the declarations of Rustem, and the treacherous king, willing to ascribe the event to an overruling destiny, readily acquitted Rustem of all guilt in killing Isfendiyár. At the same time he sent for Bahman, and on his arrival from Sístán, was so pleased with him that he without hesitation appointed him to succeed to the throne.

The Death of Rustem

FIRDUSI SEEMS to have derived the account of Shughad, and the melancholy fate of Rustem, from a descendant of Sám and Narímán, who was particularly acquainted with the chronicles of the heroes and the kings of Persia. Shughad, it appears, was the son of Zál, by one of the old warrior's maid-servants, and at his very birth the astrologers predicted that he would be the ruin of the glorious house of Sám and Narímán, and the destruction of their race.

> *Throughout Sístán the prophecy was heard*
> *With horror and amazement; every town*
> *And city in Irán was full of woe,*
> *And Zál, in deepest agony and grief,*
> *Sent up his prayers to the Almighty Power*
> *That he would purify the infant's heart,*
> *And free it from that quality, foretold*
> *As the destroyer of his ancient house.*
> *But what are prayers, opposed by destiny?*

The child, notwithstanding, was brought up with great care and attention, and when arrived at maturity, he was sent to the king of Kábul, whose daughter he espoused.

Rustem was accustomed to go to Kábul every year to receive the tribute due to him; but on the last occasion, it is said that he exacted and took a higher rate than usual, and thus put many of the people to distress. The king was angry, and expressed his dissatisfaction to Shughad, who was not slow in uttering his own discontent, saying, "Though I am his brother, he has no respect for me, but treats me always like an enemy. For this personal hostility I long to punish him with death." – "But how," inquired the king, "couldst thou compass that end?" Shughad replied, "I have well considered the subject, and propose to accomplish my purpose in this manner. I shall feign that I have been insulted and injured by thee, and carry my complaint to Zál and Rustem, who will no doubt come to Kábul to redress my wrongs. Thou must in the meantime prepare for a sporting excursion, and order a number of pits to be dug on the road sufficiently large to hold Rustem and his horse, and in each several swords must be placed with their points and edges upwards. The mouths of the pits must then be slightly covered over, but so carefully that there may be no appearance of the earth underneath having been removed. Everything being thus ready, Rustem, on the pretence of going to the sporting ground, must be conducted by that road, and he will certainly fall into one of the pits, which will become his grave." This stratagem was highly approved by the king, and it was agreed that at a royal banquet, Shughad should revile and irritate the king, whose indignant answer should be before all the assembly: "Thou hast no pretensions to be thought of the stock of Sám and Narímán. Zál pays thee no attention, at least, not such attention as he would pay to a son, and Rustem declares thou art not his brother; indeed, all the family treat thee as a slave." At these words, Shughad affected to be greatly enraged, and, starting up from the banquet, hastened to Rustem to complain of the insult offered him by the king of Kábul. Rustem received him with demonstrations of affection, and hearing his complaint, declared that he would immediately proceed to Kábul, depose the king for his insolence, and place Shughad himself on the throne of that country. In a short time they arrived at the city, and were met by the king, who, with naked feet and in humble guise, solicited forgiveness. Rustem was induced to pardon the offence, and was honored in return with great apparent respect, and with boundless hospitality. In the meantime, however, the pits were dug, and the work of destruction in progress, and Rustem was now invited to share the sports of the forest. The champion was highly gratified by the courtesy which the king displayed, and mounted Rakush, anticipating a day of excellent diversion. Shughad accompanied him, keeping on one side, whilst Rustem, suspecting nothing, rode boldly forward. Suddenly Rakush stopped, and though urged to advance, refused to move a step. At last the champion became angry, and struck the noble animal severely; the blows made him dart forward, and in a moment he unfortunately fell into one of the pits.

> *It was a place, deep, dark, and perilous,*
> *All bristled o'er with swords, leaving no chance*
> *Of extrication without cruel wounds;*
> *And horse and rider sinking in the midst,*
> *Bore many a grievous stab and many a cut*
> *In limb and body, ghastly to the sight.*
> *Yet from that depth, at one prodigious spring,*
> *Rakush escaped with Rustem on his back;*
> *But what availed that effort? Down again*
> *Into another pit both fell together,*
> *And yet again they rose, again, again;*
> *Seven times down prostrate, seven times bruised and maimed,*
> *They struggled on, till mounting up the edge*
> *Of the seventh pit, all covered with deep wounds,*
> *Both lay exhausted. When the champion's brain*

Grew cool, and he had power to think, he knew
Full well to whom he owed this treachery,
And calling to Shughad, said: "Thou, my brother!
Why hast thou done this wrong? Was it for thee,
My father's son, by wicked plot and fraud
To work this ruin, to destroy my life?"
Shughad thus sternly answered: "'Tis for all
The blood that thou hast shed, God has decreed
This awful vengeance – now thy time is come!"
Then spoke the king of Kábul, as if pity
Had softened his false heart: "Alas! the day
That thou shouldst perish, so ignobly too,
And in my kingdom; what a wretched fate!
But bring some medicine to relieve his wounds—
Quick, bring the matchless balm for Rustem's cure;
He must not die, the champion must not die!"
But Rustem scorned the offer, and in wrath,
Thus spoke: "How many a mighty king has died,
And left me still triumphant – still in power,
Unconquerable; treacherous thou hast been,
Inhuman, too, but Ferámurz, the brave,
Will be revenged upon thee for this crime."

Rustem now turned towards Shughad, and in an altered and mournful tone, told him that he was at the point of death, and asked him to string his bow and give it to him, that he might seem as a scare-crow, to prevent the wolves and other wild animals from devouring him when dead.

Shughad performed the task, and lingered not,
For he rejoiced at this catastrophe,
And with a smile of fiendish satisfaction,
Placed the strong bow before him – Rustem grasped
The bended horn with such an eager hand,
That wondering at the sight, the caitiff wretch
Shuddered with terror, and behind a tree

Shielded himself, but nothing could avail;
The arrow pierced both tree and him, and they
Were thus transfixed together – thus the hour
Of death afforded one bright gleam of joy
To Rustem, who, with lifted eyes to Heaven,
Exclaimed: "Thanksgivings to the great Creator,
For granting me the power, with my own hand,
To be revenged upon my murderer!"
So saying, the great champion breathed his last,
And not a knightly follower remained,
Zúára, and the rest, in other pits,
Dug by the traitor-king, and traitor-brother,
Had sunk and perished, all, save one, who fled,
And to the afflicted veteran at Sístán
Told the sad tidings. Zál, in agony,
Tore his white hair, and wildly rent his garments,
And cried: "Why did not I die for him, why
Was I not present, fighting by his side?
But he, alas! is gone! Oh! gone forever."

Then the old man despatched Ferámurz with a numerous force to Kábul, to bring away the dead body of Rustem. Upon his approach, the king of Kábul and his army retired to the mountains, and Ferámurz laid waste the country. He found only the skeletons of Rustem and Zúára, the beasts of prey having stripped them of their flesh: he however gathered the bones together and conveyed them home and buried them, amidst the lamentations of the people. After that, he returned to Kábul with his army, and encountered the king, captured the cruel wretch, and carried him to Sístán, where he was put to death.

Gushtásp having become old and infirm, bequeathed his empire to Bahman, and then died. He reigned one hundred and eight years.

Nizami

THE GREATEST poet of the twelfth century was Nizami (*c.* 1141–1209), whose pathetic love songs are the best productions of the kind in the Persian tongue. He lived the greater part of his life at Ganja, and is therefore known as Nizami of Ganja.

His first important work was called *The Storehouse of Mysteries.* This was followed by the beautiful poem of *Koshru and Shirin,* the theme of which was taken from ancient Persian history. In the latter part of the twelfth century he wrote his *Diwan,* a collection which was said to contain twenty thousand verses, but few of these, however, have come down to our own times. Soon afterward the great poet wrote his famous love story entitled *Laili and Majnun,* which was followed by his *Book of Alexander,* an epic which was devoted to the glory of the Greek conqueror. His last work was the *Haft Paikar,* also known as the *Seven Fair Faces,* and this was presented in the form of romantic fiction, and consisted merely of seven stories which were told to amuse the king by the seven wives of Bohram Gor. These five works are known as the *Five Treasures of Nizami.* His eulogies were sung by the greatest Persian poets who lived after him.

It was of him that Sa'di wrote: "Gone is Nizami, our exquisite pearl, which Heaven in its kindness, formed of the purest dew, as the gem of the world."

Khosru and Shireen

KHOSRU PARVIZ lived A.D. 590: he was a prince of exalted virtues and great magnificence: he fought against the Greek emperors with success, hut was at last defeated by Heraclius. He is said to have married a daughter of the Greek Emperor Maurice, named Irene, called by the Persians Shireen, or Sweet.

Ferhad's history forms a tragical episode in this romance. He was a sculptor, celebrated throughout the East for his great genius, and was daring enough to fix his affections on the beloved of the King. The jealousy of Khosru was excited, and he lamented to his courtiers the existence of a passion which was so violent as not to be concealed, and which gave him great uneasiness. He was recommended to employ Ferhad in such a manner as to occupy his whole life, and divert him from his dangerous dream: accordingly, as on one occasion the fair Shireen had, somewhat unreasonably, required of her royal lover a river of milk, he made this desire a pretext for the labors he imposed on his presumptuous rival.

Ferhad was summoned to the presence of Khosru, and commissioned by the King to execute a work which should render his name immortal, but one which, to accomplish, demanded almost superhuman powers. This was to clear away all impediments which obstructed the passage of the great mountain of Beysitoun, at that time impassable in consequence of its mighty masses of rock and stone. He commanded him, after having done this, to cause the rivers on the opposite side of the mountain to join.

Ferhad, nothing daunted, replied that he would remove the very heart of the rock from the King's path; but on condition that the lovely Shireen should be the reward of his labors. Khosru, secretly triumphing in the conviction that what the artist undertook was impossible, consented to his terms, and the indefatigable lover began his work.

The Labors of Ferhad

On lofty Beysitoun the lingering sun
Looks down on ceaseless labors, long begun:
The mountain trembles to the echoing sound

Of falling rocks, that from her sides rebound.
Each day all respite, all repose denied —
No truce, no pause, the thundering strokes are plied;
The mist of night around her summit coils,
But still Ferhad, the lover-artist, toils,
And still – the flashes of his axe between —
He sighs to ev'ry wind, "Alas! Shireen!
Alas! Shireen! – my task is well-nigh done,
The goal in view for which I strive alone.
Love grants me powers that Nature might deny;
And, whatsoe'er my doom, the world shall tell,
Thy lover gave to immortality
Her name he loved – so fatally – so well!

[The enamored sculptor prophesied aright; for the wonderful efforts made by this "slave of love" left imperishable monuments of his devotion, in the carved caverns which, to this day, excite the amazement and admiration of the traveler who visits the Kesr-e-Shireen, or "Villa of Shireen," and follows the stream called Joui-shur, or "stream of milk," which flows from the mountain, between Hamadan and Hulwan.

Ferhad first constructed a recess or chamber in the rock, wherein he carved the figure of Shireen, near the front of the opening: she was represented surrounded by attendants and guards; while in the center of the cave was an equestrian statue of Khosru, clothed in armor, the workmanship so exquisite that the nails and buttons of the coat of mail were clearly to be seen, and are still said to be so. An eye-witness says: "Whoso looks on the stone would imagine it to be animated." The chamber and the statues still remain there. As Ferhad continued to hew away pieces of the rock, which "are like so many columns," the task was soon performed. The vestiges of the chisel remain, so that the sculptures ap- pear recent. The horse of Khosru was exquisitely carved: it was called Shebdiz.]

The Great Work

A hundred arms were weak one block to move
Of thousands, molded by the hand of Love
Into fantastic shapes and forms of grace,

Which crowd each nook of that majestic place.
The piles give way, the rocky peaks divide,
The stream comes gushing on – a foaming tide!
A mighty work, for ages to remain,
The token of his passion and his pain.
As flows the milky flood from Allah's throne
Hushes the torrent from the yielding stone;
And sculptured there, amazed, stern Khosru stands,
And sees, with frowns, obeyed his harsh commands:
While she, the fair beloved, with being rife,
Awakes the glowing marble into life.
Ah! hapless youth; ah! toil repaid by woe —
A king thy rival and the world thy foe!
Will she wealth, splendor, pomp for thee resign —
And only genius, truth, and passion thine!
Around the pair, lo! groups of courtiers wait,
And slaves and pages crowd in solemn state;
From columns imaged wreaths their garlands throw,
And fretted roofs with stars appear to glow!
Fresh leaves and blossoms seem around to spring,
And feathered throngs their loves are murmuring;
The hands of Peris might have wrought those stems,
Where dewdrops hang their fragile diadems;
And strings of pearl and sharp-cut diamonds shine,
New from the wave, or recent from the mine.
"Alas! Shireen!" at every stroke he cries;
At every stroke fresh miracles arise:
"For thee these glories and these wonders all,
For thee I triumph, or for thee I fall;
For thee my life one ceaseless toil has been,
Inspire my soul anew: Alas! Shireen!"

[The task of the rival of Khosru was at length completed, and the King heard with dismay of his success: all the cour- tiers were terrified at the result of their advice, and saw that some further stratagem was necessary. They therefore engaged an old

woman who had been known to Ferhad, and in whom he had confidence, to report
to him tidings which would at once destroy his hopes.]

The Messenger

What raven note disturbs his musing mood?
What form comes stealing on his solitude?
Ungentle messenger, whose word of ill
All the warm feelings of his soul can chill!
"Cease, idle youth, to waste thy days," she said,
"By empty hopes a visionary made;
Why in vain toil thy fleeting life consume
To frame a palace? – rather hew a tomb.
Even like sere leaves that autumn winds have shed,
Perish thy labors, for – Shireen is dead!"
He heard the fatal news – no word, no groan;
He spoke not, moved not, stood transfixed to stone.
Then, with a frenzied start, he raised on high
His arms, and wildly tossed them toward the sky;
Far in the wide expanse his axe he flung
And from the precipice at once he sprung.
The rocks, the sculptured caves, the valleys green,
Sent back his dying cry – "Alas! Shireen!"

[The legend goes on to relate that the handle of the axe flung away by Ferhad, being
of pomegranate wood, took root on the spot where it fell, and became a flourishing tree:
it possessed healing powers, and was much resorted to by believers long afterward.

Khosru, on learning this catastrophe, did not conceal his satisfaction, but liberally
rewarded the old woman who had caused so fatal a termination to the career of his
rival; but the gentle-hearted Shireen heard of his fate with grief, and shed many tears
on his tomb.

The charms of Shireen were destined to create mischief, for the King had a son
by a former marriage, who became enamored of his fatally beautiful step-mother.
His father, Khosru, was, in the end, murdered by his hand, and Shireen became the
object of his importunities. Wearied, at length, with constant struggles, she feigned to

give him a favorable answer, and promised, if he would permit her to visit the grave of her husband, when she returned she would be his. Shireen accordingly went on her melancholy errand, and, true to her affection for her beloved Khosru, stabbed herself, and died upon his tomb.]

Laili and Majnun

EVERY NATION has its favorite romance of love and chivalry. France and Italy have their Abelard and Eloisa, their Petrarch and Laura, while Arabia and Persia have their Laili and Majnun, the record of whose sorrows is constantly referred to throughout the East as an example of the most devoted affection. This story, which has been versified by several Persian authors, is of Arabian origin, and hence it bears the impress of Arabic thought.

The poem contains the mystic lights and shadows of Bedawin life – the fervid loves and passionate yearnings, the hopeless grief and stoical endurance, which belong to the sons of the desert.

Majnun was the son of a haughty chief, while Laili belonged to an humble Arab tribe, but her father carried in his veins the pride of his desert race, and the bitter hatreds of the Moslems. Laili is described as being very beautiful, with the crimson of her cheek flashing through the dark olive shades of her face, and her heavy ringlets, "black as night," hanging in graceful profusion around her shapely neck.

> *"When ringlets of a thousand curls*
> *And ruby lips and teeth of pearls,*
> *And dark eyes flashing quick and bright,*
> *Like lightning on the brow of night—*
> *When charms like these their power display*
> *And steal the wildered heart away—*
> *Can man, dissembling, coldly seem*
> *Unmoved as by an idle dream?*

> *Kais saw her beauty, and her grace*
> *The soft expression of her face;*
> *And as he gazed and gazed again*
> *Distraction stung his burning brain;*
> *No rest he found by day or night—*
> *She was forever in his sight."*

But the wandering tribe to which the girl belonged folded their tents and slipped away to the solitudes of the mountains. They had left no trace of their going – no hint of where they might be found, and the luckless maid found herself far from her lover with no possible means of communicating with him, while the frantic boy was wandering through the wilds in the almost hopeless search for his love.

> *"He sought her in rosy bower and silent glade,*
> *Where the palm trees flung refreshing shade;*
> *Through grove and frowning glen he lonely strayed,*
> *And with his griefs the rocks were vocal made."*

Alarmed by the condition of his son, the old chieftain gathered his men for an organized search, and at last they found the mountain stronghold of the tribe they sought. They were challenged by a stern voice beyond the rocky barriers, which demanded:

> *"Come ye hither as friends or foes?*
> *Whatever may your errand be,*
> *That errand must be told to me;*
> *For none, unless a sanctioned friend,*
> *Can pass the line that I defend."*

This challenge touched the chieftain's pride, and he haughtily responded that he came in friendship, to propose the marriage of his son to the Arab maiden to whom he had taken a silly fancy.

> *"With shame,*
> *Possess'd of power, and wealth, and fame,*
> *I to his silly humor bend,*

> *And humbly seek his fate to blend*
> *With one inferior. Need I tell*
> *My own high lineage known so well?*
> *If sympathy my heart incline,*
> *Or vengeance, still the means are mine.*
> *Treasure and arms can amply bear*
> *Me through the toils of desert war;*
> *But thou'rt the merchant pedler chief,*
> *And I the buyer; come, sell, be brief!*
> *If thou art wise, accept advice;*
> *Sell and receive a princely price!"*

The haughty tone of the applicant was little calculated to call forth a favorable response, and the proud father replied:

> *"Madness is neither sin nor crime, we know,*
> *But who'd be linked to madness or a foe?*
> *Thy son is mad – his senses first restore;*
> *In constant prayer the aid of heaven implore.*
> *But while portentous gloom pervades his brain*
> *Disturb me not with this vain suit again.*
> *The jewel sense no purchaser can buy,*
> *Nor treachery the place of sense supply.*
> *Thou hast my reasons, and this parley o'er,*
> *Keep them in mind and trouble me no more."*

The scorn of the father's reply had been, if possible, more bitter than the insulting demand, and Syd Omri turned indignantly to his followers and ordered the homeward march. The desert fates were stern, and

> *"When Majnun saw his hopes decay,*
> *Their fairest blossoms fade away,*
> *And friends and sire who might have been*
> *Kind intercessors, rush between*
> *Him and the only wish that shed*

> *One ray of comfort round his head,*
> *He beat his hands, his garments tore,*
> *He cast his fetters on the floor*
> *In broken fragments, and in wrath*
> *Sought the dark wilderness's path,*
> *And there he wept and sobbed aloud,*
> *Unnoticed by the gazing crowd."*

The kinsmen of Laili brought to the encampment the news that a youth, insane and wild, was haunting the desert wastes below the mountain, and the fair Laili blushed when she heard the tidings, but dared not venture forth to meet her maniac lover. The Arab chief swore vengeance against the hapless youth, and ordered his followers to slay him in the desert. The father of Majnun heard of the cruel decree and sent his own followers into the wilderness to rescue his son.... Again and again he was carried to his father's home, and as frequently he made his escape, always wandering, with unerring instinct, near to his beloved.

> *"Laili in beauty, softness, grace,*
> *Surpassed the loveliest of her race.*
> *The killing witchery that lies*
> *In her soft, black, delicious eyes—*
> *Her lashes speak a thousand blisses*
> *Her lips of ruby ask for kisses;*
> *Her cheeks, so beautiful and bright,*
> *Have caught the moon's refulgent light;*
> *Her form the Cypress tree expresses,*
> *And full and plump, invites caresses.*
> *With all these charms, the heart to win,*
> *There was a ceaseless grief within,—*
> *Yet none beheld her grief, or heard,*
> *She droop'd like broken-winged bird.*
> *Her secret thoughts, her love concealing,*
> *But softly to the terrace stealing*
> *From morn to eve, she gazed around*
> *In hopes her Majnun might be found."*

An oasis with its cooling streams was near the rocky fortress of the Bedawin encampment, and here the tall palms seemed to lean against the sky, while the doves cooed in the thickets of foliage. Here the gentle Laili came day after day, hoping that her lover might venture near. She gathered the lilies that bloomed around her feet, as she wandered through the fragrant grove, but her dark eyes were heavy with unshed tears, when she reclined beneath a mournful cypress tree and softly chanted her song of faithfulness:

> *"Oh, faithful friend and lover true,*
> *Still distant from thy Laili's view;*
> *Still absent, still beyond her power,*
> *To bring thee to her fragrant bower;*
> *Oh noble youth! still thou art mine,*
> *And Laili, Laili still is thine."*

As she pensively sat one day beneath the cypress tree, a youth of kingly mien passed that way. His eyes rested a moment upon her crimson lips, and the flowing tresses which were dark as the plume of a raven's wing – he saw too the full form with its shapely curves and the beaming softness of the dark eyes, with their heavy lashes. Ibn Salam was the honored name of this young prince, who with his suite had sought for a moment the cooling shades of the palm-tree grove, and he it was who hastened to her father with a plea for his daughter's hand. Dazzled by the gold and position of the suitor, the father of Laili gave a cordial consent to the proposed union.

A Friend

The chief of the domain where Majnun wandered in his pitiful loneliness, looked with compassion upon him, for one day, while in pursuit of a bounding deer, he saw the wasted frame and wild look of the despairing lover. Dismounting from his splendid steed, Noufal, the Arab chief, came kindly to him and listened to the story so constantly told of love and suffering. With kindly words the chieftain soothed the restless spirit, and gently drawing the tortured mind away from its painful thought he offered nourishment to the sinking body. A change for the better came over him, and he took the proffered cup and drank, although he drank to Laili's name. Refreshed by Noufal's kindly ministry and drawn by gentle urging, Majnun went with his new friend to his home, and there received the best of care and hopeful cheer.

"An altered man, his mind at rest,
In customary robes he dressed;
A turban shades his forehead pale,
No more is heard the lover's wail,
His dungeon gloom exchanged for day,
His cheeks a rosy tint display;
He revels midst the garden sweets,
And still his lip the goblet meets;
But so intense his constant flame
Each cup is quaffed in Laili's name."

The generous Noufal was not content with the change so nearly wrought, but he gathered his bravest men in battle array, and marched at their head to the mountain fortress of the Bedawin encampment. The troops of Arabian horsemen were halted and sword and helmet glittered in the sun, while Noufal sent his messenger forward with a demand for the hand of the coveted bride. His request was haughtily refused, and when the messenger was again sent forward with a threat of revenge if his wishes were not complied with, his power and vengeance were alike defied. Then the word of command rang along the glittering lines. There was a rattling of helmets and spears, a twanging of the bowstring and a gallant charge was made upon the foe that was so well entrenched in the mountain fastnesses. Amidst the clangor of brazen drums and trumpets, the fearful fight went on and

"Arrows, like birds, on either foeman stood,
Drinking with open beak the vital flood;
The shining daggers in the battle's heat
Rolled many a head beneath the horse's feet;
And lightnings hurled by death's unsparing hand
Spread consternation through the weeping land."

There was no pause in the sound of the trumpets, no stay in the wild flight of the arrows, as the dreadful work went on, and the dripping swords were bathed with the crimson tide of shame.

The shades of night came down ere the fate of the battle was decided, but the assaulting party had suffered most, and in another hour of conflict the friends of

Majnun had been undone. With the coming of the morning light the assault was renewed, and the desert rang again with the sounds of war; all along the long line glittered the sword and buckler, the helmet and spear; swords clashed and the desert sands were wet again with the blood of the fallen. At last the tribe of Laili's sire gave way, and Noufal won the bitter fight, though many of his bravest men lay bleeding on the burning sand.

> "And now the elders of that tribe appear,
> And thus implore the victor. Chieftain, hear!
> The work of slaughter is complete;
> Thou seest our power destroyed; allow
> Us wretched suppliants at thy feet
> To humbly ask for mercy now.
> How many warriors press the plain?
> Khanjer and spear have laid them low;
> At peace, behold our kinsman slain,
> For thou art now without a foe.
> Then pardon what of wrong has been;
> Let us retire unharmed – unstay'd—
> Far from this sanguinary scene,
> And take thy prize – the Arab maid."

The aged father came forth with dust and ashes upon his hoary head, and admitted that his tribe was fully conquered, and offered the life of his daughter for a peace offering, while still refusing to allow her to wed with a maniac.

> "My daughter shall be brought at thy command;
> The red flames may ascend from blazing brand
> And slay their victim, crackling in the air,
> And Laili dutiously shall perish there.
> Or, if thou'dst rather see the maiden bleed,
> This thirsty sword shall do the dreadful deed;
> Dissever at one blow that lovely head,
> Her sinless blood by her own father shed!
> In all things thou shalt find me faithful, true,
> Thy slave I am – what would'st thou have me do?

But mark me; I am not to be beguiled;
I will not to a demon give my child;
I will not to a madman's wild embrace
Consign the pride and honor of my race,
And wed her to contempt and foul disgrace."

The chivalry of the desert disdained to tear the child from her father's arms, even though that father was a conquered foe. The gallant Noufal, feeling that he was himself defeated, and that in vain the blood of his brave men had stained the desert sands, sadly gave the order that the conquered tribe should be allowed to retire unmolested from the well fought field.

"And thou and thine may quit the field.
Still armed with khanjer, sword and shield;
Both horse and rider. Thus in vain
Blood has bedewed this thirsty plain."

With a heavy heart the gallant chief pursued his homeward way with Majnun, reckless and desperate, by his side. He tried again to calm the poignant pangs of hopeless love, and to bless, with gentleness and tender care, the wounded and despairing spirit.

"But vain his efforts; mountain, wood and plain
Soon heard the maniac's piercing woes again;
Escaped from listening ear and watchful eye,
Lonely again, in desert wild to lie."

In another part of the wild domain a cloud of dust on the horizon of the desert tells of the coming of a troop of horsemen, and soon a wearied and broken column is seen beneath the clouds of sand which obscure the blue of heaven. The women of the conquered tribe, who had been placed in safer quarters, come forth to meet the returning warriors. As the trampling steeds come nearer they hear the leader's angry word, as he breathes his curses, loud and deep, upon the victor in the fight, for he scarcely cares to survive the blow while burning with the disgrace of defeat. Poor Laili listens sadly to the story of her fate, but no hope of aid can enter her crushed and broken heart. And still the story of her beauty is borne on every gale, and the neighboring tribes are wondering for whom her father is keeping the beauteous gem.

The Wedding

At last, the lover comes with his magnificent offerings of embroidered robes, and carpets worked with silk and gold; the rarest gems were brought to lay at her feet, and a long line of camels, with their tinkling bells, were laden with costly presents for the bride of Ibn Salam.

Beautiful steeds were proudly stepping to the low music of his march, for a long line of the purest Arabian blood was coursing in their veins. But while the nuptial pomp and nuptial rites engaged the chieftain's household, and every square was ringing with the rattle of drums and the voice of pipe and cymbal, the stricken bride was sitting sad and lone in her retreat, mourning for her betrothed, and pleading that she might be allowed to die rather than to wed the man that she could never love. The joyous bridegroom came with gorgeous litter and golden throne for the chosen bride to occupy. He came in richest garb, with happy smiles and costly jewels, into the presence of his promised bride, but the Arabian maiden turned with flashing eyes upon the intruder, and informed him that the betrothal had been made by her father without consulting her. She declared she would rather die than become a wife unloving, for in her heart she could find only hatred for the man who was willing to claim her under circumstances so revolting, and then with the air of a queen she ordered him to leave her alone. When Ibn Salam heard her frenzied words, he turned away from the indignant girl and poured his woes into her father's ear. The pitiful pleadings of the girl were unheeded, and the fearful mockery of marriage went on amidst the glare of trumpets and sounding drum, – went on, with jewels and costly gifts for the unwilling bride, and all the outward show of happiness and joy. But though Laili's plighted faith to Majnun seemed so sorely broken, she still cherished his memory with tenderest thought, and

> "Deep in her heart a thousand woes
> Disturbed her days' and nights' repose
> A serpent at its very core
> Writhing and gnawing evermore;
> And no relief – a prison room
> Being now the lonely sufferer's doom."

Amidst all the heartaches of humanity the slow movement of sun and stars still goes on, and the bare horizon of the desert is illumined by the lamps of heaven. Night with her coolness and dews, comes down upon the burning sands with the restful touch of peace. Her primeval fountains of light have gathered for all time around the desert steppes, watching their silent mysteries, and touching with glory the far-away crowns of their palms.

Laili sat in her prison tower, looking out upon the peaceful beauty of the night, and its soft repose crept into her troubled heart, bringing with it a message of hope. For days and years she had lived within that guarded tower, shut like a gem within its stony bed, surrounded by the dragon watch which her husband still supplied. But hark! there is an unusual sound beneath her casement; there are flickering lamps and wailing cries; confused voices are bearing messages to and fro; there is a death-note in the wild chant which is ringing out upon the night.

> "Beneath her casement rings a wild lament,
> Death-notes disturb the night; the air is rent
> With clamorous voices; every hope is fled,
> He breathes no longer – Ibn Salam is dead!
> The fever's rage had nipp'd him in his bloom;
> He sank unloved, unpitied, to the tomb."

Laili looked up to the face of the moon, and thought of its chilling rays that fell upon the haggard form of her desert love. She gazed upon the flashing star that stood like a guardian above his restless sleep, and then she turned to receive the messengers who brought the formal tale that her jailor now was dead. And must she mourn for the man she loathed? Ah, yes; the Arab law must be obeyed, and she must assume the garments of woe! It was easy for her to weep,

> "But all the burning tears she shed
> Were for Majnun, not the dead.'"

The days went by with weary feet, and the night still looked upon a lonely heart, for the Arab law maintained that years must pass before one breath of freedom could be given to the woman in the rock-bound tower. But Laili arose one morn with a new light in her dark eyes, and called her faithful Zyd, the boy who had long served his gentle lady, and to whom her word was the law supreme. To him she said:

> *"To-day is not the day of hope,*
> *Which only gives to fancy scope;*
> *It is the day our hopes completing,*
> *It is the lover's day of meeting!*
> *Rise up! the world is full of joy;*
> *Rise up! and serve thy mistress, boy;*
> *Together, where the cypress grows,*
> *Place the red tulip and the rose;*
> *And let the long dissever'd meet—*
> *Two lovers, in communion sweet."*

The Meeting in the Desert

Then with her faithful attendant she went cautiously forth, and together they threaded their way over the desolate sand and through the grove of palms; but she stayed not to gather the lilies blooming around her feet – she waited not to catch the breath of the roses, or to drink of the tiny stream, whose life-giving waves had made this little oasis to bloom like a garden in the midst of the desert. But she hastened on her way, and the boy ran by her side wondering why she sped so quickly through the grove. On, beyond its cooling shade and over the barren steepes, she pressed with unfaltering feet until she saw the haggard form of her lover; then she stepped gently to his side and laid her hand upon his arm. "Ah! Majnun, it is thy Laili that has come;" his mind awoke with one glad cry, for the familiar voice with its caressing tones rang with the notes of peace and joy through the darkened chambers of his brain. For one glad moment he held her in his arms, and then, overcome with emotion, he fainted at her feet. She quickly knelt beside him, and then

> *"His head which in the dust was laid*
> *Upon her lap she drew, and dried*
> *His tears with tender hand and pressed*
> *Him close and closer to her breast;*
> *'Be here thy home beloved, adored,*

Revive, be blest; – oh! Laili's lord.'
At last he breathed, around he gazed,
As from her arms his head he raised—
'Art thou,' he faintly said, 'a friend
Who takes me to her gentle breast—
Dost thou in truth so fondly bend
Thine eyes upon a wretch distressed?
Are these thy unveiled cheeks I see
Can bliss be yet in store for me?
I thought it all a dream, so oft
Such dreams come in my madness now.
Is this thy hand so fair and soft?
Is this in sooth my Laili's brow?
In sleep these transports I may share
But when I wake 'tis all despair!
Let me gaze on thee – e'en though it be
An empty shade alone I see;
How shall I bear what once I bore
When thou shalt vanish as before?'"

Then the beauteous vision rested within his arms, with her dark ringlets flowing around her smooth neck, and the sweet confession of her love beaming in her tremulous eyes. He saw her chin of dimpled sweetness, and the soft cheek with its crimson flush, then her matchless voice came again to his ears with its message of tenderness.

"To hope, dear wanderer, revive;
Lo Zemzems, cool and bright,
Flow at thy feet – then drink and live
Seared heart! be glad for bounteous heaven
At length our recompense hath given,
Beloved one, tell me all thy will
And know thy Laili faithful still.
Here in this desert, join our hands,
Our souls were joined long, long before;
And if our fate such doom demands,

Together wander evermore.
Oh Kais! never let us part,
What is the world to thee and me?
My universe is where thou art
And is not Laili all to thee?"

The tempted lover listened, with his soul in his longing eyes, but he knew that he could not make her his wife according to the Arab law – they could not be legally wedded, and his love for her was too pure and unselfish to accept the sacrifice that she proposed to make. To him, then, was given the hardest task ever given into lover's hands – that of saving the woman that he worshipped from his own embrace. After the years of suffering that had been his, could he push the tempting cup from his thirsting lip? Was the weakened frame strong enough to carry out the dictates of his will? Nay, did God require such a sacrifice after all these years of loyalty and truth? Were they not already wedded in his pure sight? Had she not always been his own in the eyes of heaven? These questions surged through his throbbing brain as he held the woman he loved in his close embrace. One sweet taste of heaven, surely the Lord had given, in the desert of his wasted life – one moment of bliss wherein he might taste the lips he had hungered for, so long. But should he therefore outrage his own conscience, and sacrifice the woman he loved, for the temporary enjoyment of the present life? His manhood and his conscience answered, never. He clasped her closer to his aching heart – he kissed again the tempting lips – his eyes lingered with one long sad look upon the lovely face, and then he slowly answered:

"How well, how fatally I love,
My madness and my misery prove;
All earthly hopes I could resign—
Nay, life itself, to call thee mine.
But shall I make thy spotless name—
That sacred spell – a word of shame?
Shall selfish Majnun's heart be blest
And Laili prove the Arab's jest?
The city's gates though we may close
We cannot still our conscience's throes.
No – we have met, – a moment's bliss

Has dawned upon my gloom in vain
Life yields no more a joy like this,
And all to come can be but pain.
Thou, thou, adored! might be mine own
A thousand deaths let Majnun die
Ere but a breath by slander blown
Should sully Laili's purity!
Go, then – and to thy tribe return,
Fly from my arms that clasp thee yet;
I feel my brain with frenzy burn—
Oh, joy, could I but thus forget!"

With another kiss upon the silent lips – another close embrace, the manly lover tore himself away to another struggle between death and life; still warring in the unequal strife with fate, he told to the desert wind, his piteous tale:

"The fevered thoughts that on me prey
Death's sea alone can sweep away.
I found the bird of Paradise
That long I sought with care;
Fate snatched it from my longing eyes—
I held – despair.
Wail, Laili, wail our fortunes crossed,
Weep, Majnun, weep – forever lost."

Death of the Lovers

Time passed by on leaden feet, for he no longer carried in his hands the flowers of hope. No longer the bare horizon of the desert was illumined with the mirage of rivers and palms. Fate had done her worst, and Death, the great consoler, waited near to place his seal with the touch of peace upon the weary brow. The flower of the desert lay again in the tower where she had passed so many wasted years, and feeling that her life was going out with the glory of the setting sun, she called her mother to her side and pleaded that when she was gone Majnun might be allowed to weep over her grave.

"Again it was the task of faithful Zyd,
Through far extending plain and forest wide,
To seek the man of woes, and tell
The fate of her, alas! he loved so well.
With bleeding heart he found his lone abode,
Watering with tears the path he rode.
And beating his sad breast, Majnun perceived
His friend approach, and asked him why he grieved?
'Alas!' he cried, 'the hail has crushed my bowers,
A sudden storm has blighted all my flowers;
Thy cypress tree o'erthrown, the leaves are sear;
The moon has fallen from her lucid sphere;
Laili is dead.'"

His sad duty was done, and the bereaved lover lay unconscious at his feet. With gentle ministry the stricken man was roused from his swoon, and then he started toward the loved one's grave.

"Now he threads
The mazes of the shadowy wood, which spreads
Perpetual gloom, and now emerges where
No bower nor grove obstructs the fiery air;
Climbs the mountain's brow, o'er hill and plain
Urged quicker onward by his burning brain,
Across the desert's arid boundary hies
Zyd, like a shadow, following where he flies.
And when the tomb of Laili meets his view,
Prostrate he falls, the ground his tears bedew;
'Alas!' he cries, 'no more shall I behold
That angel face, that form of heavenly mould,
For thou hast quitted this contentious life,
This scene of endless treachery and strife;
And I, like thee, shall soon my fetters burst,
And quench, in draughts of heavenly love, my thirst.
There where angelic bliss can never cloy,

> *We soon shall meet in everlasting joy;*
> *The taper of our souls, more clear and bright,*
> *Will then be lustrous with immortal light.'"*

The troubled day was closing fast in night, and though he received the kindly ministry of his friends, only a few more weeks had passed away, when the stricken lover was found with his head resting lovingly upon her tomb, while upon his loyal brow there rested the peaceful touch of death. His weary heart had found rest at last, rest beyond the fevered dream of life, with all its anxious hopes and fears. Reverent hands opened Laili's tomb, and they laid the stilled heart beside her own.

> *"One promise bound their faithful hearts – one bed*
> *Of cold, cold earth united them when dead.*
> *Severed in life, how cruel was their doom!*
> *Ne'er to be joined but in the silent tomb!"*

The Vision of Zyd

No heart more loyal was left behind than that of the faithful page who so long had done the lady's bidding. He often pondered on the faith and devotion of the lovers, and one night he slept alone beneath the desert sky, when the canopy of heaven seemed to roll away. A new morning seemed to dawn in glory upon the waiting earth, and touch the distant mountain peaks with crowns of light. Beneath the radiance of its coming, the secrets of the earth, which had been written in the roll-call of the ages, were read by the waiting millions, for the age of recompense had come. The desert sands gave way to vistas of golden fruit and blooming roses; the white lilies gleamed amidst the green verdure, and the almond blossoms waved in silvery sprays upon the passing breeze. The nightingale sang in fadeless bowers, and the low, sweet voices of the ring-doves were heard among the feathery plumes of the palms. The desert voices gave way to the rich melodies from harp and shell. The fronded palms pressed upward, and a royal throne, with gems and gold, stood beneath their protecting shade.

> *"Upon that throne, in blissful state,*
> *The long divided lovers sate,*

> *Resplendent with seraphic light,*
> *They held a cup with diamonds bright."*

This cup was filled with the nectar of immortality, and, quaffing its rich contents, they wandered away, hand in hand, through the long aisles of unfading flowers.

> *"The dreamer who this vision saw,*
> *Demanded with becoming awe,*
> *What sacred names the happy pair*
> *In Irem-bowers were wont to bear.*
> *A voice replied: 'That sparkling moon*
> *Is Laili still – her friend Majnun;*
> *Deprived in your frail world of bliss,*
> *They reap their great reward in this!'"*

Zyd wakened from his wondrous dream, and, rejoicing, told the story of his glad vision. The sons of the desert took up the mystic theme, and still repeat the promise that pure and loyal love can never fail of its final reward.

> *"Saki! Nizami's song is sung;*
> *The Persian poet's pearls are strung;*
> *Then fill again the goblet high!*
> *Thou wouldst not ask the reveler why*
> *Fill to the love that changes never!*
> *Fill to the love that lives forever!*
> *That purified by earthly woes,*
> *At last with bliss seraphic glows."*

Masnavi-I-Ma'navi
Jalal-uddin Rumi
Translated by E.H. Whinfield

THE THIRD PERIOD of Persian poetry, which may be called the mystic and moral age, is assigned to the thirteenth century.

It was at this time that Genghis Khan, the Tartar chief, swept like a mountain torrent over the East. His first attack was upon the countries beyond the Oxus, where the devotees of science had taken refuge during the invasion of Persia by the Arabs. Bokhara and Samarcand were then the homes of scholars and the centres of civilization. Their colleges and libraries were celebrated throughout the Orient, but during the great Tartar invasion these cities were both destroyed, being stormed and burned by the Tartar horde, while more than two hundred thousand lives were sacrificed to the cruelty of the invading host. Bagdad was also devastated, the colleges destroyed and the most valuable books in the libraries were thrown into the Tigris.

During these stormy times the courts of the descendants of the Selucidae were sought by scholars as places of refuge, some of their princes being literary men. A prince of this dynasty, by the name of Alladin Kaikubad, became somewhat celebrated in the world of letters, and during his reign Iconium became the refuge of scholars from the Asiatic nations, who felt that on the western frontiers of the continent they were more secure from the attacks of the barbarians. The brightest ornament of this court was the mystic poet and philosopher, Jalal-uddin Rumi (1207–73).

His father was the founder of a college at Iconium in Syria, but after his father's death Jalal-uddin went to Aleppo and Damascus to continue his studies, and finally succeeded to the direction of the college. His literary fame rests upon his *Masnavi I Ma'navi*, a work in six volumes, which is a series of stories with moral maxims. A selection of stories from the first volume are included in this chapter.

The Prince and the Handmaid

A PRINCE, while engaged on a hunting excursion, espied a fair maiden, and by promises of gold induced her to accompany him. After a time she fell sick, and the prince had her tended by divers physicians. As, however, they all omitted to say, "God willing, we will cure her," their treatment was of no avail. So the prince offered prayer, and in answer thereto a physician was sent from heaven. He at once condemned his predecessors' view of the case, and by a very skilful diagnosis, discovered that the real cause of the maiden's illness was her love for a certain goldsmith of Samarcand. In accordance with the physician's advice, the prince sent to Samarcand and fetched the goldsmith, and married him to the lovesick maiden, and for six months the pair lived together in the utmost harmony and happiness. At the end of that period the physician, by divine command, gave the goldsmith a poisonous draught, which caused his strength and beauty to decay, and he then lost favour with the maiden, and she was reunited to the king. This Divine command was precisely similar to God's command to Abraham to slay his son Ishmael, and to the act of the angel in slaying the servant of Moses, and is therefore beyond human criticism.

Description of Love.
A true lover is proved such by his pain of heart;
No sickness is there like sickness of heart.
The lover's ailment is different from all ailments;
Love is the astrolabe of God's mysteries.
A lover may hanker after this love or that love,
But at the last he is drawn to the KING of love.
However much we describe and explain love,
When we fall in love we are ashamed of our words.
Explanation by the tongue makes most things clear,
But love unexplained is clearer.
When pen hasted to write,

On reaching the subject of love it split in twain.
When the discourse touched on the matter of love,
Pen was broken and paper torn.
In explaining it Reason sticks fast, as an ass in mire;
Naught but Love itself can explain love and lovers!
None but the sun can display the sun,
If you would see it displayed, turn not away from it.
Shadows, indeed, may indicate the sun's presence,
But only the sun displays the light of life.
Shadows induce slumber, like evening talks,
But when the sun arises the "moon is split asunder."
In the world there is naught so wondrous as the sun,
But the Sun of the soul sets not and has no yesterday.
Though the material sun is unique and single,
We can conceive similar suns like to it.
But the Sun of the soul, beyond this firmament,
No like thereof is seen in concrete or abstract.
Where is there room in conception for His essence,
So that similitudes of HIM should be conceivable?
Shamsu-'d-Din of Tabriz importunes Jalalu-'d-Din
to compose the Masnavi.
The sun (Shams) of Tabriz is a perfect light,
A sun, yea, one of the beams of God!
When the praise was heard of the "Sun of Tabriz,"
The sun of the fourth heaven bowed its head.
Now that I have mentioned his name, it is but right
To set forth some indications of his beneficence.
That precious Soul caught my skirt,
Smelling the perfume of the garment of Yusuf;
And said, "For the sake of our ancient friendship,
Tell forth a hint of those sweet states of ecstasy,
That earth and heaven may be rejoiced,
And also Reason and Spirit, a hundredfold."
I said, "O thou who art far from ' The Friend,'
Like a sick man who has strayed from his physician,

Importune me not, for I am beside myself;
My understanding is gone, I cannot sing praises.
Whatsoever one says, whose reason is thus astray,
Let him not boast; his efforts are useless.
Whatever he says is not to the point,
And is clearly inapt and wide of the mark.
What can I say when not a nerve of mine is sensible?
Can I explain 'The Friend' to one to whom He is no Friend?
Verily my singing His praise were dispraise,
For 'twould prove me existent, and existence is error.
Can I describe my separation and my bleeding heart?
Nay, put off this matter till another season."
He said, " Feed me, for I am an hungered,
And at once, for 'the time is a sharp sword.'
O comrade, the Sufi is 'the son of time present.'
It is not the rule of his canon to say, 'To-morrow.'
Can it be that thou art not a true Sufi?
Ready money is lost by giving credit."
I said, "'Tis best to veil the secrets of 'The Friend.'
So give good heed to the morals of these stories.
That is better than that the secrets of 'The Friend'
Should be noised abroad in the talk of strangers."
He said, "Without veil or covering or deception,
Speak out, and vex me not, O man of many words!
Strip off the veil and speak out, for do not I
Enter under the same coverlet as the Beloved?"
I said, "If the Beloved were exposed to outward view,
Neither wouldst thou endure, nor embrace, nor form.
Press thy suit, yet with moderation;
A blade of grass cannot, pierce a mountain.
If the sun that illumines the world
Were to draw nigher, the world would be consumed.
Close thy mouth and shut the eyes of this matter,
That, the world's life be not made a bleeding heart.
No longer seek this peril, this bloodshed;

Hereafter impose silence on the 'Sun of Tabriz.'"
He said, "Thy words are endless. Now tell forth
All thy story from its beginning."

The Harper

IN THE TIME of the Khalifa 'Omar there lived a harper, whose voice was as sweet as that of the angel Israfil, and who was in great request at all feasts. But he grew old, and his voice broke, and no one would employ him any longer. In despair he went to the burial-ground of Yathrub, and there played his harp to God, looking to Him for recompense. Having finished his melody he fell asleep, and dreamed he was in heaven. The same night a divine voice came to 'Omar, directing him to go to the burial-ground, and relieve an old man whom he should find there. 'Omar proceeded to the place, found the harper, and gave him money, promising him more when he should need it. The harper cast away his harp, saying that it had diverted him from God, and expressed great contrition for his past sins. 'Omar then instructed him that his worldly journey was now over, and that he must not give way to contrition for the past, as he was now entered into the state of ecstasy and intoxication of union with God, and in this exalted state regard to past and future should be swept away. The harper acted on his instructions, and sang no more.

Apology for applying the term "Bride" to God.
Mustafa became beside himself at that sweet call,
His prayer failed on "the night of the early morning halt."
He lifted not head from that blissful sleep,
So that his morning prayer was put off till noon.
On that, his wedding night, in presence of his bride,
His pure soul attained to kiss her hands.
Love and mistress are both veiled and hidden,

Impute it not as a fault if I call Him "Bride."
I would have kept silence from fear of my Beloved,
If He had granted me but a moment's respite.
But He said, "Speak on, 'tis no fault,
'Tis naught but the necessary result of the hidden decree,
'Tis a fault only to him who only sees faults.
How can the Pure Hidden Spirit notice faults?"
Faults seem so to ignorant creatures,
Not in the sight of the Lord of Benignity.
Blasphemy even may be wisdom in the Creator's si ht,
Whereas from our point of view it is grievous sin.
If one fault occur among a hundred beauties
'Tis as one dry stick in a garden of green herbs.
Both weigh equally in the scales
For the two resemble body and soul.
Wherefore the sages have said not idly,
"The bodies of the righteous are as pure souls."
Their words, their actions, their praises,
Are all as a pure soul without spot or blemish.
'Omar rebukes the Harper for brooding over
and bewailing the past.
Then 'Omar said to him, "This wailing of thine
Shows thou art still in a state of 'sobriety.'"
Afterwards he thus urged him to quit that state
And called him out of his beggary to absorption in God:
"Sobriety savours of memory of the past;
Past and future are what veil God from our sight.
Burn up both of them with fire! How long
Wilt thou be partitioned by these segments as a reed?
So long as a reed has partitions 'tis not privy to secrets,
Nor is it vocal in response to lip and breathing.
While circumambulating the house thou art a stranger;
When thou enterest in thou art at home.
Thou whose knowledge is ignorance of the Giver of knowledge,
Thy wailing contrition is worse than thy sin.

The road of the 'annihilated' is another road;
Sobriety is wrong, and a straying from that other road.
O thou who seekest to be contrite for the past,
How wilt thou be contrite for this contrition?
At one time thou adorest the music of the lute,
At another embracest wailing and weeping."
While the "Discerner" reflected these mysteries,
The heart of the harper was emancipated.
Like a soul he was freed from weeping and rejoicing,
His old life died, and he was regenerated.
Amazement fell upon him at that moment,
For he was exalted above earth and heaven,
An uplifting of the heart surpassing all uplifting;
I cannot describe it ; if you can, say on!
Ecstasy and words beyond all ecstatic words;
Immersion in the glory of the Lord of glory!
Immersion wherefrom was no extrication,
As it were identification with the Very Ocean!
Partial Reason is as naught to Universal Reason,
If one impulse dependent on another impulse be naught;
But when that impulse moves this impulse,
The waves of that sea rise to this point;

The Man who was Tattooed

IT WAS THE custom of the men of Qazwin to have various devices tattooed upon their bodies. A certain coward went to the artist to have such a device tattooed on his back, and desired that it might be the figure of a lion. But when he felt the pricks of the needles he roared with pain, and said to the artist, "What part of the lion are you now painting?" The artist replied, "I am doing the tail." The patient cried, "Never mind the tail; go on with another part." The artist accordingly began in another part, but the patient again cried out and told him to try somewhere else. Wherever the artist applied his needles, the patient raised similar objections, till at last the artist dashed all his needles and pigments on the ground, and refused to proceed any further.

The Prophet's counsels to 'Ali to follow the direction of the Pir or Spiritual Guide, and to endure his chastisements patiently.

> The Prophet said to 'Ali, "O 'Ali,
> Thou art the Lion of God, a hero most valiant;
> Yet confide not in thy lion-like valour,
> But seek refuge under the palm-trees of the 'Truth.'
> Whoso takes obedience as his exemplar
> Shares its proximity to the ineffable Presence.
> Do thou seek to draw near to Reason; let not thy heart
> Rely, like others, on thy own virtue and piety.
> Come under the shadow of the Man of Reason,
> Thou canst not find it in the road of the traditionists.
> That man enjoys close proximity to Allah;
> Turn not away from obedience to him in any wise;
> For he makes the thorn a bed of roses,
> And gives sight to the eyes of the blind.
> His shadow on earth is as that of Mount Qaf,
> His spirit is as a Simurgh soaring on high.
> He lends aid to the slaves of the friends of God,
> And advances to high place them who seek him.
> Were I to tell his praises till the last day,
> My words would not be too many nor admit of curtailment,
> He is the sun of the spirit, not that of the sky,
> For from his light men and angels draw life.
> That sun is hidden in the form of a man,
> Understand me! Allah knows the truth.
> O 'Ali, out of all forms of religious service
> Choose thou the shadow of that dear friend of God!
> Every man takes refuge in some form of service,

And chooses for himself some asylum;
Do thou seek refuge in the shadow of the wise man,
That thou mayest escape thy fierce secret foes.
Of all forms of service this is fittest for thee;
Thou shalt surpass all who were before thee.
Having chosen thy Director, be submissive to him,
Even as Moses submitted to the commands of Khizr;
Have patience with Khizr's actions, O sincere one!
Lest he say, 'There is a partition between us.'
Though he stave in thy boat, yet hold thy peace;
Though he slay a young man, heave not a sigh.
God declares his hand to be even as God's hand,
For He saith, The hand of God is over their hands.'
The hand of God impels him and gives him life;
Nay, not life only, but an eternal soul.
A friend is needed; travel not the road alone,
Take not thy own way through this desert!
Whoso travels this road alone
Only does so by aid of the might of holy men.
The hand of the Director is not weaker than theirs;
His hand is none other than the grasp of Allah!
If absent saints can confer such protection,
Doubtless present saints are more powerful than absent.
If such food be bestowed on the absent,
What dainties may not the guest who is present expect?
The courtier who attends in the presence of the king
Is served better than the stranger outside the gate.
The difference between them is beyond calculation;
One sees the light, the other only the veil.
Strive to obtain entrance within,
If thou wouldst not remain as a ring outside the door.
Having chosen thy Director, be not weak of heart,
Nor yet sluggish and lax as water and mud;
But if thou takest umbrage at every rub,
How wilt thou become a polished mirror?"

The Lion who Hunted with the Wolf and the Fox

A LION TOOK a wolf and a fox with him on a hunting excursion, and succeeded in catching a wild ox, an ibex, and a hare. He then directed the wolf to divide the prey. The wolf proposed to award the ox to the lion, the ibex to himself, and the hare to the fox. The lion was enraged with the wolf because he had presumed to talk of "I" and "Thou," and "My share" and "Thy share" when it all belonged of right to the lion, and he slew the wolf with one blow of his paw. Then, turning to the fox, he ordered him to make the division. The fox, rendered wary by the fate of the wolf, replied that the whole should be the portion of the lion. The lion, pleased with his self-abnegation, gave it all up to him, saying, "Thou art no longer a fox, but myself."

Till man destroys "self" he is no true friend of God.
Once a man came and knocked at the door of his friend.
His friend said, "who art thou. O faithful one?"
He said, "'Tis I." He answered, "There is no admittance.
There is no room for the 'raw' at my well-cooked feast.
Naught but fire of separation and absence
Can cook the raw one and free him from hypocrisy!
Since thy 'self' has not yet left thee,
Thou must be burned in fiery flames."
The poor man went away, and for one whole year
Journeyed burning with grief for his friend's absence.
His heart burned till it was cooked; then he went again
And drew near to the house of his friend.
He knocked at the door in fear and trepidation
Lest some careless word might fall from his lips.
His friend shouted, "Who is that at the door?"

He answered, "'Tis Thou who art at the door. O Beloved!"
The friend said, "Since 'tis I, let me come in,
There is not room for two 'I's' in one house."

'Ali's Forbearance'

ALI, THE "Lion of God," was once engaged in conflict with a Magian chief, and in the midst of the struggle the Magian spat in his face. 'Ali, instead of taking vengeance on him, at once dropped his sword, to the Magian's great astonishment. On his inquiring the reason of such forbearance, 'Ali informed him that the "Lion of God" did not destroy life for the satisfaction of his own vengeance, but simply to carry out God's will, and that whenever he saw just cause, he held his hand even in the midst of the strife, and spared the foe. The Prophet, 'Ali continued, had long since informed him that he would die by the hand of his own stirrup-bearer (Ibn Maljun), and the stirrup-bearer had frequently implored 'Ali to kill him, and thus save him from the commission of that great crime; but 'Ali said he always refused to do so, as to him death was as sweet as life, and he felt no anger against his destined assassin, who was only the instrument of God's eternal purpose. The Magian chief, on hearing 'Ali's discourse, was so much affected that he embraced Islam, together with all his family, to the number of fifty souls.

How the Prophet whispered to 'Ali's stirrup-bearer
that he would one day assassinate his master.
The Prophet whispered in the ear of my servant
That one day he would sever my head from my neck.
The Prophet also warned by inspiration me, his friend,
That the hand of my servant would destroy me.
My servant cried, "O kill me first,
That I may not become guilty of so grievous a sin!"
I replied, "Since my death is to come from thee,

How can I balk the fateful decree?"
He fell at my feet and cried, "O gracious lord,
For God's sake cleave now my body in twain,
That such an evil deed may not be wrought by me,
And my soul burn with anguish for its beloved."
I replied, "What God's pen has written, it has written;
In presence of its writings knowledge is confounded;
There is no anger in my soul against thee,
Because I attribute not this deed to thee;
Thou art God's instrument. God's hand is the agent.
How can I chide or fret at God's instrument?"
He said, "If this be so, why is there retaliation?"
I answered, "'Tis from God, and 'tis God's secret;
If He shows displeasure at His own acts,
From His displeasure He evolves a Paradise;
He feels displeasure at His own acts,
Because He is a God of vengeance as of mercy.
In this city of events He is the Lord,
In this realm He is the King who plans all events.
If He crushes His own instruments,
He makes those crushed ones fair in His sight.
Know the great mystery of 'whatever verses we cancel,
Or cause you to forget, we substitute better for them.'
Whatever law God cancels, He makes as a weed,
And in its stead He brings forth a rose.
So night cancels the business of the daytime,
When the reason that lights our minds becomes inanimate.
Again, night is cancelled by the light of day,
And inanimate reason is rekindled to life by its rays.
Though darkness produces this sleep and quiet,
Is not the 'water of life' in the darkness?
Are not spirits refreshed in that very darkness?
Is not that silence the season of heavenly voices?
For from contraries contraries are brought forth,
Out of darkness was created light.

The Prophet's wars brought about the present peace,
The peace of these latter days resulted from those wars.
That conqueror of hearts cut off a thousand heads,
That the heads of his people might rest in peace."
God's rebuke to Adam for scorning Iblis.
To whomsoever God's order comes,
He must smite with his sword even his own child.
Fear then, and revile not the wicked,
For the wicked are impotent under God's commands.
In presence of God's commands bow down the neck of pride.
Scoff not nor chide even them that go astray!
One day Adam cast a look of contempt and scorn
Upon Iblis, thinking what a wretch he was.
He felt self-important and proud of himself,
And he smiled at the actions of cursed Iblis.
God Almighty cried out to him, "O pure one,
Thou art wholly ignorant of hidden mysteries.
If I were to blab the faults of the unfortunate,
I should root up the mountains from their bases,
And lay bare the secrets of a hundred Adams,
And convert a hundred fresh Iblises into Mosalmans."
Adam answered, "I repent me of my scornful looks;
Such arrogant thoughts shall not be mine again.
O Lord, pardon this rashness in Thy slave;
I repent; chastise me not for these words!"
O Aider of aid-seekers, guide us,
For there is no security in knowledge or wealth;
"Lead not our hearts astray after Thou hast guided us,"
And avert the evil that the "Pen" has written.
Turn aside from our souls the evil written in our fates,
Repel us not from the tables of purity!
O God, Thy grace is the proper object of our desire;
To couple others with Thee is not proper.
Nothing is bitterer than severance from Thee,
Without Thy shelter there is naught but perplexity.

Our worldly goods rob us of our heavenly goods,
Our body rends the garment of our soul.
Our hands, as it were, prey on our feet;
Without reliance on Thee how can we live?
And if the soul escapes these great perils,
It is made captive as a victim of misfortunes and fears,
Inasmuch as when the soul lacks union with the Beloved,
It abides forever blind and darkened by itself.
If Thou showest not the way, our life is lost;
A life living without Thee esteem as dead!
If Thou findest fault with Thy slaves,
Verily it is right in Thee, O Blessed One!
If Thou shouldst call sun and moon obscure,
If Thou shouldst call the straight cypress crooked,
If Thou shouldst declare the highest heaven base,
Or rich mines and oceans paupers,
All this is the truth in relation to Thy perfection!
Thine is the dominion and the glory and the wealth!
For Thou art exempt from defect and not-being,
Thou givest existence to things non-existent, and again
Thou makest them non-existent.

Anwar-I-Suhali
Husayn Va'iz Kashifi
Selected by Elizabeth A. Reed

THERE WERE TWO collections of early fables in Sanskrit literature, called the *Pancatantra and the Hitopadesa*, and during the reign of the Sassanian kings a quaint old book containing these stories was brought to the Persian court and translated into the Pahlavi tongue. This was a notable event in the history of Aryan literature, and since that time this rare collection of simple stories has passed through more mutations than has the Roman Empire; it is now extant, under various names, in more than twenty languages, the Persian version being known as the *Anwar-i-Suhali*, or *The Lights of Canopus*. It is recorded that King Nushirvan commissioned an officer of state to procure a translation of this work, and, being obtained after years of difficulty, it was deposited in the cabinet of the king's most precious treasures, and was regarded as a model of wisdom and didactic philosophy. But at the time of the Arabian conquest, this work, with many others, was destroyed by the vandals of the desert.

The Persian version is the book which candidates for the position of interpreter are required to read, as the great number of words and the variety of its style make it the best book in the language to be studied by one who wishes to make rapid progress in Persian. The repetition of metaphor and highly florid style of composition is often offensive to the English reader, but these very characteristics form its greatest attraction in the eye of Persian *litterateurs*, and many stories are delightful to them which are wearisome to the simpler taste of the western student.

When divested of the cumbersome verbiage these stories will be found both quaint and pleasing. A few of the best of them are here given in simple phrase.

The Bees and Their Habits

THERE STOOD in the garden an old tree, whose leaves had fallen, and there was no vitality with which to replace them. The hatchet of the peasant Time had mutilated its limbs, and the saw of the carpenter Fortune had sharpened its teeth in making shreds of its warp and woof. The centre of the tree had become hollow, and a busy swarm of bees had made it their fortress.

When the king heard the buzzing of the little workers, he inquired of his sage why these little insects gathered in the tree, and at whose command they resorted to the meadow. Then the minister replied: "O, fortunate prince, they are a tribe doing much good and little harm. They have a queen larger in bulk than themselves, and have placed their heads on the line of obedience to her majesty; she is seated upon a square throne of wax, and she has appointed to their several offices her vizier and chamberlain, her porter and guard, her spy and deputy. The ingenuity of her attendants is such that each one prepares hexagonal chambers of wax, having no inequality in their partitions, and the best geometricians would be unable to do such work without instruments. When this work approaches completion they come forth from their abode at the queen's command, and a noble bee explains to them that they must not exchange their cleanliness for grossness, nor pollute their purity by evil associations. They therefore sit only beside the fair lily or fragrant rose, in order to draw therefrom the purest honey. When they come to the home the warders try them by smelling, and if they have kept their sacred trust and avoided all impure associations, permission is given them to re-enter the immaculate chambers of white wax. But there are many blossoms which, though beautiful to the eye, will poison those who touch them, and the foolish bee who is attracted by their deceitful loveliness is also polluted by their fatal breath; when he comes to the portals of the hive the quick scent of the warders detect the fact if he has been polluted by evil surroundings, and the offender is quickly punished by decapitation. If, however, the warders should be negligent enough to allow the culprit to enter, and the queen of this spotless palace should detect the offensive taint, both the culprit and the careless warders will be conducted to the place of punishment and the warders will be executed first. It is recorded that Jamshid, 'Emperor of the World,' borrowed from these wise disciplinarians the regulations respecting warders and guards, the appointment of chamberlains and door-keepers, and also the arrangement of thrones and regal cushions, which, in the course of time, perfected our customs."

Upon hearing this wonderful illustration of the effects of bad company upon the unfortunate bee, and learning that every man carries with him a portion of the vileness of his evil companions, the king exclaimed: "I have been convinced to-day that the society of some persons is more hurtful than the poison of a viper, and the association with them more dangerous than a position which involves the peril of one's life, and I reason therefrom that it may be better to live in seclusion." But the sage replied: "Great leaders have preferred the companionship of the good and true, but when a sincere friend is not to be found, then indeed solitude is better than society."

The Two Pigeons

THERE WERE two faithful pigeons who at one time consorted together in one nest, with their loyal hearts undisturbed by treachery, and free from misfortune. One was named Bazindah (playful), and the other was called Nawazindah (caressing), while every morning and evening their voices were mingled in the soft notes of love. But some were envious of the happy pair, and evil counsellors attempted to "sever love, and friend from friend divide."

An anxious desire for travel was carefully instilled into the ambitious heart of Bazindah, and he said to his loving mate, "How long shall we continue in one nest, and spend our time in one abode? I feel a desire to wander through different parts of the world, for, in a few days of travel, many marvelous things are seen, and many experiences are gained. There is no honor awarded until the sword comes forth from the scabbard upon the field of the brave; the sky is ever journeying, and it is the highest of all things, while the earth which is ever still is always trampled down, and kicked by all things, both high and low:

> 'View the earth's sphere and the revolving skies,
> This sinks by rest, and those by motion rise;
> Travel, man's tutor is, and glory's gate,
> On travel, treasure and instruction wait,
> From place to place had trees the power to move,
> No saw nor ax could wrong the stately grove.'"

To this his gentle mate replied, "My beloved, when thou removest thy heart from the society of thine own, thou dost sever the cord of unity; thou mayest unite with new comrades, but never wilt thou find them so loyal, as those which long years of trial have shown to be true. Remember the precept of the wise man, and

> 'Do not an old and well tried friend forego
> For new allies, for this will end in woe,'

Thou mayest transgress, and what impression will my word have upon thee then? Remember that

> 'He shall his foeman's fondest wish fulfill,
> Who to well wishing friends bends not his will.'"

Bazindah, however tore his heart away from his loving mate, and set forth upon the wing, exulting in his liberty and freedom from her gentle admonitions. With great curiosity, and perfect pleasure, he traveled for a while through the blue air, and passed over the bright hills and gardens of roses and lilies. After a time he came to a mountain, and at its feet lay a beautiful meadow; its green surface was delightful as the gardens of heaven, and the northern breeze swept down from the cool hills, laden with the perfume of a thousand flowers.

> "There countless roses their pavilions kept,
> The grass moved wakeful, while the waters slept,

The roses painted with a thousand hues,
Their heavenly fragrance each a league diffuse."

The setting sun was bathing the hills with its glory when the weary pigeon reached the lovely spot, and he nestled gratefully down amidst the green grass and fragrant flowers to spend the night in peace and happiness; with his head tucked under his wing, he did not see that a shadow had darkened the fair sunset; he did not see that its glory was shaded by an angry storm-cloud. But soon the restless wind was tossing the canopy of clouds into the high court of the air, and Bazindah's heart was quaking with terror as the fiery lightnings flashed around him, consuming the hearts of the tulips beside him; the pitiless hail dashed the bright narcissus to the earth, while the thunderbolts seemed to tear the very heart of the mountain.

"In pieces was the mountain's breast, by the lightning's arrows riven,
And earth to its foundations shook, at the fearful voice of heaven."

Bazindah had no shelter from the storm – no refuge from the pitiless hail and searching wind; in vain he tried to hide beneath some friendly branch or amidst the leaves and grass, still the cruel hail pelted him like some remorseless foe, and the cold rain still poured upon him.

"Night! gloomy night! – Heaven's awful voice—
What tempest shower so fierce as this?
What care the gay in banquet halls?
Our perils do not mar their bliss."

In terror and peril, the traveler passed the night thinking of the home-nest, and the gentle mate who would so gladly shield him from the storm with her own pinions, and who was even now grieving her life away in loneliness, because he came not.

But whatever feelings of penitence may have been cherished during the perils of the night, were quickly dissipated by the beauty of the morning light.

"From the east then drew the sun,
His golden poniard bright,

And through the earth's dark regions
Spread a flood of yellow light."

Bazindah again arose upon his faithful wings, and pursued his journey; but a royal white falcon was abroad looking for prey, – a falcon which descends upon the head of its quarry, swifter than the rays of the sun, and when soaring on high he reaches heaven quicker than the sight of man.

"Attacking now, it left the thunderbolt behind,
And soared more swiftly than the chilling wind."

For the pitiless bird had marked the pigeon for his prey, and the victim's heart began to flutter, while his wings, paralyzed with fear, seemed to lose all power of motion.

"When on the dove the rapid falcon swoops,
The helpless quarry unresisting droops."

In that moment of helpless terror, Bazindah thought again of his faithful mate, and quickly resolved that could he but escape this deadly peril, he would be content at home in her downy nest. He was already beneath the claw of the falcon, when the flashing eye of an eagle fell upon them, – an eagle whose talons were so sharp that the sign of Aquila was not safe in the nest of the sky, and who, when hungry, carried off from the meadows of heaven the signs of Aries and Capricorn.

"Aries itself, through fear of him
Would gaze not on the sky,
Save that Bahram, the blood drinker
Each day stood watchful by."

This fearful bird was on the wing searching for food, and seeing the falcon and the pigeon, he said to himself, "Although this pigeon is only a mouthful, nevertheless one may break one's fast upon it," and quickly he dashed at the falcon:

"The feathered rivals then to fight began,
The quarry, dodging, from between them ran."

While the fight went fiercely on, Bazindah threw himself under a stone, and crowded himself into a hole hardly large enough for a sparrow, and here he passed the day and another night, quivering with terror and distress. But the morning light again illumined the mountain peaks, for the white-pinioned dove of the dawn began to fly from the nest of heaven, and the black raven of night went to his rest like the Simurgh, behind the shades of the distant mountains. Bazindah began to flutter his weary wings, and look hungrily around him, when he gladly spied another pigeon, with a little grain scattered before him. Rejoicing to see one of his own species, he fluttered eagerly to the grain, but alas! his foot was caught in a snare.

> *"Satan's the net, the world's the grain,*
> *Our lusts the enticements are,*
> *Our hearts, the fowl which greediness*
> *Soon lures within the snare."*

With bitter reproaches upon the captive pigeon who had thus lured him to destruction, he trembled and struggled, until he broke the decayed net, and turned his tired face toward the home-nest, and flew as rapidly as his forlorn condition would permit. Fearing to attempt again to satisfy his hunger, he was nevertheless compelled to rest, at last, on a wall near a field of corn. A thoughtless boy sent an arrow toward him, and wounded he fell, but he lay so quietly that the young hunter failed to find his game, and at last, weak and wounded, hungry and discouraged, he fluttered by short flights homeward. Nawazindah heard the flutter of his wings, and flew joyously out to meet him saying:

> *"'Tis I whose eyes expand, my love to find—*
> *How shall I thank thee – thou so true and kind."*

But when she had caressed him, she saw that he was weak and thin, and she exclaimed, "Oh, beloved, where hast thou been?"

Bazindah replied:

> *"Ask me not what woes, my love,—*
> *What pangs have been my lot,*
> *All the grief that parting brings,*
> *I've tasted – ask me not.*

> *For travel's conflict I'll not lust again,*
> *With home and friends perpetual pleasures reign.*

The truth of the matter is, that I have had much experience, and as long as I live, I will not make another journey, nor go forth until compelled from the corner of our nest." Then the gentle wife flew out and brought him the daintiest food she could find, and tenderly she caressed the wounded wing with her loving bill, and no thought of reproaches entered her grateful heart. Gently she nursed him back to health and strength, and together they cooed and nestled in their quiet home.

The Blind Man and His Whip

A SAGE, who was discoursing to a king upon lessons of wisdom and morality, gave him the following illustration of an important principle:

"Once upon a time a blind man and his friend were making a journey together, and they halted in a wild place for the night; the morning found them cold and little rested, for the weather had suddenly grown severe. In searching for his whip the blind man picked up a frozen snake, which he found smoother and more nicely polished than his whip, and greatly pleased he mounted his horse, forgetting the faithful old whip which he had lost. His friend, however, could see, and when he beheld the snake in the hand of the blind man, he cried out: 'Oh, my friend! what thou takest for a whip is a poisonous snake, fling it away before it makes a wound upon thy hand.' But the blind man fancied that his friend was jealous of his great success in finding so beautiful a whip, and he answered: 'Oh, friend! it is owing to my good luck, that I have found a better one, and I am not going to be wheedled out of my good fortune by idle tales.' His friend continued to plead, but the man was obstinate and conceited, as well as blind, and he became angry and frowned upon his faithful friend, while he clung closely to what he believed to be a beautiful thing. After a time the sun rose higher in the heavens, and the air grew more balmy, the snake was also comforted by the warmth of the blind man's body, and recovering from her torpor, she turned backward, and bit the poor fool who had, clung to her because he fancied she was beautiful; he died of the venom given in the wound." Then said the sage, "I have adduced this story that thou mayst not be deceived by appearances or fascinated with outward charms, which are as deceitful as the beauties of a snake. Be not attracted by the softness and delicacy of flattery and hypocrisy, for their poison is deadly and their wound is fatal; it is far better to listen to the admonitions of a faithful friend, even though his advice may not always be agreeable, than to be led into the snare of the flatterer, by the poison of her honeyed words.

> *'Think not sweet sherbert from the world to drink,*
> *Honey with poison is mingled there,*
> *That which thou, fondly, dost sweet honey think,*
> *Is but the deadly potion of despair.'"*

Amicable Instruction

I't is said that there lived a wise and virtuous prince, who was greatly afflicted with the conduct of his sons. The young princes "knew no books and were continually working in evil ways," therefore the raja asked himself, "Of what use is it that a son should be born who has neither learning nor virtue? Of what use is a blind eye except to give pain? Of a child unborn, dead or ignorant, the two first are preferable, since they make us unhappy but once, and the last by continual degrees. A numerous family under such circumstances is poison, as is a young wife to an old man."

Considering these things, the king gave orders for a council of learned men to be called, in order that they might study the solution of his problem, and devise, if possible, some method by which his sons might be taught the lessons of morality and wisdom.

Among the wise men who were thus called together, there was a great philosopher named Vishnu-sarman who understood the principles of ethics. He declared that as these young princes were born of good family there was still a hope of their reformation, and he offered to give them the necessary instruction. His proposition was gladly accepted by the anxious father, and soon the class was called together on the roof of the palace to receive the instruction of the sage. The teacher decided to interest his listeners, and also to convey the lessons of morality by repeating fables. Therefore, with many wise admonitions, and carefully pointing the moral of each lesson, he told them the following stories:

The Pigeons and the Rat

NEAR THE GODAVARI river there stood a large Salmali tree, on which the birds found their nightly rest. One morning, when the darkness had just departed, leaving the moon – friend of the night flowers – still in his mansion, a raven who sat in the tree saw a fowler approaching like the genius of death, and he said to himself, "This morning an enemy appears, and I know not what poisonous fruit is ripening." The fowler went on, however, fixing his net and scattering grains of rice. Soon a flock of pigeons, led by their prince Citagriva, or painted neck, came flying that way. They saw the rice and were eagerly descending, when the leader counseled caution, for he feared a snare; but led away by their appetites, they all flew downward upon the rice, being followed, even by the leader, who was unwilling to desert the flock. In a moment more they were snared. But although covetousness had brought them into trouble, the leader counseled that a wise unity of action might even yet deliver them from it. He ordered that they should all fly together, and doing so, they raised the net and carried it along with them. They were followed by the fowler, who expected to see them soon fall into his power.

In a wood near by dwelt a rat, who was a friend of Citagriva's, and to him they directed their flight, coming down near his hole. The prisoned birds then besought him to gnaw the strings that held them. The rat replied that "to abandon our own is not the conduct of moralists. Let a man for the sake of relieving his distresses preserve his wealth; by his wealth let him preserve his wife, and by both wife and riches let him preserve himself." "I am but weak," said he, "and my teeth are small, but as long as they remain unbroken will I continue to cut thy strings." And gnawing diligently away, he severed their bonds and received them as guests.

Thus the sage taught the princes that "covetousness leads to lust, to anger, to fraud and illusion." He taught also that the union, even of the small and the weak, is beneficial, and also that the humble friend who stands by us faithfully, in the hour of adversity, is of more value than the flatterers, who are watching for our prosperity, in order that they may absorb our gain.

The Antelope and the Crow

I**N THE COUNTRY of Magadha there was a forest, in which an antelope and crow had long dwelt in friendship. The antelope was fat, and his flesh was greatly desired by a jackal, who sought to obtain it by gaining his confidence. Going to him, therefore, she pleaded for his friendship, saying, "I am friendless and alone like a dead creature, but having gained thy friendship I shall live again, and I will ever be thy servant," and saying this, she slipped into his home under the branches of a tree, where dwelt the friendly crow. Then the crow inquired of the antelope, "Who is this comrade of thine?" And the antelope replied, "It is a jackal who is my chosen friend." "O my beloved," said the crow, "it is not right to place thy confidence with too much celerity." But in vain the faithful bird pleaded with the infatuated antelope, who still listened eagerly to the flatteries of the jackal, until the aggrieved and disgusted friend flew away to another part of the wood.**

"My beloved antelope," said the jackal one day in her softest and sweetest tones, "at one side of the wood is a field of corn, I will take thee there." The antelope found the corn rich and tender, and going there he fed freely. The owner of the corn perceived his loss as the wily jackal had anticipated, and he spread a strong net there, wherein the antelope was captured. The jackal crept softly near, saying to herself, "It has befallen as I wished, and soon I shall satisfy my appetite on his tender flesh." As soon as the antelope perceived his false friend he was glad, for he anticipated deliverance by the gnawing of his bonds.

The jackal examined the net, and congratulating herself that it was strong, she said, "Oh, my beloved, I cannot do it to-day, but to-morrow I will come and deliver thee," and going away, a short distance she awaited for him to die in order that she might regale herself upon his flesh. The crow, however, in flying over the wood, saw the condition of his imprudent friend, and hastened to his side. "This," said the antelope "is the consequence of rejecting friendly counsel. The man who listens not to the words of affectionate friends, will give joy in the moment of distress to his enemies."

"Where is the jackal?" inquired the crow. "She is near by," answered the antelope, "waiting to feed upon my flesh." "This I predicted," said the crow. "I escape such calamities because I place no such trust; the wise are continually in dread of wicked associations. A pretended friend who flatters thee should be shunned as a dish of milk with poison at its brim. Contract no friendship with flatterers; at first they fall at your feet in their anxiety to drink your blood; they hum strange tunes in your ears with soft murmurs, and, having found an opening, they will ruin you without remorse."

The faithful crow watched until he saw the farmer approaching, then he said to the antelope, "Feign to be dead and remain motionless until thou hearest me make a noise, then run swiftly away."

The owner of the corn, with his eyes flooded with joy, saw the antelope who pretended to be dead, so he took away the snare, and was busily engaged in taking care of his net, when the crow cried out, and the antelope hearing the signal, bounded to his feet and ran away with great speed. The disappointed farmer threw a club after him, and struck the deceitful jackal, who was hidden in a bush, for thus it is written: "In three years, in three months, in three days, the fruit of great vices may be reaped, even in this world."

The Brahman and the Ichneumon

THERE WAS a Brahman named Modeva, who lived alone with his wife and their infant daughter. One day the mother went away to perform her ablutions and acts of adoration. She therefore left the child in the father's care. Soon after the mother left home a great raja sent for the Brahman to

perform a religious ceremony called the Sraddha, or offerings to the ghosts of his ancestors. It is customary upon these occasions to bestow rich presents upon the officiating Brahman or priest, and this was an opportunity that ought not to be lost.

Knowing that if he did not go promptly another would be called in his place, he committed the care of his child to a faithful ichneumon, which he had long cherished, and having done so, he hastened away to obey the call of the raja. Soon after he went away a terrible serpent crawled into the little home and approached the child. He was attacked, however, by the faithful ichneumon, who killed him and cut him in pieces; then seeing his master returning the animal ran to meet him, even while his mouth and paws were still wet with the blood of the serpent. Seeing him thus, the Brahman promptly decided that he had killed the child, and in his rage he slew the ichneumon. Then going to his house he found the babe sleeping peacefully with the mangled body of the snake beside it. Then, indeed, he knew that, in his haste and unreasonable anger, he had slain the faithful protector of his child. Therefore, he who knows not the first principle, and the first cause, and who is in subjection to his wrath, is tormented like a fool. Let not a man perform an act hastily. Want of circumspection is a great cause of danger.

FLAME TREE PUBLISHING

In the same series:
MYTHS & LEGENDS